D0321119

White Mountain

The Darkling Chronicles
Book 1

Sophie E Tallis

Safkhet
Publishing

Safkhet Publishing, London, United Kingdom

first published by Safkhet Publishing in 2012

1 3 5 7 9 10 8 6 4 2

Text & Illustrations Copyright 2012 by Sophie E Tallis
Cover Art Copyright 2012 by Kim Maya

Sophie E Tallis asserts the moral right to be identified as the author and
illustrator of this work under the Copyright, Designs and Patents Act 1988.
Kim Maya asserts the moral right to be identified
as the cover artist of this work under the Copyright, Designs and Patents Act 1988.

ISBN 978-1-908208-09-5

All characters and events in this publication, other than those clearly in the public domain,
are fictitious and any resemblance to real persons, living or dead, is purely coincidental.

All rights reserved. No part of this publication may be reproduced, stored in or introduced into
a retrieval system, or transmitted, in any form or by any means, including but not limited to
electronic, mechanical, photocopying or recording, without the prior written permission of the
publisher.

A CIP catalogue record for this book is available from
the British Library.

Printed and bound by Lightning Source International

Typeset in 10.7 pt Crimson

Production Crew:
Sophie E Tallis   Author, Illustrator
William Banks Sutton   Managing Editor
Kim Maya Sutton   Cover Art, Copyeditor
Charlotte Choules   Proofreader

 The colophon of Safkhet is a representation of the ancient Egyptian goddess of wisdom
and knowledge, who is credited with inventing writing. Safkhet Publishing is named
after her because the founders met in Egypt.

Contents

White Mountain	1
City Of Ice	7
A Strange Meeting	13
Escape from Issàtun	22
The Two Travelers	27
The Grey Forest	42
Attack in the Dark	57
The Oracle of the West	69
Kallorm	86
City of Light	99
Flight of the Dragon	110
The Falls of Tarro	124
The Encircling Mountains	131
The Flame of Fendellin	146
The Silent Watch	162
The Last March	177
Kavok's Peak	194
Turn of the Blade	205
Cavern of Souls	221
Morreck	235
Into The Light	246
Mund'harr	255
The Long Journey	267

With Special Thanks to the
Dragon Friends

Hector Adams
Harry Ahearne
Andrea Baker (Rose Wall)
Joanna Bellamy
Cherry Bevan
Linda and Simon Bingham
Sharon Brown
Sheryl Browne
The Campbell Family
Jan Chinnick
Sally Cushnan
Mollie D'Arcy Rice
Monty D'Arcy Rice
Seb D'Arcy Rice
Thor Davey
Samantha Davies
Freddie Delap
Hamish Delap
Giles Diggle
Emily Dryden
Sophie Dryden
Hannah and Jamie Edmonston
Alys and Bryn Evans
Tania Fawcett
Jane Galton-Fenzi
Theo Hall
Jessica and Hebe Heynes

Ryan Holmes
Bass Hornor
Katrina Anne Jack
Will Macmillan Jones
Thomas Locke
Gina Mather
Helen McElwee
Emily McKeon
Caroline Morgan-Grenville
Lindsey J Parsons
James William Peercy
Gill Ricks
Jeremy Rodden
Ros & Andy Sheppard
Harry, Lewis and Annabel Smith
J. Snell
Gretchen Steen
James Stevens
Andrew Tabor
Judith Clare Tallis
Ella Thompson
Esther Fiona Walker
Emma Walker
Heather Walker
Richard Wentworth
Val Wicks
Graham Wingrove

Glossary

A'Orvas – The Ǽllfren word for the First Realm.

Ǽllfr – Referred to in myth as elves or *alfarr*. The Greek letter *alpha* may have been derived from this. The ǽllfr are an ancient race with prodigious intellect pre-dating humans. They are great astronomers, fickle in nature and disinterested in the matters of others. Tall and sinuous, yet broad in frame, with great strength and agility. Angular features with notably high cheekbones, pale skin, and dark hair. The height of ǽllfren society was some 500,000-340,000 years ago, whereby it steadily declined. The first exoduses coincided with a growing human population and their intolerance of this lesser species. The final great exodus coincided with the end of the last Ice Age and the boom in human populace, some 10,000 years ago. Very few ǽllfrs remained. Ǽllfrs built their small, but grand cities, not merely among the heights of mountains, but on the plains and savannahs and even the deserts of the world. But among the great sand palaces and glistening crystal spires, the most spectacular of these cities were those oceanic pearls that perched on islands or cliff faces just above the sea, or those rare marvels that sparkled beneath it.

Ǽllfren Sanskrit – A very ancient Ǽllfren text and written language thought to be the origin of the ancient Indian Vedic Sanskrit.

Chukchi – An indigenous people of extreme northeast Siberia. The language of the Chukchi belongs to a small family also including Koryak.

Dworll – (related to dwarves) Ancient and proud race pre-dating humans. Protectors of nature and custodians of the great forests, jungles, and grasslands. Highly-skilled crafters and inventors. They have broad stocky frames, are usually stouter than ǽllfrs, especially ground-dwelling dworlls, though they are still tall by human standards. Pale to tanned skin, pale eyes, earth-toned hair. Some elders of royal bloodline may have small forehead ridges at the hairline (males only). Dworlls are divided into two principal castes. The taller and more agile mountain dworlls prefer open and airier spaces to their stouter subterranean-loving cousins. These ground or earth dworlls are shorter and broader than their lofty relatives, but older in history, heredity and lifespan, and were always by far the more numerous of the two types. Dworlls built not merely with grand designs and architectural wonder, but with expansion and population in mind. Thus, the great dworll kingdoms and metropolises, of which Kallorm was the first and greatest, sprang up. Most cities were underground, as is dworllian custom, but were breathtaking in their sheer size and ingenuity.

Dworllian – Relating to dworlls and/or dworll culture. Akin to dworlls in character or appearance.

Egglesquell – One of Mr. Agyk's unusual culinary experiments involving stewed eggles (a tiny anchovy-like fish found only in deep mountain pools) and fermented wheat.

Evenki – A member of an indigenous people living scattered through the wastes of northern Siberia. Also called Tungus. The Tungusic language of the Evenki has about 15,000 speakers.

First Realm – A'Orvas. The ǽllfren and dworllian equivalent of Heaven, Valhalla, Elysium, etc. A mythical realm of tranquility and beauty. Created by the gods, it represents a portal to another dimension between life and death, where all ǽllfrs, dworlls, dragons, or mages too burdened with the heavy cares of the world can go to live eternally among the stars. Once there, none can return.

Fÿrren – Dworllian and Ǽllfren word for any dragon, wyvern, wyrm, or fire-drake.

Fÿrullfr – fire-wolf (*fÿr* meaning fire and *ullfr* meaning wolf similar to Old Norse ulfr). Ancient demons of the old world, fire-wolves are gigantic beasts, bear-like in size with the tusks of a boar, sharpened fangs and red, fiery eyes. A portent of evil, they were greatly feared by both dworllian and ǽllfren societies for their relentless pursuit of their victims, voracious appetite for flesh and destruction, and their ability to breathe fire. Fire-wolves are bitter enemies of all dragons.

Greenling – A youngster, an apprentice, or any who is tender in age and experience.

Ïssätun – The City of Ice. A beautiful ǽllfren city made entirely of ice and crystal, and situated high within the Arctic Circle. A hidden meeting place for all the elder races to exchange news and trade.

Kalador – Ancient ǽllfren city of middle Asia (modern-day Jericho was built on its ruins) and seat of great learning. Thought to be the spiritual home of most magic-casters (mages, sorcerers, wizards, etc.). The Fall of Kalador is attributed to Morreck the Corruptor, as chronicled in the ancient Ǽllfren sand-scrolls.

Kallorm – Oldest and greatest of all dworllian cities. An enormous, hidden, subterranean metropolis beneath the Congolese jungles of central Africa. Capital of dworllian culture. Also called Dwellum in Ancient Dworllian, or Silverden in Ǽllfren.

Khanty – An indigenous tribal people living in northwest Siberia, east of the Urals; member of the Ugrian people. The Finno-Ugric language of this people is related to Hungarian.

Llrinaru – The Elder Wood, heart of the Grey Forest. These are very ancient silver-barked trees that still retain their wood nymphs, tiny tree spirits that live within the tree and extend its life.

Mimmirian – (from the Dworllian word 'mimirr' meaning wisdom or knowledge, similar to the Norse giant Mimir, who guarded the well of wisdom). An ancient mystical mirror-like communication device with a viewing panel and instrumentation for sound. Mimmirians can be any size; the knowledge of how to construct them is all but lost. A skilled practitioner may break a shard from a larger device to make a portable mimmirian. Only a few mimmirians still exist.

N'dirron – Another word for fire-wolf (fÿrullfr), any ancient wolf demon known to breathe fire.

Nabatean – An extinct language of the Nabateans, a dialect of ancient Aramaic. The Nabateans were traders who flourished around Petra during Hellenistic and Roman times.

naru'l'tarr – A forest leopard (Amur leopard).

Nenet – A member of a nomadic people of Siberia, whose main traditional occupation is reindeer herding. The language of the Nenets, the most widely used of the Samoyedic languages, with about 27,000 speakers.

Silver Greenwood tree – An ancient Llrinaru tree.

snootledown – Another word for snowdoves.

snowdoves – Birds related to white doves in appearance but much larger in size, resembling ptarmigans.

starstone – An ancient ǽllfren device for capturing, storing and creating light. Cool to the touch and everlasting, but very fragile. The millions of starstones embedded in the ceiling of Kallorm have been synchronised to exactly emulate the sun's transit across the sky, dimming at dusk and brightening at dawn, and also emulate the changing constellations during the night.

Ullfrs – Wolves.

Urallaia – Dworllian name for the region east of the Ural Mountains in Russia, and location of the Grey Forest, Wendya Undokki's home.

wærloga – (Old English word for warlock) A man who practices black magic, witchcraft. Originally, an oath breaker, from *wær* oath and *loga* liar, also 'traitor, scoundrel, monster'. Also means 'the Devil': the word was transferred in Middle English to a person in league with the Devil, and thus a warlock.

Dedication

To Mum,
For your loving support and for always being there.
Simply the best mum!
Thank you xx

To S.H.A. and my Goddaughter Esther,
For all the magical things you will do and see and be xx

Chapter One

White Mountain

he deepening sun scorched the snowy drifts turning them cherry pink as it cast its dying rays over the peaks and popular winter resorts of the skiing elite. Shadows of dusk lengthened as lights twinkled in the valley below. Above the hustle and bustle of bistro and café life, chic alpine lodges, ski schools and cable cars, White Mountain loomed. Its towering flanks gleamed in the fading light, its secret heart still safe, still undisturbed — the ancient, ancestral home of an old wizard.

Within the bowels of the mountain lived the aging scholar, a practitioner and magus of the old arts. An archetypal wizard with steely gray hair and a scruffy beard; his heavy, lidded eyes belied a keen intellect and appeared both sharply alert and ready for slumber. A powerful but rather eccentric figure, he had the bumbling demeanor of an old-world gent, a long-lost uncle back from some distant travels with stories to astound and amaze. Mr. M Agyk, also known as Marval or simply the Green Wizard, had witnessed the passing of ages. A quickening of time had brought too many great changes to the world outside; yet nestled deep within the mountain's walls he had continued to live his life mostly unaffected by the curious comings and goings beyond.

From within this dwelling sprang many hundreds of beautiful rooms and twisting tunnels, a labyrinth of chambers, which even the wizard had forgotten or lost his way in. Its endless expanse of passages and curling staircases glittered and shimmered when touched, and delicate frozen beads of water, each encrusted with crystal, hung from the corridor ceilings, swaying and tinkling like millions of tiny bells. At the core of this strange home lay a huge, round living room. Its circular walls were lined with shelves upon shelves crammed full of books and curiosities from all over the ancient world and bulged as if the mountain were pressing inwards. Dominating the center of the room stood a roughly-hewn fireplace where an ever-burning fire always flickered.

Mr. Agyk, not being the tidiest of people nor able to throw a single thing away, had, over the centuries of his life, become a hoarder on the grandest scale. Despite the size of his home and the vastness of its rooms, he had managed to fill nearly every nook and cranny with an immense collection of dust-covered clutter. The living room was no exception. Littered amongst the dozens of faded and matted rugs, their overlapping edges frayed and worn, lay little stacks of books and parchment paper piled in tumbling mounds or stuffed beneath the missing legs of tables and chairs. Above it all, and stretching to a height of some forty or fifty feet, arched an enormous, domed, and vaulted ceiling of the deepest sapphire blue, set with a thousand twinkling stars that drifted across its expanse.

Mr. Agyk lived a hermit life on the whole, unknown to the outer world and isolated from others of his kind, except for a few of his closest friends. However, to the exasperation of these friends, and despite the wizard's own aversion to modern day man, he was also deeply fascinated by humans and their complicated, chaotic lives. On occasions, when this fascination became too great, the old scholar ventured outside — disappearing for days, weeks or even months on one of his expeditions. Often the wizard could be found wandering the streets of the great industrial cities, an unnoticed elderly fellow watching the frenetic pace of humans in their never-ending cycle of work, stress, and life.

So it was, that after one of these strange days Mr. M Agyk eventually returned to White Mountain to find an old friend waiting in the cold. Gralen stood leaning against the rock face, scraping his talons down the ice-covered stone, an expression of boredom and annoyance on his face. "Where have you been?"

"Sorry, am I late?" fumbled the old man, patting his friend on the back. "You know I always get my days muddled!"

Mr. Agyk and his lifelong companion, Gralen, a temperamental and rather portly green dragon with dark, leathery wings and an amazing orange-jeweled belly, stood precariously high upon a narrow and slippery mountain ledge. The weather grew steadily worse as chilling night winds howled and curled over the rocks, blasting a flurry of ice flakes into their eyes. The wizard looked his usual disheveled self, his straggly beard and shock of wiry hair blowing around him like the mane of a mangy old lion. His ruddy features and profile were almost handsome, with pale silver eyes and an impressive Roman nose, the bulbous tip of which reminded the dragon of an unripe or scarlet-colored raspberry, depending on the weather and mood of the old man. Today, it glowed beacon-red. Gralen on the other hand, though certainly impressive at full height or in mid-flight, was a rather overweight and average example of the near extinct North Eurasian dragon.

Mr. Agyk pressed his hand against the rock, eager to get out of the cold. A large doorway appeared. "This is your home too, you should have gone in," he said quizzically, looking at the settled snow on the old dragon's scales. "How long have you been waiting?"

"A while ... waiting and watching," Gralen grumbled, crossing his arms and making no effort to hide his irritation. He looked at the old man's tweed trouser suit. "You're wearing your human robes I see ... you haven't been off on another expedition have you? I thought you'd gone off somewhere south to visit Malty, or one of the others."

Mr. Agyk smiled. "It is cold, let us get inside. After you," he bowed.

Gralen gave him a suspicious look and mumbled something under his breath, then disappeared inside, closely followed by the wizard.

Standing eight feet tall at the shoulder and fifteen feet to the top of his head, Gralen had a broad frame and huge articulated wings, which folded flat against his sides. His long, muscular neck supported a slightly outsized head with overlapping fan-shaped spikes, which splayed out from behind his ears. His large amber eyes, though swift to anger or laughter, displayed a depth and subtlety unexpected in such a lumbering bulk. However, Gralen's most distinguished features lay not in the horns that protruded from his muzzle and forehead, or the wispy chin whiskers he had grown over the years to catch stray bits of food, but merely in the remarkable fact that, in a modern world, he remained the sole surviving member of his kind. The very last of the race of dragons.

White Mountain, the ancestral home of Mr. Marval Aguk.

The dragon settled himself in front of the warm glow of the fireplace. Mr. Agyk shook his outer clothes, which promptly changed to his usual green attire, and vanished down one of the many tunnels leading off from the living room like the burrows of a rabbit warren.

"Is offal sweet-cake alright?" he asked a few moments later, from the general direction of the kitchen.

Gralen stretched in front of the flames, curling and flexing his toes in comfort. "Let me know if I can help," he yawned, closing his eyes.

"No, no," came a hurried voice amidst a clatter of dishes and a faint whiff of peppery smoke.

The wizard reappeared. Floating in front of him were two enormous dishes. Gralen sat bolt upright wrapping his tail around his huge clawed feet. The dishes gently drifted towards him, hovered for a moment, as if offering themselves for approval, then placed themselves neatly on the table in front of the dragon. Mr. Agyk sat cross-legged on the floor as another long procession of plates and dishes piled high with steaming food glided in from the kitchen. Gralen's orange eyes widened, his chin whiskers already twitching wildly.

"Well, tuck in!" Mr. Agyk chuckled and raised a crystal goblet. "A toast ... to great friends and great food!"

"I'll toast that!" spluttered the dragon, his mouth full to overflowing.

The two friends sat for hours in front of the roaring fire talking and laughing and eating until they thought they'd burst. Finally Gralen stretched out, satisfied at last, and patted his pendulous belly. Then, with a contented smile on his face, he lazily began blowing tiny, green fire bubbles into the air. He watched as they slowly drifted up almost out of view, floating higher and higher before exploding in little puffs of emerald smoke and sparks.

Gralen closed his eyes, rather pleased with himself. "I couldn't eat another thing!" he announced at last. "My scales are poking out!"

Mr. Agyk kicked his battered boots off with a satisfying thud, before resting back into his favorite rocking chair: an old wooden throne he'd picked up in the Crusades, with delicately carved intertwining wings for a back and sinuous arms that curled each side into drooping flower-heads. He mumbled a command and instantly the wooden frame creaked into motion, gently rocking him back and forth.

"My stomach is as full as a grouchal's!" he mused, remembering from his youth the giant toad-like creatures and their legendary voracious appetites.

Gralen nodded, his mind drifting towards sleep. "You know, you really shouldn't take the risks you do," he turned to face the old mage. "All these idiotic trips you go on. Sometimes, I don't understand you at all!"

The wizard sighed heavily and stared down at his toes, which were waving at him like fat little men through the many holes in his socks. He had had this conversation before, many times, and he was in no mood for another.

"Must we talk about it? I will not be traveling anywhere for a while."

"Good! I'm glad to hear it … it's about time you came to your senses," muttered the dragon, resting on his back and staring up at the ceiling. "Well, the stars are looking bright tonight," he began, at last.

"Yes," Mr. Agyk murmured faintly. "They grow brighter the nearer we get to the winter solstice."

Gralen tilted his head. "What the hell's that?"

"The winter solstice?"

"No, that noise … you can't hear it?"

The wizard strained to listen. The sound repeated itself. A rumbling tone, low and muffled, barely audible to the old man's ears, yet growing steadily louder.

"Well?" Gralen demanded. "What is it?"

Mr. Agyk shook his head. "I do not … oh, my heavens!" he laughed. "That, my friend, is a message! Someone is using a mimmirian to contact us!" he beamed. "I only use it to reach Wendya these days." He closed his eyes and muttered a bringing-incantation.

"Well, turn the blasted thing off!" Gralen complained.

Moments later, a large triangular mirror drifted into the room and rested in front of them. The noise booming from it was quite deafening. "Enough!" Mr. Agyk touched it and at once it fell silent.

The ancient communicator had been crafted by the old sage himself and allowed messages to be sent and received over vast distances; providing a means of staying in contact with allies from across the globe. The knowledge and art of making such elaborate mystical devices was known to only a few of the most learned mages. Mr. Agyk had made one such rarity for his good friend Wendya years before; few now survived and the secret of how to construct them was all but lost.

Mr. Agyk passed his hand across it. "Who seeks counsel?" The mimmirian's mirrored surface quivered and became a diaphanous liquid before their eyes: metallic yet clear. Ripples formed across it, colliding and merging with each other until an image began to form.

"Who seeks counsel?" he repeated.

Suddenly the liquid stilled and the image cleared to reveal a faint but recognizable face.

"Belloc? Is that you Bell'?" The figure did not reply.

Mr. Agyk shook his head. "Of course, he is not calling now … this is a message, perhaps a few days old."

The figure started to talk but no sound came.

"What's wrong with it?" said Gralen coming closer.

"I do not know. Something is interfering with it."

Gralen narrowed his eyes and stared at the image. "Look at him. Something's wrong. He looks … frightened!"

"Belloc? Never."

"*Look at him*," urged the dragon. "He doesn't look right."

Mr. Agyk stopped fiddling with the device for a moment and gazed at the image of his magus friend. To his surprise, Belloc appeared unusually aged and deeply troubled.

"Yes … perhaps you are right … let me try this," he said altering a small lever, while passing his hand over the mirror. "Tell us your counsel!" he demanded.

Suddenly the device sprang to life and the figure's voice emanated from the screen.

"Marvalla, please come quickly!" Belloc's voice was coarse as if every breath were a struggle. "I do not know who to turn to anymore, who can be trusted. So many have been corrupted. I dare not leave, they are always watching … You must come quickly; so much depends upon you … Marval, I need your help." He paused and lowered his voice to a whisper, his dark eyes flitting nervously around him. "Things are on the move, terrible things … a reckoning is coming, a war … it has already begun. The humans … dear gods, the humans will never be able to survive." The image began to crackle and fade. "–urdered, countless of them! We have to stop it! *You must come!*" The final plea came just before the picture was lost and the mimmirian turned black.

Gralen sat upright. "What the hell was that about?"

"A reckoning … a war?" repeated the old wizard, pressing his hand against the cold glass. "Against whom? How are humans involved?" He sat silently, lost in thought, the worry on his face evident.

"Well, this is a first," Gralen jeered, "him asking *us* for help, but then Bell' always had a flair for the dramatic! *They are always watching* … who's *they*?" he scoffed.

The dragon had never much cared for Belloc. An arrogant and ambitious idiot he thought, too interested in accumulating things, be it wealth or influence. In truth, Belloc had never much cared for the dragon either.

"It seems plain he's in some sort of trouble," Gralen pressed.

"It certainly appears that way," the old man muttered. "But what kind of trouble, –urdered he said. You are right, Gralen, I have never known Belloc to ask for anyone's help, ever. He must be in great need," he shook his head. "He looked … terrified. I have never seen him like that. Something is dreadfully wrong my friend."

Gralen looked at him; he was taking this very seriously.

The wizard started pacing the room. "Curse me for my ridiculous antics! I have been away for far too long. If I am truly honest with myself, I have felt it. Something out of balance, a shifting of energies. I am old enough to know better. I should have listened to my instincts!"

"You're not going?"

"Of course I am, we are," he faced the dragon. "He needs our help. Gralen, what would you have me do?"

The dragon sighed and sucked at his teeth with an awful rasping sound before eating a large lump of food that had dislodged from his back molar.

"Gralen, my dear friend, it will give you an opportunity to stretch your wings and for both of us to catch up with news from abroad."

The dragon shrugged and shifted his weight uneasily. "I doubt there's much news to hear. Things don't change in our world." He couldn't quite muster up his enthusiasm. "We could head off tomorrow I suppose," he said, gently flexing his huge wings and wafting the fire as he did so. "I could use some long-distance exercise."

Mr. Agyk smiled. "Thank you."

Chapter Two
City Of Ice

The next day dawned bright and clear. Sunlight streamed through narrow slit-like windows cut high in the mountainside. It was a cold, beautiful September morning. Gralen's cavernous room and the corridors outside echoed with the big dragon's snoring. Mr. Agyk had had an unusually fitful sleep, full of worrying dreams and dark, shifting images. He was tired and restless when he awoke and had a distinct feeling of apprehension.

Belloc's distressing cryptic message kept playing through his mind. He shook his head and carefully lifted the heavy latch of Gralen's door. It creaked open. The dragon was fast asleep and snoring on his huge bed of willow grass and snootledown feathers, his wings wrapped tightly round him like great leathery sheets.

The wizard stood framed in the doorway for a moment watching his old friend. A stream of autumnal light slowly crept down the walls towards the slumbering figure, igniting thousands of floating dust specks in its wake, like a trail of tiny falling stars. Mr. Agyk loved mornings, the slow awakening of the world, the beginning of things. Gralen, of course, was quite the opposite. He loved the night, especially for flying and, if his stomach didn't wake him demanding food, he could quite easily sleep the whole morning away and most of the afternoon.

"Rise and shine!" the wizard called, at last. He waved a hand at the roof and part of it promptly slid back, opening the room to the sky and the pale morning sun. Gralen stirred and opened a bleary eye.

"It's not morning yet!" he yawned, turning over and pulling the snootledown cover over his head.

Mr. Agyk chuckled. "Yes it is … and breakfast is getting cold!"

A large green head shot up and, in an instant, the dragon was clambering out of the door, "I'm coming, I'm coming!"

After a large breakfast or four, they slowly made their way down to the map room.

"Don't you think we should try contacting Belloc first?" quizzed Gralen. "We should at least know what's going on, what we're flying into!"

Mr. Agyk kept walking, "I have already tried, many times," he sighed. "Our mimmirian is working but his is not. Whether it is broken or disabled I cannot tell, but there is no way of reaching him." He walked ahead a little way, and then stopped. "Here we are."

The map room lay before them. An enormous pyramid-shaped room with tilting walls covered with strange maps, drawings, star charts and atlases, and a pointed ceiling far above, inlaid with a single starstone. The chamber glowed with an eerie luminescence as the early light poured in from small shafts burrowed deep through the mountain rock.

In the center of the chamber, directly below the starstone and its beam of soft light, stood a raised stone dais and, upon it, a large domed table showing a layered Tapestry of Time, as the wizard called it. Shimmering beneath an ever-altering veil lay an overlapping view of both the old and new worlds. Shifting borders, changing coastlines, ancient and forgotten countries, newly discovered lands, islands and whole nations swallowed by the sea. Continents and landmasses torn in two, archaic and ruined ællfr cities, the last few dworll strongholds and, glittering through the veil brighter than anything else, sparkled thousands and thousands of stars, each one a spreading human metropolis. The old scholar sighed again and studied the table; passing his hand over it, he revealed a small area below the mist.

"Now, we need to plan a route, the safest and most direct," he said seriously. "You are not as young as you used to be and my staff will not take us both, certainly not for long distances."

"I'm only 892 years old," grumbled Gralen.

"You are 1364 years old and not a day younger!" laughed the wizard. "Now, Belloc lives in Ïssätun."

"The land of the white bear … *Arrktika!*"

Mr. Agyk shuddered. "Urghh! Dreadful modern name! It has always been Ïssätun and it always will be! We have not been there for a good many years." He glanced over the map and fell silent for a moment, as if troubled by some nagging worry. "I do hope Bell' is alright — he sounded so desperate. There are so few of us left now," murmured Mr. Agyk, a strange sadness in his eyes. "I have allowed myself to lose touch with our own kind," he paused and looked up at his friend and half-smiled. "Well, it is never too late to rebuild kinships, eh?"

"Arrktika," teased Gralen, grinning as the old man winced at the name. "It's a fair way though, it'll take one or two days at least, and we'll probably have to spend the night there, and fill up with supplies," he added cheerfully.

"That is fine. I am sure Belloc will put us up. We could even make it a longer trip and call upon Wendya on our way back."

Gralen's eyes sparkled and a mischievous grin spread over his face.

"Well, that is settled then!" laughed the wizard.

The wizard leaned over the atlas and suddenly the veil parted to reveal a narrow pathway, no more than a sliver, winding from White Mountain steadily northward to the icy wastes of the Arctic.

"Good!" he chirped, "quite direct."

The wizard packed their rather generous provisions and strapped them onto the dragon's back. After changing into his green traveling clothes, the friends were ready at last. Mr. Agyk held his traveling staff aloft: a rather ordinary and scruffy looking cane of twisted willow wood with the merest sheen of silver covering the brownish fleck of its bark. He tapped it lightly on the floor and mumbled an incantation. Mounted on top of the slender stick and seemingly too heavy for its support, sat a perfectly spherical orb of translucent glass. From within this delicate sphere burst a flame, dim at first but quick to brighten, filling the room with a dazzling light.

Mr. Agyk closed his eyes as a faint milky haze emanated from the orb, enveloping them in a shroud of the finest sheer gossamer. He smiled and clambered onto Gralen's back as they slowly disappeared from view. The two invisible travelers shuffled down a long, winding tunnel until they came to a dead-end. The wizard leaned forward and touched the stone wall in front of them, which promptly fell away. There, stretched out before them as a startling, almost blinding white against the sky, stood a thousand snowy mountain tops.

"Ready? Then off we go!" cried the old man, as they leapt out of the tunnel mouth and soared up into the clear dawn sky.

A sudden gust of icy air hit them, taking the wizard's breath away. Gralen hardly noticed. He lowered his head into the wind, arched his back, breathed deeply, and shot forward. As they soared higher and higher, he couldn't stop smiling.

On and on they flew, sometimes above the cloud, sometimes below, following the ridge of mountain peaks as they curled into the north. Hours passed and slowly the mountains thinned, falling away to hills and rolling green countryside. Gralen looked down at the tiny houses and gray, thread-like roads as they rushed past, and licked his lips as they swooped over fields full of grazing cattle and sheep.

Still further they flew, Gralen quickening his pace now, his great wings finding their natural rhythm. Mr. Agyk sat high, perched on the ridge of the dragon's back, the wind billowing his robes, his silver hair streaming behind him, his keen eyes scanning the skies around for airplanes.

"There! A flying craft straight ahead!" the wizard warned.

Gralen dived below it.

"Never had to worry about those in the old days," he grumbled.

The morning and the afternoon waned, and the landscape blurred beneath them as vineyards became industrial outlets belching out thick clouds of chemical smoke, and farms gave way to factories and endless parking lots. The travelers continued north but avoided the larger cities. Soon they were flying over sea, then land again, then sea once more, on into the darkening night as the acidic glare of a million street lights burned the skies behind them.

Time passed quickly now and, just as dawn crept over the eastern sky, the dragon and wizard flew over the last expanse of wintry sea and were soon skimming low over ice and snow, a white blanket as far as the eye could see.

They were journeying onwards when suddenly Gralen veered off to the left, as if following some unseen road sign. Less than two hours later, the companions passed through a strangely dense fogbank and beyond it, a veil of gray mist known as The Dome: a protective shield encompassing Ïssätun and its surrounding land, shrouding it from unfriendly human eyes and acting as an enchantment to any creature that entered.

The land began to change now, as a series of jagged ravines and crevasses appeared, each dropping to a fathomless depth. Large and beautifully sculpted canyons of ice gaped open beneath them.

"It is not far now!" Mr. Agyk shouted.

At that moment, the ground dropped sharply away into a deeper chasm: a vast, sunken ice crater. Nestled at the bottom and surrounded by sheer cliffs of white, stretched Ïssätun, like a sparkling diamond in the sun.

"I had forgotten how beautiful it is!" Mr. Agyk gasped, in awe of the sight before them.

Ïssätun was huge. An immense and vibrant city of ice under a single roof. It covered the entire crater floor in a dazzling array of turrets and steeples all made of glittering white rock, crystal, and snow. Rising above its parapets in undulating waves bobbed vast glassy spheres and huge galleried domes. Along the high walls, towers rose, flanking each entrance and glistening in the late morning sun. Hundreds of pale ribbons stretched across each gateway, dancing in the cold air like welcoming prayer flags or offerings to the gods.

The frozen city was more than just an immense collection of shops, traders, and bustling markets. It remained one of the last outposts for any of the old races to gather: a vital meeting place, a refuge from the modern world, a center of magic and learning, and a crucial link to the past. Its great archives and records were known to be the largest and most complete in existence and a source of immeasurable knowledge. Most importantly, amidst its labyrinth of twisting streets and busy alleyways and its cavernous open spaces, it was the best place to hear news.

A sense of excitement and frenetic activity pervaded the air as the friends eventually landed. Their invisibility veil fell away as they made their way towards one of the entrances.

Gralen glanced up at the fluttering flags, trying to read their scrawled inscriptions as they walked inside. Frozen sculptures and ice-trees celebrating the coming winter solstice and New Year were already in place and a million twinkling star lights decorated the snowy walls. It was busy. Enchanted polar bears wandered past, a large group of pixies were frantically trying to remember where they had parked their branch, teams of faeries and sprites were everywhere, busy hanging up the last decorations and, amongst the general chaos, a witch's convention from Bermuda had just arrived.

"Wendya could be here" smiled Gralen, smoothing down his scales.

"I doubt it," Mr. Agyk replied simply. "It would be too crowded for her. In fact, I doubt if she has ever been here!"

Gralen shrugged, but still kept a lookout for a head of long, raven hair.

Ïssätun was packed. The two friends wandered further in and finally decided to split up. "I'll try to find some information out ... see what's going on ... oh, and I could get a New Year's tree!" chirped Gralen excitedly.

New Year's Day, although it fell considerably earlier in both Ællfr and Dworllian calendars, was the only human festival commonly celebrated. It was also the only event the dragon enjoyed, due entirely to the receiving of presents and the copious amounts of rich food and drink.

"Alright," answered the scholar. "I will head to the information center, then try to find Belloc. He used to live in the old quarter. I will meet you by the main waterfall in about three hours and we can have a late lunch."

An hour passed quickly and Ïssätun got busier and busier. Just before half past twelve an announcement echoed over the speakers.

"Mr. Nicholas is visiting us today, he's on his way. Could the owner of a large orange and red patterned flying carpet, registration W.O.O.L.L.Y.1, please move their rug as they are parked in Mr. Nicholas's space? Thank you."

Less than ten minutes later, an enormous and rather flamboyant sleigh pulled up outside the city. The glitzy wizard, Mr. Nicholas, got out, signed a few autographs, and then wandered in carrying several large empty sacks. The figure, dressed entirely in white arctic fur, darkened his sunglasses and disappeared into the swarming crowds, as his reindeers untied themselves and trotted in after him.

"Humph! Not an attention seeker, eh?" scoffed Mr. Agyk. "He breaks just about every rule and *I* get roasted for interfering in human affairs!"

Another outbreak of excitement filled the air, even greater than before but mixed with something else, awe or perhaps fear. Mr. Agyk looked up at the kafuffle and was amazed to see his old friend Belloc arrive, looking surprisingly robust and followed by a group of very serious young wizards and dworlls. Before he could utter a word, the somber group swept past in a flurry of capes and hushed whispers, as all around fell deathly silent.

"Bell'! Belloc! It is Marval! BELLOC!!" Mr. Agyk called after him. He tried to follow but his friend had disappeared in the throng. "Blast!"

"That's bin happenin' a lot round 'ere lately," came a croaky voice.

The wizard turned to see a shopkeeper behind him. An old and stout, leathery-skinned dworll, his white hair neatly brushed back into a tight ponytail, his platted beard adorned with minute silver and blue beads.

"Pardon?" Mr. Agyk asked, distracted by the dangling beads.

"It's just I saw ya watchin' those youngsters an' that grand magus … I'm sorry sir, I should mind me own business as like it is."

"No, no … please, what were you saying?" asked Mr. Agyk, curious at the look of concern on the old seller's face.

The dworll hesitated and looked suspiciously at the wizard, as if gauging his character.

"I meant nothin' by it sir," he started at last, digging his hands into his apron pockets. "But, well … I bin 'ere longer than most and I seen a great deal of things, some good, some not so good. But I've noticed, like most of us that live and work 'ere, stallers and sellers and traders, ya know … that things 'ave not bin as they should be. There's changes afoot, and not changes for the better, I'll warrant."

The old dworll seemed unduly nervous and looked intently at the wizard again. Then, nodding to himself as if he knew he were somehow safe, he came closer. He lowered his voice, and it seemed to Mr. Agyk that he had been laboring under a great and troubling weight for some time, a worry he had been unable to unburden himself with until now.

"I'm a 'seer', ya see … not a powerful one mind you, but I can tell about people, an' I can tell, that yer to be trusted," he began slowly, "well, we get all sorts 'ere ya see and all sorts bring news from far forgotten parts most of us 'ave never even wondered about!

And, well, by all accounts the rumors and stories of late 'ave bin dark, very dark ... worrying ripples." The shopkeeper leaned against the edge of a large cauldron. "We get more and more of those young wizard an' dwizard types arrivin' every day ... don't buy nothin' mind you, just rush past like that, all frownin' and secretive."

Mr. Agyk's curiosity was well and truly roused. "What stories?" he asked.

"Ah, that's the thing! Whatever's going on they've bin tryin' t' keep a lid on it ... deal with it quietly themselves I'd guess ... but things 'ave a habit of gettin' out and stayin' out. Whatever's got 'em worried we'll probably all know soon enough ... when it's too late!" he added. "In either case, folks say they're tryin' t' get the ol' Order back together, t' discuss things ... can't see it happenin' meself. Most of those folks, beggin' ya pardon, have long since gone."

Mr. Agyk gazed over the shoppers. "I wonder," he mused.

"Anyway," the seller went on, clearing his throat, "I'm sure they'd want a distinguished fellow such as yerself t' help in matters, bein' learned as you are and wise no doubt beyond count!" he said with a false sort of laugh as he tapped his fingers on the cauldron.

Mr. Agyk understood the old seller's meaning. "I will take the large cauldron ... the expensive one," he smiled.

"Oh, oh ... fine choice sir, fine choice!" cooed the old dworll.

The green wizard wandered over to the gilt-edged cauldron. It was quite horrid.

"Have you heard anything specific? Any name or place mentioned? Anything at all?" he asked slowly, opening his drawstring purse.

The shopkeeper looked around furtively. then lowered his voice again. "Well ... only about the disappearances ... mostly. People just vanishin', no warnin', nothin', just gone! We've even had some 'ere!"

"Here?"

"Oh yes sir, nasty business. Started a few years ago it did ... we'd get one or two a year maybe. No one knew where they went, all their stuff would be 'ere but not them! A mystery t' be sure ... but it was all kept quiet though," he tapped his nose. "It would always be worse in the dark months too ... no matter what magic they'd conjure up t' try an' keep the sunshine shining, once winter's 'ere an' that sun sinks, things got worse. Some folks think that's why them flags fly ... that they're lost souls or prayers t' the missin' ... most likely dead! But recently? Well, it's just bin plain bad!" the dworll shook his head, clearly upset over the whole matter. "We had another four go missin' just a few months back ... fine youngsters like those wizards, and two more before that! Came 'ere they did, for a conference or some such grand meetin', and up and vanished right under our noses!"

"They were never found? Nothing was found?"

"Not a whisker! Mind you this is a huge place and no doubt there are parts of it that no soul would want t' go pokin' in. But the search went on for weeks and weeks." The shopkeeper hushed his voice again. "Then, only about four or five weeks ago, some torn robes were found frozen at the bottom of an ice cave out there." The seller waved his hand nervously towards the nearest exit. "Torn t' tatters they were and there was blood an' bits all over 'em! Terrible, just terrible it were. Folks reckon it might be the giant wolf, A'kllut, come back to curse us, or somethin' worse. I hope it weren't those younguns. Anyway, all I know is people got more than a little scared an' folks stayed away. Business has bin very bad!"

"Murdered. Do you know who they were?" Mr. Agyk asked, greatly disturbed over the whole thing. "Do you know their names or where they came from?"

"No sir, I don't, but records might 'ave them, over in the archives."

"Thank you …," Mr. Agyk paused.

"Oh, Limmol sir, me name's Limmol."

"Thank you, Limmol," smiled the wizard and, giving the old dworll twice what the cauldron was worth, he turned to leave.

"Yer ewer, sir!"

"I will pick it up later … thank you again," he nodded, leaving another pile of coins floating in the air as he quickly left, concern etched on his face. "I have been away far too long," he murmured, shaking his head as he watched the shoppers jostle past. He thought of the message again, of Belloc's words, of the fear in his voice. "Something in this place does not feel right," he paused, looking at the faces around, their eyes seeming nervous now and downcast, "something terrible … No, I do not like this at all … I must speak to old Bell'!"

Mr. Agyk walked off at a swift pace, following in the general direction he had seen Belloc, past countless brightly decorated shop fronts and noisy market stalls, past crowded alleyways and smaller offshoots, in search of his old pal. Meanwhile, Gralen, who had bought an enormous ice-tree, was now sitting and waiting for his friend and busy stuffing his face with his fifteenth lizard burger and tadpole shake.

Chapter Three
A Strange Meeting

Where is he?" muttered Gralen, looking round the atrium in a sulk. He'd been waiting for ages, and more importantly, lunchtime had long since passed. He sat, perched awkwardly on the lip of a wide, circular pool, its crystal sides sculpted into scenes showing the founding figures of Ïssätun and the struggles that the ice city and its people had faced. Gralen tapped his claws impatiently on the side and resisted the temptation to deface it a little.

The waterfall thundered behind him, a constant gushing torrent, frothing and cascading into the shallow pool, before dividing off into hundreds of little streams that carved and snaked their way across the icy floor, like the writhing vipers of a gorgon's head. Tiny rainbows sprang and danced in the misty air, as the amber of the

13

late afternoon sun spilled in from the domes, filling the city atrium with a golden glow. From somewhere, Gralen could hear distant music, classical and haunting, drifting in the air and seeming to soar and echo in the glassy canopies far above, as if each crescendo had wings of its own.

The atrium was one of many large gathering places dotted around the city. Although it was busy, the dragon noticed that most people, who seemed shocked to see a living dragon in their midst, were now meeting up and getting ready to leave. Gralen ignored the stares and whispers of gawking passers-by and met them with exaggerated toothy grins and the licking of chops. This seemed to do the trick and had the desired effect of emptying the entire space around him.

"Late … as usual!" he complained.

He eyed the half-empty luncheon basket beside him. Long ago, he had got used to the old scholar's legendary tardiness, and a host of other irritating habits, but it still annoyed the hell out of him. He glanced around once more. There was no sign of him.

"Well, it's his fault!" he grumbled, before grabbing the basket and tucking into the last of its contents.

Hours passed and Mr. Agyk seemed to have been walking for miles and miles. Ïssätun was simply too vast, too confusing and too crowded to look for one person.

"I will have to try a locating spell," he thought as he hurried past another busy arcade of shops, markets, and hostels offering a safe bed for the night.

The wizard walked on looking for a private alcove in which to concentrate, when, out of the corner of his eye, he caught a glimpse of his old friend Belloc. He appeared high above, on one of the upper levels, on what seemed a perilously narrow bridge spanning one of the main squares.

Even from this distance, Belloc seemed remarkably taller than Mr. Agyk remembered — an imposing and silhouetted figure. Belloc stood motionless, his black hair and dark robes billowing about him as if kindled in some mighty solar wind. He stood in the midst of a large host of young wizards and dworlls, some standing, some kneeling, but all utterly mesmerized by him. They pitched forward, straining to get closer, spellbound by his every word and gesture.

"How strange. Looks like a gathering," mused Mr. Agyk.

The old wizard rushed across the square, its glassy floors sparkling beneath his scruffy boots, and over to a lifting platform. Hesitating for just a moment, he gingerly stepped onto the flimsy-looking rectangle. Instantly, the platform shot up.

"Top floor," he mumbled, trying not to look down and feeling rather unsafe as the small oblong wobbled and screeched its way upwards.

The wizard counted each level as he passed it: there were nine, each one supported by colossal ice pillars that rose up from the floor, making the whole place look like the frosted tiers of a wedding cake. He stepped off and found himself in a light and airy gallery dominated by a huge dome above.

This quiet and calming area of the city was lined with a dozen or so smaller and more bizarre boutique shops, selling beautiful silk scarves, tailored cloaks, brocade flying capes, and strange jarred ingredients and potions, some of which still twitched and squirmed in the window fronts.

Mr. Agyk looked across the bridge but Belloc and the other young wizards were nowhere to be seen, in fact the entire space seemed suddenly deserted.

"Blast!" he muttered.

He lifted his face to the sky, it was getting late. He could feel the tingling heat of the setting sun as it streamed through the crystal dome and filtered its way to the ground in hazy strands of rainbow colors. Everywhere the white walls were turning to a sparkling pink and gold in the fading afternoon. He leaned over the railings and looked down, past the numerous bridges and gantries that crisscrossed the square below, to the distant shimmer of the floor and the few ant-like visitors that scurried this way and that across it. It had been many years since he'd been here and, although the appearance of the place remained unchanged, the feel of it was completely different. It had become cold, an uninviting metropolis with only a small number of permanent residents. Somehow, the heart of it had gone.

"I will definitely take the stairs down," he thought, feeling queasy at the idea of descending on the same flimsy death trap.

The sun sank in a brilliant haze of orange, then crimson. Ïssätun, as if in reply, awoke in a breath-taking array of a million or more tiny lights and starstones, all illuminating the city for the coming night. The bridge glittered pink and lilac in the dusky evening. As Mr. Agyk walked aimlessly across it, he felt as if he were stepping into a dream of a time long passed but never forgotten. He glanced around; there was no sign of Belloc or indeed anyone. The city was clearly emptying.

"This is strange … I have never heard of Ïssätun closing for the night!"

He jolted, frozen to the spot.

"Something does not feel right," he whispered slowly, his senses alert, his heart thumping against his chest as a chill ran down his spine like the sharp point of an icy nail.

The very air around him seemed to grow deathly still, colder and darker somehow, as if a veil of shadow had fallen and was dimming the starstones around the city. An electrical charge pulsed through his body. Slowly but unmistakably, he sensed a presence like nothing he had felt before. Something foul and menacing drawing near, silently rearing up behind him. Suddenly, he felt the chilling clasp of a hand on his shoulder.

"Are you looking for me?" whispered a cold, silken voice, so close he could feel its freezing breath brush against his ear.

He spun round and stumbled backwards, astonished to see Belloc, not standing right behind him but quite some distance away on the far side of the bridge.

"I must be losing my faculties!" he smiled awkwardly and rushed over to shake his old friend's hand. "Oh, Bell'! You gave me quite a fright!"

Belloc stood tall, an elegant, sinuous figure of a mage, perfectly groomed and supremely confident. He was swathed in simple robes of deep blue and gray and, as he shifted his slender weight, his drapes moved around him like sails caught in a sudden breeze. His black hair, which held no trace of gray or silver, was swept back from his face and his chiseled features and smooth pale skin glistened with a vibrancy which belied his age. He smiled as if reading the old man's thoughts, his dark eyes fixed on Mr. Agyk from beneath heavy brows. Though far younger and lither in years and appearance than the old scholar, he looked quite different from when Mr. Agyk had last seen him. He had grandness about him now, almost imperial, like a regal conqueror back from some triumphant campaign. This was thoroughly in contrast to the disheveled and ever-shabby Mr. Agyk, with his receding tangle of wiry hair, his wrinkled clothes, and his well-worn face. Belloc smiled again and tilted his head to one side as if puzzling over the wizard.

"Well … Marvalla Agyk!" he murmured slowly, pondering the words. "I am so very pleased to see you. I was hoping you would come." The magus looked at his rather untidy and unkempt friend, the dark purple of his eyes scanning every inch of the old man.

Mr. Agyk smiled. "All this is progress I suppose," he said with a nervous laugh, gesturing toward their surroundings, and feeling more than a little edgy under the wizard's gaze.

"Indeed," Belloc replied at last, "we must all embrace change, don't you think, or be left behind?" his eyes were still fixed on the green wizard. "You are looking well though, very well. Stronger and wiser, I'd say, than when we last met."

"Well, we all age," shrugged the scholar, "but not you it seems. You look better than when I saw you last, very youthful. What is your secret?"

A look of uncertainty — almost anger — flashed across Belloc's face, then passed just as quickly. He smiled broadly and, pursing his lips, he replied, "determination, my old friend. So, you received my message?"

"Oh, yes. Though I must say, I am glad to find you in better spirits than you appeared in the mimmirian. We were quite concerned. It will be good to catch up on news … I have been out of circulation, as they say, for such a dreadfully long time, and without the old network, I have completely lost touch!" he chirped, still feeling strangely uneasy.

"We? Ah, I take it you're still with the fÿrren then?"

"Gralen? Of course. In fact, I am awfully late. I should have met him hours ago!"

Belloc stroked his beard, as if recalling some distant memory of the dragon, or considering a course of action yet to be taken. The silence, though brief, made the old man evermore uncomfortable and he found himself staring at Belloc's hands, watching his long, spindly fingers slowly wind around the hem of his robe. Mr. Agyk noticed he wasn't wearing his usual rings and there was something odd about the pallor and texture of his skin.

"You must want to know the meaning of my message?" the magus asked suddenly.

"Oh, oh yes." Mr. Agyk lowered his voice. "And, well, I have just heard some very disturbing news myself. I wanted to discuss matters with you and offer my services if they are needed. I remember you always had your finger on the pulse, but you seemed in trouble," burbled the wizard, feeling increasingly anxious.

"Yes, but where did you hear this 'disturbing news'?" asked Belloc, studying his friend closely.

Mr. Agyk paused. He couldn't explain why, but he was suddenly and intensely aware that he did not want to reveal the shopkeeper's name, despite the mage's eyes pressing him for an answer and a strange overwhelming desire to tell him. He struggled for a moment, then replied.

"Oh, I do not know the place," he lied at last, "but I take it there are troubles to discuss? Worrying news from abroad?"

Belloc shifted his weight. "Abroad yes and closer, but it's best if we don't talk here," he said quietly, glancing around.

Mr. Agyk looked at him. "Is it not safe?"

"No, not in the open, not after sunset … not anymore." Belloc replied seeming nervous himself for the first time. "You may have noticed that Ìssätun closes for the night now. I'm afraid it has become a very dangerous place for anyone to venture out after dark. I'll explain everything later. We should leave. Come, a nice hot cup of herbal tea and a roaring fire will ease conversation."

Mr. Agyk hesitated. "But Gralen?"

"Will be fine. He's far stronger and safer than you or I," Belloc smiled, placing his arm around his friend's shoulder. "I'm sure he's busy eating, or has found some comfortable corner in which to snooze. Come, we must go, my place is not far from here."

"I thought you lived in the old quarter?"

"I did, but I like to move around … find somewhere quieter and nearer to the center of things," he explained, gently but firmly guiding the old wizard away from the railings and urging him onward.

Mr. Agyk faltered for a moment unsure of what to do, then, casting one last glance downward, he nodded and followed his friend back over the bridge and down a narrow alleyway. Pausing briefly, Mr. Agyk passed beneath a strangely carved arch and disappeared into the yawning mouth of a tunnel beyond.

The muffled noise of the city faded and died away as the two wizards found themselves encased in icy silence. The green wizard shook his head. He was quarreling with himself, as usual, and losing. Nevertheless, he couldn't shake a gnawing fear that seemed to plague his every step. Belloc remained silent and strode ahead, swiftly, as if wanting to find safe shelter before the night truly took hold.

Onward they marched, turning downward now, through tunnels and curling stairways that reminded the old scholar of White Mountain. Only, these passages were not the familiar soft sandy steps of home, nor the reassuring comfort of mountain granite, but were frozen and icy to the touch and lit by strange long starstones that glowed mournfully from above. Still further they went — Belloc's robes and black hair fluttering behind him as he quickened his pace once more — and the passage pressed in around them like the closing of a tomb. Mr. Agyk reached out and traced his fingers lightly over the frozen walls. They were unusually slick to the touch, not the dry ice and snow of the city.

"Well it is not getting any warmer," he thought. Certainly, if there was some heat source ahead he couldn't feel it, in fact, if anything, it was growing increasingly bitter.

He drew his cloak tightly about him. "Is it far?" he asked, finding it difficult to keep up as they passed down yet another gloomy tunnel.

Belloc seemed to be visibly trembling as well. "Not far my old friend," he smiled as the darkness grew deeper.

The stars glinted clear in the coldness around Ïssätun as luminous lights of green, blue and red snaked and danced across the northern skies, ebbing and flowing in curling waves above the glistening towers of the city.

Gralen woke up with a start. He'd been dreaming of distant white peaks under milky blue skies, vast sparkling waters, darkling woods of green and glistening seas of grass as far as the eye could see.

Half the night had passed and the city was silent and bathed in an eerie, blue glow. The waterfall continued to pound incessantly behind him sending fine clouds of cold water vapor into the air. Somehow, Gralen had managed to roll over and melt the ice-tree he'd bought, which now lay in puddles about him. He stood up and shook himself. He was freezing, wet, miserable, and now very worried. The old man had been later than this before, much later, but his guts told him this was different. He looked around. The atrium was utterly still. The whole place seemed depressingly desolate. Markets were closed, shop shutters were down, and black windows were gaping ominously in the shadows, like so many doleful eyes. He listened. Somewhere in the distance he could hear ice-chimes echoing, sounding out twelve o'clock. But there was no sign of life anywhere.

"What the hell's going on? This place isn't supposed to close at night!" he snorted.

There was no moon. The darkened night seemed to menacingly creep in through the walls and close in around him. The only shimmer of light came from the millions of dim starstones embedded in the wintry walls and dangling from the frosty bridges and walkways. Gralen shivered. Mr. Agyk was nowhere in sight but, more worryingly, he couldn't sense any trace of him either.

"Mr. A?" he called out, his graveled voice seeming lost amidst the churning waters behind. "Marval!" he roared. Nothing.

Fear gripped the dragon.

"Something has happened. I know it … I know it!"

Pain, searing, ripping pain, pulsating through him, from him, power surges cleaving him in two, draining and draining him!

Mr. Agyk tried to open his eyes but they were too heavy, like leaden weights were pressing down on his eyeballs. He felt himself struggling. Something had caught him tightly, as if in an iron vice, unable to move, hardly able to breathe. He could hear terrible screams, close by, and familiar — his own? Hisses, half-cackles, half-snarls filled his ears. Mingled voices — haunting, mocking. Dark voices — whispering insidiously to him inside his head, pulling at him, tearing and lashing at him. Nightmare flashes. A face — recognizable, a friend, pale, hollow, disintegrating, melting, and changing before him. Horror! Familiar eyes rolling back, becoming dead, empty, blank.

He fought to open his eyes again, to struggle free. His body felt as if it had been pummeled and pounded by a train and was now being slowly and deliberately torn in two, disemboweled organ by organ. He could feel himself dividing. One heavy, leaden part was sinking into the floor and another lighter, spirit part, hovering above for a moment, then drifting away, escaping into the ether. He tried desperately to catch it, hold onto it, but it slipped through his fingers and beyond his grasp. Darkness fell again. He felt something smothering his face, numbing his senses, an icy blanket dragging him down into the blackness.

Hours passed. Suddenly, the darkness seemed to lift a little as if split. A tear, small at first, then growing, opened up above him and through it tumbled words like jagged shards of glass, cutting and clear. He was aware of a voice, silken, corrupt, dark and cruel, full of trembling excitement and triumph and malice — terrible malice — speaking to him now, stabbing at him with each venomous word.

"You were gone too long Marvalla, but you should have stayed away!" it gloated. "I thought at first you had left with the other cowards … you certainly have kept yourself hidden from the others and from me. Imagine my delight to have you here, finally …," the voice became a whisper, shrill and harsh and choked with hatred. "The others, the lesser ones, faded fast, disintegrating flesh. The young ones took only days, a week at most, a mere snack. Not much feeding to be had there!" It laughed and the sound of it seemed to pierce the heart and wrench the stomach. "But Belloc … your *great friend*." it mocked. "He lasted almost two months. Oh, how he pleaded, how he screamed! I have enjoyed wearing his skin, you know. But you! What a feast! You have immense power — wasted power — yes, older and far stronger … you should last at least twice as long. What's left of you I'll throw to my pets to finish!"

The voice came closer, invading Mr. Agyk as an insidious, sliding thing behind the membrane of his eyes, coiling round his eardrum, spreading its poison.

"You will fulfill my plans sooner than I had expected," it whispered. "You'll be mine, every last drop of you …," it moved even closer, prolonging the moment, "power feeding my own, becoming my own, completing my transformation."

"NOOOO!" shouted the wizard, forcing his eyes open.

The blackness shifted around him. He was alone. He blinked, trying to get his eyes to adjust to the darkness, making sure he was awake and wasn't dreaming, or blinded. He found himself lying face down on the dirty floor of a small dungeon. Every part of him pained. He took a sharp breath and slowly managed to turn himself over. The walls rose smooth and cold around him, like a tomb, except for one wall near his feet, made entirely of narrow crystal bars, shining black.

Mr. Agyk struggled to sit up. Blood pounded in his ears. Every bone, every muscle, every sinew felt heavy, weakened and weary beyond any toil of his long life. He tried to steady himself and get his bearings but his head was swimming. It felt inflated somehow. A wave of pain and nausea flooded his body as he tried to catch his breath, then, instinctively, he felt the back of his head. His fingers found a mass of congealed stickiness, his own blood. He'd been struck heavily from behind.

The old wizard scrambled to his knees, clawing at the wall, he eventually got to his feet. He stood motionless for a moment, allowing the room to stop spinning. Then, stumbling towards the bars he clutched the cold crystal between his fingers and pressed his face against them.

"What is this place? Where am I?" he gasped, squinting into the blackness beyond, and then turning to look at the bars. "Obsidian? No ... Black diamond ... too strong to break," he thought.

The corridor outside, if it was a corridor, was plunged in a deeper darkness. Mr. Agyk listened carefully, trying to silence his racing heartbeat and the throbbing in his head.

"Focus. Focus!"

He could hear echoes now, far off ... whimpers, crying. Shuffling feet, many feet, something heavy being carried, no, dragged. Suddenly, like a sharp prickling sensation down the back of his neck, he was terrifyingly aware that he was not alone.

There, almost out of view amidst the pitch outside, he could see a pair of glassy black orbs, eyes staring back at him from the shadows. He recoiled in horror. A laugh or hiss, different from the other one, younger, thicker and fleshier somehow, escaped from its lips. The eyes came closer, silently gliding towards the bars, hovering and swaying, all their malice fixed on the wizard. Mr. Agyk could just make out the figure of a lean young man like one of the youthful apprentices he had seen following Belloc, only this one was different, this one terrified him.

It was empty and mindless — *demonic*. An unthinking, unquestioning machine. It was as if this miserable creature had had his very essence, his soul and mind, sucked out, leaving only the hideous and obedient shell behind. It moved closer and now the wizard truly felt fear and pity. The man was indeed young, painfully young, no more than a child or a greenling, as he would say. It stood silently, rocking gently from side to side, all its will, all its hatred bent on the wizard, staring at the wizard through dead, lifeless eyes.

"Another one and on the Master's new moon!" it hissed at last. "We do get busy down here!" it cackled feverishly. "But you won't last long. Master will return soon, His Darkness will keep you until he can feed you dry, then you'll be ours!"

"Who?" shouted Mr. Agyk, his voice sounding as hollow as the creature before him. "Who is Master?"

The creature laughed hysterically. "Master of us all, of course ... underground, over-ground, hidden and seen."

Mr. Agyk's head cleared a little. "Belloc? Where is Belloc?" he asked.

The laugh came again, only crueler this time. "Why, dead of course, a long time ago." the eyes stared blankly at the old man, then, with a snigger, they slowly retreated back into the shadows. "We ate him, after Master was finished," the voice hissed again: a lingering horror before the creature disappeared entirely from view.

Silence fell.

Mr. Agyk could hear his own heart pounding once more.

"Hello? Who are you? ... Who is Master? Where am I? Answer me! What have you done to me? ... What have you done to me?"

The wizard's frail voice echoed, but no reply came. He was alone again.

"I have got to get out of here!" he whispered, as his head reeled and his knees buckled and gave way beneath him.

"What have they done to me?" he gasped slumping to the floor in utter exhaustion.

He felt different. Something was drastically wrong and he knew it. He instinctively clutched at his chest, then his face, as if expecting to find a gaping hole there. He couldn't explain it, but he felt changed inside, as if his organs had been removed, leaving a vast and empty void. The image of the horrifying and mindless creature he had just seen came back to him, that awful hollowness. His strength, his life-energy and powers all felt as if they had been forcibly ripped out of him and drained away.

"Impossible!" he muttered.

He closed his eyes and tried to focus, tried to channel his powers. Nothing. The wizard shook his head and tried again. He slowed his breathing, slowed his heart to a soft steady beat, outstretched his hand and focused his every thought, every cell, every nuclei. From his eyes and the tips of his fingers a pale glow emanated, spreading out in long, coiling tendrils of green and silver, then faded and disappeared.

The wizard fell back.

"My powers!" he gasped. "They are gone! ... Gone! They have taken them!" he tried frantically to clear his head again.

"Think Marval! Think! ... No, no they have not taken them all, not yet or I would be dead. Think ... before he ... *it* returns!"

Mr. Agyk paused. His head was swimming again.

"Poor Belloc ... dead ... a long time," he whispered the words and a sadness flooded him as he knew, instantly, that it was true.

"I do not understand ... How could I have been fooled? *What* was that thing imitating him?" He paused again, closing his eyes as the pain and dizziness returned.

Flashes of memory danced before him, a jumble of incoherent images coming back to him, blurred, overlapping, nonsensical ... horrifying.

"Belloc," he murmured again. "Master? The creature *playing* him? Was that him? A shape-shifter ... a changeling?" The idea seemed impossible.

Suddenly he froze, he could hear the dragging sound again, only nearer, then silence, then five or so minutes later, a loud splash like a dead weight hitting deep water.

The thought flashed through his mind. "Getting rid of the leftovers," he winced and shook his head. "I have got to get out of here!"

Chapter Four
Escape from Ïssätun

The city lay under a shroud of brooding silence. Gralen had spent the last four hours recklessly flying through its endless arcades, looking for his friend and growing evermore worried and angry in equal measure. The entire expanse of Ïssätun was deserted, as if its inhabitants were forbidden, or were too afraid to venture out at night.

After searching every street and alleyway and circling the city's many squares and domes, the dragon eventually found one place still open. At the heart of the ice city in the oldest quadrant, stood the great learning centers: Ïssätun's ancient Archives. In front of these towering structures, these great edifices of education, stood a tiny and rather pathetic little information kiosk manned by a few nervous dworlls, unhappy to be doing the nightshift. The Information Centre, if you could call it that, had been doing a fine job doing nothing.

Gralen slowly and deliberately scraped his long talons across the desk making a deep groove in the top and a lasting impression on everyone, as he demanded information. Smoke rings billowed out of his nostrils, spiraling into the air like little green hoops; it was clear that he was not happy. After the initial terror and shock of seeing a real dragon — after so many centuries — swooping down out of the galleries and crashing in front of them, the staff were now huddled together deep in conversation, trying to solve this rather large and volatile problem.

At last, and very reluctantly, the eldest dworll, a gaunt figure with wispy hair and a complexion the color of lard, was 'elected' to address the creature before them, after a helpful push from the others. He inched forward, his face turning slightly gray now.

"Sorry ... s ... sir," he stuttered, clearing his throat. "We've triple-checked our files. No description has come in of the gentleman you refer to. He's not registered at any of the taverns or any other facility and we have no current records of your other friend, Mr. Belloc. He must have left some time ago. Perhaps you sh ... could wait until morning? It's only a couple of hours from sunrise. I'm sure he'll turn up. Most people simply forget the time and reappear from a long night's entertainment no worse for wear!" the dworll explained, trying to smile.

"Not Mr. Agyk! Now, as much as I hate this city freezer of yours, I hate irritating little dworlls who can't do their jobs even more!" Gralen bellowed, trying very hard to restrain his temper and the liquid fire that was welling up inside. "Now tell me, how are people supposed to be enjoying themselves if everything is CLOSED?!"

The dragon took a deep breath, which made them all throw themselves to the floor simultaneously. Then, towering above the desk, he leaned menacingly forward, his nostrils fuming, his orange eyes burning with anger. "Now. It has been over twelve hours since he disappeared and if I have to wait one more hour I'm going to start melting things — starting with YOU!"

Mr. Agyk sat huddled by the bars of his icy cell, his mind racing, his senses alert to the slightest noise. A foul, rotting stench drifted through the air, cloying and churning his stomach as the bitter cold closed in, gnawing through his torn robes as if it had teeth, though he almost welcomed the distraction it brought from the throbbing of his head.

"If I stay any longer I will be beyond the point of escaping!" he reasoned with himself. "Whatever creature this Master is … it must be some sort of drainer. A wizard-thief of some kind, one of the ancient evils perhaps. Dormant and now awoken. Whatever it is, I will not be its next snack … now come on, think!"

He concentrated for a moment and listened for any approaching sounds. Still silence.

"What was it he said? *He'll keep you until he can feed you dry* … He obviously could not take all of my powers at once or I would be dead, perhaps it can only feed in stages."

A whimpering sound came, a quiet sobbing at first, then growing louder and more desperate to an awful pitiful wailing. What hellish forsaken place was this? The old wizard listened until the noise finally died away. He had the unmistakable and sickening feeling that his was just one of many cells. Perhaps hundreds in some huge underground network of ice-dungeons. A nightmarish, nest-like labyrinth full of mindless drones slaving away, tirelessly providing victims for their Master. He shuddered. How long had this been happening? Why had nothing been done? Was this the tormented fate of all those lost souls, all those prayer flags?

"How many others are there caged in the dark?" he wondered. "Come on, you cannot help anyone if you are stuck here or dead!" he muttered to himself. "I still have some powers left, not many but some. Now, invisibility will not help, teleporting needs too much strength and they have taken my staff. Think! The bars are too strong to bend, break or melt. I will probably only have enough energy for one spell, so I've got to make it count! Think Marval, think!"

Amidst the blackness the old man could now hear a strange scratching and scrabbling sound, very faint but drawing nearer. He moved away from the bars as the noise approached, closer and closer, and braced himself, hardly daring to breathe. He strained his aged eyes into the darkness, expecting to see another horror, another mindless thing with black eyes staring back at him, when he suddenly caught sight of it. There, almost indistinguishable from the pitch, came a little moving shadow, shuffling and scampering along the walls, nervously venturing through bars, looking and sniffing for food.

"Hello little fellow," whispered the wizard crouching down and outstretching a hand. A rat appeared out of the darkness. Slowly, driven by curiosity or hunger, it crept forward.

"Come, I promise I will not hurt you. Now, where did you come from, eh?"

The rodent hesitated, then cautiously slipped through the bars and over to Mr. Agyk's hand. It was a half-starved thing, but somehow its bony frame gave comfort to the old man. "No fleshy diet, at least," he thought.

"No food I am afraid and no enchantment I see," he sighed, hoping that this little visitor might suddenly start talking to him. "If you help me find a way out, I will make sure you have enough cheese for ten lifetimes!"

The wizard wondered if rats were as partial to cheese as mice. He stroked the creature, an emaciated, scrawny little thing with the ridge of its spine and the contours of its ribs poking out from beneath its velvet fur.

"Why you idiot!" he exclaimed, louder than he intended. "If I cannot break the bars I will go through them!" He stared down at his nervous little friend as if seeking some counsel.

"If I do this, I doubt I will have the strength to return to full size."

The rat tilted his head, its dark eyes darting to the side, as if startled by something, then suddenly he scampered off back through the bars.

"Exactly! I can worry about that later and how to confront this Master and get my powers back."

The old man sat cross-legged and closed his eyes. Echoes drifted in the darkness; the whimpering again and now an awful moaning from somewhere below.

"Come on! Concentrate, concentrate!" he argued with himself.

He focused his mind, blocking out the horror. All turned to silent darkness. Pinpoints of light suddenly appeared, sparkling around him, growing into towering clouds of colored gases mixing and sizzling with life and energy. Galaxies full of stars collided and streamed through the old wizard's mind, as passing planets became animated blood cells pumping — charged with electricity — green and silver power, his life force, depleted, weakened, but still evident and flowing in his veins … power still … centuries old … down through his ancestors, older than mountains, stronger than stone … hard to destroy.

The great wizard's heart thudded slowly, filling his senses, throbbing behind his eyes. Incantations, ancient verses, Old Dworllian and Ællfren Sanskrit, Nabatean chants, Phoenician poems of lament, sacred Zoroastrian writings, and a myriad of spells in a myriad of ancient tongues all flooded his brain. All his great knowledge, all his long years condensed into one moment, as every particle of his being burst into life.

"Smaller than man, rat sized …," he murmured.

Power pulsed, weakened, and then faded. The wizard fell forward, his body utterly exhausted, his energies spent.

"Uh … not enough!" he gasped. "Not enough!"

Darkness embraced him and he fell formless into its arms.

When at last he awoke, he was hardly able to lift the heavy weight of his head. As he lay there, he gazed up to find himself staring at an enormous, scraggy-looking rat. Its tawny fur and startlingly sharp yellowed teeth faced him with an expression of puzzlement and alarm.

"What? My friend! It worked! It worked!" he cried, glancing up at the cavernous cell he now found himself in.

Suddenly, he became aware of a sound akin to a dog or a feral child, growing louder and more fearful, as if it sensed something moving in the darkness, padding along the corridor.

"Quick! Move!" he shouted to himself, trying to rouse his leaden limbs into working.

The little wizard staggered across the floor and reached the bars. The rat had disappeared into the blackness beyond, but the wizard could still hear him scuttling away. He quickly slipped through the bars and, with one panicked glance around, he ran as fast as his little legs could carry him, on into the darkness, blindly following the sound of the rat.

Seconds later and frighteningly clear, the echoed sound of footsteps resounded, scraping like chalk from an opening above. Someone or something was coming!

Mr. Agyk ran wildly on, half-stumbling, half-falling, until he slammed into a wall. Then, fumbling and feeling his way in the darkness, and still sensing the rodent just up ahead, he followed the line of the wall, away from the growing sound of the footsteps behind.

The animal squeaked, its tiny claws scrabbling on the smooth floor. Mr. Agyk could just see it now, a scrawny shadow bounding away. Onward he ran, as fast as he could, until he thought his legs would buckle beneath him.

"If only I could speak 'Rat', I could have asked him for a lift!" he mused.

The wizard puffed on but his heart sank as the ground before him began to run downward, ever further into the icy earth. Deeper and deeper it plunged until the wizard could almost slide down the floor, so sharp was its incline. Still he ran on, exhaustion plaguing his every stride until he finally came to a fork in the tunnel and had to stop. Here, the passageway divided and ran off in two quite opposite directions. There was no sound or sign of his furry companion.

"Well, he has certainly deserted this sinking ship! So which way now?"

At that moment a blood-curdling screech that turned to a terrifying and guttural roar, like the splitting and cracking of rock, thundered down the passageway behind him, seeming to shake the very ground.

"They have found the empty cell!" he cursed. "Quick! … think, you old fool, which way?"

The little figure stood momentarily poised between the two paths, as the heavy pounding of many footsteps could now be heard coming along the tunnel behind. Mr. Agyk could falter no longer and, grasping his tattered green robes, he raced down the right passage. To his relief and delight it began to rise steadily upward and, as the little wizard climbed, he could now sense a faint draft of fresher air coming down the tunnel towards him. The wizard hurried onward, his legs paining with every step. As he turned a corner he could see, far up ahead, a faint glimmer of blue light.

"Yes! One good decision today at least!" he panted, then froze.

The footsteps behind him were much louder now and cruel voices, rasping and half-crying, full of malice, but also fearful themselves, could be plainly heard.

"Where is he?"

"Master will have our skulls and skins for this!"

"He couldn't 'ave gone far … find him! FIND HIM!"

Mr. Agyk anxiously ran on, the gradient now slowing his progress.

The light ahead, a misty pale blue, grew steadily brighter, along with a strange rushing sound. The wizard pressed on. A delicious chill of fresh icy air flowed down to meet him. Not far now, not far.

He turned and paused for a moment, listening. His pursuers had reached the fork already.

"Come on!" he cried, urging himself forward as the red flicker of torches glimmered in the tunnel behind.

The rushing sound grew louder and louder until it became a deafening roar in his ears. The wizard had no choice but to head towards it. As he passed a final bend in the tunnel he could see a clear opening straight ahead, and beyond it, pure brilliant white. He struggled on, racing forward. Suddenly, in shock and dismay, he skidded to a halt … To his horror the tunnel came to an abrupt end and there before him yawned a huge chasm of ice, a gigantic crevasse too deep and too wide to cross!

He looked frantically across the void. At some point an ice bridge had spanned the abyss, joining the tunnel to another in the far wall, but now only a few broken remnants remained. He was trapped!

"A dead-end! Trapped!" he cried, his little voice echoing round the chamber, before being swallowed by the roar of tumbling water.

The wizard looked up. Far, far above he could see a distant sliver of pale, milky sky and the first glimmer of daylight. He was still deep underground but he could sense the coming morning outside. A glacial waterfall thundered nearby, charging through the chasm, its icy waters rushing down the crevasse walls and into an underground river below.

In horror, the little figure realized that he was not alone. He spun round and gasped. Eight, no, nine torches filled the passageway, blocking his escape, and were now moving menacingly and silently forward, as one solid wall.

"There you are!" the voices hissed as one. "Shrunk! So that's how he got away. No matter. Master will have you tall or pocket-sized!" they cackled, only their glassy, lifeless eyes visible, glistening and black in the torchlight as they moved ever closer.

Mr. Agyk glanced down. He couldn't see the bottom of the crevasse but he could hear its churning waters. He sighed and shook his head. It was hopeless. Then, with an expression of grim resignation, he turned slowly and faced his enemies alone. He watched calmly for a moment, letting the creatures draw nearer, their limbs trembling with excitement, their voices harsh and shrill in his ears. He spoke, striding forward, a bold little silhouette against the light. His voice made them cower in their tracks, as if suddenly unsure of how dangerous their quarry still remained.

"Give your Master, the murderer and thief, a message from me!" he bellowed, his voice booming and as cold and clear as the torrent behind him. "I will find him and I will take back what is mine! My powers shall never be his! NEVER!" Mr. Agyk raised his arms in defiance, and despite his size and battered appearance, the drones recoiled, sniveling and snarling as if his very words were barbed and cut them like steel. "Your

Master will pay for his crimes!" he thundered, stepping back toward the edge. "I will find him and finish this!"

All of a sudden the creatures howled as one, aware of the little wizard's intentions. "NOOOOOOOOOOOOOO!" they screeched, dropping their torches and rushing forward … but it was too late.

To the wretched sound of shrieks and cries, Mr. Agyk turned, took a deep breath, and threw himself from the broken bridge. He plunged into the frozen abyss, the void erupting in a cacophony of angry hisses amidst the deafening roar of the falls … then utter silence. The icy water took him, numbing his senses and filling his ears and lungs, as he fell into its torrent and was swallowed whole.

Chapter Five
The Two Travelers

Darkness swirled around him, blinding his sight. The little wizard found himself carried in a swift-flowing soup of glacial water, spiked with jagged shards of ice which cut him, stinging and freezing him to the bone. Water currents cascaded and churned like so many clumsy hands grabbing at him, dragging him down and under. Ears muffled and filled with a thunderous roar.

Mr. Agyk desperately tried to grasp air, grasp anything. The flow slid past faster and faster, surging over him, slamming him against the icy walls of the channel. He could feel himself slipping, losing consciousness, losing the last of his strength, losing the will to stay alive.

The torrent hurled the little figure forward, shooting him through ever-narrower waterways. At last, he was squeezed into a duct that climbed steeply up and spilled him out into the light. The falls continued to pound, indifferent to the little wizard that fell out half-dead amongst its tumbling flow, to the shallow pool beneath.

Streams of pale blue — the first rays of dawn — crept nervously through the domed roof far above and sparkled in the cold waters. Mr. Agyk opened his eyes and grabbed the side of the pool. Using what little strength remained, he slowly pulled himself out of the water, slid off the lip of the pool and collapsed on the floor, very near to where his old friend had been waiting the day before.

The wizard lay completely still and closed his eyes. Never, in all his long life had he ever felt so exhausted and so spent. Images flashed through his mind: … Belloc … the dungeon … the pitiful whimpering … the horror of the young man with the dead eyes. But worst of all, he could still hear the Master's voice curling inside his brain, its whispering malice stabbing like knives. He felt a dreadful aching loss, a gaping emptiness.

"A wizard-thief!" he muttered deliriously, "a … changeling!"

He tried to fight his fatigue but finally succumbed. And so, as the early morning sun started to fill the city with a reassuring light, the inn-houses, marketplaces and shops began to stir, the little wizard lay motionless; a small figure of stone against the floor.

"What is it?" came a voice nearby. "Is it dead?"

A tiny, winged figure approached the mage and stared at the wet, tattered robes entangled about him and nearly frozen to his skin.

"Gabel, don't get too close!" warned another voice.

"I think it's alive … just," proffered the delicately-winged figure, as he bent over the old man and cautiously gave him a prod.

The wizard groaned and the sprite jumped back.

"Yipes, he's definitely alive!"

"But what is it? … It's not one of us," said another, a burly-looking chap standing behind the leader with a look of puzzlement on his face.

"Well obviously! It's a magus I think … something's happened to him though," answered Gabel.

"Well, if he stayed out here overnight, he's asking for trouble!"

The sprite gave his companion a stern glance. "It looks like he came out of the waterfall," he said bending down again, lightly touching the wizard's hand. "He's icy cold … he won't last long if we leave him here … we should take him to the healers."

Mr. Agyk stirred and mumbled something. He thought he heard the distant *Song of the Sirens* calling to him softly over the waves. He was vaguely aware of being lifted by many small hands, lots of nimble fingers tugging at his clothes and light, soulful voices around him, like music or birdsong, but whispering.

"My name is Gabel," said a kind voice near to him. "You'll be alright."

Mr. Agyk reached out. "A wizard-thief," he muttered, his voice slurred and barely audible.

"What does that mean?" sneered one of the others.

"Shh! … Don't wake him!"

"Gabel, he's probably connected to all the trouble … He probably caused it … we should take him to the council and dump him there, let them deal with him!"

"If they are there!" answered the sprite firmly, while staring at the face of the bedraggled wizard. "No, he deserves our pity and our help … look at him, he's not evil, I'd stake my wings on it!"

"Better yours than mine!"

Mr. Agyk forced his eyes open for a moment and found himself flying. Higher and higher he rose until he was almost within touching distance of the white crystal roof. He turned his head slowly to see that he was being carried by four or five youthful-looking sprites, each one only a little smaller than him, their delicate features and keen eyes staring ahead. Their hair, like strands of frost-covered silk, glistened in the light.

The leader, Gabel, smiled at him. "Hang on! We're taking you to be healed … you've been hurt," he motioned toward the back of the wizard's head.

Mr. Agyk blinked and tried to look down. Far below them — miles it seemed — he could see the city bursting into life again. Shoppers, traders and visitors, oblivious to the horror that lurked beneath their feet, scurried this way and that like busy little insects. None looked up to witness the strange sight above them.

"Who are you?" he asked, trying to focus.

"My name is Gabel Ngalla. We are Ïssätun sprites … but we prefer the term 'flyers'," he smiled and motioned to the figures next to him. "This is Berae, Lesal, Temin and Calis."

"Where are you taking me?"

"To the Sanctuary to be healed … you've been badly injured." Berae replied bluntly.

Mr. Agyk closed his eyes, blocking the throbbing in his head. "No," he said at last, "I need to find Gralen. I have got to get back … got to get back …," he sighed and dropped his head.

"What's he talking about?" asked Lesal, wishing he were anywhere but here.

Gabel looked at the disheveled figure and shook his head. "I think something terrible has happened to him," he said quietly, "perhaps those stories we try not to hear, are true … about the disappearances."

"Shh!" Temin snapped. "It's not our business … whatever has happened to him, is his fault for staying out."

Gabel gently squeezed the wizard's hand, trying to rouse him.

"Can you tell me what happened?" he asked.

Mr. Agyk opened his eyes once more and seemed to half-laugh and half-moan. "Drained … I have been drained," he stammered, "by a changeling."

The flyers fell silent and looked at each other in fear. They'd heard the word before. Whispered in dark corners, hushed warnings uttered but never repeated. They flew higher and faster now as the early morning sun warmed their wings and backs and brought some measure of comfort.

Suddenly the city's speakers chimed and burst into life. "Security! Security to the main desk! Security needed urgently to the Information Cen …"

A roar, more akin to a demonic growl, interrupted the announcer and bellowed out of the speakers, echoing through the ice city and stopping everyone in their tracks. Mr. Agyk roused himself and smiled.

"I know that roar! Take me there!" he gasped. "Gralen … that is where he will be. Take me there, please!"

Gabel nodded to the others and, swooping down, they turned sharply left. Flying above a large suspended gantry, they followed it towards the heart of the city. Within half an hour the little scholar could see, far off in the distance, the familiar green shape of his friend. Gralen stood surrounded by rising plumes of thick gray smoke and, in this steamy haze, occasional bursts of emerald flame could be seen shooting into the air.

29

The dragon was furious; he was raging.

As they drew closer, a scene of absolute chaos greeted them. The information desk lay in ruins. All about were dworlls, some scattered, some cowering or running from the crazed beast, while a few of the security troops attempted to surround and subdue the dragon.

The long line of sprites, each carrying Mr. Agyk by his tatty robes, fluttered down from the ceiling, unnoticed, toward the bedlam below. Relief flooded the wizard to see his old friend again and slowly his senses, and a little of his strength returned. He thanked his rescuers as they carefully set him down amongst the rubble.

Gabel looked nervously toward the rampaging creature as it blasted another large hole in the floor. "Are you sure?" he asked, a worried expression on his face. "We could take you to the Sanctuary ... somewhere safe," he added.

"I am quite safe now I promise you. Thank you, all of you. May our paths cross again under happier circumstances!" Mr. Agyk smiled and tried to bow.

"I hope you find what you're looking for," Gabel replied quietly. "Peace be upon you." They waved and, just as quickly, in a dazzle of light, they shot up into the air and vanished from view.

Mr. Agyk turned to Gralen as he spread his wings to their full height and width and, with a single swish of his tail, completely obliterated what remained of the map stand.

"If I have to tear every rotten ice cube of this place down I will! People don't just disappear!" he bellowed. "There's evil at work here, I can smell it! ... And you ... YOU! ... You're all too frightened of your own shadows to do anything about it! ... Cowards! The lot of you!"

"Harsh words but perhaps true. You are right my old friend ... as usual," spoke a small but familiar voice behind him.

The dragon swung round and nearly fell backwards. His eyes widened in disbelief, his wings suddenly listless. "Mr. A? Marval? ... What the hell? How? Is that you? ... You're tiny!" he spluttered.

The little wizard sat amongst the icy wreckage of the front desk, his battered appearance almost as shocking as his size. Gralen's posture instantly changed from rage to worry as he knelt down before his friend.

Only once in his life had he witnessed the old mage so shriveled and minute, when, in centuries past, he had watched the wizard experimenting on shrinking potions as a way of reducing the endless piles of clutter he had accumulated. But even then, his diminutive stature had been robust: a tiny but hearty figure full of life and vivacity. Never had he seen him so wizened and so frail. It was as if he had gained a thousand years overnight. His face was sallow and drained, his eyes sunken, even his hair seemed whiter and without its usual luster.

"Marval? What ... what has happened to you?"

Mr. Agyk sighed heavily. "Oh dear friend," he stammered, feeling his tiredness return. "I do not know quite where to begin ...," he paused, trying to find the right words, "I was attacked and held prisoner. I do not know by whom or what exactly ... only I fear ...," the wizard gasped as if struck by a sharp pain.

"Mr. A? What?" Gralen shouted, trying to control his temper.

The little scholar swayed for a moment and looked as if he might fall, then motioned for the dragon to pick him up. "I need help …," he murmured, "we need to get to the city's council chambers … I think they may be trying to gather the old Order back together."

"B … begging your pardon," came a timid voice from behind the rubble — it was the dworll announcer, his face even paler and clammier than before. "There is no council here, not anymore. It was disbanded … There hasn't been a proper council in session for years … I mean … I heard they've been trying to reform it to deal with … er, problems … but its members keep … er … ."

"Disappearing?" answered the wizard grimly.

"Ermm, yes, or leaving," shrugged the dworll, wishing he'd kept his mouth shut.

"What authorities do you have round here then?" Mr. Agyk asked.

"Just security. We report to a few elders when they're around … which is rare … people tend to govern themselves nowadays, but there have been a few troubles we can't … ."

"TROUBLES! You call this 'troubles'? Look at him!" thundered the dragon. "He's been attacked in your city!"

Mr. Agyk held up his hand. "Are there any elders here now?" he asked.

The dworll shook his head. "Sometimes there's talk of the elder mages like yourself visiting, but none stay."

"Oh, what a surprise!" Gralen sneered sarcastically. "Don't expect any help here, Marval. They're all terrified of something, that much is clear." he snorted, staring down at the dworll through furious eyes. "What about Belloc? These fools couldn't find him … I know he'd help us!"

"You are right again, old friend," sighed Mr. Agyk shaking his head. "But Belloc is beyond helping us, or even himself now …," he paused and sighed again. "He is dead … and his end was not a pleasant one. I very nearly suffered the same fate. No, this city has changed beyond my knowing. A shroud of evil hangs over it now and festers beneath our very feet!"

His weary eyes strayed over the scene before them. "Evil can only exist here, or anywhere, if people allow it to, if they turn their backs and hide their faces from it … Apathy and ignorance are its closest allies!" he murmured, looking at the dworll announcer.

The old wizard, his robes torn and wet and clinging to his wiry frame, climbed onto the dragon's back and took a final glance at the dworlls gathered there.

"Come on, Gralen … We must help ourselves!"

With that, they took to the air in a sweeping gesture of disapproval and sped toward the ceiling far above. Gralen flew quietly, listening to the wizard's laboured breathing as he began to tell him of his terrifying ordeal in the ice dungeons.

The dragon turned his head. "We should get you to a healer," he said worriedly.

"I will be alright. I am alive at least, but poor old Bell' …," he murmured, lost in the horror of it. "Ghastly! … I think he may have been murdered some time ago," he continued solemnly, his heart heavy with grief and fear.

"What about the message … was that him or this 'thing'?"

"I do not know. Perhaps it was Bell'. The message could have been made months ago and only sent now … to ensnare us." He closed his eyes. "Gralen, there is an unspoken evil here, a darkness behind the façade, beneath the ice, ages old … People have been vanishing for a long time, unnoticed and unlooked for." He winced in pain but continued. "What greatly concerns me is that if evil can grow here, in a place such as this: once a realm of ǽllfrs and all the old races … then what of other, more isolated lands, dworll kingdoms, and ancient citadels? … Is the danger that lurks here, only here?"

"What did they do to you?" whispered the dragon softly.

"I was struck from behind … I remember long dark tunnels, I was following Belloc to his home, or so I thought. Then something dropped down behind me. I think I turned … and that was it. I woke up in darkness."

Mr. Agyk felt the back of his head. It was still very painful and he could feel clots of blood glued in his hair, but at least it was slowly healing. No, the head wound didn't worry him now. His thoughts turned to what they would find … what forces and perils would be waiting for them in the dark, especially for Gralen. And what of the other poor souls still trapped down there?

"No one to help …," he murmured.

"Don't worry about that. I'll sort it out!" growled Gralen.

Mr. Agyk could sense his bristling fury, the ferocity of his rage ready to ignite. He simply did not have the strength to stop Gralen doing something rash and impulsive and he knew it. Despair filled him. How could he hope to face such a powerful adversary with countless drones under its command?

"Can you remember anything else about the place?" Gralen pressed.

Mr. Agyk hesitated. "There were dungeons, lots of them, going deeper into the bedrock, and other poor souls trapped … being fed upon." He paused.

"Fed!" gasped the dragon in horror.

"Yes. This Master has been hunting people … dworlls, mages, young greenlings … trapping and feeding upon them. I think he must be a shape-shifter, a changeling of some sort … like the stories of the Carpathus Magus, *as many shapes as Proteus.*" He paused, his eyes full of bewilderment and grief. "But it looked and sounded exactly like Bell'!"

Gralen shook his head. "A changeling? Are you sure?"

He remembered old stories, myths really, the stuff of idiot fiction he'd thought. Such creatures were unheard of, except for the deepest, darkest rumors — tales to put fear in even the sturdiest dragon.

Mr. Agyk paused again. "An old fool like me should have known better than to ignore my instincts. I knew there was something wrong, out of place about him."

The little wizard looked down at the blur of white streets and shops below and felt as if he were sliding back into a dream, fading into darkness.

"Mr. A? You've got to stay awake!"

"Sorry, I … where was I? … Yes, a shape-shifter or the best trickster I have ever seen."

"And?"

32

The scholar had never been so tired in body and spirit but he could sense his friend's impatience. "I cannot explain but I … I felt … that it drained me, drained my powers and my life force. It tried to consume me. Like the old fables, the first of the ancient evils, the wizard-thieves … Gralen, we have got to find it and stop it!"

"This is bad," muttered the dragon, "I'll feast on its miserable bones!"

Mr. Agyk fell silent as they retraced his journey back to the narrow bridge where he had first seen Belloc.

"Is this it? This place looks all the same to me," scowled Gralen looking round.

The green dragon with his small companion walked across the bridge, its fluted balustrades glistening bright in the morning sun. They followed the path Mr. Agyk had taken the previous day, but couldn't go far.

"Where is it? I do not understand! This is it! … The beginning of the tunnel should be here! … This was a huge archway with strange carvings around it!" he slipped off the dragon's back and pressed his hand against the wall, now no more than a blank panel of ice.

"Are you sure this is the place?"

Mr. Agyk gave him a look that shut him up. "Where is it?" he whispered running his fingers over the frozen surface. It was completely solid with no edge or hint of a doorway. "The entrance must have sealed after me … no way in … no way to get back," he mumbled, slumping to the floor in despair. "And the others … we have got to save them!"

Gralen slammed against the wall with all of his might, digging his talons into the floor to push harder, but it was no use.

"It is gone. He is gone!" Mr. Agyk sighed. "We are too late."

Gralen looked at the ragged little figure and gently scooped him up in his hands. "Well, let's see what a little heat can do!" he smiled and blasted the wall with a focused jet of green flame.

Steam filled the air … but nothing. No sign of melting or even a mark could be seen on it.

"Why isn't it melting?" He tried again and again.

"Stop. Stop! Gralen … a magic stronger than mine has sealed that. Fire, even yours, will not undo it," the wizard sighed again. "Those poor souls."

"We'll free them all, I promise and when we find him …"

"I will deal with him," interrupted the wizard sternly, "If you kill him, I will never get my powers back!"

"Alright, but I can toast him afterwards, can't I?" smiled Gralen belching out a quick green flame.

At last Mr. Agyk relented and tried to smile. "You can wear him as a hat if you like … only let me deal with him first." He pressed his hand against the cold wall once more. There was no sign of any entrance or even a crack. "He is gone. I can feel it," the wizard closed his eyes. "There is no trace of him at all."

Gralen turned and looked at him, his eyes full of worry. "What happens if we don't find him? … If you can't get your powers back?"

33

The little wizard shrugged, he knew the answer all too well.

"After a time, the powers he stole will become his, including the few I have left. I will grow weaker as he grows stronger ..."

"And?"

"Then I will fade."

"Fade? ... You mean die?!"

Mr. Agyk nodded. "You know all this. A wizard's life and powers are one and the same; without either we cannot survive."

Gralen stood silently and for the first time in the dragon's long life he was truly petrified.

"How long?" he said in barely a whisper.

"I do not know," Mr. Agyk answered. "I may have a few weeks or a few months ... What I do know though is that I am not as easily killed as *he* thinks. These bones may be old but they are as tough as boots!"

"Months? Weeks?!" the dragon's voice crumbled as he felt his knees begin to buckle.

"Gralen, I am not giving up, so you must not! We will find this creature and we will make him pay for what he has done," he replied firmly.

Gralen nodded. "Back to White Mountain then?"

"Yes, there is nothing more we can do here. We cannot hope to free those imprisoned below, not yet. Even you cannot burn through mile-thick ice! ... No, I need to gather my strength. Come, let us leave this awful place!" he clambered once more onto the dragon's back.

Mr. Agyk clung to the dragon's scales and, without another word they flew at full speed through the city and burst out into the fresh morning air. Mr. Agyk blinked at the brightness, but as they rushed past the pale flags, he remembered the old seller's words "They're lost souls or prayers to the missing."

"Yes ... and probably dead," he mumbled to himself.

Gralen shot up into the misty blue. Together with the wizard, he had never been so pleased to see the morning and the sun. They sped on, leaving Ïssätun far behind, cold and hard, frozen in the ice. Passing through The Dome without a backward glance the two travelers raced forward with a new urgency.

Once more over endless fields of ice and snow they flew, the empty whiteness stretching before them and dazzling the dragon's eyes. Finally one of them spoke.

"We must fly high my old friend, I have no spells to hide us from view," the wizard sighed. "I am afraid this may take longer without my staff to guide us."

The day passed without event, and as early evening came, wisps of snow began to fall. The first stars crept into the darkening sky spreading a barely visible sheen over the clouds below. Gralen breathed out a long torch of flame, making a path of light in the darkness. The snow fell thickly, making it impossible to see more than a few yards in front. He shook his head.

"This is no good," he complained. "Dragons aren't made for flying through this!"

"I am sorry, old friend," answered the wizard, lifting his head and feeling the soft brush of the flakes against his face, soothing his aches and pains. "When we get home I will be able to regenerate a little and you can rest." His mind still filled with the voice of his captor.

Onward they flew, into the moonless night, trying to find the quickest route home as Gralen swooped and dived through the snow clouds. Utterly exhausted, the little wizard had to concentrate hard to cling on for dear life. The flurry was thicker now and the dragon's wings were getting weighed down in a heavy coating of white.

"Hold on!" Gralen cried as he soared upwards, bursting through the snow clouds and into the thin air of the clear night sky above.

Mr. Agyk looked up at the stars and sighed. "Lovely … just like home."

Far below the twosome could glimpse dark lands, sparkling lights and the orange glow from a hundred sprawling cities. Night turned to day and still the two traveled onwards. Eventually, as the next afternoon passed and the sun hung low in the sky, they dared to drop beneath the clouds. Flying swiftly over the ridges of extinct volcanoes and jagged mountaintops they finally arrived at the tallest peak. Like a towering sentinel covered in pure white … White Mountain!

They landed quickly.

"Home!" Mr. Agyk stepped inside and felt instantly better. "A tonic for the soul!" he sighed.

He hastily changed into some fresh, dry clothes, which shrunk to fit. After tending to his head wound he joined his friend and rested in front of the fire. The wizard stared into the hot coals, lost in thought. Neither of them could fail to notice that the ever-burning fire seemed smaller and less bright, as if it too had diminished.

"What next?" asked Gralen quietly.

The old man looked mournfully into the pale flames, his mind wandering. Gralen watched as the firelight flickered across the lines and cuts on his face which, thankfully, seemed to be healing.

"Let me rest awhile. We will have something to eat … then we will try the books," he answered wearily.

The friends sat quietly for many hours, Gralen's eyes never leaving his slumbering friend as he dozed in and out of sleep. Eventually they ate a small supper and Mr. Agyk found his 'secondary staff', a dual power source similar to the one taken from him, though weaker in strength. The staff instantly shrunk in the wizard's hand, its lustrous sphere shimmering pale green.

"We need a name," he said suddenly, color returning to his cheeks. "We need to know who this Master is and exactly what we are dealing with … the library should help us."

"You said he was a 'wizard-thief' and a changeling," Gralen shook his head, "able to look like Belloc?"

"Exactly … and the voice too. He was a perfect mimic … He described it as 'wearing his skin'" Mr. Agyk shuddered at the thought.

"So, doesn't that mean he could be pretending to be anyone?"

The wizard nodded. "Presumably. He will probably keep playing Belloc until it suits him to pick another victim and another identity … but, as powerful as he is, he still needs to feed."

"I haven't heard of any drainers for over a thousand years, not since I was a young drake. They were all killed, so who is he?" Gralen asked, itching to get his talons into the thing.

"A more powerful mage than me," replied the wizard simply, "I wonder how many lives he has taken, how many bodies and souls he has fed on?"

"Can you remember anything more?" asked the dragon softly.

Mr. Agyk sighed. "I know I felt compelled to follow it. That despite my own instincts I still had the urge to … obey. I could feel it taking me, bending my will."

The wizard paused and looked very serious.

"I have never felt power like that before, Gralen. He is more dangerous and far stronger than you know," he said grimly. "Such terrible power and frightful malice. I have never felt anything like it."

A few hours later they left the warmth of the fire and made their way down the long winding stairs and maze of corridors that led to the Great Library. Gralen walked in front and lit the candles and torches as they went.

The Great Library, the largest of all White Mountain's chambers, lay deep in the roots of the mountain and was a testament to the wizard's obsessive nature of having to collect — or 'hoard' as the dragon called it — as many books as possible. Over the passing centuries the library had expanded again and again to become legendary. One of the largest personal collections of books and artifacts in the world. Only the ancient public libraries and temples of Kallorm and Ïssätun's Archives could match it. Within its shelves lay virtually every book written by mage, witch, ællfr, dworll, dragon, or man from over the last forty thousand years. From ancient manuscripts to engraved steles and stone tablets, from forgotten scrolls to lost treasured texts, everything ever written or carved or painted lay somewhere within its walls.

They turned the last corridor and found themselves in a large vestibule before the mighty library doors. The doors were triangular and dwarfed the green dragon, protruding before them like a great pyramid. Despite the layer of dust that covered them, the doors still glinted bronze in the torchlight and were adorned with thousands of beautiful carvings of one-horns, dragons, wood nymphs and a procession of flying horses, which seemed to dance in the flickering light.

Gralen strolled up and carefully pried the doors open with a satisfying thud. The library inside was quiet and dark and absolutely enormous. A waft of cool air greeted them along with the faint smell of parchment and old bound leather.

Gralen smiled. He didn't care for books as the old man did, but nevertheless this had always been his favorite room and the only one large enough for him to spread his wings and fly in. He marveled at how such a vast space could fit inside a mountain, even one as big as White Mountain. The dragon looked up. Even in the dim light his sharp eyes could follow the smooth granite walls as they rose to such a height that the ceiling above was not visible, only the strands of cloud that floated far above their heads. Fluttering in the gloom flew hundreds of nesting snowdoves, cooing from unseen ledges or swooping and weaving between the library's colossal pillars and shelves, dropping white feathers as they went. Gralen licked his lips. "Fast food," he thought.

Halfway up each pillar dangled clusters of pale glowing orbs like bunches of grapes. As Mr. Agyk walked in they sprang to life flooding the entire library in a soft, golden light. "Everything ever written is in here," smiled the tiny wizard, proudly gazing toward the rows and rows of impossibly tall bookshelves that stretched from floor to ceiling each side of the library. "This will help us."

Gralen squinted and could just make out the far side of the library wall, with its opposing set of pyramid doors, but could not see the length of the room in either direction.

"I love it here," he smiled. "It's great for flying!"

"I doubt the birds agree," chuckled Mr. Agyk.

Gralen turned and looked at his small friend, worry in his eyes once more.

"Will you have the strength to return to full size?" he asked.

"I may have that now," replied the wizard simply.

The dragon looked puzzled.

"Gralen, I need to conserve my powers, especially if I have to confront this creature," he began seriously. "I must use them sparingly. Wasting them on reverting to my normal size will not bring me any closer to my enemy. In this state I can preserve my strength far better." Mr. Agyk winked at his friend, his silver eyes sparkling. "Besides, if this Master thinks he has weakened me more than he has, so much the better. For now, I shall remain small!"

Turning quickly, he strode ahead. His little figure was perfectly reflected in the floor, which, though glassy hard, changed color with every step, shifting and shimmering beneath his tiny feet as if he were walking on oily water. Gralen tapped his foot and watched the rainbow ripples spread outward.

"Hmm … nothing like home," he sighed, swishing his long tail.

Mr. Agyk marched out across the floor until he reached the middle and stood within a thin inlaid circle of silver. "Right!" he said raising his arms to the roof. "Let us get to work!"

He threw his little cloak back and started to chant, half-singing, half-speaking at first, in whispering ancient dialects that the dragon couldn't begin to understand. He recounted spells and incantations in the tongues of old and new and, as he spoke, his words seemed to flow into the air as pale silver strands of light.

He tapped his staff on the ground three times and it burst into flame. At that moment, a strange rustling sound could be heard that grew steadily louder and louder, spreading throughout the room. Within minutes, a thousand books of every size, color and shape started to lift themselves off the bookshelves and fly down to meet the wizard. As each book descended, it opened itself to the right page and started to gently float in a wide, spiraling circle around the little scholar.

From every floating book sprang an amber haze, as the words on each page lifted into the air, fluttering like strange butterflies. Gralen sat down on the shifting floor, enjoying the show but keeping a watchful eye on the old man.

"Please, help him," he whispered, then quietly watched the little wizard as flashes of light came streaming from his staff and subsequently his entire body.

Suddenly, the library began to shake. Books rattled on their shelves, all the snowdoves took to flight; the orbs of light blazed like wildfire. The floor seemed to become a boiling liquid beneath them and the floating books began to spin faster and faster until Mr. Agyk was standing in the middle of a swirling book tornado: the maelstrom completely blocking him from sight.

"Hold onto your horns!" laughed the wizard's voice through the whizzing books.

Then, just as suddenly, the whole library was plunged into darkness and deathly silence. Gralen could only hear his own breathing and the loud drumming of his twin hearts.

"Mr. A? Marval?"

"Well," sighed a voice in the black. "It is a warlock. An ancient wærloga, as I feared, and a powerful one," he paused. "The books have shown me a name, an old and accursed name but it seems ... impossible!"

Gradually, the light came back and there stood Mr. Agyk looking very grim and pale once more. He walked over, exhausted by the effort and slumped down beside his friend.

"An accursed wizard-thief — Morreck ... M'Sorreck of old ... an elder and an evil name I have not heard for many long years," he closed his eyes conjuring up the past. "Morreck was a name whispered in stories to me when I was only a young apprentice, a mere greenling. A phantom of the dark past. I remember my mentor, Larrkis Corniel, and all the old scholars, forbade me or any of us, from even speaking his name, as if the very mention of it would harm us. Corniel destroyed any record in the archives from our prying eyes, even an ancient sand-scroll that spoke of him and the fall of Kalador."

Mr. Agyk sat back, his little head resting against the wall. "According to our books he was a member of the Order but became an enemy of it and was cast out. Banished for foul arts of some kind," the wizard shook his head, "but that was centuries ago. There are fragmented reports of him. I remember hearing the name myself in Kallorm once, but not as a wizard-thief or a changer of shapes! ... No, no. Dark mages and tales of wizard-thieves disappeared from the world after the great wars, long before you or I were born," he paused. "Such creatures were the strongest of wizards, strong and corrupt, using their powers for their own benefit. Turning all things to evil. They craved more power, more life, more influence. An addiction I suppose ... feeding off the weak and the fallen until eventually they started to feed off their own kind ... vulturines!" His voice was full of contempt and weariness. Gralen said nothing but listened quietly.

"Trickery and deceit were their tools, stealing life and magic whenever they could. Parasites of the worst kind," he continued, "only, I have never heard in any legend or verse, of even the most powerful wizard-thief, having the ability to shape-shift! ... There are no real accounts or records of any changelings, other than vague references in folk tales. The underwater *A'Baullka*, for instance."

"The what?"

"Never mind ... Anyway, the books cannot explain it. Changelings do not exist!"

"Like dragons you mean?" retorted Gralen. "Well ... I don't care who or what he is, one thing in life is true ..."

"Which is?"

"If it breathes you can kill it! ... We will find him and finish him!" he said resolutely, feeling the liquid fire in his veins and his own desire to go 'rampaging'. "And when we do," he spat, "he'll meet his match, the last wizard-thief and the last dragon ... he won't expect me!"

Mr. Agyk looked at him grimly. "I am afraid, that is not true ... He does know of you ... when he took Belloc's body he took his voice and his memories too," he sighed again. "Morreck ... the name of my captor and Belloc's murderer is a ... changeling!" he said slowly, pausing over the word.

"This is not good," Gralen blurted out in his usual blunt manner. "All enemies of the Order were destroyed or exiled to the First Realm, A'Orvas, weren't they?"

Mr. Agyk nodded. "A'Orvas, yes. Or sent out into the world where, by all accounts, they eventually died. It does not make sense; any of it ... Why come back, why now?"

"If this Morreck is really as ancient and powerful as you say, then we're going to need more help."

"Yes I am afraid we are ... but ... there is more," Marval fell silent, pulling his knees up under his chin. He was never any good at disguising his thoughts, an atrocious liar — as Gralen would often tease — and he couldn't hide his doubt and worry now.

Gralen studied him and became aware of a startling thought. "How long have you ... we got? Did the books tell you? How long did they say?"

Mr. Agyk avoided his gaze. "At the very most, no more than six new moons ... if I have not regained my powers by the sixth new moon, by the first light of that new dawn ... then it is all over."

"Over? What d'you mean over?! But that's only six months ... at the most!" gasped Gralen, too shocked to think clearly.

The wizard nodded calmly, there was no point lying about it. "Less than six months ... the first new moon was two nights ago. The clock is already ticking ..."

Gralen jumped to his feet. "Where do we find this fengal beast?" he asked.

"The books did not know exactly." Mr. Agyk thought for a moment, his eyes flickering with uncertainty. "The best place would be to find his home. Like me or any mage — even a creature like *that* ... they are strongest in their home, the source and seat of their power."

"But surely we don't want to fight him when he's strongest?"

"No, but if we could find his source, the source of his power and destroy it ..."

"It would kill him?" Gralen said hopefully.

"No ... but it would greatly weaken him, it would give us the advantage, a chance at least," the scholar got up and started pacing, working things out. "Finding his home would bring him to us."

Gralen looked puzzled again.

"Goodness me, you really have been using the library for nothing but flying practice! ... It is an old legend but a true one. The home is the source of strength and if you threaten the home of a wizard, wherever he is, he will sense it and return."

"But how do we find Morreck's home?" asked Gralen impatiently, glad to see the familiar spark in his friend.

"The books only hinted at some of the way. Morreck appears to have a connection to Kallorm ... and that is certainly where I heard the name. But they also showed me somewhere else, a strange and distant land surrounded by mountains ... a place I do not know. It was difficult to see but I glimpsed a golden mountain rising like a thorn out of the earth and surrounded by seas of grass ... and a dark valley full of fire with two crooked horns and a structure, a fort I think at the far end." He shook his head. "It could have been a glimpse of the past, or perhaps one of the ancient realms now lost to us, some hidden forgotten kingdom. But which one and where, I do not know. No name was given."

"We'll start at Kallorm. Someone there may know of this other land," the dragon paused — the old man looked so gray. "Kallorm, the dworll city in Africa, under the jungle?"

"Yes ... Dwellum in Old Dworllian or Silverden in the ǽllfr verse. Wendya used to live there, so she should be able help us ... but Gralen, there is more."

"Great!" he chirped, excited for a moment. "And what about Malty? He could help us."

Mr. Agyk glanced down. "No ... not anymore I fear."

Gralen looked confused.

The wizard sighed. "I asked the books about Malthasar, about any who could help us, and they showed me ... that he no longer lives."

"What!? Malty?"

Mr. Agyk shook his head. "The books have never been wrong."

"Gods! How? When? You think Morreck killed him?"

"I do not know. For his sake, I hope not ... but something has happened to him."

"Malty, dead? ... Wendya! What about Wendya?!"

"She is alright, she is alive, thank the heavens. But we must head for her first. If Morreck is hunting our kind ... Wendya is alone. She is too vulnerable." He turned to the dragon, his voice somber. "Gralen, I am an old fool who stumbles into trouble because I do not have the horse sense to look where I am going! And this time I have stumbled into something beyond the strength of me," he paused and sighed heavily. "Everything tells me that this is only the beginning ... that we may have a very long journey ahead of us and a dangerous one. I cannot ask you to blindly ..."

"Now hold on! If you go, I go. No discussion!"

"Gralen, I do not want you getting yourself injured, not on my account. First Belloc and now perhaps dear Malty too …," he paused. "We must ensure that Wendya is safe, yes, but after that … without my powers I cannot protect you."

"Protect me! Gods! Marval, I'm big and ugly enough to look after myself and you … and without me? … No, no … you're going to need as much help as you can get, and you know it! Besides, if you're right, then this fengal, Morreck is a threat to all of us!"

Mr. Agyk relented. "You are a stubborn fool …," he smiled and sighed, "but thank you, dear friend. I will be relying on you. There will be a lot of traveling."

"Not a problem. I'm as fit as an ox!" he boasted, feeling twinges already in his back and wings at the mere thought of more exercise. "So, let's get Wendya!"

"Very well … we will set a course for the Grey Forest, then probably Kallorm afterwards."

Together, the two companions left the vastness of the Great Library behind and headed once more for the map room and the start of their journey.

"The route from Wendya's home down to Kallorm is a long and difficult one. You have never been to Kallorm, have you?" Mr. Agyk asked, trying to gauge his friend's flying abilities.

Gralen shrugged and shook his head. "Kallorm is full of dworlls and dworlls tend to get nervous around me. I think they think I'm going to eat them or something," he moaned.

"Nothing to do with your temper?" Mr. Agyk half-smiled. "Well, I have not seen the city myself for nearly three hundred years. We may both be traveling to places neither of us are familiar with," he fell silent.

Gralen looked at him. "Everything will be fine," he replied, being uncharacteristically optimistic. "Who knows … if wizard-thieves and changelings still exist, then we may even find some dragons lurking!" he said with a wide tooth-filled grin spreading over his face.

"Perhaps … but time is against us."

All the rest of that night and the next day the two companions worked tirelessly, making preparations for the journey to come. At long last, on the forth night since leaving Ìssätun, when the merest sliver of moon was riding high in the western sky and the last map and provision had been packed, the two friends said goodnight to each other. With tired eyes and heavy hearts they went to bed. Gralen soon fell into a deep, dreamless sleep but the little scholar was plagued by haunting images and insidious whispers.

Chapter Six
The Grey Forest

They had only a few hours of sleep before the sun rose, pale and misty, above the mountaintops. Mr. Agyk woke first, weary after a dreadful sleep full of dark visions and the faces of his fallen friends. His little bones ached and the back of his head still throbbed with a dull persistence. Exhausted and unaccustomed to being the size of a rat, he had eventually settled in the living room in one of the tattered armchairs beside the hearth, as the ever-burning fire grew steadily weaker with each passing hour.

Sunlight flooded the upper vaults and chambers of the mountain as the dragon stirred and the mage kept busy. Once the dragon was awake, the two sat down for a hearty breakfast but, amongst the steaming plates of egglesquell and the crispy bacon loaves, nervousness crept over them: a dread they would not name or even voice. They sat in silence, each lost in their own thoughts, until Gralen had finished his forth helping.

The little wizard felt a wave of exhaustion come over him. "Right," he said taking a sharp breath. "Time to go. The quicker we get started the quicker we will get there!"

A few moments later they left the confines of the mountain and were soaring high in the early morning sky. They climbed steeply through feathery clouds, past v-shaped flocks of geese, who were startled to see a dragon rushing by, and up into the hazy blue where only the warming sun kept them company, and no unfriendly eyes could reach them.

It had been several years since they had last visited the Grey Forest and their good friend Wendya Undokki. Somehow the months had slipped by since they had last spoken to her using the wizard's mimmirian.

"Wend', she'll be alright won't she?"

"Yes," replied the scholar quietly, "… the books never lie. Wendya is alive and well for the moment. But she will need to come with us … at least as far as Kallorm. The Grey Forest is too isolated. I am sure she will protest, but I do not want to leave her there, not now."

"Have you spoken to her on that stupid mirror thing of yours, told her what's happened? I tried working it. I just ended up looking at myself!"

Mr. Agyk fell silent for a moment. "Yes, I have tried … many times. She is not responding."

Gralen turned his head and looked at him. "You're not worried about her, are you? She is alright isn't she?"

"I am sure she is. Like you, she has never been accustomed to working the mimmirian … But it has been a long time since we spoke, longer than I would have liked … ." The old man paused, a shadow of doubt creeping into his mind. "I would feel happier if I had made contact with her. I do not like the idea of her being alone, especially with these disappearances, and Morreck somewhere out there hunting for his next victim."

They flew on in silence for a while until Gralen finally spoke.

"How far is it again?" he asked, gliding on the air thermals to rest his great wings.

"A fair way and it will take longer without my powers to help us," Mr. Agyk answered, happy to distract his thoughts away from Morreck and the loss of his two friends. "The Grey Forest and the Elder Wood, Llrinaru, lie many hundreds of leagues from here," he began. "Urallaia was its ancient name. My human geography is not what it should be, but I believe they call it Siberius or some such place, not far beyond the Ural Mountains."

"I hope I can still find her," Gralen said. "That place confuses me. One tree looks the same as another!"

"I would not say that to her," smiled the old man. "But it is very sizable and the Llrinaru, being the oldest part of it, has always been notoriously difficult to locate."

Gralen peered down through the clouds as they passed over the distant, sprawling grayness of yet another town. "How old is the forest? Is it older than you and me?" he asked, casually.

The little wizard laughed, his straggly beard and cloak billowing in the wind. Gralen smiled; it was great to hear the old fellow sound like himself once more. "Why Gralen, there are saplings older than you, my dear friend, and some as wizened as me!" he chuckled, squinting his eyes towards the hazy sun. "In fact, some of it is so ancient, that its roots reach down to when the world was young. The trees in Llrinaru still retain the wood nymphs and spirits that once lived in the bark and marrow of every tree," he paused, pondering the last time he had seen one of the elusive creatures.

"Legend tells that the wood nymphs, or dryads, were able to manipulate the trees to stretch their roots and branches and send trembling messages through the earth to their kin in other forests hundreds of leagues away!" recounted the little wizard, pulling the hood of his cloak down to enjoy the full force of the air on his face.

"The Llrinaru hold an ancient magic of some sort, which may come from the nymphs or from the trees themselves," he sighed. "But they are the only enchanted part of that forest left now," he said sadly. "If it was not for their 'tree magic', humans would have found that secret place long ago and probably cut down and cleared the entire area, as they have done in so many places … root, branch and bark!" muttered the wizard slowly, a melancholic expression drifting over his face.

"I often think of old tales about Merlin," blurted the dragon wistfully, "trapped in that great oak. I always imagine trees know far more than any of us … all the hidden and secret places in the world."

"Yes … great knowledge locked in wood and memory of earth … only the rock itself is older. In fact Wendya's cottage and its garden are as old as some of those trees. She is a guardian of the forest, they protect her and she protects them," Mr. Agyk continued. "If a human ventures into the forest, the nymphs and the trees know. They somehow disorient the intruders and frighten them away," the wizard deepened his voice, "never to return to such an accursed place!" he smiled. "Despite this modern age, the enchantment over the forest is still surprisingly strong, an ancient and potent power. Local tribespeople have many wonderfully superstitious tales about it."

"Well it makes it damned difficult for us to find!" grumbled Gralen, using his tail as a rudder in the wind.

The little mage tugged at the heavy linen of his cloak, pulling the hood back over his head. His tiny bones seemed to feel the chill of the air more keenly now. He was aware of his weariness and constantly growing pain, a dull ache that came with every movement he made. Wrapping his shabby green robe about him, he snuggled into the dragon's back as they flew higher.

Onward they flew into the late afternoon. Mr. Agyk sat quietly, scanning the surrounding skies. Nearly a week eked slowly past and still eastward and north they flew, with the two adventurers finding shelter and sleep where they could. The sun burned behind them in a violent, orange haze on the closing of another tiring day. They dropped below the clouds and decided to rest for the night near the lapping shores of a vast inland sea.

Gralen started a small fire and the two sat quietly in the glowing light looking up at the clear autumn sky and out across the dark waters. Lights twinkled in the far distance and a faint acrid smell of burnt oil wafted over the shore from an industrial rig or tanker, lost amongst the gloom. They ate a light supper, their spirits low, and then settled down for the night.

"We should be there tomorrow, three days at the most," said Mr. Agyk softly. "If we do not get lost that is."

"Good," Gralen yawned, stretching his wings. "We'll need to leave early and keep out of sight. I saw some towns and lights not far from here."

"I agree … There are so few unspoiled places left in the world now," Mr. Agyk answered, leaning against a boulder and staring up at the stars. "I wonder where *he* is?" he whispered into the darkness, then fell silent.

The friends said goodnight and curled up next to the fire. Again the dragon fell into a deep, snoring sleep, full of bouncing tender sheep and floating beefsteaks. Mr. Agyk lay awake for some time watching the fire spit and crackle and its dying embers drift into the blackness above; until, at last, it seemed to come down to meet him.

"Morreck," he murmured, as sleep took him. "Where are you?"

The next morning came cold and clammy. Mist rolled in from the sea and the pale sun broke its first rays amongst the tussock grasses and the low-lying mud flats of the shoreline. Mr. Agyk was already awake, staring out to sea and watching the blue dawn slowly brighten across the east, revealing a mournful sight in its wake. There lay the remains of ships, rotting amidst the oily sands and shallow waters, or beached high upon the shingles with the drifts of sea foam and detritus that lined the coast. Great metal hulks abandoned and rusting, their carcasses strewn about like driftwood.

Such wanton waste, such madness. How could a people capable of such astonishing feats of imagination and inventiveness behave so mindlessly? He shook his head. Despite all his travels, all his 'expeditions', he was still no closer to understanding humans. Perhaps Gralen and Wendya were right. Perhaps they were all ungrateful greenlings, infants whose abilities far outweighed their understanding, who could so easily save or destroy the planet if they chose. He looked across the waters to the half-shrouded shapes of sea trawlers and fishing boats moving silently in the fog, only their lights visible from shore. The somber air reflected his mood and yet there was something else, something in the wind, imperceptible but there nonetheless — a sense of imminent change.

He wandered back to camp. It had rained during the night and the bitter chill had turned the ground to a hard frost. He soon realized that the dragon had folded his wings into a canopy so he would stay dry.

"The most gracious fellow I know," he whispered.

He busied himself. Soon a fire was lit and breakfast was cooking.

"Up you get. Rise and shine!" he smiled, patting his old friend on the tail.

Gralen rolled over, his chin whiskers covered in drool and stuck to the side of his face. "Is breakfast ready?" he yawned, revealing an impressive mouth of very sharp and expectant teeth, and more than a little bad breath.

Mr. Agyk nodded. "Of course … but I think you may need some mint herb after!"

Following another plentiful and unusual meal, one of the scholar's own experimental recipes, Gralen sat on the fire to put it out.

"We should start flying over the forest by lunchtime, shouldn't we?" he asked, already feeling hungry again.

"With any luck, yes, if my directions have not gone awry."

They traveled on, daring to fly lower over the last lakes and grasslands. Winter seemed to have come early to this vast steppe land. Semi-frozen wastes and barren, open plains flowed beneath them as a formless gray landscape, occasionally dotted with the odd lonely birch or a thin, winding ribbon of broken road or disused railway. Amidst these endless, sloping hills lay abandoned concrete and metal-framed factories, their corrugated roofs missing or half-dangling, as they stood forlornly at the ends of dirt tracks leading to nowhere.

Finally they spied the faint but unmistakable line of trees far ahead and, racing onward with a new urgency, they were soon flying over the first treetops.

The taiga, the great boreal forest, lay before them as far as the eye could see, a dark, coniferous carpet stretching into the distance. It covered everything and seemed, in its vastness, to swallow hills and mountains. Only its cold rivers and streams remained free, breaking the green sea in front of them and twisting through it like precious silver veins.

A strange feeling overwhelmed the friends as they flew over its hidden depths. It seemed to both of them that this was a truly enchanted place on the edge of some distant, forgotten dream, a place entirely out of time, where magic beings still lived and walked in the modern world, and a poignant reminder of ages long past.

"It's huge," gasped the dragon, "I'd forgotten!"

Gralen cast his mind back to his last trip here, many years before, and how beautiful the forest had looked in the late spring. He remembered seeing a few ramshackle wooden huts and hunting lodges sprinkled amidst the outer forest, and how he had even squeezed into an abandoned one and slept there for the night.

"Is Wend' the only one who lives here?" he asked.

"Oh no, the forest has always supported a wondrous number of creatures, winter leopards, snow tigers … though far fewer than it used to," Mr. Agyk paused. "So many changes … It is still the largest forest in the world," he smiled, as if the thought pleased him.

I believe humans still live around its fringes: the Evenki, the Nenet and Khanty tribesmen, and the Chukchi still dwell here, up in the North and Far East … but not within its heart. Even Wendya does not know all of it and she has lived here most of her life …," he paused again, watching as the trees slipped past in a blur, "deep and wild parts that only the wood spirits and the trees know."

"A stony clearing in the ancient Grey Forest,
danger lurking in the shadows.

Gralen dipped his head, looking at the thick carpet below and sighed heavily. Further on they flew, almost clipping the upper branches, while scanning the horizon for a tumbled-down cottage, a wisp of chimney smoke or the silver glint of the Llrinaru trees.

The forest darkened steadily beneath them, trunks thickening, aged and lichen-covered, their branches gathered together and entwining to form an almost impenetrable barrier above the forest floor. Slow-moving elk picked their way tentatively through the mossy and needle-strewn ground, while herds of smaller fleet-footed deer darted through the shadows, their keen senses alert to the green creature that wheeled above their heads.

The trees rose up in endless and towering waves before them, following the contours of the land, flowing down into primeval valleys and deep hollows, then falling away to reveal a few open glades; sparkling jewels that sprang into view and were lost just as quickly.

Onward they glided.

Slowly the landscape began to change. The young lithe-limbed pines and firs gave way to larch, alder, then rowan, oak and ancient birches, their silver barked branches arching toward the sky. These trees faded, giving way to the oldest parts of the forest. Its sacred heart. As old as the earth's granite bones, which protruded here and there as lonely sentinels, ancient weather-beaten tors rising above the dark canopy.

Gralen flew on but could feel the ache of his muscles, his huge shoulders pumping his tired wings forward with each joint feeling the strain.

Hours passed and the day waned, with still no sight of Wendya's cottage or any familiar point of reference. As afternoon slipped into dusk, an unearthly stillness lay on the forest, a brooding presence as if the trees had sensed their arrival and did not welcome it. Gralen felt unusually nervous, he could taste something in the air.

"I've changed my mind, I don't like this place … it's too quiet. It's dead down there!"

Suddenly, as if in reply, the forest seemed to erupt beneath them. Hundreds of birds flew up into the pink sky in a thick cloud and a chorus of wild calls. Insects filled the air and could be heard clicking madly in the shadows below, as if startled by something.

Gralen turned his head. "That's not my fault!"

Just as quickly, the forest fell silent again. Mr. Agyk felt the burn of the sun on his back. It was sinking quickly now, a deep, red flame burning low over the forest and seeming to catch the countless treetops on fire in a carpet of visceral scarlet.

"We can't go on much further," moaned Gralen at last, his wings feeling terribly heavy.

"Oh I am sorry … of course, we will find somewhere to rest," sighed the wizard uneasily. "Well, it looks like another night under the stars!"

"Great!" grumbled the dragon as he swooped even lower, his clawed feet skimming the top branches.

They circled, looking down between the dark shapes and spaces below until they spied a small clearing ahead. Flying closer, they could see that it was a raised, stony hill with a group of limestone tors huddled together. Stacked like many squashed and tumbling pancakes, the smooth rocks glowed salmon pink in the fading sun. It reminded the little wizard of the haunting beauty of Dartmoor which he loved so much — it reminded the dragon of breakfast.

"That looks like a good site. No bumpy tree roots and disgusting crawling things at least!" he snorted feeling exhaustion overtaking him.

Mr. Agyk laughed. "You may be fierce my friend, but you are not fearless! … Well, I for one will sleep under the trees if it rains," he said, pulling his robes tightly round himself as he felt the temperature begin to drop. "It will be cold tonight … It feels like snow," he murmured, looking doubtfully at the deepening sky.

The night was icy and clear. The two friends sat close to a small camp fire nestled between the giant rocks and ate their supper quietly. The forest seemed quite black now and full of moving shadows, of things unseen, lurking in the darkness between trunk and twisted root.

The stars glinted cold and bright, arcing slowly across the sky. A strange and deep foreboding fell upon the two once more, and though neither could explain their fears, they both felt reluctant to close their eyes. Finally with heavy eyes, they succumbed and drifted off into an uneasy sleep of eerie noises and strange dreams.

The hours creaked past slowly. The yellow moon waxed high above them, then began its inevitable decline. As flakes of snow began to swirl out of the blackness, the little wizard awoke with a start.

"Ragnarrok!!" he shouted. "Ugh! What a horrid dream!"

Mr. Agyk, who had been sleeping close to Gralen's side, sat up with a jolt, his senses alerted.

"Something dreadful is happening … tonight … something evil," he whispered, shaking off his grogginess and feeling a sudden creeping fear come over him.

He glanced at his friend. The green figure was snoring loudly, as usual, and intermittently mumbling in his sleep. The fire had died down and only a few of the ashes still showed any sign of life. All was still and silent, muffled by the growing mantle of white.

"You are being an absolute fool, Marval," he scolded himself, "now, come on … get some rest or you will be no good to anyone!" he shook his head and yawned. The air was crisp and the snow seemed cleansing, almost comforting. He stretched, pondering whether to go for a short stroll, when something stopped him short.

There, almost out of view, but no further than fifteen feet away under the darkness of the trees, he could see eyes, red piercing eyes! He gasped and quickly looked again. There were lots of eyes now, multiplying, fanning out around the edge of the clearing, slowly surrounding them. All the fiery stares fixed on him. He jumped to his feet and blinked, convinced he was dreaming, then dared himself to move nearer to the edge of the rock. He squinted down into the dark, his little heart pounding in his throat, and was met by a terrifying pair of burning red eyes staring right back at him.

"Uhh! Who … who are you? … What do you want?" he called.

No sound came from the darkness, but the wizard thought he could hear a rasping growl or a snarl, almost like laughter. He stepped forward to the very brink of the tor and was just about to shout and wake Gralen, when all of the eyes moved and rushed forward.

Mr. Agyk stood rooted to the ground in horror, rather than bravery. The eyes faltered for a moment, uncertain of their opponent. To his relief they stopped but revealed themselves more fully in the moonlight. The sight terrified him.

The snow fell in a thicker blanket now, settling on the hides of a monstrous group of creatures, their huge shoulders crooked and sloping, their backs arched. Wolf-like, yet not wolves. One foul beast, far larger than the others, and quite clearly the leader of the pack, emerged from the tree line. Menacingly, and in complete silence, it strode forward, an abomination of fangs and fiery breath. Its pelt was greasy and matted in clumps, its eyes blood-crimson and full of malice. Mr. Agyk could smell the stench of it from here, like petrol and rotting flesh, and it churned his stomach. As he stared, the beast stopped, barely five feet from the base of the rock. Fumes rose from its putrid skin and its colossal bulk seemed to tremble, swaying from side to side as if enthralled in some frenzied trance, though its fiery gaze never left the wizard. A curdling hiss escaped from its mouth and reverberated through the little wizard's body, chilling his blood; and instantly he knew what it was.

"A fire wolf! A fÿrullfr!!" he uttered in disbelief.

At that moment and to his horror, he became aware of more eyes joining the others, moving closer in the shadows, coming behind, haunches to the ground, mouths snarling, teeth and claws ready for the order to strike.

Mr. Agyk froze, hardly daring to breathe. He could feel his heart hammering against his ribs, and his head started to throb again. He looked around. All the wolfen creatures, including the vile brute in front of him only a short jump away, were rocking violently to and fro and appeared to be under some spell. It reminded the old man of Morreck's mindless drones, obedient and utterly ruthless.

"Be gone foul N'dirron! Demons of the underworld! I am not alone!" he shouted, his voice seeming small and altogether swallowed by the night.

The creatures stirred and awoke from their stupor.

"*Death* … Pain and death will come to you and all who follow you, V … ery soon." the words hissed on the wind and seemed to rattle through the trees, yet no creature appeared to speak.

Slowly, one by one, as if obeying some unseen and unheard instruction, the fire hounds retreated back into the forest. Their hulking shapes lost quickly amongst the shadows, until only their scarlet eyes remained, before they too vanished from view. The green wizard remained perfectly still, as the leader of the beasts lingered, its fire-rimmed eyes blazing. Then, with another rasping snarl like a warning or promise of violence, it faded slowly into the darkness, until even its stare was lost in the pitch. All fell quiet once more. The flurry of snow, oblivious to the horrors that had just visited, continued to fill the clearing covering everything in white silence.

When at last Mr. Agyk moved, he returned to the dead fire and the ever-warm shelter of his friend. For the rest of the night he sat rigid, staring into the forest, expecting to see the eyes again.

It was just before dawn when the little wizard gave in to sleep, exhausted, cold, and unable to stay awake any longer.

"Come on Mr. A., time to get up. You're getting as bad as me!"

Mr. Agyk felt a gentle nudge and opened his weary eyes to see a huge pair of hairy nostrils and an enormous smiling mouth only inches from his face.

"So much for an early start! Well come on!" chirped Gralen, unusually good-tempered, especially for a morning. "I couldn't wait any longer so I've fixed breakfast meself."

Mr. Agyk dragged himself upright. "Uh … oh, is it morning?" he mumbled, as a waft of roasting pinewood and smoke passed over him.

"Morning? It's nearly afternoon!" replied Gralen, crossing his arms. He was clearly eager to get started. "I've been trying to wake you for ages! Are you alright? You look terrible!"

"Oh, sorry, uh, yes," Mr. Agyk looked at him, "ah … did you sleep well?" he asked nervously.

"Not very," muttered the dragon, brushing stone dust off his bottom. "It snowed last night, started to melt when it touched me of course but it meant I woke up in a puddle this morning! Well," he said belching loudly, "third breakfast is ready!" he smiled and shot out a flame to make the fire hotter. "Nettle tea?"

Mr. Agyk managed a smile. It was clear that his green companion was in fine spirits and had slept solidly throughout the night. So, after another hearty breakfast eaten mostly by Gralen, the wizard felt much better and had convinced himself that he had imagined it all, just one of many night terrors he'd had since Ïssätun.

Soon the fire was put out and they were off. Gralen wheeled up into the sky, glad to be leaving the hard rocks behind. A fine dusting of snow and ice still clung to the trees, glistening in the midday sun, while their silver trunks seemed to sprout from the ground like so many winter thickets amidst the white. Here and there patches of rich, dark earth could be seen peeping out from beneath the melting drifts and even the foraging shapes of solitary wolverine and capercaillie could be glimpsed from between the shadows.

The forest lay still and quiet; it seemed a pensive threatening thing to the travelers. They continued on for another three or four hours until they finally spotted what they were looking for. In the hazy distance, Gralen's keen eyesight caught a faint wisp of dark smoke spiraling up into the sky. As they drew closer the smoke grew thicker and hung like a heavy cloud over the familiar sight of Wendya's battered old cottage, most of it obscured in a tangling mesh of ivy and weeds.

"There it is!" Gralen blurted and swooped down with such speed, that he almost turned his little passenger green.

They approached the small patch of open land, but an unfamiliar sight greeted them and caused their hearts to sink. Gralen suddenly stopped and hovered in mid-air. They could now see that the dark smoke billowing into the sky was not from the chimney but from the cottage itself. The entire site lay decimated, blackened and smoldering as if caught in some terrible firestorm.

They quickly landed beside the charred remains of their friend's home, little more than a shell now. Scorch marks and strange scratches rose up the sides of the crumbling walls as if something had been gnawing at the building. Its wooden eaves and the roof had completely collapsed, leaving only a crooked and mournful-looking chimney stack and a few unstable beams from what had been the floor above. Every charred door, window and shutter had been ripped apart or smashed into splinters that littered the floor.

Panic gripped them. There was no sign of their friend, no sign of life anywhere, even the birds were silent.

"Wendya? Wendya! Where are you?" they called. "WENDYA!"

No response came.

Mr. Agyk slipped from the dragon's back. For a moment they stood, staring in horror at the destruction all around. Then, gingerly treading on the debris of what remained of the front porch, they looked inside.

"Wendya?" Mr. Agyk whispered, his gaze drawn from the mess before them to a large smeared bloodstain on the floor and deep gash marks in the walls nearby. He froze. The blood was not the oily black slick kind from all fÿrullfr veins. This was crimson.

"There's been a struggle in here," Gralen mumbled, almost unable to speak. He bent down and picked up a broken chair, trying to set it straight. "It looks like the doors and windows were barred from the inside … but they didn't hold … and …," he sniffed the air. "Wolves. Wolves have been here!"

Mr. Agyk remained silent, a paralyzing sickness growing in his stomach.

"Wolves couldn't have done this! I don't understand." Gralen knelt down and grabbed a small piece of shattered wood, a split table leg, from which hung a length of foul smelling fur, greasy and matted. "It smells like … fire!" he muttered, holding the rotten thing in his hand. "These were no ordinary wolves … Wendya! WENDYA!" he bellowed and, dropping the rancid thing, he turned and charged out to the garden.

Mr. Agyk stood motionless. A little figure, lost.

Wendya Undokki had remained their dearest friend since she was a young witchling, and the closest that the old fellow had ever come to having a child of his own. Since her early days after leaving the hidden city of Kallorm, when the wizard had appointed himself as her guardian, she had chosen to live alone in the wilds of the Grey Forest. A hermit in a truer sense than himself, she seldom ventured far from her forest home, even seeming reluctant to have her friends visit and intrude upon her solitude. Though intensely private, she was a caring figure, with a sharp intellect and a quiet disposition prone to melancholia at times. Her vast knowledge lay not in books and histories but in the intricacies and mysteries of the natural world. Though all practitioners of the herbal and mystic arts had an interest and instinctive trait in such matters, hers stemmed from her own profound and spiritual love of all living things. She had always jested that her friends were akin to the sky and the stars, while she was akin to the earth; by all accounts, there were few plants, trees or creatures that she could not name.

Wendya had dedicated much of her life to protecting her beloved forest and garden, which had always been so breathtakingly beautiful in any month. It was full of the most exotic orchids, moonflowers, sweet-smelling herbs and plants from all over the world, which Mr. Agyk had lovingly sent her from his many travels. It now resembled no more than an ugly, blackened field of ash. Shrubs had been brutally torn out of the ground, bushes still smoldered and every flower had been deliberately trampled and burnt. The very earth looked scorched and scarred. Any trace of her ancient and beloved garden now lay in ruins, like her home.

Desperation took hold of them. They shouted her name again and again, scouring the wreckage, the great dragon bounding through the billowing fumes. Gralen felt as if his two hearts were about to explode through his chest, when they suddenly noticed through the plumes of rising smoke and cinders, a small gray figure near to the edge of the forest clearing, slumped beside an old tree stump. They caught their breath.

"Wend'?" Gralen called softly. He raced over and placed a hand carefully on her back.

The figure turned slowly, her face blackened and streaked with tears. "They destroyed it all," she whispered, "every last seed and sapling."

The young witch sat in a disheveled heap. Her long hair — which 'sparkled as black as a star-filled night,' according to Gralen in one of his more poetic moods — was tangled, singed, and full of soot. Her clothes were torn and covered in the fine gray dust that now filled the air, swirling up the ruins of her home in little pirouettes.

She sat mournfully as if in prayer beside the hewn trunk of a colossal and beautiful old tree. Tears stained her pale freckled cheeks and her deep green eyes were full of grief, and weary from crying. She held her right arm awkwardly and clutched at the bloodied sleeve. Gralen could see she'd been injured, slashed deeply across the shoulder and down her arm as she had tried to escape her attackers. He stared at her and felt the burning of anger rising in him.

"You're hurt! What happened? Who did this?" He settled beside her.

"It's not bad, it's just a cut …," she murmured, half to herself, and then stopped, "Gralen? Gralen! Is that really you? … How? … How did you know? … Oh, I'm so glad you're here. They ruined the garden … they burnt everything!" she wept, hugging him tightly. "They set fire to the trees … and they killed one of the ancient ones! Look!" she cried. "It's stood here since the mountains were formed … look at it! … And the poor spirit inside … burnt alive!" she sobbed and pointed to a small mound of ashen earth where she had buried the nymph.

She laid a single remaining blue flower on the grave and smoothed her hand over the hewn trunk, her delicate fingers tracing its ancient rings back into history. All gone now. The old tree, parts of its silver-green bark still glistening in the afternoon sun, had been slashed horribly, its branches hacked or chewed off, its roots mutilated and torn.

"It was one of the Ellda … one of the first ones of the forest," she said brushing aside her tears.

"What happened?" asked the little wizard gently.

Wendya turned and nearly lost her balance. There before her was a rat-sized Mr. Agyk, leaning on his tiny staff and standing beside Gralen's tail.

"Marval!?" she gasped.

"It is a long story my dear. I will tell you everything later," he smiled. "But first, you must tell us: what has happened here? When we saw the state of the cottage we feared the worst … Are you sure you are alright?"

She nodded, staring at her old friend in bewilderment. But it was not merely his diminutive size which shocked her, but his frail appearance. She had never seen him look so old and so weakened.

"Honestly! I am fine," he smiled awkwardly.

Wendya sighed and wiped the dust out of her eyes.

"I know it sounds mad … but they were fÿrullfrs, demon wolves from the ancient realms!" She shook her head, hardly believing it herself. "For days now the trees and I have felt a strange presence in the forest, something we've never felt before. Of something moving very fast between the trees, something old, but very powerful … closing in. You could almost feel it in the air."

She sat on a large stone and wiped her face with her sleeve. Mr. Agyk said nothing but he could feel the throb in the back of his head again.

"Well," she continued, "last night, soon after sunset I heard a strange noise, like a snarl or a hiss carried on the wind. Now, we have plenty of wolves and brown bears and, thankfully, even some naru'l'tarr … but this was like nothing I've ever heard before. All the trees were nervous and the birds and insects suddenly flew up into the air as if they were escaping a predator in the forest. Something awful frightened them."

"Yes, we saw that," replied the wizard, trying to conceal his worry.

"I thought it was because of me!" mumbled Gralen.

"No, it was them, I'm sure of it … fire wolves," she repeated the words slowly. "Where did they come from? They are extinct. An ancient race of demons from the elder days. How could they be here now?"

"Oh that's not the only ancient and foul thing that's been out hunting …," started Gralen.

Mr. Agyk glared at him and shook his head, then motioned for Wendya to continue.

"What do you mean?" she asked nervously.

"I will tell you everything, I promise, but not here, not now … Please go on," he urged.

She paused and looked puzzled. "Alright," she said quietly, picking up a handful of scorched earth. "I can't explain it … but they seemed to know me, I'm sure of it. They knew exactly how to find me, exactly where I was. I've felt an awful anxiety for the last few weeks, months even, all building up to something … It's ridiculous I know but I have the feeling … I think … they were hunting for me!"

She paused again. She felt utterly miserable and couldn't shake the feeling that something catastrophic was happening. Dread seemed to close in around her, drenching her along with the late afternoon drizzle.

"Well," she whispered, "they found me last night. I was close to the cottage when they came … All I could see were eyes, hundreds of terrible, terrible eyes!" she shuddered. "I was working late, just tilling the soil, when I heard that awful sound again, only closer. It sort of froze me to the spot. I looked up and that's when I saw them," she hesitated, feeling the chill of the air through her wet clothes. "They all rushed at me. They were so quick! … I barely made it to the door when the first brute smashed into it. I tried boarding the windows and barricading the doors but there were too many of them! They were so vicious, so … relentless … whatever I did they just kept coming!" she shivered and shook her head. "They tore up the garden and set everything on fire. They were frenzied, rampaging. They broke into the house and charged straight at me … I only just managed to climb up the chimney! It was horrifying!"

Gralen comforted her but the wizard remained stony-faced and gray, and took to muttering to himself in a low whispering babble. "Ullfrs. Fÿrullfrs. How?"

"They're extinct!" Gralen roared. "The stinking beasts died out when I was a draken, the same time as the last of the dragons … didn't they?"

Mr. Agyk nodded, but remained silent.

Wendya sighed. "Well they were here and very much alive. The great ugly brutes. Apart from eating me, they seemed to be looking for something too," she said, brushing ash from her tattered dress. "If I ever see those filthy beasts again I'll …"

"… toast their hides!" snapped Gralen getting fired up again. "Fight fire with fire that's what I say, and my flames are stronger than theirs!"

"Not if they are hunting in a large pack," warned the wizard. "Wendya, how many were there?"

"I don't know … twenty, maybe thirty … It was dark, all I could see were their red eyes, all around me …," she shivered again and tried to block the image from her head.

The drizzle began to fall heavier now, making thick black splashes in the ash. Wendya looked at her two friends, so dear to her. She was elated to see them, but somehow their being there brought her little comfort … and it was plain that something dreadfully wrong had happened to them.

"Let's get some cover from this rain. I need some tea, then you can tell me what's going on!" she said, looking at the haggard little wizard.

Gralen wrapped a protective arm around her and helped her inside. The place was gutted. The roof and most of the upstairs floor were gone, opening the house up to the heavens, except for a small rickety area still joined to the chimney stack which the three huddled under. The rain came down in gray sheets now as Gralen lit a fire in the blackened chimney, then insisted on tidying up some of the smashed glass and pots and the broken furniture to see what could be salvaged. Finally, in resignation, he fixed some of the floorboards above to form a temporary shelter and the three sat down amongst the ruins.

After a comforting mug of tea they sat in silence for a while, listening to the rain, until at last, the old scholar spoke. He quietly told Wendya of the events that had happened since their fateful visit to Ïssätun, though he left out the more disturbing details. In such a vulnerable place he didn't feel safe naming his captor, or voicing his suspicion that the attacks on the witch and him were somehow connected.

Lastly, and briefly, he spoke to them about the strange wolf-like 'visitors', which had come the night before.

The dragon looked at him. "What in hellfire's name is going on? Demonic changelings, stinking firedogs!" he snorted, puffing out a cloud of green smoke as the rain pounded around them. "Why didn't you tell me these stinking dogs came to us last night? Why didn't you wake me up? I would've sent them packing! Foul carrion! Fengal beasts the lot of them! Killing machines, mindless, with no mercy and no reasoning. They've always been our bitterest enemy. In the elder times good dragons were blamed for killing cattle and even attacking and killing dworlls and humans and we never did; it was always them!"

"Why this sudden reappearance? Where did they come from?" Mr. Agyk glanced at the witch. "What do you think they were looking for?" he asked quietly.

Wendya shrugged. "I've no idea ... I have nothing of any value."

"I wonder ...," the wizard stopped suddenly. "I wonder if they may have been looking for us, Gralen and me. The night before, in the woods, there were not enough of them to attack a full-grown dragon, but clearly there were more than enough of them here at the cottage. Perhaps they were expecting us to have arrived here earlier than we did, then split up and went hunting for us. In any case, if there are fire demons roaming once more, then this is a worrying sign of things to come."

"They're evil to the marrow," replied Gralen "D'you think they were conjured by Morre—"

"Do not speak his name! Not here!" snapped Mr. Agyk "We are not safe yet," he paused. "We must all be careful. Belloc's memories of us will be his now. Through poor Bell' he will know of you and Wendya and the Grey Forest and White Mountain ... and every other person or place we hold dear!" he sighed and turned to Wendya. "He could have unleashed the fÿrullfrs on us. In any event, it is not safe here, for you or any of us, especially after dark. We must leave tonight or I fear more of them will come and we may never leave at all!"

"Let them come!" roared Gralen. "Those fengal beasts will have a match in me!"

Mr. Agyk gave him a look which shut him up.

"But the trees ...," exclaimed Wendya.

"Will have to fend for themselves! You cannot be a guardian to them or the dryads if you are dead!" he warned "Fire wolves are far too good at tracking and they never give up until they have found and killed their quarry! We must go tonight. The trees will have to look after themselves ... *We* should try to find some safe shelter though."

"Somewhere close by," said Gralen. "Only, it'll take us at least two days to be clear of the forest, and I'm not sure if I can fly straight through without some rest."

Wendya nodded. "There's my old tree lodge up on the mountain ridge, my summer house. It's high up in the canopy so it should be safe there."

"Good. That sounds perfect!" smiled Mr. Agyk "Now, Wendya, see if you can gather some essentials, dry clothes would be good and anything else you can carry ... and we must fix your poor arm properly."

After sifting through the debris of her home, the witch had managed to collect a few prized belongings that had escaped the flames. Those she couldn't take with her she carefully hid in the cellar and, with Mr. Agyk's help, put a simple barring spell on them to keep them from harm.

"How are her skills these days?" whispered Gralen.

Mr. Agyk smiled. "She is a better practitioner than you think, she just lacks the concentration needed," he replied, as Wendya tentatively climbed up what remained of the stairs. "There is power there, quite a lot I think. She just has to channel it properly."

An hour passed. The wizard stood on the windowsill, a small silhouette against the sky. The rain had eventually stopped. A cold, autumnal chill blew in from the north. Mr. Agyk stood silently, watching the sun sink lower in an ominous haze, turning the sky from pale gold to blood-red.

"The sun is setting! We have got to go now!" he called.

"Sorry. But I can't believe I nearly forgot this!" she said nervously.

Gralen looked at the huge book tucked under her arm. "What is it?"

"Only the most important thing I own ... my holy book, so to speak! My 'Wiccadian'. Everything is in here, this'll help us!"

"We will look at it later," replied the little wizard jumping onto the dragon's arm. "Come. Time to fly ... the wolves are on the move again, I can feel it!"

The forest around them lay silent and gloomy. Even the trees themselves seemed tense, as if waiting for the falling night. Wendya took one last look at the wreckage of her home and garden, then, climbing onto Gralen's back, the three friends took to the skies.

The young witch felt a sickness clutch at her as if she would never see any of it again, then blowing a kiss goodbye, she said farewell to her beloved trees.

"I hope they'll be safe," she whispered.

"It is not the trees I fear for," replied Mr. Agyk grimly as they disappeared into the deepening skies.

Chapter Seven
Attack in the Dark

The three friends turned south, and then east with the sunset burning behind them. The forest grew darker and more foreboding as they peered into its shadowy depths expecting to see a carpet of red eyes at any moment.

As the harvest moon rose full and pallid, they could just make out a black line of mountains, rising like the long arching back of a whale out of the dark sea around. Following this ridge of tree-covered peaks northward they came to its highest point, an overhanging crest of rock and thin earth that perched precariously above the folded hills below. At the top of this spur of weathered stone stood the tallest and most ancient trees in the forest and hidden amongst the loftiest of these was the witch's summer home.

An enormous structure, yet almost invisible from the sky and the forest floor, it rested in the strong upper branches of a massive Silver Greenwood tree, its pale trunk and branches towering into the sky far higher than any others. Its smooth silvery, green bark — almost velveteen to the touch — was luminescent in the moonlight. Tiny white flowers that smelled of sweet jasmine and honey, dangled from its slender limbs and fluttered in the breeze. The house was reached by a broad, hidden stair carefully carved from inside the marrow of the tree itself. It was larger than Wendya's entire cottage and made exclusively of living branches twisted and woven together.

Two airy platforms greeted them and, perched above these, at the very top of the tree, stood a high observation tower. Inside, the cool, breezy rooms were divided by beautifully carved wooden pillars and woven screens of rustling leaves and flowers. Reed rugs covered the floors and, in two of the smaller rooms, hammock beds swung gently from the ceiling, their silken fibers made of soft golden grass and lined with dove and ptarmigan feathers. Every room in the house stepped out onto a large pillared veranda, a circular walkway that encompassed the entire tree and from which could be viewed the limitless forest below.

Gralen circled the great structure twice, and then carefully landed on one of the larger balconies.

"It's magnificent Wend'!" he said, a little uncertain of how sturdy it was.

"Don't worry," she said with a gleam in her eyes. "It's as strong as granite!"

Gralen promptly dumped their provisions in a tumbling heap and together they lit the many papery lanterns which dangled from bower and branch, each one a beautifully shaped lily or upturned bellflower. The young witch made a small fire and they sat down, their spirits low.

"Welcome," she said, her voice quiet and full of sadness. "You should see it in summer, all pale green and gold and full of the music of the forest ... I don't know why ... but it feels as if summer will never come again."

The young witch felt the cold chill that now blew in from the north. "I'll make us something hot to eat," she said softly and left for the kitchen.

Gralen stared into the fire, his mind consumed with the smell and thought of those foul dogs rampaging through the forest and attacking his beloved Wendya. The mere stench of them made his blood boil. Mr. Agyk, however, sat impassively, watching the darkening skies and feeling a growing unease.

"It won't be long, only half an hour or so," she said returning with three cups of herbal tea.

"Wendya, I need to tell you the rest ... I did not want to speak his name before, but I feel we are safer here ... The books told me the identity of the warlock who imprisoned me and murdered dear old Bell' — and possibly Malthasar too. His name is Morreck."

Wendya gasped and stared at the little wizard.

"I see you have heard that name before," he said, studying the witch's face.

"Swallower of the world," she muttered. "Uhh, yes, a lifetime ago. M'Sorreck ... Morreck!" she repeated slowly. "Are you sure? Could the books be wrong?"

"No, they were quite certain," answered the wizard grimly. "What can you tell us?"

Wendya looked shocked and turned to the fire. "That is a name I have not heard since I was a child ... though he used many names, Molloch, Molkorr ... but all of them evil ... an evil name for an evil creature."

"Molloch ... yes, I remember the story ... the evil deity who seduced parents into sacrificing their own children to him ... for him to eat!" the old scholar shivered and shook his head. "They are the same?!"

Wendya nodded and stared once again at the old man. Fear gripped her as she began to understand. "He did this to you? Morreck? He is this Master, this changeling at Ïssätun?"

"Yes." Mr. Agyk looked at her plainly.

"If Morreck has drained you ... gods! Oh, Marval!"

"Please, go on," he whispered.

She swallowed, her voice lost for a moment.

"Please, we have not much time," implored the wizard softly.

"Alright," she whispered, "but I only know a little, from whispered rumors. Morreck used to belong to the Order many years ago. He was a very powerful magus, even then."

"Yes, the books said as much, and that he was cast out."

"Well," Wendya sighed, "when the old ways passed and the great decision was made, Morreck — like a few others — refused to abide by it. To relinquish the earth to mortal men, lesser beings, was unthinkable to him."

"I hate to say it, but he was probably right," Gralen replied gloomily. "They haven't exactly helped the world, have they?"

Wendya looked at the old scholar. "Morreck was the most influential and powerful elder at the time, with a following of devoted zealots. He was the bitterest opponent of the Order's decision and became consumed by a fury that became ... insatiable. He hated all humans and the Order alike and vowed vengeance on them all."

Wendya's summer home in the Llrinaru treetops of the Grey Forest.

She paused as if remembering something long forgotten. "I think I met him once, when I was very young, in the woods above Kallorm ... before my family disappeared. He was plaguing the city. There was fighting almost every day. I remember this strange figure appeared suddenly in a clearing. I don't know what I was doing, picking berries I think, but I shouldn't have been out. It was a dangerous time ...," she looked at them. "I can't tell you what he looked like ... but I remember thinking that he seemed as fair and as terrible as the sun. A burning, scorching presence. I couldn't see his face clearly and his eyes were veiled, but he seemed untouched by age, but not in a youthful way ... like something preserved yet rotted from the inside." She glanced at her two friends.

"It was only for a moment. The scouts were tracking him. You could feel his power. I had nightmares for a while after ... King Dorrol wouldn't speak of it but he sent out an army to capture him," she drew her knees up under her chin. "Kallorm has a long and terrible history with Morreck. Many, many years ago, he was accused by the City Senate of massacring five entire human settlements, down to the last man, woman, and child. It was widely believed that he was behind the disappearances and murders of many others, dworll and human. Forest tribes, years before, had been mysteriously wiped out ... in any case he was expelled from the Order. I think they were fearful of him, of his growing power and his corrupting influence. Like a dreadful canker, he and his followers would spring up all over the place, causing death and destruction ... the King of Chaos."

"We're in trouble aren't we?" Gralen asked, not liking what he was hearing.

Wendya paused, her mind drifting back into memory. When at last she spoke again her voice was full of fear and doubt.

"Morreck is ... the epitome of evil," she shook her head in despair. "An adversary like him ...," she looked at Mr. Agyk and fell silent. How could they possibly hope to defeat such an enemy? She stood up and wandered over to the balcony. "He was put on the 'Watcher's List' as a danger to others and banished from Kallorm forever, as an enemy of all free peoples. It was then that matters grew worse."

"Worse!" Gralen scoffed. "How could they get worse?!"

She looked at him uneasily, then continued. "Rumors circulated that he broke the sacred oaths we all live by, that he made a sickening discovery. That ... he could possess greater and more terrible powers by feeding off his own kind. By stealing the souls and draining the powers of others he could become ... invincible," she shook her head. "Any who stood in his way were killed, or simply vanished," a look of melancholy fell across her face.

Gralen watched the wizard who was listening intently. "Go on," he urged.

Wendya sighed and looked disheartened. "Uhh ... well, you know ... there were accounts of wizard-thieves, rumors of them back in the elder times. Tales of them descending on battlefields after the fighting, to prey on the dead or dying. But stories tell that Morreck became the worst ... he *sought out* his victims, hunted them, some say. No one could control him. He attacked the city many times and tried to incite a war between our peoples. Then, the attacks suddenly stopped and he disappeared," she shrugged. "Everyone thought or hoped he had died."

"Until?'

"About two hundred years ago, sometime after I'd left. I only know what Halli, the King's daughter told me, that he suddenly reappeared. There was a terrible battle led by Morreck and some awful wargol army he'd conjured. Halli said they only just defeated them and that before he vanished again, he stirred up some great evil beneath the city to plague all those who defied him!"

Gralen looked at her. "Wargols? That's bad!" he leapt up and started pacing the room. "Morreck keeps popping up like a foul smell!" he sneered.

"Yes," she agreed, "but that's why he's so dangerous. He's unpredictable."

"No, no there is method in his madness. Divide and conquer," muttered the wizard slowly, "I think his plans go far further than any of us can imagine," he said worriedly. "Do you think he was behind the Kallorm riots and the Dworllian Wars?"

"I don't know. Probably. I don't know how far back his history goes or how old he is. When I was growing up in Kallorm, Morreck was never openly talked about but he was common knowledge, part of folklore and fear. I know King Dorrol refused to ever mention his name, but Halli was always fascinated by him, she told me most of it. Morreck is Kallorm's bitterest enemy, even though he was once its most brilliant son."

"Son!" exclaimed the wizard. "He was born there?"

"No, but he was raised there and did wondrous things for the city, once. I think one or both of his parents was originally Kallormian … It was all long before my time though."

"Do you know where he was born then?" asked the dragon hopefully.

Wendya shook her head.

"Please carry on," said the old man, growing increasingly fearful.

"There's not much more to say," she sighed. "When Morreck reappeared the last time, Halli did say that he came in another form …," she turned solemnly toward the old wizard, her voice hushed as if she feared unfriendly ears. "He's very powerful, Marval. He may have been defeated then, just … but he will be even stronger now. If he has already taken Ïssätun."

Mr. Agyk looked at her. "What do you mean 'in another form'? Had he shape-shifted?"

"I'm not sure. Halli only said that he tricked his way into the city. But if he has the ability to mimic …"

"Either way, he's not beyond a good hammering!" exclaimed the dragon.

Mr. Agyk's mood was more subdued, as was Wendya's, "Morreck has had centuries to gather himself and grow stronger. Centuries of stealing others' powers …," she shook her head, her eyes staring off into the firelight. "I can't believe he's still alive."

"One thing is certain; Morreck has not wasted these past centuries. Our enemy has been neither dormant nor idle," whispered the wizard.

Gralen stopped pacing for a moment, all this chatter was making his brain ache. "Why the hell hasn't anyone stopped him?" he yelled, itching to get his talons into the thing.

"Who?" replied Wendya. "How? There are too few of us left. Our cities lie abandoned or ruined. Even Kallorm is a pale shadow of her former glory. When I left, the city's population was half of what it had been. Those of us who choose to remain here now are either oblivious or afraid of him or believe, as I did, that he was dead and gone, no more than a whisper of the past," she sighed.

Mr. Agyk looked at them both. It was blatantly clear that this adversary was a match far beyond his skills. "We must find a way to stop him and we shall," he answered firmly. "The fate of all those trapped beneath the ice at Ïssätun and my own future not least, depends upon it … and perhaps the fate of others," he added grimly. "Kallorm seems the place to start. King Dorrol will help us," the little wizard looked at the young girl and paused. "We will need your help, my dear. I have only visited Kallorm a few times in my life and many years ago. I have a feeling your expertise will be greatly needed. In any event, the forest is no longer safe for you."

She hesitated for a moment, then smiled. "Of course, anything I can do to help."

"But we still have to find his birthplace don't we?" asked the dragon. "Does this Dorrol know? … Because without that, we might as well sit here and count squirrels until the world ends!"

"We will find it," reassured the old man, feeling anything but confident.

"How?"

"I do have an idea … if we are really desperate," replied Wendya nervously, "I could try … well, it'll be in my Wiccadian," she said, pointing to her large book.

Mr. Agyk looked at the young witch. "Of course! The last page? I had quite … forgotten. The Oracle?" he asked solemnly.

The witch nodded but Gralen immediately froze, as a sudden chill ran along his scales.

"You call that an idea? That won't help us; it'll only make matters worse! We want to get out of trouble not fly straight into it!" the dragon scoffed.

"It makes sense Gralen …"

"Yes, to a five legged toad!"

"Gralen …"

"No! … We should try Kallorm first … Marval? There must be another way!" he pleaded.

"I do not think there is, old friend," answered the wizard wearily. "Kallorm will help us, I am sure, but it is not Morreck's birthplace. Only an Oracle could give us that information."

"If it doesn't kill us all first!" Gralen argued. "Oracles are not to be trusted! None of them! They're devious, malignant things. It is well known that the one at Delphi used to eat more people than she helped! … Besides, even if they still exist, we could waste time we don't have trying to find one," he replied crossly.

"That's not exactly true," answered the witch slowly, as she opened the book. "As a child we were taught about them … the twelve great Oracles. In every Wiccadian, in the last few pages, it always has instructions on how to find the closest one."

Wendya flicked through the heavy sheets and turned at last to a strangely blank leaf. She smoothed her hand over the parchment and whispered something the dragon could not quite hear. The page shimmered and strange symbols slowly emerged before them in a sparkling ink that seemed to change from silver to red, then back again. Wendya touched the page again and through the markings emerged a map, unclear at first, then growing steadily brighter. It showed a huge jungle beyond a vast sea, with a mighty river snaking through its heart. Wendya translated the signs carefully.

"If in great haste
And help you need
Go to the West
With all your speed."

"In forest foul
You'll find your goal
Near twisted rivers, behind waterfalls
Lives the mighty Oracle."

"Search dark places
Walk through fear
Answer three riddles
And your path will be clear."

"Well I don't like the sound of that!" snorted the dragon, letting his disapproval be known from the outset, before everything went 'tails up' and he got the blame. "If that isn't a warning as plain as damn it, then I don't know what is!"

"I agree," said Mr. Agyk. "But I think it is the only route for us to take. Time is short my friend and we cannot waste a drop of it," he said glancing toward the moon. "We should seek this Oracle first, and then go to Kallorm for any aid the King can give us."

Gralen's head drooped in his customary scowling manner as he proceeded to scrape his claws along the floor.

"One of the Oracles of Wisdom!" whispered Wendya, excited at the prospect of actually seeing such a thing.

Gralen shrugged and slumped in front of the fire. Wendya sat beside him.

"The Oracle will probably be some kind of old sage sitting in a rocking chair … knitting," she smiled.

"Yes, and I'm a flying one-horn!" he grumbled.

Mr. Agyk smiled at the witch as she got up and disappeared back into the kitchen.

"Gralen, there are worse things out there than Oracles … and I have a dreadful feeling that we may meet most of them before this is over," the wizard fell silent as a wave of tiredness flooded over him again.

Gralen looked at him seriously. "Are you sure we should bring Wend' along?"

"I thought you would jump at the chance?"

The dragon shrugged. "I know, but I know how dangerous this could all be!" he whispered.

"You want her out of harm's way?"

Gralen nodded sheepishly.

"I quite understand," the wizard smiled, "I could not bear to see her hurt, you know that, or you for that matter. In any event, harm has come to her door and we cannot leave her here, to face it alone. The forest is too dangerous now and we will need her help with the Oracle and in Kallorm. After that, well ... I will see if I can persuade her to stay in the city." He wandered over to the balcony. The forest below lay utterly black now. The watery moon peered down, pale and mournful somehow.

"Not long until the next new moon," he mumbled and felt a strange queasiness come over him. Looking out across the dark expanse of trees, something suddenly caught his eye. "What is that?"

"What's what?" yawned the dragon.

"A light in the forest, over there," the small wizard pointed to a faint glimmer in the blackness, only a few miles away, just below the rise of a low hill.

Gralen lumbered over and scanned the horizon. "That's no light ... that's a fire!" he bellowed. "The trees are on fire!"

At that moment a clatter came from the kitchen and Wendya raced in. "The forest is burning!" she cried.

Across the darkness of the treetops rose a tall, twisting pillar of flame and, as the three companions watched, to their horror there sprang another fire, then another and another.

"The forest is on fire! The forest is burning!"

As they rushed round the balcony to see more fires appearing, a sudden fear clutched at the little wizard and drew his gaze downward. Far below in the shadows, the entire forest floor seemed to be shifting. Something was moving. Mr. Agyk grabbed the railing and squinted into the gloom. He was met by a pair of fiery eyes.

"Ullfrs! Fÿrullfrs! Look! They are here! ... Fire wolves!" he shouted. "They have found us! We are under attack!"

All at once it seemed hundreds of gleaming red eyes appeared in the darkness around the house. A snarling mass of them gathered and swarmed round the trunk of the great tree while others could be seen moving silently through the undergrowth, their eyes betraying them in the shadows. To their horror, many of the foul beasts had already managed to scale some of the nearby trees and were now clambering into the canopy, dangerously close and almost within reach of their own branches.

"There are hundreds of them!" cried Wendya. "They're everywhere! They're climbing the trees!"

Howls and hisses rose from below, a cacophony that froze the blood of all — except for one of the companions.

"I'll show them!" shouted Gralen, his belly blazing with fire. "I'll send these bloody dogs running!"

"No! There are too many of them!" cried Mr. Agyk.

"Yes, but they can't fly!" bellowed Gralen, shooting out of the tree before the wizard could stop him. "Now … I'll show you a real flame!" he roared as he flew straight up into the night sky, took a deep breath, and then plummeted towards the wolves. Green fire spewed from his mouth like a mighty river, engulfing the fell beasts in the treetops and slamming into those trying to climb or cling onto the tree trunk below; sending them hurtling to the ground and their death in a blaze of fur and flames.

Wendya gasped. "That was a sight!"

But the largest creatures remained on the ground and were unafraid. In reply, they opened their snarling mouths and blasted back a wall of orange and crimson fire. Gralen swerved too late, nearly hitting a tree, and was caught in the assault.

"NO!" cried Mr. Agyk and, using all the strength he could muster, he threw a torrent of lightning bolts down towards the red eyes. Yelps and screams could be heard as the wolves scattered. Suddenly Gralen emerged from the firestorm and, bursting through the inferno, he swooped down as they ran into the forest. Fury fuelled the dragon onward as he poured flames upon their miserable hides.

"They're leaving!" cried Wendya. "Look! They're leaving!"

"No … they are massing for another attack! Gralen get back here! … GRALEN!" shouted the wizard as the dragon whizzed by, circling higher and higher.

Amidst the burning trees and thick smoke, the wizard and witch could see a carpet of red eyes surging forward again, their howls piercing the night with their mindless hatred.

"They are coming!" Mr. Agyk cried, feeling utterly spent.

"There are too many! We can't hold them back!" shouted Wendya, throwing down pots and anything she could lay her hands on. "I could try a spell … a spontaneous combustion spell, perhaps?"

"NO! No! GRAAAALLLENNNN!" the wizard shouted once more.

With that, the dragon careered past, looking triumphant. "Did you see that? I said I'd toast their filthy paws!" he panted, puffing out smoke rings before shooting off again.

Mr. Agyk steadied himself. "He is going to get himself killed!" he shouted, trying to find the strength for another volley of lightning.

Gralen soared into the sky, then hurtled down once more, weaving at reckless speed through the burning trees as he descended upon the hounds. Fire met fire. The dragon burst through another barrage of flame and managed to tear the heads off of several large beasts before being beaten back.

He could feel the pain and hear the crackle of his own burnt skin, raw and bleeding.

"Time for toast!" he roared and, ignoring his own injuries, he shot through the trees.

Skimming perilously low to the ground he tried drawing as many of the creatures away from his friends as possible, before doubling back for another assault. The entire ridge seemed ablaze now. Clouds of green fire fell upon his enemies, smothering them in flame, but still they kept coming back, still they regrouped and attacked.

"Don't they stop?"

"GRALEN!" boomed the green wizard as the dragon made another pass.

The dragon faltered, torn for a moment, then glided down into the tree, the victorious warrior.

"You're hurt!" Wendya said, seeing the burns and gaping tears along his sides and wings.

"Just a little singed that's all," smiled the dragon.

"You are a … a blasted fool! You are impossible!" Mr. Agyk snapped. "There are too many of them! You could be killed you idiot!"

Gralen looked enraged for a moment.

"I cannot lose my dearest friend after all these years!" Mr. Agyk said, trying to calm himself. "You have been very heroic, but we must leave! These fetid beasts cannot be stopped. I feel a greater force is at work here. They do not fear death or pain!"

"Quick!" shouted Wendya. "They're coming up the tree!"

She leant over the balcony to see a mass of dark, crawling shapes swarming up the trunk towards them like horrid black spiders.

"Watch out!" shouted Gralen, pulling her back just as a ball of fire shot past her face. "Don't give them a target!"

Suddenly, amidst the chaos of hisses and the roar and crackle of the flames, the three friends could hear a terrible scrabbling sound, distant at first but getting louder. Wendya turned and raced over to a small door carved into the trunk and prized it open. The stairwell inside was pitch black and dropped, for several hundreds of feet, down to the ground below.

"Hand me that lantern," she said and shone the dim light into the shaft, "I can't see anything … no … wait … they're coming! They're coming!" she screamed, as a wave of things filled the stairs, teeming up the steps, falling and clambering over each other to reach them. "They've found the passageway! They're coming up!"

"Bar the door! … Come on! We have got to go NOW!" shouted Mr. Agyk just as he spun round to see a huge pair of eyes, rimmed with fire, crawling over the balcony behind him. "Look out!" he cried as the enormous wolfen beast, bear-like and larger than the rest, reared up ready to pounce.

Before either the dragon or wizard could react, Wendya sprang into view and, holding a small table, she smashed it into the creature's face, shattering it into hundreds of splinters that sizzled in the air. The wolf roared, its flames shooting upwards, black and venomous, as it fell back in pain and surprise.

"That's for trespassing!" she shouted, picking up a large shard of broken wood, "and that's for my house!" she hollered, stabbing the creature in the chest.

The wolf screamed as the wood burst into flames in her hand.

"Come on!" boomed the wizard as Gralen grabbed Wendya's arm and dragged her away.

Crimson eyes now appeared all around them as the witch and wizard scrambled onto Gralen's back and the door to the stairwell blasted open.

"GO!" Mr. Agyk shouted, "GO!"

"Hold on!" the dragon warned, sending his full fury towards the beasts in a torrent of green fire.

He quickly grabbed the Wiccadian and as many provisions as he could carry, then ran wildly towards the beasts, punching through the balcony and up into the sky in a blaze of flame and triumph.

"I showed them!" he roared.

They bolted up into the night through curling smoke and flying embers. As they flew, the forest seemed to explode beneath them in a horrifying chorus of howls. Hundreds of blood-chilling voices screeched from the forest floor and the canopy heights they had just left, as the fire wolves went wild. Caught in the firestorm, they threw themselves from the treetops, setting everything ablaze or turned on each other as if madness had taken them.

"The forest! It's burning! It's all burning!" cried the witch, beside herself as her beloved trees were caught in the spreading inferno and ignited like roman candles below them.

Mr. Agyk said nothing, but closed his eyes. He could feel his strength waning with each passing day, but there was still a little left, just a little. Power pulsed through his body, coursing through every minuscule cell as he silently finished his incantation. His tiny staff blazed for a moment, then died and as its light faded in the growing dark, the three friends could hear the rumble of heavy rain clouds overhead and felt the first wet, icy splashes upon their skin.

Wendya looked up. "Rain? ... Thank the gods! Rain!" she cried as the water came down in sheets, quelling the fires and preventing any more from taking root.

Gralen kept his eyes fixed on the horizon but he knew what the wizard had done.

Onward they flew, through night, rain and bitter chill, ever aware, ever feeling the ominous presence of their enemies in quick pursuit below them, running somewhere in the shadows. The three friends flew on in silence; though Gralen's wings hurt with every beat, he never uttered a single word of complaint, for they all knew that they could have no rest until they had left the mighty boreal forest.

Despite Wendya's directions, the escape seemed painfully slow. And so, after the remaining night and the next day had passed, and the blue light of yet another dawn pierced the eastern sky, they could see the ending of the trees and the pale glimmer of the grasslands beyond.

Gralen flew on for another hour, pain and exhaustion plaguing his every wing-beat, until he could go no further. Utterly spent, the dragon glided down into the long, soft grass near to the southern shores of the inland sea they had camped beside only four days earlier.

He slumped down, barely able to move. The thick, leathery skin between each wing bone had been badly burnt and torn in places. Ignoring this, and the deep gashes he bore on his chest and back, he fell instantly into a deep sleep.

The day matured and Gralen slept on as the two friends worriedly watched over their charge and tended to his wounds. Wendya glanced at them both, so different yet so similar in so many ways. Clearly visible, the dragon's injuries looked more severe and yet the heavy weight of her heart lingered on the wizard. She looked at the frail wizard, a person who had always been such a strong force of wisdom and vivacity. He seemed even smaller and older than the day before. A wizened figure bent beneath his clothes, as if the effort of battle had stolen the remaining strength from him. For the first time the witch truly understood the great urgency of their quest and how little time remained, and the thought of losing him terrified her.

"We must try to stay awake if we can," he murmured, "I do not think those demons can travel as far or as fast as we … but we cannot be certain."

She nodded and turned her head, trying desperately to fight away tears. Her voice caught in her throat.

"Go to sleep, Marval," she whispered. "Save your strength, I'll keep watch."

The wizard didn't argue and soon fell into a fathomless sleep beside her.

At last, with her friends in a peaceful slumber, the witch relented and wept quietly until the ache of her heart could take no more and the sun rose in the clear, midday sky.

The day passed without event and a cool breeze, like a memory of summer, rustled through the grasses. The smell of roasted root herb and flower-stem drifted through the air, as the old dragon finally awoke. The late afternoon sun sank slowly, turning the autumn sky to golden peach and the nearby waters to a rippling copper.

"We were worried about you, old friend," said the wizard, chewing on some willow grass.

Gralen yawned and, stretching his wings, he immediately noticed the carefully wrapped bandages. He winced, then smiled.

"They're only a little sore," he lied. "Now, what are we eating? I'm starving!"

Mr. Agyk smiled. "We are on rations I am afraid. The supplies you managed to salvage will not last us long … we will have to start finding our own food soon."

Before long, the group were tucking in: although there was no sign of their pursuing enemies, each kept a watchful eye on the horizon as they ate.

As evening fell, they were soon flying once more, but progress was slow. The quickest route to the Atlantic meant passing over many cities and populated areas, but this was too dangerous without the wizard's protective spell to conceal them. So, reluctantly they now traveled only by night or by soaring high enough not to be seen, the higher altitude making it harder to breathe and more arduous for the green dragon.

For a while, Wendya managed to create a blanket of clouds to cover their flight, although this resulted in Gralen almost crashing into a plane, and being struck by lightning twice, which caused his chin whiskers to resemble a brush.

Nearly three long weeks had passed since the company left the forest and the second new moon came and went, when they finally set down. It was a cold and drizzly morning. The group stood poised on a rocky cliff, overlooking the gray expanse of the Atlantic, as dark clouds raced across the sky. The three friends made camp beneath a straggling, twisted, old fig tree and sat by the fire watching wisps of smoke drift into the air, as the crashing waves and the seas' constant pounding drowned all conversation. It was just after noon when, amidst another curtain of rain, the silence was finally broken.

"The world is changing," the wizard said quietly. "There are … events happening. I can feel it … a turn in the wind, a shift, something is changing and not for the better," the old scholar seemed lost in a vision of some kind. "There are older and more monstrous forces living in the earth than we know and he is awakening them … Stirring things that have slept for eons, since Ogygian times. Things that should remain undisturbed."

Wendya glanced at Gralen, and sat beside the wizard. "Everything will right itself," she said softly.

The friends sat huddled together against the downpour, a lonely group lost amongst the gray rocks. Wendya peered up into the darkening skies and the heavy rain clouds. "There's a worse storm coming," she said.

"I think you'll find we're already in it!" grumbled the dragon.

They decided to stay on the barren cliffs, to rest for the journey ahead. That night, their sleep was filled with the sound of the crashing waves below and the foul voices and howls of the fire wolves haunting their dreams. The sky lit up with crackled flashes as thunder broke above their heads and rumbled out across the sea. Mr. Agyk's mind could only hear an icy hiss and see a pair of fire-rimmed eyes staring at him, moving closer and closer inside each curling wave.

"Marval?" Wendya gently woke him.

"That was a big storm last night," sniffed Gralen, looking out over the shifting ocean. "It headed out there, so we'll probably be flying right through it!" he griped.

"Well, I'm surprised you noticed anything over your snoring!" the witch laughed.

The company ate quickly before setting off.

"To the Oracle of the West!" Wendya announced chirpily.

Gralen shuddered.

Mr. Agyk stared out to sea. "Yes, but what will we find when we reach it," he mumbled as he clambered once more onto the dragon's back. "Well," he sighed, "now our journey truly begins, and I fear it will be a perilous one!"

Chapter Eight

The Oracle of the West

nxious and dreary days followed tireless, black nights as the three adventurers set off across the ocean. Endless it seemed, an impenetrable blanket of deep and turbulent water with little place for rest or sleep. On occasion, a thin wake or trail of churned foam led to a silver jewel; a ship or tanker, where by night they could steal a few hours of sleep amidst towering funnels of billowing steam.

A hunter's moon shimmered above the dark water, red and bloated, an unsettling face staring down at them amidst the pitch. After nearly two weeks since leaving the gray shoreline, the weary travelers eventually found land once more and a safe haven for aching wings and heavy eyes.

They spent the next day and night resting, hauled up and hidden from view on the muddy sandbanks, beneath a cluster of shady mangrove trees. As first light dawned, the friends tentatively began their journey again. They ate a light breakfast and were soon flying low over dense mangrove swamps, the twisted roots and deadened stumps rising out of the waters like a mass of tangled snakes. They flew on warily, following the map from the young witch's Wiccadian.

Gralen remained silent and watchful.

The vegetation below thickened, clogging and choking the many inlets and tributaries of the mighty river, and causing the muddy, silted waters to turn black. Soon, the rainforest grew in height. Canopy rose above canopy, trees rivaling each other, competing for the sun and the moisture-laden mists, until their uppermost branches stretched greedily into the sky. The entire place had the distinct feeling of being one giant, breathing organism, throbbing to its own savage beat. The verdant green below seemed to stretch out in infinite flatness, its emerald heart more ominous than the Grey Forest they had left behind.

Wendya felt it. The jungle had a different character, an unpredictable wildness. It was as if, as unwanted strangers, they had entered a sacred place and were about to be swatted for trespassing.

Onward they flew, over huge swathes of flooded forest, letting Wendya's book lead the way deeper into the jungle. As the sun climbed higher, heat began to rise from the forest tops in long curling mists. The heaviness of the air was only matched by its humidity, covering the travelers in an uncomfortable, sweaty film that seemed to permeate everything. All around, the sounds of life could be heard. Exotic birds hooted and called from lofty perches or glided above black ox-bow lakes, isolated and scattered like giant boomerangs across the forest basin, their ominous and abyssal depths unknown.

Onward they went, following the dark river as it sparkled and snaked its cloudy waters further inland. The forest buzzed with millions of insects and animals rustling and bustling in the treetop canopies or foraging below on the hidden jungle floor.

At last, as afternoon started to wane, they could go no further.

"We must find a place to land. We will walk from here," said Mr. Agyk. "No flight can lead to the Oracle."

Wendya glanced down at the open book. Its map and inscription glowed scarlet on the page and seemed to be growing brighter. "We follow the book to find the twisted river," she murmured.

"What do you mean 'the twisted river'? Look at them, they're all twisted!" Gralen snapped. "Like serpents, slimy and slithering! … I hate this place already!" he moaned.

The dragon wished he could keep flying. He loathed the oppressive heat of the jungle but far worse was the thought of being swallowed inside of it, with all the crawling things to keep them company.

Before long, the great dragon reluctantly landed in a small, brown clearing, tangled with a myriad of rotting and shaggy growths, and the three travelers continued on foot.

Progress was slow and the little light that reached them from the canopy above was failing fast. Thick, straggling undergrowth seemed to hamper their every route. The forest floor became a spongy matt of decaying leaf litter, which squirmed and shifted beneath their feet, a moving carpet alive with an unthinkable number of creatures. Mr. Agyk perched himself on Wendya's shoulder and together they struggled through the jungle, past hanging lianas, vines and dangling mosses, over rotting stumps and flowering fungi. They trudged round the spindling roots and massive buttresses of colossal trees towering up into the air and under giant heliconias and umbrella ferns, all dripping ceaselessly from above.

The jungle was stifling and dark. A thick gossamer of spider webs stretched across their path and hung ominously in great billowing sheets above them. Morpho butterflies fluttered in the gloom, a startling flash of iridescent blue, flitting between the shadows of tangled trees, a dazzling sight when caught in the misty shafts of light that stabbed through the jungle.

They passed through the murky forest, unseen by most of its inhabitants. Gralen, on the other hand, made his presence and his discomfort clearly evident to all and lumbered behind as a truculent child, muttering incessantly under his breath as he swatted at the clouds of midges that had congregated around him. He hated the sinking feel of the ground beneath his feet and the sense that he was already covered in a crawling layer of things, all burrowing and nesting beneath his scales. He shook himself and squeezed his bulk between the trees, but even with his wings tucked in tightly he still managed to break nearly every branch and vine he passed.

The ground began to rise before them and, as it did, the jungle seemed to close in. With every passing footstep it soon became increasingly difficult to cut through, and the humidity was beginning to take its toll. The weary troupe rested for a while, then pressed on again.

Gralen unhappily took the lead, with strict instructions not to blast a fire path through. Instead, he simply used his great bulk and sharp talons to cut a track. Eventually, after a long and tiring day, the travelers reached the top of a steep incline, a ridge where the trees were thinner and they could at last see the dimming sky above.

It was late. The sun had already set, casting the last streaks of orange over the forest. Standing on the ridge-top, as evening deepened to dusk, they could see the jungle disappearing in a misty gray haze. Howler monkeys screamed from the treetops around, as the jungle awakened in a cacophony of night sounds.

Far below them, on the other side of the ridge, lay a deep gully from whose eerie silence a dread seemed to emanate. The sheer sides of the valley appeared as if they had been clawed at and, from within the gully no living thing, plant or tree could be seen. They stood silently in the dimming light and strained their eyes into the dark shadows below. From one end of the ravine they saw a faint sliver of water snaking its way into the tapering valley mouth, and from the deepening gloom they could hear the muffled roar of a waterfall.

"That's it! The twisted river," whispered Wendya glancing at the book. "That must be it!" She looked at the Wiccadian as its pages shimmered in the gathering darkness.

"Great," Gralen muttered as his keen eyes focused on the gully.

"Yes, this is the place," answered the wizard quietly. "Down there lies the entrance to the lair and the Oracle itself. We will stay here tonight. Better to find her in the comfort of the day I think."

Gralen peered into the valley and smelt a foul stench rising up from somewhere below. He shuddered. "I'll say again, for the record … this is a bad idea," he stared into the dark gulf as if expecting to see it rise up to attack them.

Mr. Agyk patted the dragon's back. "Nonetheless, we must attempt to find her tomorrow. Let us try to get some sleep if we can. Rest now, old friend."

They trudged back from the ridge along the trail they had cleared and out of sight of the valley. Settling in the forked buttress of a huge mahogany tree they made camp. The wizard seemed particularly exhausted and declined any food before curling his cloak tightly round him and falling into a deep sleep.

Wendya and Gralen stayed awake, talking quietly into the night, each taking comfort in the glow of the fire. Despite the croaking of a thousand tiny tree-frogs and the constant rustling and clicking that filled the air, the thought of meeting the Oracle made Gralen quite forget the jungle around them and all the nasty crawlers in it.

Morning came early, though the light of dawn barely reached them. The air was already humid and the jungle was steaming. Great wafts of swirling vapors rose from the dark floor and streamed off the canopy far above, as if the rainforest were being boiled.

The company had had a miserably wet night and another restless sleep. Mr. Agyk and Wendya waited as Gralen finished off the last of the now soggy breakfast, then, with heavy hearts, they set off. They reached the ridge-top quickly and, without looking down toward the valley, they started the descent. Mr. Agyk remained with Wendya as, once more, Gralen took the lead, clearing a path. The ground ran sharply down and became perilously rocky and slippery in places. Thorny bushes tore at their arms, loose stones slid beneath their feet. The whole gully side seemed unstable. Gralen spread his wings to stop a fall or save the others. Little by little, the friends carefully wound their way down the steep ravine and stood at last on the shadowy ground.

A strange stillness greeted them and a nauseous smell of decay hung in the air. The company had heard nothing but the relentless sounds of the jungle, of monkeys and birds, jaguars and a million other things, yet in this place no sound, save that of the distant waterfall, could be heard.

The group continued warily, leaving the shelter of the gully sides. Here, the stony ground was cut by a shallow gray river, little more than a fast-flowing stream that snaked its way into the shadows ahead.

They followed the river's course. Peering into the grimy water they could see the rotten carcasses of countless dead fish and fallen birds, being carried away by the swift current. Everything seemed dead or decaying. Gralen shivered and wished he was anywhere but here.

"What a dreadful place!" Wendya muttered.

The morning ebbed away and a deeper dread crept over the friends. They seemed now to be passing in perpetual shade. No sunlight appeared ever to reach the drabness of the gully floor. The few plants that could be seen between its barren rocks were all yellow and withered. Gralen found himself looking up at the narrowing slice of clear blue above. The sight of sky comforted him. However, Mr. Agyk's gaze never faltered from the waterfall, which could now be seen in the deepening gloom at the head of the ravine.

The three travelers finally reached the river's end and stood before a slick black rock face. From a narrow slit high up spewed a dark gray cascade of water into an even darker pool.

The friends had seen many waterfalls in their lives, and things of wonder and beauty they had always been, yet this seemed quite the opposite. A hard, steely outpouring with a putrid stench of death that rose from its bowels, as the dark pool was churned from the flow above and vomited its waters into the stream below.

At last the little wizard spoke. His voice was subdued and it seemed to Gralen that he was speaking from the edge of some dark dream, on the brink of an abyss, dreading the first step yet resolved to taking it.

"The Oracle's lair," he sighed and slipped from Wendya onto the ground. "Beyond the waterfall and any tunnels or chambers that lie within will be one of the ancient tellers. Never have I met one of their kind," he paused and climbed onto a sharp spur of rock near the pool's edge. "How can I ever thank you? I needed your help and help you gave me, gladly. Two braver, better friends I could not have," he said gravely. "But I cannot ask you to follow me now, it is too dangerous. It is for friendship that you have come this far. The finding of Morreck would not concern you directly were it not for me. I alone must face the Oracle. Any risk that lies within must be mine alone."

The dragon swept forward and hurled a green fireball into the water. "Wait a minute!"

"Gralen, listen to me!"

"No, you listen to me! I knew you'd do this. We all go or none of us go!" he boomed, puffing out a large smoke ring, he folded his arms defiantly. "For a wise man you do spout a lot of tripe sometimes! Marval, it is true, if it wasn't for you I would not be here at all … because your friendship has *saved* my hide countless times! … Even if you were to forbid me from coming, I should still follow you, even into the very pits of hell itself!"

"I certainly hope it will not come to that!" Mr. Agyk smiled grimly. "If you or Wendya were hurt, …," he shook his head and sighed, his heart burdened with worry yet filled with pride at his friends' loyalty and resolve.

73

"You can't stop us!" Wendya added. "Besides, to defeat an enemy like Morreck will take all of us working together and as much help as we can get! This battle will affect far more of the world than just us!"

He looked at them both and reluctantly nodded, knowing that the dragon and witch intended to come and could not be dissuaded. And so, together, they clambered up the rocks and disappeared behind the waterfall and into the gaping cave beyond.

The tunnels, unlike the warm, dry passages of White Mountain, were cold and wet. A thin, slimy layer of mucus coated the walls and drips hung from the ceiling in ghastly tendrils. The air was suffocating and choked with a foul, rancid smell. Gralen clasped his nose.

"You still think this is a good idea?" he spluttered. "It stinks like a fetid cesspit!"

Still they pressed on, following the dim light of Mr. Agyk's staff into the gloom.

After what felt like an age, winding down into the growing darkness, the air became hotter and a pale, sickly yellow light could be seen glowing ahead. The travelers went slowly now, feeling the slippery ground beneath their feet and stopped. Though the passage walls were growing wider, the ceiling was now becoming so low so that the dragon and the witch had to crawl. Gelatinous wisps of jellied slime dangled from the tunnel roof and sides and became a thick, sticky blanket on the floor ahead.

"Marval, you can't walk through that!" said Wendya brushing a glutinous strand from her face. The wizard poked the strange mass with the end of his staff: it was several inches deep.

He nodded and climbed once more onto the witch's shoulders. "Now remember," he whispered. "This Oracle, much like any other, is not wholly evil … or good. It will no doubt be cunning and wise and very learned, but its foresight may come at a price," he paused. "Be wary … . I do not believe it will be able to read minds but say or think nothing, unless it addresses you first!"

The friends took a deep breath and waded through the thick slime until the last glutinous veil was broken, and they were finally in the Oracle's nest.

The tunnel stopped abruptly before them. The company could see countless other tunnels leading away from the cavernous space they now found themselves in.

The cavern was huge. A gigantic cylindrical shaft with sheer sides that dropped down into a black pit beneath. Rising up to a great height near the ceiling, there seemed to be a sticky mass of twisted and tentacle-like roots.

Emerging from the tunnel they stepped down onto a small rocky ledge. And there, to their utter horror, sitting expectantly on an opposite ledge, as if waiting for them, was the Oracle. The sight of it filled them with terror and revulsion. A hideous, bloated thing, insect-like in body and features, with six legs that twitched as it sat before them. The Oracle appeared as a giant hybrid creature of some sort with the head of a praying mantis and the body of a scorpion, all merged into one terrifying nightmare vision.

The dark jungle path towards the Oracle of the West.

Each bulbous segment of its body glistened with a silken dew, and fine hairs rippled along its spindling legs and up to the quivering tip of its venomous tail. By far the worst sight of all was its broad, flat head with its enormous cluster of glassy eyes, like hundreds of mirrored orbs all looking at them. Below that, its serrated jaws and protruding mandibles snapped together like a set of huge pincers.

Gralen, who knew a little of the Oracle fables from Mr. Agyk, was horrified and couldn't help letting out a gasp. Instantly the creature's attention switched to him and she seemed to smile.

"It's been a very long time since I've had a fÿrren," she hissed mockingly, "I didn't think there were any of your kind left … in captivity."

The Oracle's stare filled Gralen with a sick dread and, for the first time in the great dragon's life, he was truly frightened.

Mr. Agyk climbed down from Wendya's shoulder and, stepping forward, he threw his tattered green cloak open and stood small but straight before the thing.

"I have come before your mighty wisdom with my friends here, to seek for your help and counsel. And the answers we need to fulfil our quest," his voice seemed thin and hollow as it echoed round the chamber.

The Oracle clicked its jaws together, never taking its gaze off Gralen.

"What strange sights enter my domain … What do we have here? A tiny rat of a wizard. A fool of a witch and a pet dragon! And you want my counsel? My help?" she laughed. It felt like a thousand steely daggers stabbing the air. "Of course you do!" she sneered.

The great beast shifted her huge body and, leaving her foul ledge, she came towards the three friends, suspended on only a few long strands of slime. There she stopped, far too close for comfort, dangling in front of them as if she were some hideous plaything.

"Well," she said slowly, her voice gliding over them like bitter honey. "You, at least, magus, know the price of my help. The terms are clear and unchanging since before you were born. Three riddles I will give to you, the time shall be short and of my choosing. If you answer all three correctly I will help you, I will show and tell you the things you seek. But, if only one of the riddles is answered incorrectly, you forfeit your lives. Understood? Do you accept these terms?" said the Oracle smiling again.

"No, we do not!" burst Gralen.

He turned imploringly to Mr. Agyk, hoping the wizard would know his mind and leave, escape from that foul and evil place.

Mr. Agyk turned and smiled at his friend. "I know what I am doing," he whispered, then turning once more to face the Oracle he spoke at last, and his voice filled the chamber. "I *alone*, which is my right, am here to ask for your help and I alone accept your terms and whatever fate awaits me."

"NO!" shouted Wendya.

The Oracle looked disappointed. Taking her gaze at last off the dragon, she looked down at the tiny wizard.

"You have lost nothing," said the wizard, his voice rising to a clear resonating boom. "Though small I seem, if I fail, a tasty and powerful meal you will still have, for wizards of any size would be a prize indeed."

"No!" bellowed Gralen, getting ready to snatch his friends and bolt.

The Oracle twitched its long barbed legs, as if in contemplation, its claws scratching at the rock. At last the creature spoke.

"I agree, but you cannot use your staff or your friends to help you. If they are not to share your fate, they must leave now!" and with that the hybrid threw two of her huge black legs out and, before they knew what was happening, a thick shroud was cast around the dragon and the witch, and by magic or force they were thrown back into the tunnel behind, along with the tiny wizard's staff.

Gralen roared and cut through the viscous layer with his tail and claws, then charged forward.

"STOP!" shouted Mr. Agyk. "I am sorry old friend, but the deal has been made. There is nothing you can do now. I had no choice, but if I fail, you must look after Wendya and she must look after you."

"NO!" cried the dragon, refusing to accept it. "I won't leave you!" he yelled, feeling as if his chest would burst.

"Do not worry," the wizard smiled, "I have not failed yet!"

With that the Oracle turned once more to the dragon.

"The pact has been made, fÿrren. If you help him, he shall fail and none of you shall ever leave here," she hissed. Holding up a leg as if to dismiss the impudent dragon, he was pushed back once more into the tunnel. A thick wall of ice and frozen slime sprang up, sealing the entrance and trapping the witch and dragon behind it.

"Don't!" cried Wendya struggling to hold him back. She pressed her hand against the wall and recoiled. "It's magic, you won't be able to break it. There's nothing we can do for him now."

"I'm not leaving him in there to be eaten!" he roared.

"Gralen, listen to me! Listen! It's too late. Once a bargain has been struck with an Oracle it cannot be broken. If we try, we'll be killing him ourselves!" Wendya sighed and reached for his hand. "Please ... there really is nothing we can do for him now. We have to trust in Marval, I'm sure he knows what he's doing."

The dragon gave her a doubtful look but, taking her hand in his, he squeezed it gently and grudgingly nodded. "Well, I'll tell you this ... if Mr. A gets any answers wrong, nothing will stop me getting him and you out of here. She'll not be munching on any of us! ... We'll see if she likes her foul hide toasted!"

Gralen puffed out a smoke ring while they pressed their faces to the ice and watched on helplessly.

The Oracle moved back towards her ledge, but remained suspended in the air, while she instructed Mr. Agyk to step forward onto a single column of rock that rose up from the depths below.

The wizard looked tiny, dwarfed by the hybrid that dangled menacingly before him, her scorpioid tail poised above as the long spike of its bulbous tip dripped with venom and excitement.

"You are courageous or foolish, either way we shall see," she hissed.

Mr. Agyk could feel and smell her foul breath and he almost lost his footing. She reeked of death.

"The first riddle: What is black and red in a viper's bed?" she smiled.

Mr. Agyk stood deep in thought. A thousand books and words flashed through his head, everything he had ever read, ever learnt. Suddenly his old mentor and master appeared in his mind and the endless teachings and debates he had had to absorb. Herb-law, astronomy, biology, entomology, geology, alchemy, ornithology, birds ... BIRDS!

"It is a play on words ... it is a læwerce, a laverock ... a skylark!" he shouted.

The Oracle showed no response.

"Next," she sneered. "Second riddle: Where can you find a Dioclan?"

"Dioclan, Dioclan," repeated the wizard and closed his eyes. "Ancient Dworllian or Ællfren, no, Harrapan lore, no, Ogygian, Sumerian, Akkadian, no, think ... Capsian, Illyrian ... no, no ... Atlantean?"

"Is that your answer?" taunted the hybrid.

The wizard hesitated. "No, no ... in the sky! ... In the sky! In the stars!" he shouted.

Malice flashed across the creature's repulsive face and one leg began tapping angrily against the tunnel wall.

"Third riddle," she hissed, edging closer, her glassy eyes transfixed on the little wizard. "Who shattered the ties?" she whispered. "You have less than a minute," she gloated.

Panic flooded the little wizard as his mind raced. He had no idea.

"Who shattered the ties?" he repeated, his mouth dry, his heart seeming to pound in his throat. "Shattered the ties ... the ties ..."

His mind sped through all the stories he had heard, legends, myths, ancient manuscripts, archaic languages, magic lore, the origins of dragons, the earliest recorded histories of ællfren and dworllian society.

"What is your answer?" laughed the Oracle. "Time's up!"

Mr. Agyk swallowed and slowly lifted his eyes, to see his own reflection mirrored in a hundred glistening and eager orbs. The Oracle spun leisurely before him, a look of excitement and triumph on its face, its jaws almost drooling and its foul breath covering the little wizard in a nauseating cloud, when suddenly a strange verse popped into his head. He paused for a second trying to get the translation right.

> "The breaker of bonds, the breaker of oaths;
> The circle was riven by one of the few,
> An oath that was taken was broken anew,
> The bonds that were given were made untrue,
>
> And the breaker escaped with the knowledge he knew.
> The trust of the wise was shattered apart,
> By the magic that hid a blackness of heart,
> And evil did fester in the breaker untrue
> And long did he reap the souls that he knew."

The wizard stopped, incredulous at his own stupidity.

"Morreck!" he shouted. "Of course! Morreck was the breaker of bonds! He shattered the ties, he broke the sacred oaths! Morreck, M'Sorreck of old!"

The Oracle snarled contemptuously and its foul stench seared the air.

"There, I have answered all your riddles correctly and fulfilled my part of the bargain," declared the wizard as he stepped very carefully off the pillar and back onto the ledge.

The Oracle hissed again and spun round on her thread of mucus, faster and faster, like some ghastly spinning top. Then, without a sound she vanished into the darkness above.

"We made a pact!" the wizard shouted after her, his voice echoing off the walls. "You cannot break your word Oracle, we made a deal! ... Answer me! Oracle!"

All was still. A deathly silence fell, overpowering the air. The wizard glanced behind him toward the frozen wall and his two friends trapped in the tunnel behind it. He wished he had his staff.

Suddenly a voice, distant yet as clear and hard as steel and full of hatred, echoed from above. Mr. Agyk squinted into the darkness, but nothing moved.

"I will uphold my part of our bargain," whispered the voice, "but first ..., tell me how you knew my last riddle?"

"For one simple reason ... Morreck is the very person I seek!"

A violent rumble came down from above that sent shudders through the rock. Mr. Agyk stood very still and listened. He could hear an awful crunching and cracking sound, like the ripping of bone and flesh. Fear tingled through him as he sensed a shift in the Oracle and became acutely aware of how small and vulnerable he was. Silence descended once more, a tightening shroud to encase its victims.

"I ... I have asked for your help," he continued nervously, his eyes scanning every hole and burrow about him and the shadows above.

"M'Sorreck murdered my friend and many others, and tried to kill me. He held me prisoner and by some foul device he robbed me of ... something dear to me," he hesitated. He did not feel safe in revealing any details of his attack to this creature, or how weak it had truly left him. "Morreck has been killing his own kind. We must find him urgently. It has to stop!" Mr. Agyk paused.

"You do not name the 'valuable' thing taken ... but I can guess," whispered the voice.

"I must find him and stop him ...," mumbled the wizard in reply.

Silence. The waiting was torturous. With every passing moment, fear rose in the little figure like a dark flower slowly unfurling its petals. Suddenly, after what seemed like an eternity, the silence was broken by a low, rumbling sound that rose to a thunderous din as the Oracle's laughter filled his ears.

"A wærloga thief!" she exclaimed with delight. "That is what you speak of but will not name! M'Sorreck is not merely killing your kind; he is feeding off of you!"

"Yes," he replied quietly, straining to see his questioner in the gloom above.

"The breaker of bonds!" laughed the hybrid. "Yes, yes. The veins of evil run deep and very old. A cruelty unmatched and unyielding, a monstrous nature," she smiled proudly. "Such intensity of hatred and horrifying power. What you seek may be found, but it is impossible to stop. A great change is coming, green warlock, for all of us. A change to end all things. It has already begun. It started long ago, secretly, quietly. Preparations made, foundations built. Slowly, but strongly. Time is already running short and shorter still for you my friend," she hissed, a gleeful smile flickering in the darkness.

"You were but another victim of his malevolence. One of many. Already you feel yourself frailer, day by day. It will not be long now, before you succumb and fade. You have little strength left to find M'Sorreck and less to fight him … for fight him you must if you are ever to regain your full powers. Ah! … but strong is he … far stronger than you, little magus!"

Gralen pressed his face against the frozen wall. "I don't like this. I can't hear what's going on and I can barely see through this stuff," he grumbled, butting his head against the ice. "It's been too long. We can't just stay here … I don't care; I'm going in to get him!"

Wendya pulled him back. "No! We may have to, but please, for his sake and ours, give him a little longer!"

The voice stopped. Once again, Mr. Agyk could only hear his own breathing and the rushing of his blood, except now he could also discern the sound of rushing water from somewhere deep below. Perhaps an underground river or the flow of the waterfall. Dread fell over the little figure, as if he were the main-course to a meal.

"Mighty Oracle, you are the greatest seer of all. I have passed your test, you must fulfill our bargain and help me."

A voice pierced the air. It was cold and full of malice, and far too close.

Mr. Agyk spun round to see that the foul, six-legged beast had silently dropped behind him blocking his escape.

"I will tell you what you need to know … for an Oracle never breaks its word," whispered the creature towering over him. "You know already that you must find the wizard-thief's home and destroy the orb, the vessel and source of his power. This alone will not kill him. You will have to fight him … a bitter fight to the death. One of you will not survive," she smiled. "There is betrayal in your future green wizard … One you know will turn against you … and at least one of your 'beloved' friends will not survive!" the hybrid jeered, edging forward, its mirrored eyes enjoying every exquisite second of the wizard's pain.

"My friends? … Who? … Who will die?! Tell me! TELL ME, PLEASE!"

The Oracle shook its grotesque head, its jaws and mandibles spread wide now in the most hideous grimace, showing row upon row of needle-like teeth.

The creature edged her bulk forwards again and was almost upon him. With nowhere left to go he stepped back onto the lonely pillar of rock and desperately tried to block out the Oracle's words.

"W … where does Morreck live?" he asked, avoiding the gaze of her eyes.

"His ancient home and the place of his birth, is in the northern lands of the Lost Realm of Fendellin, The Kingdom of Dragons, what the humans call Shambhala. It lies beyond the roof of the world, the Great Range, and deep within the heart of the Encircling Mountains at the world's edge."

"The Great Range? … The Himalayas?"

"As the humans name it. There you will find his home, in the mountain fortress at the roots of the highest peak, Kavok, amidst an army of enemies and a sea of woe," she cackled. "But … you cannot enter a warlock's domain without his leave, you know that. You will never find him and regain your power without the means of entering his lair first."

"Then what are we to do?" cried the wizard.

"In Kallorm, the hidden dworll city, you must find the only thing, save an invitation from M'Sorreck himself, that will gain you entrance to his home. A small, silver key in the shape of a dragon, from the mixed blood of that beast and the wærloga himself. It has two green gemstones for its eyes and a single stone, red as blood, for its heart," she paused. "This is his birth-key and the key to his fortress home," she smiled acidly.

"Who has this key?"

"That, I cannot see. One of the dworll lords, perhaps, or the King himself, or one of the Ancient Order he broke with … but it should be an easy task to find," she said slowly, her eyes glistening.

"Kallorm is a huge city. It has been many years since I visited it. Can you not tell me where in the city I might find this key?" Mr. Agyk pleaded, wanting desperately to leave that creature and its horrid stench behind.

"One of your party will lead you there," replied the creature smiling a jagged smile, "for they know it well."

"And the Lost Realm of Fendellin? How do we find it? The Himalayas are vast."

"I cannot tell you this as part of our bargain," answered the beast twitching its front legs. "Beyond what I have told you … if you seek further directions, then go to Kallorm's great libraries. They may hold maps and journals to help you, and the Royal House will know at least a little of its ancient location."

The creature paused for a moment.

"But you may need none of that. Once you are on the path to the Kingdom of Dragons, the source of all primordial dragon races, it may draw you to it. For it is said that only a fÿrren, or one who was born there, can find it and pass beyond its secret borders. As you have a dragon in your company, this should not prove difficult."

Viscous drips fell from above, splashing at the wizard's feet and covering the narrow column of stone in a slippery film. The wizard felt every part of his being ache to escape.

"Thank you, Oracle," he said, taking his hat off and bowing.

The hybrid laughed at such a ridiculous display.

"So, have I not fulfilled our bargain?" she said gliding slowly forwards.

Mr. Agyk hesitated. At that moment his deepest fears were realized. He knew the creature's mind, and it filled him with terror. He stepped back until he teetered on the very edge of the pillar, with nothing but oblivion below.

Trapped in her nest!

"You cannot break your word Oracle!" he cried raising his arms in defiance.

"I won't," she hissed, "I'll eat it!"

With that, the beast suddenly lunged forward. Mr. Agyk sprang to the side and darted beneath its stinking hide as it careered onto the pillar and nearly fell off it, then recovered and spun round, a tangle of limbs and hisses.

"No you DON'T!" Gralen roared through the ice. "Stand back!" He threw himself against the wall.

"It won't work! It's magic!" cried the witch.

The dragon reared up. "Wend', get behind me! ... I knew that filthy thing was up to no good!" he shouted as he stood back, took a deep breath and blasted the wall with green fire.

Wendya hurriedly flicked through her Wiccadian. "Melting spells are what we need ... WAIT! ... I've got it!" she cried and placed a piece of the slimy ice in her hand. *"Lai bantium sorl tol`e kinum`e mathalium tol kierre`."*

The tunnel started to violently shake. Cracks, hairline at first but growing wider, appeared in the floor and walls and, from each opening fissure, oozed a foul-smelling liquid that quickly began to fill up the passageway.

"Well this is better!" snorted Gralen. "Wendya! What the hell are you doing?"

"Sorry! Sorry! I read it the wrong way round! ... *Kierre` tol mathalium `e kinum `e tol sorl bantium lai!"*

The ice and liquid receded, melting back into the cracks, which then disappeared. The wall, which Gralen had only managed to make a small dent in, began to dissolve.

"It's working! It's actually, truly WORKING!" she cried.

Mr. Agyk was cornered. "You have broken your word Oracle!" he shouted wildly.

"No! I kept my word," she said softly, her mandibles chittering, her swollen tail poised and aching to sting the little rat before her. "You have the answers you sought, the answers to your quest ... only, you'll never fulfill it," and with that the great creature lunged forward again.

"Pero tine!" the wizard cried, *"Pero tine!* Freeze!"

The hybrid halted and looked stunned for a moment, then slowly shook its legs and head as if something had ensnared it for an instant before falling away. Its dry cackle filled the air.

"Your magic is failing, wizard!"

At that moment, the great dragon's head smashed through the hole now made in the dissolving wall, and he hurled a fire bolt at the creature. It whistled over the wizard's head and hit two of the scorpion's legs, sending it stumbling sideways; it screeched in pain and nearly lost its balance. Then, just as quickly, the Oracle recovered and tried to block the tunnel once more. But it was too late, the wall was collapsing quickly now.

The beast turned back, glowering down at the little wizard, a ferocious wildness and panic in its eyes. Then, in an instant, before the wizard could move or shout, it snatched him up into its claws and disappeared into the blackness.

"NO!" shouted the dragon and witch and, with one last push, they broke through the wall.

In a split second, Wendya leapt onto Gralen's back and they hurtled into the space and up towards the shifting darkness above.

They were just approaching the top part of the chamber, when a myriad of smaller tunnels opened around them, like nesting chambers. They flew past and shot up toward the ceiling, still high above their heads. As they climbed higher, they could just make out a squirming and matted mass of gnarled tree roots and slime. Wendya spotted, out of the corner of her eye, something dark and fast racing towards them.

"Watch out!" she screamed as the huge beast rammed straight into the dragon, knocking her off his back.

Gralen was flung against the wall, all talons and wings, crashing into the rock. He shook his head and, to his horror, saw the screaming figure of the witch falling into the abyss.

"Wendya!" he cried but couldn't move.

A thick layer of congealed mucus had caught in his wings and glued him fast to the wall. He struggled but it seemed to make it worse. The scorpion creature silently dropped down in front of him, excitement drooling from its foul jaws.

"At last!" it hissed, and pulled back its fangs just as Gralen shot a fire ball towards its face, and blasted at the sticky mass holding him.

The slime ignited and flames rose around him like a curtain. He could hear the shrieks and screams of the Oracle nearby, but his thoughts were only with Wendya.

From within the blaze, the dragon ripped at his bindings. Seconds later, after struggling wildly, he freed himself and dived down after the witch at an incredible speed, pushing his wings and shoulders back as far as they'd go to become a dart.

The young witch tumbled toward the churning mass of dead water and rocks below, and was just about to hit them, when she was caught in Gralen's arms.

"Hold on!" he cried as he opened out his wings and lassoed his tail round a passing spur of rock to stop them from falling into the whirlpool below.

The pair dangled upside down just above the waters, with Wendya coughing from the rising fumes churned up beneath them.

"I've got you!" panted Gralen. "I've got you! You're alright," he said as he tried to curl his tail tighter, but felt his grip loosening.

At that moment, the dragon looked up and a terrifying panic filled him. Silently descending upon them, like some hideous, black cloud with sprouting limbs, came the Oracle.

"NO YOU DON'T!" he roared and, using his tail and all his remaining strength, he quickly swung them up onto the spur of rock, just as the hideous creature shot past.

Missing its target, the Oracle squealed in panic, its limbs making a terrible scrabbling sound against the rock as it quickly spewed the awful stuff from its bulbous body and cast down a thin membrane to save it from the waters.

Gralen and Wendya clambered up onto a higher ledge of rock, just as the hybrid once more sent a tangling mass towards them. In a flash and without hesitating, Wendya grabbed her cloak and, tearing it from her shoulders, she threw it over the creature's eyes.

"NOW!" she shouted.

With that, Gralen's fury exploded upon the hooded beast, setting the cloak and membrane on fire. The dragon quickly took another deep breath and hurled fireball after fireball at the thing and the supporting net under it. Suddenly the membrane snapped and, with a scream that would curdle milk, the creature plunged into the black waters and was carried away.

Without pausing to catch their breath, the dragon and witch shot upwards.

"Marval! Mr. A!" Gralen bellowed.

"Mr. Agyk!" cried Wendya, "Marval, where are you?"

Approaching the top of the chamber and its ceiling, they could clearly see that it was moving. Globular sacks hung in translucent clusters like phlegm-covered grapes and, from within the foul mass of each dangling cocoon, creatures were stirring. Thousands of them.

"Oh gods! Look at them! … They're eggs and they're hatching!" Wendya cried in horror at the squirming sacks.

"More of those creatures? … Marval! … MARVAL!" called Gralen desperately.

"Over here!" replied a muffled voice from a tunnel just below them.

Gralen swooped down to see, amidst a sticky mass of vines and slimy tendrils, a small and rather angry Mr. Agyk, half-covered in the awful stuff.

"Well, you were right as usual, my dear friend. That is the first and last time I trust an Oracle!" he said, trying to peel off the gelatinous bonds. "We must hurry. She may not have been destroyed, and these eggs are beginning to hatch!"

Wendya hurriedly untangled the little wizard and they jumped back onto the dragon.

"We must get my staff!" he said, feeling more shaken than he wanted to admit.

"I have it here," Wendya said handing over the little wooden stick. "Are you alright?"

"I am fine, but I will be better when we leave this accursed place!" he replied, glancing up.

The nest above was horrifyingly full of feverish movement, as each sticky sack began to tear open from the inside.

"Quickly, towards the tunnel!" he cried.

They darted back into the low passageway, Gralen bumping his head and firing jets of flame before them, making sure the path was clear.

Behind them, in the gloom, thousands of hybrid offspring were bursting out of their birth sacks and crawling down the chamber walls. The entire space became one hideous moving blanket, and far, far below, something wounded, angry and blood-red was crawling out of the water.

The three friends hurtled along the winding tunnels as fast as Gralen's wings and legs could take them. Before long, they emerged from behind the waterfall and were flying low, back along the dead river and over the stony ground of the gully floor.

Afternoon had nearly passed and a wedge of pink dusk could be seen above.

"We must hurry!" cried the wizard again, feeling the pursuit behind.

"Hold on, let's get some height!" boomed Gralen, desperate to take to the skies.

"No! Not yet! We'll get trapped!"

At that moment, as if deliberately chosen to demonstrate the wizard's point, Gralen saw what he meant. Out of the jungle canopy swooped a huge crested bird, a beautiful harpy eagle, flying effortlessly on the air thermals before gliding down into the gully looking for food. Suddenly it floundered, fell a little and screeched out in distress. Looking up, it seemed to be caught in some huge invisible net, its massive black and white wings frantically beating the air. The bird struggled valiantly. Then they saw them, hundreds of creatures swarming out of the rocks and along invisible membranes towards the stricken animal.

"Urghh! It's like some awful fly paper!" Gralen said looking up at the teeming mass. "They'll not catch us! Just keep your eyes open though, make sure none of them drop down."

"Look!" cried Wendya, turning in horror to see a moving carpet of black, swarming from the waterfall behind and rushing toward them.

"Come on!"

Wasting no time, they shot forward, with the great dragon's wings skimming just above the valley floor until they had reached familiar ground.

"There, straight ahead!" Wendya called. "That's the path we made!"

The dragon flew on as fast and as low as he could. Soon, they reached the gully sides and the path they had made only that morning. Then, scrabbling over the stones and up the steep slope as fast as they could, it seemed to Mr. Agyk that a shadow was slowly lifting.

Two exhausting hours later, as the sun blazed crimson across the jungle canopy, they finally reached the summit of the ridge and, for the first time since they had left the Oracle's cave, they stopped to rest and dared to look back.

The rainforest around them, now comfortingly noisy, seemed to be waking up as the last rays of sun sank below the treetops. The stars were glinting cold and bright in the deepening sky and the last quarter of the waning moon, was rising up pale and mournful.

The company's gaze wandered back into the dark gully below. When they were sure that no pursuer had followed them, they rested fully and ate a little food from one of the sealed sacks they had left on the ridge top.

"Let's go further into the jungle and sleep," said Gralen quietly. "Away from that place."

The others nodded, and with weary bones they trudged down from the hill, following the wide path Gralen had made, and back into the heart of the jungle. Then, cowering beneath the dappled moonlit shade of a large acai palm, and huddling close to the shallow roots of a Brazil nut tree, the three friends made camp and slept with no fire until morning.

Yet always, the mighty dragon kept one watchful eye and ear open to their surroundings.

Chapter Nine

Kallorm

After a clammy and disturbed night, the morning came dull and cheerless to match the solemnity of the camp. The friends ate a small breakfast in silence, wanting to leave the heat and oppressive threat of the jungle behind. They set off early making good progress following the path they had made only two days earlier, before taking to the skies.

By late afternoon, they arrived once more on the muddy shores of the Atlantic. Amidst the soft, lapping waters and the shelter of the mangrove trees — alive with the chatter of ibis birds, their scarlet plumage a startling sight amongst the green — they could finally relax.

Wendya looked at the old mage. "He's awfully gray," she whispered to Gralen, as they made camp.

The dragon nodded. Mr. Agyk, who had remained unusually quiet, now sat watching the amber sun dance across the tops of the waves and shimmer on the horizon. The endless sea stretched before his eyes as a sheet of glass veiling a hidden and violent nature. As the wizard stared into the distance, he wished he could be consumed by those cruel waters.

Gralen and Wendya busied themselves collecting firewood and making some semblance of a meal, but their gaze always turned to the silent figure.

The wizard seemed distant, lost in some troubling thought. His silence since the morning had not gone unnoticed. At last they settled beside him and asked about the Oracle.

The wizard spoke softly as if a stray word might bring disaster upon their heads. Yet, as he spoke, it seemed to Gralen, that he stopped short of saying something and this troubled the dragon. He watched his friend intently, but knew not to press the matter. Wendya too, sensed that something was wrong.

The companions sat late into the evening, their feet dug into the cool, muddy sands watching as the last rays of light disappeared and the stars took flight.

Mr. Agyk spoke again, his tone considered and low. "The Oracle spoke of a key — the means to finding Morreck. It lies somewhere in Kallorm. The Oracle knew that one of you was acquainted with the city. Wendya, you grew up in Kallorm. In all your time there, did you ever hear of Morreck's birthkey?"

Wendya stared at him. "No," she murmured, "… are you sure the Oracle said it was in Kallorm?"

Mr. Agyk nodded. "It is quite likely that in the troubled history between Morreck and the city, he may have left it there."

"To be found by someone else?" Gralen asked.

"It may not have been intentional; he may have been forced to flee before he could recover it. I do not know," he said, turning to the witch.

"Kallorm …," she whispered and sighed heavily.

The dragon and the old man watched as she got up and wandered down to the shoreline, a thin strip of curving sand now bathed gray in the moonlight.

"What's wrong? What did you say?"

"Too much," replied Mr. Agyk, his gaze fixed on her as she stood looking out to sea. "All of our kindred have known great loss in our lives, but Wendya has known more than most."

"Because of her parents?"

Mr. Agyk nodded. "Yes … her adopted family."

Gralen looked towards her. "I've never really heard her speak about them, only what you've told me. She just … doesn't talk about her past."

Mr. Agyk sighed. "Umm, there is still much pain there."

"And they never found any of them?"

The old mage lowered his eyes, his face strangely unreadable. "No," he answered simply. "She ran away from Kallorm, from it all and never returned. I think this journey will be difficult for her."

"Tell me again, what happened?"

Mr. Agyk looked at him. "You want so much to know her heart."

Gralen blushed.

The wizard smiled. "Very well," he paused and lowered his voice, his eyes flitting back toward the beach. "You know her birthparents were killed when she was an infant? She never knew them … a wargol attack I think, though I have a feeling her grandfather told her that humans killed them, a superstitious fear of witchcraft or something," he shook his head. "I believe her mother was a beautiful human woman and her father a dworll … very frowned upon in those days and now," he smiled sadly, "… I understand it was a forbidden love between a village maiden and a low ranking dwizard, which would account for her powers."

87

"Such as they are," Gralen grinned.

"Oh, you would be surprised. There is power there, but it is unfocused … it does not quite fit her somehow."

Wendya walked along the beach, a lonely figure lost amongst the deep shadows. Gralen got up to follow her.

"No, Gralen. Let her be alone for a while."

He reluctantly sat down but his eyes never left her. "Go on, what happened next … after her parents died?"

Mr. Agyk heaved a sigh. "Her grandfather, a traditional sort of dworll, took her to Kallorm where she would be safe. But he was too old and frail to look after an infant, so she was adopted by a family. They were good people, solid and honest," he sighed again. "Vallok was a mining engineer, as I remember, who lived with his wife Kailla and their only son Lorrem in one of the city's suburbs. They raised her and loved her as one of their own. She had some wonderfully happy years in Kallorm. That was when I first met her, a tender greenling of a thing," he wrapped his cloak tightly round him. "Then one day she returned home to find the place empty … the entire family gone, just vanished! The fire in the hearth was still burning, the evening meal was cooking, but they were gone. She spent months and months, years, looking for them, trying to understand what had happened. She was completely distraught …"

"They just disappeared?"

"Yes," he looked grimly at his friend. "There was a spate of disappearances back then, a mixture of exodus and wargol attack it was thought."

"Disappearances! Isn't this seeming familiar?"

"Gralen … our people disappear on a frequent basis. As the world becomes more alien to us, more and more of our kind leave. … It is just the cycle of things, you should know that."

"Yes but to vanish without telling her? No goodbye? Not even a note?"

Mr. Agyk conceded. "I know. Perhaps you can understand now why Kallorm holds such painful memories for her. She loved them so dearly. She searched for many years, fruitlessly, before finally giving up and leaving … she has never returned."

At that moment the pair heard a voice, thin and clear and full of sadness, singing softly in the darkness beyond.

"Beneath a canopy of stars
Its whispering waters flow,
Beneath the towers standing tall
Lies my heart and home.

A city great of Dworllian past
Three mountains and a palace white,
Nine gates to pass and bridges all
To reach the secret realm of light.

A veil of silver, a thundering roar
A crystal dome, a rain-bowed beam
I hear the song of Kallorm call
Within my heart, its mists must fall.

Kallorm, Kallorm, come call me home
To dance and sing in Tarro's spring,
Kallorm, Kallorm, come call me home
To rest amongst your sheltered stone."

Wendya came back, picking her way through the twisted mangrove roots, her hair damp from the sea spray, her eyes downcast. She sat next to the fire.

"I used to sing that ballad as a child but the true melody is sadder …," she murmured.

Gralen wrapped a blanket around her and blew on the fire. "Are you alright?" he asked.

She smiled weakly. "Uhh, Mr. A was telling me about the city, from what he remembers of it."

"Yes, he used to visit it and me from time to time …," she looked up, "I'll give you both a guided tour when we get there. I can show you all its parks and hidden spots … unless it's changed."

Mr. Agyk reluctantly pressed her. "Wendya, I am sorry, but are you sure you do not remember any stories about a birthkey? Any rumors at all about a hidden object of power? Anything belonging to Morreck?"

She shook her head. "Only what I told you, that Morreck was our most feared enemy."

"I see. Well, perhaps King Dorrol will have knowledge of it …," he trailed off.

Gralen gazed into the fire, the flames reflecting and dancing in his amber eyes. "What's it like, Kallorm?"

She smiled. "It's an amazing place, The City of Light. Carved out of the earth, it stretches for leagues and leagues, far bigger than Ïssätun. Its ancient name was Dwellum, Silverden in the Ǽllfren tongue, the oldest and largest dworll city ever built!"

"Go on," Gralen said, propping himself up, eager to hear more while the little wizard sat quietly and listened.

"Alright," replied the witch. "There are towering spires and domes of glistening silver and bronze. Huge buildings of crystal and quartz that sparkle in the light. Citadels and cathedrals, bell towers and great libraries — really beautiful!" she smiled. "There are hundreds of walkways that crisscross the city, columned arcades and water ducts that rise above the buildings. The older parts of the city are closely packed but there are wide open squares and amphitheaters … and the best marketplaces you'll find anywhere, really amazing, especially in the old sellers' quarter of the city …," she laughed at seeing the dragon's eager face. "Yes, lots of good food!"

Wendya smiled. "There are so many beautiful bridges, streams and waterfalls that seem to go on forever. Then there are the famous, Three Pillars of Kallorm, gigantic mountain columns, perhaps as big as White Mountain, that support the ground above."

"Why build it all underground though?" asked the dragon amazed.

"It is dworll tradition," Mr. Agyk sighed.

Wendya nodded.

The wizard mused. "I have visited a few dworll cities in my life. Those that were built above ground were the first to fall. Kalador and K'tall Hüyük …," he sighed. "It is wonderful that cities like Kallorm still survive … first and grandest of the old Dworllian kingdoms!"

Wendya stared into the fire. "Its days are less grand now I think …," she said, casting her mind back to the epic tales of her childhood. "It's been many years since the High-Time."

"Ah yes, but Kallorm is still beautiful I wager," Mr. Agyk replied, "not earthy and dworllian at all, airy and light … All those starstones."

The witch stared into the flames and turned towards the dark waters. "I was very happy there, for many years," she sighed. "My family, they were wonderful people," she paused and sadness passed over her face.

"You don't need to say anymore," whispered the dragon softly.

"No, it's alright …," she answered, pulling her knees up as she gazed over the dark ocean. "The city was always visited by magic folk of one kind or another, like Marval. I was actually one of the few resident wiccans. I would help out when I could. Anyway, news reached us that trouble had been brewing in Gwallor, one of Kallorm's smaller sister cities. The City Council summoned me to advise them. I was gone no more than a few days … but when I returned, Vallok, Kailla and Lorrem were gone. Vallok's mining boots were still in the hallway, Kailla's washing was still drying … but Lorrem's room … was completely destroyed …," she paused. "Lorrem had spent years collecting precious gems and metals, all carefully described and labeled in thousands of little glass jars. They were all smashed. The guards said there had been a violent struggle, that Vallok and Kailla had probably tried to protect their son. But no one knows what really happened." She shook her head.

"They weren't the only disappearances …," she continued, "others had vanished in the middle of the night. Rallies and meetings were held sending countless search parties out. King Dorrol and the Council sent trackers up into the jungle, but nothing … I know they wouldn't have left me, not without a word … no, they were taken, forcibly, by someone or something."

Wendya shook her head again. "All I know is that I never saw them again. The more I searched the more hopeless it became. I waited and waited for news, but without them, Kallorm just wasn't a home to me anymore … so I left and I've never been back."

"I'm so sorry," said the dragon, placing a hand on hers.

She sighed. "They meant everything to me. Apart from you two, they are the only family I've ever known …," she paused, looking down at the glistening grains of sand between her toes. "I know, in my heart, they are dead … but I still miss them."

"Perhaps we will find the answers one day," whispered Mr. Agyk.

Wendya blinked away the tears, and without another word, settled down to sleep by the dying embers of the fire. Gralen's great chest heaved, then the dragon curled up beside her and within minutes, he was snoring.

Mr. Agyk sat silently for hours, watching his friends sleep under the twinkling stars. He took a deep breath and sighed, his eyes glistening in the darkness as he gazed up at the sky. The third new moon was nearly here, half his time had already been spent, yet always it was the Oracle's words that came back to haunt him. *One of your friends will not survive.*

Waves lapped gently onto the beach and, through the fresh, salty air, a smell of Sunday morning kippers disturbed the dragon's sleeping.

"Kippers! Kippers? I must be dreaming!" he snorted, half-awake.

"Not quite kippers. Some kind of red snapper but fish all the same," said a small voice nearby. "Good morning!"

Wendya opened her eyes. The morning was pale and misty and a cool breeze wafted in from the sea. The sky above promised glimpses of sunshine, yet where the gray of the sea melted into the horizon, Wendya could see dark storm clouds gathering.

It was not long before they set out across the ocean.

Thirteen uneventful days and nights followed. The three friends had at last crossed the Atlantic. They left the coastal margins and flew inland over a vast continent, beautiful but ravaged by the scars of war. Mr. Agyk glanced at the waxing moon. Time was running through their fingers as grains of sand, yet still they were no closer to facing Morreck.

"It is a long journey. Kallorm is in the heart of the Congo basin, many leagues from here," said the witch.

"More bloody trees!" moaned Gralen, longing for hard rock and mountain top. "We've only just escaped from one stinking jungle and I'm in no hurry to go to another!"

"There's nothing wrong with jungles," Wendya snapped. "Only what people do to them!"

The next week and a half passed as if in a dream. Mr. Agyk remained quiet throughout. The company flew during the night and found shelter where they could during the day. When they reached the less populated areas they risked flying in the daylight once more.

The troubles in Gralen's heart grew evermore acute as the great dragon watched the wizard closely. It seemed to him that with every passing day a grayness was creeping over his old friend. His strength appeared to be ebbing away.

On the fourteenth day since leaving the western coasts, they came at last to the fringes of the old rainforest kingdom of Wendya's childhood. They followed the meandering path of the great river for a while, before leaving its torrents and sandbars and turning back into the steamy interior.

"This is it! I'd know those hills anywhere!" cried the witch, pointing down at the green expanse below. "Those ridges you see lead away to the high central plateaus to the east, towards the volcanoes and Great Rift Valley lakes."

Within the hour, the three friends had landed in a large clearing, or *bai*, a surprisingly bright and open space amidst the density of the surrounding forest.

"These are magical places," she sighed. "We used to come here and watch the forest elephants and gorillas."

These remote spots, though long known to the forest peoples and the dworlls themselves, had lain untouched and unspoiled since the beginning of time. Rare gems of light amongst the towering depth and darkness of the jungle. Some of these places had recently been 'discovered' by man — encroaching upon the fabled 'heart of darkness' — but despite this, their mystery and beauty lingered still.

The three friends looked across the lush stretch of grassland before them — much of it waterlogged — as one of the river's tributaries snaked through the jungle and into the clearing, leaving only the higher ground above the level of its sparkling flow. They watched for a moment as clouds of swallowtail butterflies gathered to soak up the morning sun, dancing and tumbling over each other in constantly moving columns above the water-meadows. Small birds darted and flitted through the reed-beds. A family of giant forest hogs was snorting their way to one of the muddy holes. Wendya smiled at the others. Then, following a winding path through a sea of willowy grass, the group disappeared under the dappled shade of the jungle ahead.

Gray parrots squawked above, flashing red tails as a warning. Gralen looked around. The forest seemed quite different; lighter and airier than the Amazonian jungle. The trees, though mighty and ancient, appeared fresher and greener, although the constant buzz of insects remained the same. The friends wandered through ferny glades, under the canopy of native iroko and sapele trees, past banks of wild begonias and impatiens, their pods bursting as the dragon lumbered by. A clean mist of fresh rain hung in the air. The forest floor was covered in crumbling, soft, brown earth and the growing shoots of new trees struggling to reach the light above. As they traveled on, it seemed to all of them that the seasons held no sway here.

"When I was a child we used play in these woods, chasing bongos and butterflies or watching the BaAka forest people," said Wendya, feeling a mix of nostalgia and sadness. "We used to scare each other with stories of the lake monster, Mokelle Mbembe. They were wonderful times. I'd forgotten how beautiful it is here," she sighed, bending to pick up some sweet-smelling sedge.

"More infernal trees," mumbled the dragon, trudging behind, with a quiet Mr. Agyk perched on his shoulder. Suddenly, he stopped and sniffed the air, trying to scan the forest. He felt certain that something or someone was following them.

"Come on," Wendya called and strode ahead. "There are many entrances to Kallorm; each one has nine gates to pass. I know this track, it's a little worn but it takes us to the tunnel I used the most."

"Wait!" Mr. Agyk said. "It is not for vanity's sake … but I think it would be better for me to address King Dorrol at my full height. We are asking for his aid. I do not wish to seem …," he paused nervously. "It would be better to appear strong rather than weak."

Gralen looked at him. "Are you sure?"

"Quite certain," he replied slipping from the dragon. He stepped away from the others and whispered an incantation. A soft, green light emanated from him for a moment, as he grew back to his full size.

"That's a show!" laughed the dragon, wandering over to hug the old man. "It's good to have you back!"

Wendya stared at him for a moment, rushed over and embraced him tightly, burying her face in the folds of his tunic, as if she were a little child seeing her father for the first time after many missed months away.

"I would have done this sooner if I had known I would get this reaction!" he smiled.

She looked at him, still fragile and awfully pale. "How do you feel?"

"Fine. Now come on children, we have a city to find!"

Another hour or two passed under the shade of the trees. The group waded across a small, swift-flowing brook and came at last to a high, sloping bank of red earth. Hidden behind a thicket bush lay a small cut in the bank, as if the earth had dried in the sun and cracked.

"We're here!" gasped Wendya. "Come on!"

She rushed over and quickly disappeared into the crevice.

"Well that's impressive!" Gralen announced sarcastically, expecting something far more imposing and extraordinary than a crack. "I'll never fit through that!"

"You do not know unless you try," answered the wizard, striding ahead.

Gralen mumbled something under his breath as Mr. Agyk vanished into the fissure and passed into the shadows beyond. The dragon reached the earthy bank and, to his amazement, the crevice bulged outward and widened, allowing him to squeeze through.

Behind the hidden entrance lay a narrow tunnel that dropped before them, running deeper into the ground. The friends followed its course but the witch was growing uneasy.

"This is strange," she said. "There's something wrong here."

"What is it?" Mr. Agyk asked as he held his staff aloft, lighting the passageway in a dim glow. Wendya looked around anxiously.

"This all looks abandoned to me. I don't think it's been used in years," she whispered.

She pressed on. The tunnel fell sharply and at the bottom of the steep incline stood a low, ancient archway. Beyond that, the tunnel ended abruptly at a wall. The witch walked over to the crumbling rock face, picking her way through the rubble and debris that showered the floor, and pulled at the draping creepers covering it.

"This should be the first gate," she whispered, "but look, it hasn't been used in years."

Wendya looked closer and stooped down, running her fingers over the craggy surface. "This makes no sense. There are cracks here, but these doors are thicker than tree trunks!" The witch felt the stone once more and slipped her hand into one of the crevices. "It's as if something is pushing against it, pushing it out."

Mr. Agyk weaved his way between the broken chunks of stone that littered the floor and examined the half-hidden door. "I would say that the tunnel behind has been filled," he said, placing both hands on the cold rock. "Yes, it is completely blocked."

"But why would they block off an entrance?" Wendya asked.

"To keep something out?" Mr. Agyk replied grimly.

"Or keep something in!" Gralen mumbled, "and *we're* trying to get in!"

Wendya pushed up against the door. "Can we move it?" she said, turning to the dragon who sat hunched against the wall picking soil out of his talons.

Gralen shrugged casually. "I'll give it a go … Stand back."

With an enormous and surprising burst of speed, the dragon lunged at the door, throwing his whole weight behind him. He crashed into it with a heavy thud. Nothing. The door, though crumbling, stood defiantly before them, the great dragon's efforts only managing to dislodge a termite nest.

"That's not moving!" he huffed, as he tried a handful of the squashed ants.

"We will have to try another gate," sighed Mr. Agyk turning to Wendya. "Do you remember the other entrances?"

"Most of them, but this was one of the busiest trade routes. I don't understand why it's like this."

Mr. Agyk leaned heavily on his staff and watched Gralen munch on another handful of termites. "The answer will probably present itself," he reasoned.

"Anyone want some? They taste like … crunchy meat!"

The company swiftly left and went in search of another way in. Hours passed and still each great gate they found lay blocked, broken or in ruins. More alarmingly, many of the doors bore the scars of battle. Gralen however, was far more concerned with the strange scent he caught snatches of every now and then — not animal, but not human or dworll. Something was definitely watching them, tracking them. He said nothing to the others but kept his senses alert.

The day was darkening quickly. The friends began to doubt whether they would ever see Kallorm's great towers if, indeed, the city still existed. "Well, this is the last entrance I remember," Wendya sighed, leading the dragon and wizard down yet another tunnel.

"This looks more hopeful," Mr. Agyk commented, noticing the trodden path and lack of cobwebs. "I would say this has been used quite recently."

Wendya looked about, her spirits raised again. "I think you're right. The ceiling hasn't caved in. Here we are!" she said excitedly, as they turned the last corner and stood before a perfectly smooth stone wall.

"So is this the door?" grumbled Gralen, nervously watching the entrance behind them.

"A door, yes. Dworll doors are like wizard doors, they're not built to be seen by outsiders," she replied, feeling the sandy stone.

The young witch ran her fingers over a protruding notch of rock, and pressed her finger onto it. To her companions' amazement, her finger, and then her entire hand disappeared into the stone.

"*Narrock see,*" she whispered. "*Kallorm Sigh `e tari mon Narrock see.*"

She pulled her hand free, stood back and waited.

"Well?" said the dragon impatiently. "What happens next?"

"Shh. Wait!" she whispered, staring at the stone wall. "Come on. Come on."

Gralen looked at the wizard. Suddenly, a strange grating noise could be heard from behind the wall and a perfectly cut square window miraculously appeared in the rock before them.

"What do ya want?" Came a sharp little voice from inside.

"Oh … I … we want to come in," Wendya replied, leaning forward to speak through the opening.

"I'm sure you do," snapped the voice, as a pair of angry eyes flashed into view for a moment. "Now be off with ya!" he scowled, promptly shutting the window.

"Hey!" shouted Gralen.

"It's alright," said Wendya, pressing her finger firmly into the stone once more. "It's been a while."

The window appeared again and a small, mean face, like crumpled newspaper, filled the space. "What do ya want? Who are you?" said the dworll, his eyes blazing with suspicion and distrust.

"My name is Wendya Undokki. We have traveled far. This is …"

"We don't let outsiders in, not without a permit!" interrupted the dworll.

"Since when?"

"Ah! Well that proves you're an outsider. We've had permits for as long as I've been a gatekeeper, and that's bin a long age!"

"Well, age hasn't improved your manners," answered the witch, feeling more than a little irked. "I'm not an outsider. I'm a citizen of Kallorm and a good friend of the Royal House. I was even an adviser to the Council!"

Mr. Agyk stood silently in the shadows, sensing fear in the gatekeeper.

"Well I don't know you. You're not a dworll … you're a wicca I'd say, and we've had more than our fill of trouble with types like you! … Magic folk bring nothing but grief! Yar' not welcome!" shouted the dworll, sneering through a set of crooked yellow teeth. "Now be off or I'll call the sentries!"

"Well I don't know you!" snapped Wendya. "And magic casters of all types were always welcome here. This certainly isn't the homecoming I was expecting!"

The dworll narrowed his eyes. "Alright witch, what's the password and where's ya key?" he scoffed, squinting to try and see what was in the passage behind.

"*Narrock see* is the password … I don't have a key," answered Wendya, crossing her arms in defiance.

"HA! Not an outsider eh? That password hasn't been used for over 200 years!"

"Well I haven't been here for nearly 300 years!" shouted the witch, getting really angry. "Now let us in!"

"Us?" he scowled. "Who's there?"

At this point, the dragon had had quite enough and stormed forward. The dworll was about to slam the window shut again, when he suddenly looked up to see the end of a dragon's snout no more than two inches from his face.

"A ... a ... fÿrr ..."

"Yes!" growled Gralen, his eyes flaming. "A fÿrren! A dragon! And if you don't let us in NOW, I'll burn this door down and you with it!"

The dworll gulped and almost fainted. From behind the door came an even sharper voice, the gatekeeper's wife.

"Ullan, you're not letting them in! Do you hear me? ... They're not coming in!" she shouted.

"It is alright my dear," said Mr. Agyk coming into view. "My name is Mr. Marval Agyk, I visited your fair city long ago, and Wendya here was a resident in Kallorm for many years. We will not harm you. We are loyal friends of King Dorrol and the Royal House. Now please, we have traveled a great distance to speak to the King! Let us pass."

As the wizard spoke, it seemed to the witch and dragon that his calming voice became a soft honeyed whisper that glided on the air like a golden mist toward the dworll.

Almost immediately, a crack appeared round the edge of the wall forming a perfectly hewn door, and then the slab of rock quickly slid back revealing a beautifully carved, dimly-lit, passage beyond. The company passed through the doorway and watched as it instantly slammed shut behind them.

"Well, this certainly is a friendly place!" griped Gralen, peering down at the dworll as he cringed in the corner and his wife stood scowling behind him.

"It always used to be," Wendya replied anxiously. "There's something wrong."

The gatekeeper, an odious little figure, looked as if his own shadow would terrify him. He stood pressed against the wall, a look of petrified horror on his pallid face as the green dragon lumbered past and gave him a tooth-filled grin. His wife, Rreth, a bony stick-like unsavory looking dworll, with a pinched face and a shrill voice, stood behind him, nudging and prodding her husband while making snippy remarks.

"Well, Ullan, you've really done it now! I told you not to let them in! I told you! We'll both be in trouble now, you old fool!" she snapped.

Wendya hesitated for a moment and looked at the sad little couple. The wife glowered at her defiantly and tapped her foot on the floor. She had the emaciated figure of someone whose meticulous energies were focused, with microscopic intensity, on fixing others.

"Ullan, come on ... make them hurry past! Tell them to go faster!" she bleated, almost pushing her harassed husband forward.

Wendya looked at the forlorn guard with his bent shoulders, rotten teeth and porridge-colored complexion and couldn't help feeling a twinge of pity.

"What is the new password?" Wendya asked. She was losing her patience. "The password!"

"It's *Rikanum bri* but that won't help you at the other gates, they'll stop you for sure ... they change the password nearly every week."

"Why?" asked the witch, recognizing real fear in the dworll's face.

"B ... because of the trouble. There's trouble every few months and it's been getting worse. In the old times, hundreds of years or more would go by with nothing, but now the attacks happen every few weeks. There's talk of an endless war coming to Kallorm, of an invasion," he looked at the dragon, "t … tr … troops are mustering, on the move … you'll find the rest of the gates heavily guarded."

"Shut up you idiot! Don't tell 'em anything!" ordered his wife, who promptly shut up as Gralen leaned over her and snarled.

"So they left a weak, rude, old goat and his hag of a wife to protect this door?" laughed the dragon. "Sounds like a great plan!"

"My guess would be that he is more of a watcher than a real guard," said the wizard. The dworll nodded.

"Th … that's right, if trouble comes I'm to warn the troops," he said, pointing to a strange horn-like device, "… and I'm not allowed to let anyone pass the gate!" he muttered, bowing and shaking his head.

"No one is allowed to pass, no one! And now you've let in three of them!" shouted his wife. "They'll exile us both!"

Mr. Agyk sighed and placed his hand upon her shoulder. "Be at peace," he whispered as the harridan slumped to the floor, fast asleep.

The gatekeeper stared at him with a look of amazement and mild relief. "Th … thank you."

"Now, what sort of trouble? What are these attacks?" Wendya asked.

"Oh … the worst kind. We've had t … terrors, wargols and rock demons bombarding the tunnels, appearing out of nowhere. Fÿrullfrs rampaging around. I haven't heard of those since the old place was built! There's worse things they don't tell us about, dark rumors …," the dworll shook his head as if it were all too much for him. "There's trouble in the Council too. I don't know me politics but the city's preparing for something … it feels like we're getting ready for a siege or worse."

"Thank you," Mr. Agyk smiled. "Do not worry, you have not failed in your protection of the city, in fact, you have greatly helped her. The King will reward you for your courage in letting us pass."

"Well," snorted Gralen. "I think I understand why those two were posted all the way out here!"

Mr. Agyk strode ahead. "Come, we have a long way to walk and many gates to pass. I, for one, would like to speak to the King and the Council before the day is over."

The witch and dragon followed. As they descended, each corridor and tunnel became more splendid and ornate than the last. High, vaulted ceilings sparkled above with starstones that lit the path. Friezes covered the walls, intricately carved panels, each one depicting a famous scene from Kallorm's long and illustrious history, from its architecture, commerce and trade links, to its wondrous inventions and its heroic rulers of old. They looked at the height of its power depicted in glorious detail, but there also, carved into the rock, was Kallorm's decline, the mindless assaults from its enemies and the slow but incessant exodus of its people. Wendya walked quietly, feeling an intense and heady mix of emotions overwhelm her, and a deep anxiety at the old gatekeeper's warnings.

Before the travelers had reached the next sentry, word of their presence had arrived at the Royal House, and they were ushered past each gate with subdued reverence and more than a little curiosity. As darkness covered the jungle above and the moon rose pale and yellow behind drifting fingers of cloud, the three friends finally passed the last city gate.

They were now in a huge, cavernous space, with rock walls towering up to unseen heights. These sheer mountain walls were divided by a deep chasm below, which could only be breached by two narrow and parallel bridges.

They walked down the steep road that clung to the mountain face and wound towards the bridges. As they trudged along, keeping away from the edge and the frightening drop beyond it, they passed dozens of dworll soldiers sitting hunched around campfires, all marveling at seeing such a strange sight.

The company stood before the two bridges, spanning the abyss like arching arms. The left, and more ornate, bore high balustrades on each side, bearing the anvil and star of the city. The older crossing bore a series of twisted arches from plainer and rougher hewn stone.

"We need the left one," whispered the witch, pointing to the ornate bridge as she glanced over the edge into the darkness below.

They quickly crossed the bridge and disappeared into the tunnel behind. As they emerged from this dark passageway, they found themselves on a high pass overlooking the entire city. They stood in stunned silence as the great sprawling metropolis of Kallorm stretched its vastness before them. An endless expanse of spires, turrets, glistening towers and shimmering domes pierced the eye line. Great arches and statues rose amidst the jumble of sandstone buildings; aqueducts towered above.

Countless bridges and walkways crisscrossed the city, dividing the older and newer quarters, as sheltered avenues and colonnades joined one imposing building to another. Vast market places jostled for space. Over the nestling rooftops of homes, shops and the carpet of buildings that stretched in every direction as far as they eye could see, rose Kallorm's grand palaces, perched high above on spurs of raised rock.

"We're here!" Wendya sighed.

They gazed over the ancient city. In the near distance was the most incredible sight of all. Rising from the streets, stood one of the Three Pillars of Kallorm, a truly gargantuan mountain column of rock that supported the entire jungle above.

The roof was studded with millions upon millions of starstones, which gave the city its wondrous light, and was so immeasurably high that it was always swathed in drifting mists and clouds.

"Kallorm!" gasped Wendya, fighting back her tears. "I have missed you!"

Mr. Agyk turned to a stunned Gralen. "Well, is that impressive enough for you?" he smiled. The dragon, for once, was lost for words.

Chapter Ten
City of Light

ome on," called the wizard, striding ahead. The travelers descended from the pass and, joining a wide, curving road, they came to a deep water channel, cut into the rock, which lay across their path. The fast-flowing river skirted the city and its walls like a giant moat, feeding its many streams and fountains, its waterfalls and resting pools, before disappearing underground in a thousand tributaries. The weary group crossed a wide, low-lying causeway, just inches above the flow, and passed beneath Kallorm's towering, honey-colored walls.

"Huh. No welcoming committee then, very friendly," scoffed the dragon.

"They'll be waiting for us at the Royal Palace," Wendya replied, ignoring the dragon's sour tone. "It's tradition not to hamper a traveler's path but to greet them at their journey's end."

The city around them lay quiet and peaceful. Street torches flickered from every corner. Pale lights from the spires and towers glimmered in the darkness, casting silver shadows on the buildings below and reflecting in the little streams that trickled through the cobbled city streets, like so many dancing fireflies.

It was late, past two by Mr. Agyk's reckoning. The light that filled Kallorm's skies during the day, from the millions of starstones embedded above, was extinguished now, leaving only a few shimmering points.

All about them, countless lanterns twinkled in the glowing city as they continued on. Gralen looked up, marveling at the ingenuity of it all, but wishing he could see a real night sky and real stars.

The friends followed Wendya deeper into the heart of the metropolis. They trudged down road after road, through twisting colonnades each side lined with pillars of beautifully carved amber marble, which glinted as they passed. Every so often the dragon would stop, as if listening or sniffing for something.

"What is it?" Mr. Agyk whispered, glad to rest for a while.

Gralen hushed his voice. "I didn't want to alarm you … but I'm certain of it now, my senses don't betray me."

"Certain of what?"

"Something's been following us, tracking us. Since before we crossed the channel …, out in the jungle, I was sure we were being watched and here, now … I can smell it. Something not human and not dworll!"

"Your senses are better than mine, but I have felt it too."

"If we're going to fight, I'd rather do it up there on one of those rocky hills and not trapped like rats in these streets!" Gralen said, glancing around nervously.

Mr. Agyk patted him on the shoulder. "I could be wrong but I do not think it will come to that. I do not think they mean us any harm … unless Kallorm too has changed beyond my reckoning. Let us catch up," he smiled.

They continued on. Mr. Agyk's banter belying any problem and Wendya's excited chatting seeming altogether too loud and unwise to Gralen's ears. His keen eyesight scanned every alley and avenue they passed, waiting for some kind of attack. As they passed ever deeper into the city, somewhere in the darkness, eyes followed them and the glint of sharpened steel.

Most of Kallorm's buildings were made of ancient sandstone of various yellows, reds and browns. However, its grander buildings, spires and towers had been carved out of different quartz and crystals, which sparkled like strands of pearl and diamond caught in clear stone.

Wendya walked briskly, pointing out the sights of her childhood.

"This is the Great Forum, often called The Oval, where public meetings are held," she said eagerly.

The company climbed a long stairway to a high, circular platform surrounded by tiers of benches and stone steps and, around that, a circle of high, fluted arches. Unlike the stillness of the town outskirts, lights now shone from most of the towering buildings, with the promise of life.

"We're near to the seat of the Council and the Royal House … the White Palace," Wendya said excitedly.

She led her companions along a viaduct that rose from the city floor and wound its way towards a steep promontory, an enormous plateau of rock that jutted abruptly before them. Perched high on this elevated mount stood an imposing complex of glimmering white buildings, which overlooked the city.

"Palace Rock, I can't believe I'm here," she whispered, as they climbed higher and approached an avenue lined with tall statues that led the way to the top. "I shouldn't have stayed away for so long."

"We shouldn't have come here at all," muttered Gralen under his breath, still keenly aware of unfriendly eyes watching them.

Before the travelers reached the summit and passed beneath the outer walls of the palace grounds, they came to a small viewing platform. The views from here, over the city below, were truly breath-taking, eclipsed only by the roaring beauty of the Falls of Tarro nearby.

The falls bubbled up from a deep reservoir within the rock, where the thunderous flows of sparkling water joined together to form a series of magnificent cascades, which roared down the plateau sides giving an ethereal mist to the palace above. Wendya stood quietly for a moment, letting the soft wind catch her hair. Gralen watched her.

"It feels like home," she sighed, unable to stop her eyes from tearing.

The friends continued along the path. White Palace stretched before them, a magnificent creation of crystal walls, which shone with a brilliance that illuminated all who walked within. From its many archways and porticos hung a thousand silver points of light, shimmering in the darkness. Spiral minarets sprouted from its luminous walls. The friends could now glimpse an enormous central dome, arcing above the building like an encrusted jewel, shining light from its every cut facet.

In the distance, a young girl appeared from beneath one of the glowing arches. A slender dworll clothed entirely in amber and pearl. She glided toward them as if from some dream. Her hair flowed behind her in a trussle of bronze-colored braids and, on her face, was a warm smile of recognition.

"Halli? Halli!" Wendya cried and rushed forward.

"Wait!" called Gralen.

"It is fine," Mr. Agyk smiled. "Remember, they are old friends. Halli is the daughter of King Dorrol. They have known each other since they were greenlings."

The two girls embraced as sisters who had been parted too long and both burst into tears.

"Oh, Halli, I have missed you!" Wendya cried.

The dworll laughed as tears streamed down her face. "We heard from the gate sentries that you were coming! I had to keep asking them, I couldn't believe it ... I still can't believe it! You're really here!" Halli hugged her again, "I never thought you'd come back. I never thought I'd see you again!"

The friends wiped away each other's tears and embraced once more.

"I have so much to tell you," smiled the dworll, clasping the witch's hand, "but that will have to wait. My father and the Council are all waiting for you inside. Come, I will take you."

The two girls strode ahead, arms interlocked, deep in conversation. Mr. Agyk and Gralen smiled at each other, followed behind and soon disappeared within the glowing walls of the palace.

Moments later, the company was strolling through a glass-covered arcade, its marbled floors and galleried walls leading to the Council Chamber and Throne Room beyond. The old wizard looked up at the staring faces of great rulers, their statues standing mournfully in every alcove. The dragon's gaze never left Wendya, despite the constant stares and hushed gasps from passing dworlls on the gallery above.

At last the travelers reached the Council Chamber and the inner sanctum of the palace.

An enormous and magnificent circular room greeted them. Its walls glimmered with copper and gold and, looking up at the ceiling far above, Mr. Agyk could see the crystal dome that had been so visible from the outside, sparkling like a blazing star above their heads. From a central ring below them, steep steps and benches rose to create an enclosed amphitheater. The entire chamber had a hallowed grandness about it, but an antiquated feel, as if its greatest days were now behind it and would never come again. The friends entered the chamber and descended the stairs. They could see a raised platform at the far end, upon which stood a long line of beautifully carved chairs, and a central throne glimmering in pure white. Waiting for them sat the aging King and the Grand Council of Kallorm. Standing silently behind, almost as a statue of granite himself, was a tall, dark-haired man with sharp, unfriendly eyes.

Gralen viewed him suspiciously. "That's who was following us ...," he thought and sniffed the air. It was the same strange scent he had detected back in the forest. Not human but not dworll. He noted that the grim figure stood with his hand poised threateningly above the hilt of his sword and that his narrowed eyes were fixed solely on the dragon. "If you want a fight ... just step this way!" he glowered back.

The King, a rather frail but lively old fellow, slowly rose from his throne. "*Narrock see.* Welcome all, dear friends," he said with a warm smile. "The King and Lord of Kallorm greets you," his eyes sparkled darkly as he glanced toward the dragon, "I am Dorrol, ninth Lord of the Heirs of Edral and I welcome you all," he bowed graciously and nodded to the wizard before turning to Wendya. "Well, Wendya Undokki, it is especially good to see you again. You have been greatly missed my child, by my daughter not least of all!"

She smiled, overwhelmed and shocked to see how the years had aged the King she had known so well.

Dorrol smiled and stood proudly like some grand conquistador overseeing a great parade in his honor. A small-framed and wiry old man, his thinning hair was flamboyantly swept forward in the old style — though once a brilliant, fiery red it now shimmered with the pale russet and silver of age. His bearded face, with its extravagantly curled moustache, bore a weariness and worry that lay heavily upon him.

"Come, sit down, we have much to discuss if your tired eyes can wait a little longer," he said, showing the visitors to a nearby bench. "Your rooms have been readied but we have food and drink here to keep your spirits high before sleep beckons," he motioned to several tables laden with exotic foods of every wondrous variety.

Mr. Agyk stepped forward, his eyes wandering over the aging panel of councilors behind. Their silence and stony faces disturbed him. Gralen gave the dark-haired man a fiery scowl, then headed straight for the food. It had been many years since Wendya had seen the great chamber and its beauty was still a marvel to her.

King Dorrol sank back, his keen eyes now lingering on the aged wizard and his green companion. "I must say, I find you changed, Marvalla. I was glad when I was told of your arrival but, I confess, I hardly recognize you," he paused. "You carry the look of having survived something ... barely. Some strange adventures no doubt. Well, I am glad to see such welcome, if unusual, visitors. Your help was not looked for but it is sorely needed."

"It is actually for your help that we have come," replied the wizard, bowing graciously.

Dorrol looked closely at the old figure before him. "Our help you say. How may we help you?" he asked.

Mr. Agyk recounted their story from the beginning, and though the old King seemed greatly concerned, the news of the disappearances and the attack on Wendya's cottage seemed to trouble him the most. Mr. Agyk paused when he reached the telling of the Oracle, and once more he spoke guardedly of what she had foretold.

"I must say, I am truly surprised that you survived such an encounter," Dorrol answered with wonder in his eyes. "The Oracles of old were always wise but treacherous. We have long since known of her existence and would no sooner take her guidance than that of M'Sorreck himself!"

The Falls of Tarro and Kallorm's great mountain pillars

He paused and, staring through deep, amber-colored eyes, he gazed at his daughter, then at Wendya. When he spoke again his voice was mournful and full of sadness. "This news troubles me more than you know: … evil growing in the roots of Ïssätun, the most northerly of our ancient realms. Morreck is becoming a great shadow over the entire world it seems. Long has he been a darkness over this land and blighted the lives of all who live here," he shook his head in despair. "It is an unfortunate cycle that we Kallormians know well. We have peace for an age and fall into a kind of slumber, daring to think, to hope, that we are finally free from his tyranny. Then he or his insidious followers return, attacking the city and its people without warning or mercy. Every time they return they find the city weaker and its people lessened."

Dorrol sighed and Mr. Agyk perceived his great age and the weariness of a burdened heart.

"All we can do now is to protect our city. I fear we are presently in the calm before the next storm breaks," he sighed once more and gazed towards the dome. "When that storm breaks, all elder races left in this world must set their differences aside and unite to face it, or fall. Kallorm … has no choice but to keep fighting against the host of evil that M'Sorreck has roused; a host that may well have grown greater than all of our armies."

"Host?" asked Gralen between mouthfuls.

"Yes, it has long been held by the wise, that M'Sorreck has discovered the power of 'awakening'. That he is searching out all the ancient and dormant evils of this world — primordial beings — and rousing them into battle, into an unparalleled force, for a war to end all wars! … I for one believe this to be true."

Silence fell over the chamber.

At last the mage spoke and his voice was thin and wavering. "I had no idea Kallorm was so beleaguered! Times have changed since my halcyon days here," he said, feeling a surge of fatigue wash over him.

Dorrol lowered his eyes. "Yes, times have changed — worsened — greatly. But our fates were cast long ago, when even I was young," he answered grimly. "Foul warlocks, opposers of the Order and of all peace-loving peoples started to unite under his banner as they had done in the dark years. Morreck may not have been the first corruptor but he was the worst. The evil line ran deepest in him …," the King hesitated as if remembering some event, which had caused him deep pain, and then he continued again.

"Alas, history shows us our mistakes and, as one of the Order that cast him out, I must share the blame. We never fully understood the power and ambition he had. We never imagined that his malice ran so deep and could corrupt and incite so many. To our folly, when we had the opportunity to stop him, we did nothing … Well, our ignorance has cost us dearly. I fear now, that any chance of dealing with him has long since passed … he is simply too powerful and we are too weak," he took a deep breath and looked over the company.

"Shadows grew in the jungles above. We were plagued by strange disappearances which became ever more frequent. Violence seemed to spread through the forest like a canker. Here and there killings were reported. Entire villages were found massacred, horribly, human and dworll settlements alike. The promise of wealth corrupted many. Then the rape of the jungle began: minerals, ore, gold — anything of worth. These lands are rich in such metals … M'Sorreck infects everything. Bitter wars have raged ceaselessly in these forests in recent years. I fear it may all be his doing," he faltered for a moment before he continued. "At first his power seemed limited, his followers few, yet his true strength lay hidden. He had sown the seeds of evil within the very heart of our great city and, in time, those agents and traitors began to kill, corrupt and undermine the city from within, weakening us all."

King Dorrol glanced at the silent council members who flanked either side of him. "The fault is mine alone. It lies within the house of Edrral. So desperate were we to purge ourselves of his threat that we … that *I* — sent out sortie after sortie to destroy him, only to have them slaughtered or corrupted. Then, for my sins, and against my counselors advice, when Morreck returned again, I gave the order once more and sent out an army of hunters to rid us of him once and for all. Not one returned … more cannon-fodder for him. I had played into his hands. I helped to deplete Kallorm's precious forces and give more cause for grief," he paused, and again a look of pain flickered on the dworll's face. Gralen felt sorry for the old man, ruler of a dying kingdom.

Dorrol continued, speaking in a quieter voice as if he were talking to himself. "Unease grew in the city, so long a citadel prized for its safety. Then, a little over two ages ago, after you had gone, Wendya, we were visited by a mage … an unusual occurrence these days. He was well known to me, an old ally and a close friend. In his day, he presided over the Order itself. You may have known him Marval, Kirrem Hal was his name." The wizard nodded but remained silent. "How absurd that neither I nor even the wise among us knew his true nature before it was too late. A cancer in our midst … a changeling. It was, of course, M'Sorreck himself. I can only guess why he came here, what his purpose was. How long he assumes the faces and guises of his dead victims, who can tell?" the dworll shifted his weight uneasily and glanced toward the wizard.

"Perhaps he may have been looking for this birthkey you spoke of. Yet I do not think he found it. In any case he disappeared into the catacombs beneath the city and, since then, trouble has never ceased."

"Trouble?" asked Mr. Agyk.

The old lord shook his head. "Cave wargols and demons appeared. Allm'ettans and miners delving in the deeper caverns were attacked and killed. There were rumors of dark mytes, which we all fear … Fÿrullfrs too and other demonic beasts surfaced and multiplied in the jungles. But, most worryingly, we believe that Morreck stirred or bred some great terror in the deep recesses below the city itself! What evil it is, we do not know."

"Filthy fengal!" muttered Gralen stuffing a clotted havel into his mouth.

The King looked over the faces of his visitors, gauging their character, unsure whether to say more.

"When M'Sorreck finally emerged from the catacombs," he went on, "it was at the head of a wargol army. The ensuing battle was terrible, the worst we have known since the days of my forefathers. So many perished ... but our people fought bravely. We destroyed many of them. We drove them screaming into the dark pools and drowned them ... yet, as with all our history with him, our losses were bitter and great," his eyes flickered to the silent figure behind him whose hand still remained poised above his sword, then, turning towards the dome for a moment as if recollecting past atrocities, a deep sadness passed over the King's face.

"Our victory was at hand but, even at that moment, Morreck managed to escape with a host of wargol captains, leaving our vengeance unanswered ... ." He turned to his daughter. "It has taken us a great time to recover from our wounds. We were greatly weakened. And so, reluctantly, the choice was made to block Kallorm's entrances to prevent further attacks and become the fortress city you see now," the old dworll sighed and all could see that the decision weighed heavily upon him. "We have lost nearly half of our population through battle, disease or abandonment. I cannot blame families for leaving in search of safer homes. But our troops, though fearless, have dwindled to dangerously low numbers. Now we wait and watch for the next attack, whether from above or from the threat that lurks below, ready to well up and overwhelm us," he turned to the visitors. "You can understand, can you not, why we were hoping for your aid?"

Mr. Agyk nodded. "I am deeply sorry for your troubles. M'Sorreck has much to answer for. This threat, this evil thing that he roused ... have you sought it out?" he asked, trying to conceal his growing anxiety.

"Of course," replied Dorrol solemnly, curling the ends of his moustache through his ring-laden fingers, "regiments keep sentry on the passages below and we regularly send our best trackers to hunt out the darker places to keep the city safe. Only a very few claim to have seen the thing itself, though many have heard it. But those who have gazed upon the horror of it have been driven to madness."

With an effort he rose from his throne, the dark sable of his robe falling behind his bent shoulders in great bear-like folds. It seemed to Wendya and the other travelers that his kingship was nearing the end of its days.

"Father!" said Halli, rising to help him down the throne steps.

Dorrol placed a hand gently on his daughter's arm. "We have attacks and sightings of fell shadows frequently now, while the jungles above explode in violence. One human killing another. However, I feel in my bones that the worst is yet to come," he said wearily.

He stood, as if making some silent prayer and let the soft light of the dome bathe his face in its warmth. Then he turned to his daughter. "I am old now, even by the count of our race. Though the Grand Council is wise and will command over this fair city, the lordship alone can only pass to my heir and I would not see her take this great burden in such dangerous times."

Halli smiled and clasped her father's hand. "You are not so old and I am not so young," she said and turned to the company. "In the past, others had sent help, for which we were grateful. But we fear they too have been swallowed by Morreck. We have not received any news from our old allies for a long age now. Our ancient mimmirian was destroyed in the last battle and we have no means of creating another," she paused. "We have sent countless messengers to make contact with our kin. But either they do not return, or they tell us that our kindred have disappeared, that the old cities we have long traded with have been utterly destroyed. To protect the city, we dare not send any more."

"We are too isolated," sighed the King, "and the world above is closing in."

"I am afraid, my Lord, that that is the malady that affects us all," the wizard answered grimly. "Too long have old neighbors lost contact with their sister cities and diminished as a result. I too have been guilty of this neglect. How can we hope to fight, or even survive against such forces, if we stand alone? We must unite, all of us, as we once did!"

Despite Gralen's sloppy eating noises, Wendya had been listening intently. When at last she spoke her voice was strange and distant. "Morreck desires to be master of all: all realms, all kingdoms, and all peoples. To destroy any who stand in his way, and place himself as supreme ruler. The swallower of the world," she whispered.

"Yes," replied Mr. Agyk. "To conquer our world and the human world. To break the will of all."

"Humans. No great loss there then," muttered Gralen to a barrage of icy stares. "All I'm asking is what have humans ever done for us, other than to kill us or drive us underground? They're no better than Morreck!"

"He has a point," Wendya replied mutedly. "They worship at the altar of their false gods, when they should be worshipping at nature's altar ... They should be serving the planet they live on instead of ruining it! They ravage the land; poison the seas and the skies. They're destroying this planet far quicker than any device of M'Sorreck's could hope to do!"

Mr. Agyk looked disappointed. "Even if that were true, they are mere children. They do not deserve enslavement and annihilation!"

Dorrol turned to the mage. "You think he would reveal himself and attack the human population?" he asked.

"Why not? They are as weak as us and as divided. My Lord, we are all interconnected, though we may choose to deny it. Every living organism on this planet is dependent on another. As surely as night follows day ... if one world falls, the other will follow," Mr. Agyk sighed. "Human technology, no matter how ... clever, will not stand against the forces Morreck wields. A changeling with his abilities could easily assume the mantle of power and the identity of any ruler he chooses! Think of it: ... a starter of wars, a corruptor of minds ... . How many evils, how much genocide in the world can be attributed to him already?" his silver eyes darkened for a moment, the gravitas of his voice defying his frailty. "No, I think Wendya has guessed his true intent ... to be master of all. He would destroy this world and create another in his own image. An enslaved realm where all creatures, human or not, should cower before him as groveling worms — or perish."

Gralen lost his appetite and lurched over.

"Sire, what do you know of M'Sorreck's birthkey?" asked Mr. Agyk bluntly as he leaned his full weight on his staff and stared probingly at the King.

Dorrol held his gaze, unruffled by the bold tone of the question, then glanced toward the dark-haired man behind. "I believe it does exist and lies somewhere beneath the city. We can scarcely spare the soldiers but we have tried many times to locate it, in the vain hope of using it. We had hoped it would give us some leverage. It is important then?" he asked, stepping from the dais and beckoning for the travelers to walk with him.

The wizard nodded. "Very important. In fact everything could depend upon our finding it."

The old dworll sighed. "Then we will help where we can. We will give you the best trackers we have. I ask only this … that if you find the key and succeed in your quest to locate and destroy M'Sorreck, that you remember us in your victory and return to help us scourge the darkness below."

"You have my oath, Sire," replied the wizard smiling, "and my promise to construct a new mimmirian for your fair city."

Gralen puffed his chest out. "We promise to defend Kallorm whenever you need us!"

"High words indeed!" the King laughed.

"You have our solemn pledge," Wendya said quietly, her eyes drifting to the dark stranger who seemed to shadow the King's every move … a bodyguard perhaps? Had things become so bad that Dorrol needed protection in his own chamber? She looked at him. There was something unusual and unsettling about him.

King Dorrol smiled. "Never have I been so glad to receive such strange guests: a fÿrren and a grand magus! You have traveled far, so I insist you must have at least a full day's rest before you go in search of the key. You will need it to conserve your strength," he added. Dorrol glanced at them. "You understand I cannot risk large forces, nor leave our own defenses abandoned, but I will give you every spare soldier we can muster to help you in your search. Let us hope that it yields fruit. I see you are all tired. Halli will take you to your rooms," he smiled, motioning to his daughter. "Sleep well and may peace be upon you," he bowed and turned to the wizard, "Marvalla, may we speak awhile longer?"

The wizard nodded.

Dorrol bid the rest of the company goodnight and Halli showed them through long, glistening corridors of glass and crystal to their rooms, overlooking the roaring waterfalls.

For the first time since he had left the comfort of White Mountain, Gralen slept in a real bed with silken sheets, to the sound of trickling water and fountain showers. Wendya too, had never slept so soundly and happily since she had left her little cottage in the woods.

King Dorrol stood leaning on a balcony, perched high above the twinkling city. His amber eyes sparkled in the light with a depth and melancholy that the wizard had never seen before.

"We have missed Wendya, especially Halli. How is she?" he asked.

Mr. Agyk sighed. "As you see, my Lord. She has grown into a wise young woman. She is no longer a child. She does not need my protection anymore, only my friendship and love — which she has, wholeheartedly."

Dorrol smiled. "I am glad. We have much in common, Marvalla. I can see that she has become like a daughter to you," he paused and sighed, his voice no more than a whisper in the night. "Dark times are ahead of us Marval, very dark. I would have her safe."

Mr. Agyk looked confounded. "As would I. That is why I ask that she stay here. She will object vigorously but ...," he hesitated. "I could not bear for any harm to come to her or Gralen but I know that I cannot stop Gralen from coming with me and that I cannot enter Fendellin without him. Wendya though is a different matter. She has suffered so much and our path is so perilous. I must leave her here in your care."

Dorrol looked at him. "You cannot."

"Sire?"

"I am sorry Marvalla, but she cannot, must not, stay here," he said firmly.

The wizard couldn't disguise his shock and puzzlement. There was something in the old King's manner, in his face that worried him deeply. "Sire ... I do not understand. Despite the troubles, surely Kallorm is a far safer place than where we are heading?"

Dorrol sighed. "No, Kallorm is no place for her. It may seem safer here, but it only seems it."

Mr. Agyk stared at the frail figure. "You are protective of her, I know," he said narrowing his eyes, "but that is not it. What are you not telling me? Surely, after all these years, can you not trust me?"

The King sighed again and shook his head, his eyes fixed off in the distance. "I dare not," he whispered. "Do not ask any questions of me Marval ... I have feared this day for so long," he looked at the green wizard, his face resolute. "No, I am bound to my promise, as you are to yours. Do not ask me what I cannot tell. Just keep her close and keep her safe."

Mr. Agyk studied him, then nodded reluctantly. "I have said nothing to the others. But, I must tell you — and this may change your mind — that ... the Oracle prophesized that one close to me ... one of *them* would die!" He turned away sharply as if the words cut him, his gaze lost somewhere amongst the glowing lights of the city. "I beg you to reconsider. She should stay here!"

"No," answered the King firmly. "Pay no heed to the Oracle's venomous words; they are as false as her promises. The Oracle may have told you half-truths about the key and M'Sorreck's birthplace as part of your bargain, but that is all. Her prophetic warnings are known to be as treacherous as the beast herself."

Dorrol paced along the balcony, his hand ever reaching for the rail, his weary feet scraping like chalk across the polished marble. And when at last he spoke again, it was with such deep sorrow that even the starstones above seemed to dim for a moment.

"Keep her with you," he sighed. "Whatever journeys and dangers you face, be it here or out there, she will be safer with you than with me. This city can never be her home again."

Chapter Eleven
Flight of the Dragon

The following morning came pale and golden. A soft yellow light streamed through the crystal shutters of the windows, splitting into honey-colored shadows that danced across the floor. The muffled sound of morning bells echoed over the city rooftops and the very air seemed filled with light and peace.

Wendya woke first, out of a distant dream of hazy days and sparkling water. From her balcony she looked out across the city she had so loved. There, cascading from the side of the White Palace, not far from her room, was Kallorm's greatest waterfall, The Tarro. She watched silently, tracing its thunderous flow over the crest of Palace Rock to the foamy bottom. Amidst the plumes of vapor and the pools below, little streams snaked through Kallorm like silver ribbons before joining the great channel that surrounded the city.

Wendya watched, entranced, as rainbows arched and sprang from its white plumes, before evaporating into the air. "I've missed you," she whispered and smiled.

Within the hour they had woken and eaten their fill. Gralen still felt hungry after eleven helpings. They met up again in the Council Room. King Dorrol and Halli greeted them warmly. The wizard noticed how drained the King looked. Once seated, he beckoned to the dark-haired man they had seen before, who now stood silently beside the door.

"This is Korrun of Koralan, an honored dwelf and loyal member of the Royal Guard," smiled Dorrol broadly. "You knew his elder brother I think," he said turning to Mr. Agyk. "Korrtal? He was a brave soldier and Captain of the City Defenses."

"Yes, yes. He was an empath as I remember and an extraordinary fellow. He had honed his skills so finely it was impossible to deceive him, especially at cards!" Mr. Agyk smiled and looked toward Korrun. "He spoke proudly of two younger brothers. One was a great warrior and Captain. I am pleased to finally meet you. I was saddened to hear of Korrtal's death … he was a good friend and a gifted ally."

"Honored to meet you," replied the man solemnly.

Dorrol patted him on the shoulder. "Together with his second in command, he is our best tracker. He knows the catacombs better than anyone. He also knows much about this key and its owner, though I'll let him tell it."

Korrun towered far taller than most. He was a broad-shouldered, slender-framed man with dark skin and strong features. His high cheekbones gave him a regal air, yet behind his rugged face lay the weary look of a soldier who has seen too many battles. His black hair hung in loose braids and, about his person, he bore many emblems and weapons of war. The dwelf glanced over the strange troop, the deep blue of his eyes catching the morning light and lingering on the dragon and wizard.

"Korrun will help you. What soldiers I could spare are ready for you," Dorrol said; turning to Wendya, his face gray with worry, he lightly kissed her forehead. "Be careful my child … good luck," he said quietly. Then, with a glance at the wizard, he turned and disappeared through a small doorway under one of the marble arches beyond.

Following Korrun, they left the White Palace for the clear morning air. On the plaza steps below stood a small battalion — a contingent of about twenty dworll soldiers — their bronze armor glinting in the early light.

"A dwelf?" mumbled Gralen, looking suspiciously at the tracker as they followed the others over dazzling white flagstones, towards the waiting soldiers. "Not human or dworll …," he muttered to himself.

"Half dworll, half ællfren," whispered the wizard. "Such unions were very rare even in the elder times. There must be few of them left now. He may very well be as rare as you!"

Korrun walked ahead and spoke quietly to the soldiers, then turned to the visitors, his voice monotone. "This is Narral," he said pointing to an older member of the regiment. "He and I will be your guides. Please follow all our instructions exactly. I suspect that the key lies somewhere in the Draellth chamber network, far below the city. The Draellth were tunneled out when Kallorm was first built and are the oldest of the ancient burrows. I believe M'Sorreck was there, trying to find this key, but instead disturbed something."

"This evil thing, do you know what it is, Captain?" the wizard asked.

"I am not a Captain," the dwelf mumbled, then shrugged. "There are stories, but none who have lived to tell."

"Why haven't you found this key if you know where it is?" Gralen asked, feeling increasingly dubious about this strange dwelf.

"You do not stroll into those passages alone. Many who have tried have never returned. I myself have gone many times with soldiers such as these and been turned back by wargols or, worse … dark mytes, parasites and demons that lurk in the shadows waiting for flesh and soul to feed from. It is doubtful that we will get any further today, but we will try."

Wendya shuddered. "How did the key get there?" she asked.

Korrun looked at her blankly. "Legend says that M'Sorreck's mother kept it. She was a dignitary of some sort. She lived here many years ago. I am sure you know that all dworll mothers keep the keys of their children's birthplace — it's tradition," he replied, giving a cursory glance over the others. "The birthkey of a dwizard or dworll magus will hold a power of itself."

Wendya nodded in agreement.

"Anyway," he continued in a flat tone. "She was well-respected and had a noble lineage but, knowing what her only son had become, she hid the key from him and cast herself into the Falls of Tarro," he sighed, picking up a long sword and hanging it onto his belt, before looking closely at each of the group. "Some say, and I believe it, that he threw her in, murdered his own mother when she wouldn't give him the key … This will be very dangerous you know. Are you sure you want to go?"

"Want? No. Must ... yes," replied the wizard simply, returning the dwelf's stare.

"Then let us go. Come," said the tracker abruptly and strode ahead.

"Friendly chap isn't he?" muttered Gralen as Mr. Agyk gathered his strength for a long walk. "He's got all the personality of a root vegetable!"

The travelers followed Korrun at a brisk pace, with the soldiers falling in behind. Taking the dwelf's secret pathways, the company made their way down a steep, narrow set of hidden steps cut into the cliff face of Palace Rock, before passing through an unseen entrance behind the mighty Tarro waterfall itself. Then, leaving the waking city behind them, they descended into darkness.

Korrun lit torches as they progressed, his keen eyesight scanning every footfall and contour of the tunnel ahead. As they wound ever downward, they became aware of shadows along the path, of hidden guards and sentries silently watching the dark passages that ran off and disappeared into the earth. Korrun nodded to these shadowy sentinels as they passed until at last, after nearly four hours of continuous walking, they came to a stop.

A dark junction lay before them with two giant stone doors, one eastward, one westward but both of them closed and sealed shut. There, in front of them, sat ten heavily-armored dworlls huddled round a lonely campfire, their tired faces earth-stained, their eyes weary of the dark but still vigilant. Korrun knelt beside them and talked at length in a hushed voice. Wendya listened.

"They're speaking Old Dworllian; I can only understand parts of it. They've been stationed here for six weeks I think ... without a break. They say they've seen nothing in that time, but they've heard strange noises, scraping sounds in the depths ... I can't understand the rest," she whispered, acutely aware of eyes watching her.

Finally, Korrun returned. "This is the last sentry post ... The eastward passage leads to the catacombs — there's been a lot of fighting there in recent weeks. The westward passage is older and unused — it leads to the great caves and beyond, to the lower levels and the most ancient parts of the under city, including the Draellth chambers. The westward path is darker, more unknown and more dangerous, but that is our route. We have sent scouts and bearers in there from time to time, to assess the tunnels and bring back any dworll remains they find. Many never return ... From here there is no more light, only what we take with us."

"That's not a problem," Gralen boasted.

The dwelf looked at him and, for the first time, a bemused smile flickered across his usually somber face. "Well, if we meet any wargols they'll certainly be surprised by you!" he said, then turned and looked more seriously at Wendya. "I am not worried about the fÿrren and his companion, but unless you have weapons and can use them, it may be safer to stay at the back and keep with the soldiers."

"I can fend for myself, thank you," the witch answered icily.

Korrun shrugged. "Well, if we're extraordinarily lucky we'll find the key and nothing else."

Cautiously and without a sound, the sentries unsealed the westward door, and then slowly prized it open. Its huge hinges groaned under the weight and a stench of decay and stale air rushed in through the door. The dworlls instinctively drew their swords but the way ahead seemed clear and devoid of any life. Korrun bid the guards farewell and, picking up a torch, he led the company through the black doorway and into the darkness beyond.

As the last of their group stepped into the passageway, they turned to see the faces of the sentries and the last glimmer of firelight disappear as the heavy door was shut behind them, like the slamming door of a tomb.

Korrun sent a small party of dworlls ahead to scout out the path and report back, while the others silently divided and enclosed around the friends — some to the front some to the rear — an ever present and ominous reminder of their dangerous path. Gralen walked closely behind the tracker, his eyes never leaving the figure.

Darkness surrounded them. Narral smiled at the witch and took out what appeared to be a small smooth pebble and cupped it gently in his hands. The pebble seemed at first to be no more than a common crystal but, floating inside, Wendya could just see tiny strands of gold glinting keenly in the dark.

"A starstone," the dworll whispered.

Suddenly, as if awoken, the stone sprang to life in his hand, casting out a soft yellow light that grew brighter as the shadow around them grew deeper. Narral turned and nodded to the others, then, walking on, he held the shining stone in one hand and his blade in the other. The pale light of their torches, starstones and the dim glow of the wizard's staff, prevented them from walking blindly into the abyss, which opened up in front of them.

"This wasn't here before!" said the dwelf uneasily, as he knelt beside the fissure and peered over its edge into the gaping void below. "This is new," he said, touching the fractured rock, "a section of the path has just disappeared ... but we haven't had any tremors or quakes for over a century!" He sighed, shaking his head.

He glanced at Narral, his voice low. "The scouts should have warned us of this ...," he said, then turned to the others. "We'll have to jump. This may be only one of many obstacles and many of them may not be natural," he said grimly. He sprang across the chasm onto the other side. "You should decide now if you want to continue."

Gralen scoffed and, helping the wizard, he leapt across the void with ease. As he did so, the dwelf jumped back and offered to help Wendya across.

Once the rest of their number had safely reached the other side, they continued. Worryingly, there was no sign of the scouts. Korrun reluctantly sent out another tracker to survey the ground for any unforeseen dangers.

"Report back the moment you find any trouble," he said quietly. "Be alert. Good hunting."

Hours passed achingly slowly. Once more, the dworlls surrounded the friends or followed doggedly behind, their keen eyes piercing the darkness. Eventually, after many hours, they stopped to eat. Gathering as much light as they could, they found themselves in a small, hexagonal vestibule surrounded by the first signs of battle they had seen. Debris dotted the floor or seemed to be stacked in strange neat little piles against the walls, dworll and wargol alike.

The secret passageway behind the Falls of Tarro leading to the catacombs beneath Kallorm.

The dragon quickly proceeded to make a fire using the nearest piece of this detritus, an old broken dworll shield, much to the disapproval of Korrun and the soldiers. After a light meal in silence, they set off again — creeping deeper into the bowels of the earth.

"We're getting closer to the start of the Draellth tunnels. See these markings?" Korrun whispered raising his torch to a broken pillar. By the flickering light, the others could see ancient Dworllian symbols scratched into the stone. "This says 'Orollum, Tenth Lord of Kallorm'. His son was the first Heir of Edrral, King Dorrol's forefather. We are walking through history," he said quietly. "Be careful, there have been attacks near here."

They walked on cautiously. Gralen recognized the brown stain below the markings as being dried blood. Korrun looked at the dragon's face and nodded. Onward they crept, with the dwelf ever stopping and listening, or placing a hand on the wall and floor as if expecting to feel a signal from his scouts or the vibrations of something heavy.

Though most of the carnage of past battles had long since rotted away, or been cleared in reverence to the dead, the scars on stone and rock and the fragments of broken and splintered armory could still be seen littering the floor. The carcasses of the enemy had been burnt, and the bodies of Kallorm's fallen taken away with respect and great veneration, to be laid in the tombs of their kin, or placed in small boats and cast over the Falls of Tarro — to be accepted by the spirits. For every Kallormian knew the sickening truth: that unless the bodies were taken away, they would be sullied horribly and eaten by the creatures of the dark, their bones sucked dry and sharpened into arrowheads and cruelly serrated blades to be used on the kin of that fallen soldier. Everywhere, Gralen could see the bitter sight of spilt blood, or could smell its awful presence, sprayed on the walls and staining the floor.

The group passed through pitch-black corridors, the darkness seeming so thick that even the light of the torches and starstones appeared diminished. They felt the oppressive weight of the earth closing in around them.

As the company traveled deeper, they came at last to a small round antechamber with a low drooping ceiling and were pleased to see the young scout.

"Korrun, I have seen and heard nothing of the others and have seen no sign that they ever reached this point! The ground and dust are undisturbed!" gasped the young scout, clearly as concerned and puzzled as the dwelf.

Korrun placed a hand on his shoulder. "I know. There is nothing we can do. Let us hope that they merely took the wrong path and will return. We have to go on."

The room, unlike the many they had seen before, was devoid of any decoration, and had seven stone doors carved into its walls. Wendya looked around nervously. Each of the doorways had been blocked with rubble and larger slabs of rock. In the center of the room lay a low, flat dais with a deep well cut in the middle. Korrun pointed toward the hole.

"There are a series of giant caves beneath us. That is our only way down and back out again," he said in a whisper, then looked at the dragon. "We must be quiet. Dark mytes and other fouler creatures are attracted by noise. Let us hope we meet none of them."

He spoke to the battalion in a hushed voice and, though Wendya tried, she couldn't understand what was said. The soldiers all nodded, their faces tense and troubled by the dwelf's words. Two tall and sturdy looking dworlls stayed behind in the chamber as sentries, their swords drawn, their senses alert, as the rest of the company descended into the pit. The well-hole was narrow and tapered inwards. The group clambered down carefully, with Gralen finding it an especially tight squeeze, but soon they all found an unexpected obstacle.

"We don't have enough rope!" Korrun called up quietly, as he dangled from the end of the line. He lowered his torch to see the ground, far below. "It looks as if the entire ground level has sunken somehow or caved in!"

"Well, where ropes fail, wings will have to do!" Gralen said, crawling to the end of the well-shaft, and nearly knocking the dwelf to his death in the process, as he dropped like a heavy stone, inches from Korrun's face. Mr. Agyk grabbed onto the dragon's back before he spread his wings and swooped into the darkness below.

They landed softly on the rocky ground beneath and Gralen blew out a long jet of flame to illuminate the cavern. Once he was satisfied that all was safe, he tentatively left the little wizard and flew up to get the others. Korrun and the dworlls reluctantly accepted and soon they all stood on the slippery floor below.

The cavern was immense and pitted with holes and sulfurous smoking vents, billowing wafts of steam and foul-smelling vapors into the eerie space above. Strange, contorted shapes like layers of vomited rock grew from the floor and ceiling and, as the black of the cavern walls glinted faintly in the torchlight, an incessant sound of dripping echoed through the dark.

"Follow me, but watch where you walk. Some of these pits are dangerous," said Korrun, as he picked up a small stone and dropped it carefully into a nearby pool of dark water. The water started to boil and fizz, spitting clouds of venomous fumes into the air. "Acid," he said simply. "Tread carefully."

The travelers wound their way slowly over the razor sharp rocks, bypassing every fumarole, crater, hole and bubbling pool that blocked their way.

After many hours, they eventually reached the far northern end of the cavern where the ground dramatically sank further, falling away sharply until it met the base of the wall. Above their heads, halfway up the wall, the group could now see a small, low-cut door.

"The ground has sunk," said Korrun worriedly, glancing again to Narral, "Come on."

They scrambled up the wall and, with the help of Gralen, they passed through the door and found themselves in a long and winding labyrinth of antechambers and tunnels beyond.

"This is the start of the Draellth chambers," whispered the dwelf, listening to the walls again.

Once more, dworlls were posted to stand guard behind them as the travelers proceeded on. Looking back, Wendya saw the four sharp-eyed soldiers disappear into the shadows either side of the door, their blades drawn and ready, their dark eyes glistening.

Onward they trudged: Korrun light-footed, Gralen padding softly behind, making an effort to walk quietly — tucking his wings in and stopping his tail from swinging around too much. Mr. Agyk and Wendya could only be heard as a rustling of garments and, finally, the remnant of the dworll soldiers, all heavily armored, passed silently.

They made their way down the central corridor. Black, gaping doorways opened up on either side leading to more rooms and passages. Korrun and two of his troupe disappeared into each of these, but quickly returned.

"We must check each chamber before we can go on," whispered the tracker, looking at the dragon's impatient face. "This is our only route back. We'll be trapped if anything comes up behind us." Each chamber was examined and the many dark tunnels leading off were quickly and quietly blocked or posted with a guard. In such a way, progress was painfully slow.

At last, when they had reached the end of the main corridor, the travelers stopped. The passageway ended abruptly in an archway and a straight flight of stairs led steeply down to a large, pillared hall below.

"The resting tomb of Draellth, First Lord and Protector of Kallorm," Korrun said quietly, feeling the rough stone of the archway before silently dropping down onto the top step. "I am surprised. We've come much further than many. I myself have not been able to come down here with any soldiers for a long age, so full of wargols and demons have these chambers been. Look," he whispered, pointing into the hall.

There, amongst the hewn and broken stones, stood two parallel lines of vaults, the tombs of the ancient lords; all of them vandalized, cracked and split apart, their contents devoured and scattered. Wendya shuddered; such demons had never been a part of the Kallorm she knew.

Korrun stared at the young witch with pity in his eyes. "Much has changed since you were here?" he asked softly, as if reading her thoughts. She nodded and averted her eyes from the desecration below.

"What about wargols?" Gralen asked, being in no hurry to see one. "What if they have taken this key?"

"No, they are mindless animals. They care only for flesh and bone. Trinkets hold no sway over them. No, These chambers are the most likely place to find it. The key should be somewhere down there, either in the Main Hall or in one of the crypts below it. We are nearly there," he whispered with a smile. Whether encouraged forward by his words, or by the stifling sense of dread that lay like a heavy shroud upon them, the group pressed on.

Korrun motioned to some of the dworlls. While most of the company stayed at the head of the stairs, he and four of the soldiers silently descended, their torches and starstones flickering off the scarred walls. Once in the hall, they briefly knelt and bowed their heads in front of the broken tombs, in a sign of respect, before disappearing to check every alcove, entrance, crevice, and corner. Once secure, they beckoned the others down.

"The key is made of sillvaf'yrren, dragonsilver," said the dwelf in a whisper, "as is my pendant here," he said taking a thin, silver chain and locket out from beneath his clothes. "Dragonsilver is a very rare and sacred substance, as you know. It becomes hot and glows when it is near to other sources of the same metal, or if it is forged with the wearer's own blood, a birth gift like mine."

Wendya stared at the pendant. It showed two mighty dragons entwined round a tower. Upon the turret, and each of the dragon's heads, shone a small star of ǽllfrpearl or moonstone. Already the pendant felt quite hot and glowed with a pale luminous red light. "It *is* here! We must be close. This will lead us to the key," he said holding it in his hand. Gralen couldn't take his eyes off of it.

The group quietly searched the hall, taking care not to make a sound or disturb any remains. Korrun shook his head, feeling the pendant between his fingers. "It must be below," he whispered at last, "it's not ..."

"Shh!" Gralen hushed. "Listen!"

The company stood motionless, rooted with a sudden fear, their torches wavering as if caught in some unexpected updraft or breeze. The noise came again, undeniable now from somewhere beneath them, directly under their feet. A low scraping sound like the grating of rock against rock. They looked at each other, barely daring to breathe.

"What is it?" Wendya whispered. The dragon shook his head and glared at Korrun, whose face seemed frozen in concern and disbelief.

The scraping sound grew louder and louder and could now be heard quite clearly. The troop looked desperately around them. Nothing stirred in the shadows but a tenseness and a foreboding hung in the air ... a feeling that something had been awoken after an age of sleep. Quickly, the space seemed to fill with the awful noise, rising like a slow scream wailing off the walls and echoing through the pillared hall. A searing dread gripped them.

In that instant, the ground shook and heaved in one almighty motion, knocking them off their feet, as if it were being pushed up by something moving underneath. The walls rocked violently and giant cracks and fissures appeared in the floor all around the company. With a terrible groaning sound, the pillars buckled, broke and splintered like glass, sending huge chunks of masonry showering down on their heads.

"Look out!" Gralen shouted as part of the western wall collapsed. "This whole place is caving in!" he cried.

"We have to get out!" Mr. Agyk called as a huge part of the ceiling came crashing down.

The entire hall shuddered and the floor rose up.

"Take cover!" shouted Korrun but, as he did so, the ground heaved once more, was riven in half and shattered under their feet.

Within seconds, most of the hall had buckled and collapsed. The entire company was hurled into the air before falling into the chasm which had now opened up beneath them.

There, dormant for centuries, had lain Dwellum's Bane: an obstacle too great to conquer, a creature older and fouler than the monster that first awoke it. It had a will of iron that could not be bent or controlled by any being, good or evil. Most feared of all the primal beasts, it remained a last and terrible remnant of a time long passed. It was an ancient evil of the old world which Morreck had, by design or not, roused from its age-long hibernation to unleash its terror on the present.

An enormous and hideous snake-like creature it was. Its ribbed body coiled in sickening twists, its bloated girth filling the crypts and lower chambers below the Great Hall, its sickly, pale shape winding deeper and deeper into the earth.

From its arched neck and flattened head rose a ridge of black, needle-like spikes, which matched the glassy deadness of its eyes; both of which were now fixed on the scattered figures, half-buried, half-struggling out of the rubble like so many wriggling maggots.

"A Gorrgos!" cried one of the dworlls. "A Gorrgos! Spirits save us! A WORM BEAST!"

The creature's dead, black eyes reflected the horrified dworll for a second as it swayed and tilted its giant head, as if trying to understand the terrified wails of its victim. Then, quicker than an arrow, it shot forward and took the dworll whole.

"Band together!" cried the wizard as he emerged from the carnage. "Keep together! Band together!"

As two of the dworll soldiers struggled to get free of the fallen stones and regroup with the others, they too were swiftly consumed, their screams silenced in the worst possible way. Korrun struggled to his feet and, half-stumbling, half-running, raced over to save his friend.

"Narral!" he cried, clawing at the rubble.

The Gorrgos swayed its mighty bulk and fixed its gaze on the two frantic figures.

"Leave me!" shouted the dworll, looking up in horror to see the creature's face peering down at them. "Korrun, leave me! Go!"

"Not a chance!"

"Korrun ... get out of there! MOVE!" cried Mr. Agyk.

A second later and the tracker pulled the dworll free and they sprang to the side, just as the Gorrgos smashed into the rocks. Gralen burst from the wreckage and raced over to help Wendya and the old man before he reared up, spreading his wings like a dark sheet, and blasted a wall of fire towards the beast.

The worm dwarfed the dragon but reeled backwards, letting out an ear-curdling scream that filled their heads and then turned to a piercing cackle. Before their eyes, the great snake's skin rippled with diaphanous pigments like the skin of an octopus, flushing and changing itself from sickly cream to crimson, then to a deeper shade of black, its foul hide thickening and protecting itself in the process. Again, the dragon blasted the creature, his veins raging with the fire within.

The beast, as quick as a viper, lunged toward him. Gralen veered to the side before taking to the air, whirling above the coiled shape, sending fireball upon fireball at its black head.

To the amazement and dismay of the others, each of these fiery mortars merely burst into a thousand sparks against its blackened sides but appeared to do little else.

Venomous fumes spewed forth from the thing. Suddenly, it opened its hinged jaws, articulating and extending them outwards. From these foul organs came a tongue, black as night and edged with thorns that lashed out into the air like a whip. It caught the great dragon's wing and hurtled it toward the ground. Korrun's sword and those of the soldiers rang out in response as they rushed forward slashed at the great beast's girth. With one movement, it crushed one dworll and sent the other attackers flying back.

The dragon recovered and charged at the creature again, letting the full force of his rage explode into molten fire.

"Gralen, stop! Flame and sword cannot help us!" Mr. Agyk shouted. "This is a creature of dark magic; only that dark magic can stop it!"

Gralen didn't hear. He lunged towards the beast, fire and flame pouring from his mouth, his talons ready for damage. The Gorrgos coiled its head and body back, waiting to strike, its tongue whipping into the air once more. Suddenly, just as Gralen was circling for another attack, it shot forward with terrifying speed and clamped its jaws around the mighty dragon, trying to crush him or snap him in two, before violently shaking its head and sending him plummeting into the walls like a rag doll.

"GRALEN!" Wendya screamed.

Mr. Agyk turned to the witch, who had been frantically looking through her Wiccadian to find some suitable counter-spell. "Help me!" he pleaded, standing amongst the hall ruins. "My strength is leaving me! This is an enemy far greater than any of us … we cannot destroy it, but we may hope to contain it for a while. I need you to be my vessel."

Wendya nodded. "Tell me what to do."

The dragon lay dazed and hurt, only his hard scales had saved him from being torn in two. Korrun rushed between him and the creature, as the others banded together for another assault.

All of a sudden, the witch and wizard stepped out from the shadows and stood before the mighty beast.

"What the hell are they doing!?" cried Korrun, as the monster switched its gaze to the small figures.

Wendya placed her hands on either side of her head and closed her eyes. "Come on … focus … focus!"

The wizard clasped his staff tightly and, when he spoke, his voice boomed cold and clear like an unyielding knife through the air. "By the Order I cast you into oblivion! I banish you from our sight! Seek your sustenance from the dark creatures of this realm and threaten us NO MORE!"

With that, the mage suddenly grew taller still, almost to the height of Gralen, and a blinding light flared from his eyes and hands, then sprang to his staff, before shining out in a blaze of white and green fire around him. Korrun stumbled back, amazed at the sight, as the wizard rose up into the air and floated defiantly before the giant snake.

"De'ravenn kal e garu tal minoana vile sorru kal … sorru kal!" Mr. Agyk shouted, his voice breaking like thunder, his eyes shining, silver orbs.

He flung his arms back and a huge wave of lightning and white fire sprang from him, blasting the beast with full force. *"Pero tine sorru kal ... pero tine sorru kal!"* he cried, and then turned to the stunned dwelf. "Hurry! It is frozen but only for a little while ... hurry! Find the key!"

The wizard closed his eyes. "I can see it ... in an old throne room there to the far left. In a box in a cavity behind the throne ... Get the key, hurry. HURRY!" shouted the blazing figure.

Korrun raced forward, bounding over the creature's enormous body. Clambering over the mountain of filth and rotting carcasses stacked behind it, the tracker could now see many crypts, stone doors and passageways snaking off into the darkness. Without hesitating, he scrambled over the wreckage and ran to the far left doorway, kicking it open, then squeezing through. He found himself in a long, narrow and crumbling chamber. At the far end, on a low dais, stood a lonely throne, its canopy nothing more than a hanging sheet of dust with a few strands of faded silk. Dashing toward it, he forced the stone chair back.

"HURRY!" called the wizard, his body shaking under the strain.

"NO!" gasped Korrun, tearing the cobwebs and dust away. The wall behind was bare. Nothing. No recess, no box, no key.

"HURRY!"

Korrun smashed his fists against the rock until his knuckles bled, forcing it to give way. Like some wild animal he clawed and scratched away at the crumbling stone, and behold, there, behind a thinly-concealed wall, was a small hole cut into the rock. Amongst the dust and dirt lay a tiny, copper-colored box. Korrun's pendant burnt like fire against his skin.

"HURRY KORRUN!" cried the wizard, pain filling his voice, "I can't hold it!"

Korrun grabbed the box, prizing the lid open as he ran. There, glowing red and wrapped in an old piece of parchment cloth stained with age, lay a small, silver key in the shape of a dragon.

"I've got it!" he cried, racing back.

Gralen, bleeding but recovered, continued to blast the foul creature in a vain attempt to barbeque it, while the few remaining dworlls hewed and hacked at its sides, but to little avail. Korrun burst from the shadows and raced forward. Then, clearing the giant worm in nearly a single leap he darted over the rubble, just as Mr. Agyk's light began to waver and wane. Wendya lay nearby in a deep trance, protected by Narral and two other soldiers, pain and effort furrowing her brow and a strange light emanating from her closed eyes to the wizard above.

"Go! Now!" said the wizard through gritted teeth. "Take Wendya ... flee! ... Gralen, take them ... GO!" he shouted, then collapsed, his light extinguished, his size diminished once more as he fell to the ground.

"Marval! ... Mr. Agyk!" shouted the dragon bounding towards him as the great beast began to stir behind him.

Wendya was motionless and, to the dwelf, it seemed that a soft but deathly veil lay upon her. He picked her up gently and stared in bewildered horror at the shrunken wizard, no larger than the size of a rat.

"Leave him! Go! Take Wendya!" Gralen cried bending over the tiny figure. Korrun nodded and, together with the dworlls, they sprinted over the rubble and towards the base of the broken staircase, now far above their heads.

The Gorrgos roared with fury behind them, its terrifying screech shaking the crumbling walls around. It jerked its foul head from side to side and convulsed its coiling body as if stretching off the paralysis.Suddenly breaking free of its unseen shackles, it fixed its black eyes on the dragon and the miniscule figure before it, and dived forward.

Gralen looked up and instantly flew at the creature's throat, knocking the wind out of it. Swooping down, he scooped up the little scholar in his hand and carried him off — just as the rest of the hall gave way.

Behind them they could hear the cracking sound of stone breaking and splitting apart as the Gorrgos pursued them. Gralen glanced back to see the enormous black snake dragging the rest of its body out from the collapsed tunnels beneath.

Flying low over the broken ground, the dragon raced over the heads of the company, circled around and crash-landed. "Hurry! … It's coming, climb onto my back!"

"You can't carry us all!" protested the dwelf.

"Are you going to argue about it? Now, come on!"

Korrun threw Wendya up first, helped Narral and the others, and clambered up himself.

"Hold on!" cried Gralen, and, using all of his strength, he launched himself into the air as the rest of the hall disintegrated beneath the rush and heat of the Gorrgos.

"It's coming!" Korrun shouted as he drew his sword. "It's right behind us!"

"Well, it has to catch us first! Hold on!" called the dragon, then, pulling his wings, he darted through the doorway at the head of the staircase just as the beast shot towards them.

Gralen, unable to use his wings to fly in such narrow corridors, used them to boost himself forward and, together with his back legs, he propelled himself onward at an alarming speed. In this way, he swam through the dark passages, but always the pursuit behind was swift, as the crashing and roaring of the monstrous beast became ever closer.

They hurtled on past the numerous Draellth chambers and down the long corridor they had come, acutely aware that none of the posted guards could be seen anywhere, when a yellow light appeared at the far end.

"Are those your soldiers?" asked the dragon racing toward the glowing light.

Korrun turned and squinted his keen eyes into the gloom ahead. "I don't think so," he replied simply as a rising tide of fell voices could now be heard coming from the great cavern all around them.

Suddenly, from every passing doorway and every chamber they had blocked or guarded, poured hundreds of hulking creatures, their bulbous eyes gleaming red in the blackness.

"Wargols!" cried Korrun. "Wargols! They've broken through! We're trapped!"

"I'll toast their toes, every one of them!" bellowed Gralen, shooting a jet of flame down the passageway.

Cries and howls went up as their miserable hides ignited and engulfed them in fire. A wild panic took them and they fled, scurrying like beetles before such an unexpected enemy; though many of the larger and slower creatures could be heard screaming in the corridor behind as the Gorrgos approached and tore through them.

"I said they'd be surprised by you!" laughed Korrun, as Gralen, in a final and glorious spurt of energy, burst out of the corridor and into the huge cavern beyond.

As they did so, they passed the bodies of their fallen comrades; none of the guards had survived. Onward they rushed. Gralen, at last able to stretch his wings, flew at such incredible speed that he quite forgot the cave's many obstacles and nearly crashed several times. Korrun stared at the slumped and unconscious figure of the witch, being cradled by Narral. Hearing only silence behind, he dared to look back once more and was horrified to see the huge glistening head and dead eyes of the Gorrgos following right behind, its jaws open.

"Faster, faster! It's here!" he shouted, turning to hew at the beast as it bore down on them.

"Hold on!" cried Gralen.

The dragon shot through the cavern, weaving and twisting like a ballet dancer, trying desperately to outrun the silent terror behind as acidic fumes choked in his throat and rocky needles and outcrops tore at him. As the Gorrgos was gaining, they saw the well-hole they had come from and flew straight up towards it.

At that same moment, a wail went up around them, echoing through that cavernous space like some primitive war cry. Unable to stop, the great dragon could only go on and chance what lay ahead.

"Lie flat, everyone and grab on!" he shouted, as he folded his wings and shoulders back and darted up into the well.

As they burst into the small, round chamber above, they were suddenly caught in the midst of blinding light. Surrounding them was a mass of dworllian soldiers, their helms gleaming in torchlight.

"Hail!" they cried in unison, as the escapees crashed into view.

"I am the Captain of Kallorm," said a stern figure stepping forward.

"Urell!" shouted the dwelf as he leapt from the dragon. "We cannot linger, the Gorrgos is close behind us!"

"A Gorrgos! Korrun! I was told you came down here, though I couldn't believe it. The wargols are on the rampage. Something has disturbed them. But there is no time for further talk. We must all go now ... go!"

The sound of the approaching snake could be heard, like close thunder. The dragon, carrying Mr. Agyk and Wendya, didn't hesitate and, closely followed by the dworll host, they fled the chamber moments before the monstrous thing broke through.

"Run! To the western door! Run!"

Seconds later, a tremendous explosion rocked and heaved the ground, followed by a deafening scream that pierced the tunnels and every ear, as the entire chamber and the cavern below collapsed.

"Fly!" shouted one of the dworlls behind. "We will cave in these western burrows! Run, run, faster! Run!"

The earth shook violently and cracked, causing zigzagging fissures to appear all around the walls and the fleeing company, and each one seeming to issue foul-smelling steams or vapors of some kind. Korrun turned back to see a massive fireball rolling through the passageway behind them, engulfing and destroying everything in its path and overtaking some of the fleeing dworlls, before finally dissolving into a thick, blue smoke. More rocks crashed and tumbled; more shudders rocked the ground. Suddenly and eerily, all fell silent and dark.

"Keep going! Do not look back!" called one of the dworlls.

The entire lower levels of the western chambers and caves of Kallorm's great catacombs were gone forever. And there, somewhere buried beneath thousands of tons of rock and granite, amidst the lost tombs of Kallorm's forefathers, lay the mighty beast, the terror of the deep, destroyed.

Chapter Twelve

The Falls of Tarro

How are you feeling?" said a familiar voice. Wendya opened her eyes slowly. She was lying in a soft bed covered by a canopy of silken drapes that swayed gently in the breeze from the open balcony. Nearby, she could hear the comforting roar of the Falls of Tarro. The purple dusk of the city danced in shadows across the marble walls and pearly mirrors, filling the room in a shimmering light. Halli sat perched on the edge of the bed, her eyes full of concern.

"It's evening," she said softly. "You've been here five days, since the cave in."

Wendya blinked to clear the mist from her eyes. Her body felt heavy and her eyes wanted desperately to close again. She gazed up at the ceiling, her mind drifting to the sound of the water outside.

"Marval? ... Gralen?" she said suddenly, as if jolted to her senses.

Halli rested her back. "Gralen is fine, a little bruised and battered, but he heals remarkably quickly. He's been here by your bedside every day and night, as has Korrun."

"Marval, Mr. Agyk, how is he?" Wendya asked worriedly, her eyes searching for an answer.

Halli paused and glanced down and Wendya knew at once that something was wrong.

"The attack took a lot out of him," the dworll replied gravely. "He was weakening anyway, as you probably knew, but he has lost much of his strength."

"But he will recover … won't he?"

Halli shrugged. "I am sorry, I don't know," she said gently. "The shamans have been working hard, but the battle drained a lot of the energy he had left. He couldn't have fought the Gorrgos alone, not without borrowing some of your powers," she hesitated. "Wendya, he is fading. If he doesn't regain his powers soon, he will die."

The witch choked, her eyes filling with tears. "Where is he?" she whispered, a sickness rising in her throat. "Please, I must see him!"

Halli nodded. "He is being tended to by our best healers; Gralen's with him now," she replied quietly, taking her hand. "I shall take you to them."

Wendya rose slowly, her head throbbing. Ignoring the weakness in her legs and the ache of her limbs, she slipped on a robe and followed the young dworll.

As if walking in a dream, they passed through countless rooms and colonnades out of White Palace and across open gardens and paths to the Resting Rooms of Kallorm, perched on the highest point of Palace Rock.

The two girls arrived in a peaceful courtyard that opened outward on one side to the bustling city, its lights twinkling beneath them. The courtyard was surrounded by beautifully carved arches and twisting pillars covered in delicate white flowers. Its flagstones glittered in the evening twilight and water trickled from a hundred springs and fountains, mixing with the sweet fragrance of the white blossom.

Halli led Wendya through this oasis of calm water to a large, domed building of green jade and glistening white marble. They passed under vaulted ceilings and through sheer muslin drapes that hung and billowed like great sails from each open archway.

The light inside was quite dim, but Wendya could see the green dragon at the far end of the room, asleep. He sat hunched in a corner with his back propped up, his wings wrapped like sheets about him, his long tail coiled in a mass on the floor as he dozed in the cool evening air. Beside Gralen, on a marble bed covered in mattresses and woven fabrics that somehow resembled a mortuary slab, lay the tiny slumbering figure of the old wizard.

Halli squeezed Wendya's shoulder. "Let them rest another day," she whispered, seeing the distress on the young witch's face.

The fourth new moon passed blackly in the jungle outside, as one more unsettling day slipped away. Wendya waited nervously, but could find no rest or comfort.

While most of the city and palace slept on, the witch dressed quickly in the new clothes Halli had given her, and made her way to the Resting Rooms. To her utter amazement, this time, the little wizard was awake, dressed and sitting up in bed while Gralen was busy tucking into his third breakfast of the day.

"Marval!" she cried and rushed over to him.

Mr. Agyk sat bolstered against the marble wall and seemed altogether lost amongst the bedding. Despite his usual cheerful demeanour and the great effort he took to conceal his true condition, Wendya was shocked to see how frail he looked. His face was painfully gray and drawn and a thin milky mist clouded his eyes.

"I am fine," he smiled at her. "I just got the wind knocked out of me! And you?" he asked looking at Wendya, who nodded. "Well, do not look so glum ... we have succeeded, we have the birthkey! The first part of our journey is over and the battle is half won!"

She tried to smile, but wasn't convinced by the act.

"I must say," he continued chirpily, gazing at the young witch, "I was surprised by you ... your mind-seeing skills have certainly improved, as has your strength. I was rather impressed! We could not have found the key, and I certainly could not have fought that thing, without you. Thank you," he said earnestly, patting the bed for her to sit down.

She perched herself on the marble beside him. The dragon looked decidedly put out about something.

"Well, I hope you have better luck with him than me!" he grumbled with his mouth full.

"What do you mean?" she asked.

"He means — if he can stop eating for a moment — that I intend to leave today. Time is running very short, I can feel it, and as much as I love this old city, I have spent too long here already," replied the wizard in a matter-of-fact sort of way.

Wendya stared at him. "But ... you're not well enough ... you need to rest, to get your strength back," she protested, astonished that he was even considering such a thing.

Mr. Agyk sighed and gave her one of his trademark sympathetic but determined smiles. "My dearest Wendya," he said gently, "I know what the healers have said ... I am dying. If I do not leave soon, I shall probably never leave. I am fading, I know it. I can feel it!"

Gralen clattered the breakfast tray down, his appetite gone.

Wendya glanced at the dragon. "We can handle it ... you should stay here and rest, we can deal with Morreck, Gralen and me! We'll get help!"

The little mage laughed grimly and Gralen sighed, as one who has spent much time saying the same thing. "Wend', it's no good, he's made up his mind. He says if I don't take him he'll go by condor or walk! Oh, and then you'll love this ... I'm supposed to leave him there and return back here to get you, then we're both to go back to White Mountain where, presumably, you and I can while away the days playing cards while he gets himself killed ... and Morreck destroys everything!" complained Gralen folding his arms.

"Both of you listen!" Mr. Agyk snapped, looking more like his old self. "You cannot deal with M'Sorreck on your own ... If you haven't understood anything then understand this ... he is a very powerful warlock, extremely powerful. Even if I had all my powers restored and had your help, I still do not know if he can be defeated ...," the wizard paused and looked at his two treasured friends, "—but I have to try."

His voice was subdued and deadly serious. "I do not want either of you in this fight. You are too dear to me. My heart could not cope if anything happened to you. All of this has taught me just how dangerous this journey has become. There is every possibility that before we confront Morreck, we may have to face a sea of enemies!"

"But we did escape the Gorrgos and the Oracle and every other thing that has tried to kill us!" Wendya answered in a defiant tone, "because our strength lies in our friendship! How many times have I heard you speak about the importance of unity? Well? We are far stronger and safer together than alone. You know that. You have to take us with you or we'll follow anyway, and probably get ourselves into more trouble!" she said with a wry smile. "Besides, between my ... skills as a spell caster and Gralen's recklessness, we need you!"

"I resent that!" snorted the dragon with a smirk, feeling his appetite return and rewarding it by stuffing a large ham sideways into his mouth. "After all," he said, showering tiny pieces of pink meat all over the white linen, "Wend' is right, we'd hound you anyway, you can't stop us!"

The wizard threw up his arms in resignation. That was that. They were coming with him and nothing he could do or say could dissuade them. The course of their fates was now set, he only hoped and prayed that the Oracle was wrong.

"I give up! Foolish you are and loyal to the bone," his face became serious once more, "but remember that he has stolen my powers. If I am ever to regain them, in the end, only I can confront him. No one else."

"Fine, but you'll need our help to find him," exclaimed the witch.

Mr. Agyk smiled. "I will need help in a thousand different ways, not least in getting to Fendellin and finding his fortress. If he has gathered an army of dark followers, which I suspect he has, I will need help in dealing with them. My goodness," he laughed. "I will need help getting more help if that is the case!"

Wendya nodded, feeling anxious, but relieved.

The mage sighed. "Time is ticking away. By full light we must have left the city and be on our way," he glanced at them both. "Let us not forget that the special item we have risked our lives for, M'Sorreck's birthkey, is our only advantage. He is desperate to find it, but we have succeeded where he has failed! If we are to stand any chance of using it against him, it must be kept secret ... or the fight will be lost before it has begun."

Gralen watched him closely, reminded of how strange he had been after his encounter with the Oracle.

The old man stood up, his face grim but determined, his wiry mane of silver hair tied back in a wild mass of braids behind him. He quietly fixed a belt around his tunic, threw on his tattered green cloak, and looked at them both in turn. "The road from here will be a very dangerous one indeed, more dangerous than the one we have left ... none of us know what we will find once we get to the end of it!"

The morning wore on and the city awoke. The three friends finished their preparations and made their way to the Council Chambers to bid their hosts farewell.

"Welcome," said Harrum, one of the Council Elders. "King Dorrol will be here shortly, please sit down."

Moments later, the old King shuffled in, accompanied by his daughter and his chief counselor, Drellm, a broad-shouldered dworll with keen eyes. Korrun walked in and sat beside the counselor.

"Our parting has come," King Dorrol sighed. "It is good to see you recovered, though not quite the same as when I saw you last," he said staring at the little wizard. "Korrun has told me how bravely you fought. I cannot repay you for such courage and for saving our city from that terrible creature. We are forever indebted to you."

He sat down slowly. "Had I truly known the nature of the terror that dwelt there, I should never have let you go, or at the very least I would have offered you more soldiers. Life is precious and has to be more sacred than tradition or history; perhaps it is time to put heritage and reverence aside and collapse all of Kallorm's great catacombs and underground halls."

"Rest easy my Lord," Korrun replied solemnly. "The Gorrgos has now been destroyed."

"Let us hope so," answered the King. "Well, my friends! It saddens me to see you leave, but leave you must. To help you achieve your quest, I give you our city's finest warrior … Korrun of Koralan. He is our best tracker and has been a great friend to this Royal House for many years. He is eager to join your company. I think his skills will be very useful."

"His bravery has certainly earned him a place," smiled Mr. Agyk.

Korrun bowed graciously. "If I can be of help, I will."

"If you are sure you can be spared, then yes, your help will be much needed and appreciated," the little wizard replied and bowed in turn.

Mr. Agyk and Wendya smiled, a sense of relief on their faces, while Gralen remained stonily silent and seemed to mutter something under his breath.

The King nodded. "Good, then it is settled. Korrun will go with you. For our part, we have gathered as much information on M'Sorreck as we could from our main archives and vaults. I have given all this to Korrun. He can tell you of it and his own history with the warlock."

Wendya stared at the dwelf.

"Thank you," Mr. Agyk said, his eyes catching the King's gaze for a moment.

Dorrol smiled and sighed. "Only I and a few others, including young Korrun here, know where this forgotten land lies, Fendellin, Kingdom of Dragons. It is the most ancient of all realms and a legend to most folk. It has been called many names through the years. I believe the Indian Vedas heard distant tales of a land beyond the Himalayas and called it Shambhala, a land of great beauty and magic circled by high peaks. We know its true heritage. Fendellin was the first ǽllfren realm on earth, given by the ǽllfrs to our mountain dworll cousins, when Kallorm was young. The Kingdom of Dragons has long protected itself from outsiders …," he turned to the dwelf. "In his youth,

Korrun tried to enter Fendellin, but none can pass beyond the Encircling Mountains that border it, unless they are born there."

"Or unless you are a dragon!" Gralen boasted proudly.

Dorrol laughed. "Yes … and I hope the legends are true and there are more like you, my friend!"

Gralen's eyes lit up at the prospect. "The Kingdom of the Dragons …," he sighed heavily. "I've waited my whole life to see one of my kind. To see them flying … What a sight! Dragons still alive in the world!"

Dorrol laughed again. "You might just get your chance!"

The garrison lay quiet. Korrun stood emptying his locker and fiddling with a tangled piece of leather strap.

"So, I hear you're leaving us again?" sneered a voice. "It's about time this 'Great Leader' was on his way."

The dwelf turned to see a small group of dworll soldiers back from patrol rotation. He knew them all. "What do you want, Kevall?"

"Huh, I'm constantly amazed why King Dorrol and the others hold you in such high regard." he mocked.

"But then … he is an old fool!" jeered another one.

Korrun stepped forward, bristling. "If you got something to say, Sallom, just say it!"

Sallom unwound the protective wrappings from his hands and threw them at the tracker's feet. "Don't rush back! We'll all be glad to see the back of you!" he spat.

Kevall sauntered up, inches from Korrun's face, and smiled acidly. "Maybe, King Dorrol feels sorry for a hybrid freak like you!"

Korrun grabbed him and slammed him against the wall, kicked the other one in the stomach, and dropped him to the floor. At that moment, Narral and Urell, the Captain of the City Guard walked in.

"What's going on?" Urell shouted. "Take your hands off him right now!"

Korrun let go, a look of anger on his face.

Narral took him aside. "Are you all right?" he whispered.

"Yes … just a farewell committee."

"Are you going to defend him?" Kevall shouted.

Narral turned and glared at him. "The war is over. Let it go!"

Captain Urell shifted his weight uneasily, uncomfortable with the scene. "Narral, you should take him away. Let everyone calm down."

The dworll nodded and took Korrun's arm. "Come on," he said quietly.

"You think I should forget about my sister and my brother?" Kevall shouted after them. "How about my best friend? Well? What about THEM?"

They walked in silence until they reached one of the training courtyards. Narral sat on a bench. "Korrun, ignore them. I want to talk to you," he said, motioning for Korrun to join him.

The dwelf seemed agitated. "I don't have a lot of time."

"I know. But I want you to hear me. Ignore those dogs in there."

"Why? Most of them used to be loyal to me. They're good soldiers ...," Korrun started.

"They're trolls!" Narral said. "You have the King's trust and respect, that's what counts!"

"You are a good friend, Narral. But I do not need you defending me."

"Korrun ..."

"I mean it! I can't blame Kevall and the others. Everything they said is true. I have to live with what I did."

Narral shook his head. "Korrun, for once listen to me," he sighed. "You really think volunteering for every dangerous mission is the answer?"

The tracker stood up and started pacing.

"You've done your penance!" Narral continued. "You've saved hundreds of lives, maybe more, with no gratitude, no recognition."

"It is not enough."

"Will it ever be?" he implored and stood in front of him. "I may only be an old fool myself, but ... you made a *mistake*, you paid for it. King Dorrol doesn't punish you, so why do you punish yourself?"

Korrun looked at him and smiled. "You are a good friend. I know you mean the best, but I have to do this. It may be my only chance to set things right."

The adventurers were finally ready.

Korrun collected Morreck's birthkey and gave it to Wendya. "For safe keeping," he smiled.

She laughed. "Let me guess, too big for Mr. Agyk ... and too important for Gralen?" she whispered.

"Yes," he admitted, smiling. "Well, we don't want to lose it ... and, this way, it'll stop mine from burning!"

Wendya placed the glowing key on a strong silver chain around her neck and hid it beneath her clothes. Already, it seemed quite warm against her skin.

Korrun gathered a rather shocking array of weapons; long and short bows, several quivers of slender arrows, swords, spears, lances and his trusted battle-axe. He also took Krael blades, ancient, deadly, two-headed long blades.

Gralen watched all of this with obvious amusement, as the dwelf slung many of the weapons around himself and loaded the rest into backpacks.

"Are you sure you have enough?" he smirked.

The tracker gave him an icy look before walking over to Wendya. "This is an Ikan blade," he said, handing a short sword to the witch. "It is light and strong and less cumbersome than a broadsword. It will turn the hardest weapon, even a wargol blade ... It would be safer if you carried something."

Wendya unsheathed the knife and gasped; it was beautiful. Its blade spiraled to a fine point and on its gilded hilt were dworllian symbols etched in an ancient tongue she could not read. The blade glittered like white fire.

"It is partly made from dragonsilver, very rare," Korrun said softly. "It should bring you luck!"

"Thank you," she smiled, looking up at the tall dwelf and running her fingers carefully over the strange inscriptions.

"Well, are we going?" Gralen snapped.

Moments later, the company bid farewell to King Dorrol and the Council and started the long walk through Kallorm. Halli accompanied them, never leaving Wendya's side until they reached the city's outer walls and the deep water channel that skirted it. The waters had risen sharply during the night, swollen from days of heavy rain in the jungles above. The causeway was flooded, leaving it visible but submerged under a shallow, fast-flowing torrent of cold water.

Here at last Halli said her final, and tearful, farewells and waved them off on their long journey. She watched silently as the travelers waded across and trudged up the muddy road beyond. The young dworll stood on the causeway, a lonely figure in the early light, with the icy waters swirling around her feet.

"Keep safe. May you find hope when all seems lost," she whispered, tears stinging in her eyes.

She stayed there for a long time, watching as the figures became distant spots and finally disappeared from view.

"Farewell."

Chapter Thirteen
The Encircling Mountains

The four travelers walked on in silence, their spirits solemn, each one troubled with their own thoughts. Fearful of leaving the last safe haven and uncertain of what might lie before them. Wendya found the parting a bitter one. As they walked up the long road from the causeway, memories flooded back with every step she took, of a lonely journey she had taken many years before when, in grief, she had turned her back on Kallorm and those that cared for her. The pain of that farewell stayed with her, grown sharper now as she regretted the lost years away from Halli and King Dorrol and the city she had loved so much.

Korrun watched the young girl with puzzlement. She seemed so familiar and yet so distant, so melancholic. She reminded him of one of the tragic figures in the old sagas

131

he had read as a child, heroines of great beauty, delicate and vulnerable, yet capable of great courage and strength.

The company pressed on. Word had gone ahead and all nine gates lay open, their sentries standing in silent salute as they passed. Even the cantankerous gatekeeper and his harridan of a wife bowed in reverence. They quickly ascended beyond Kallorm's borders, climbing toward the bleak afternoon sun and the world above.

As soon as they had left the great dworll realm, they clambered onto Gralen's back and took to the skies. A deep anxiety fell on them as they traveled in silence through the remainder of the day and well into the night, with no rest or sleep.

Gralen's great wings pounded to the rhythm of his twin hearts as he tirelessly sped onward, with the sunset blazing behind them, and on into the starry darkness. Passing as a shadow over jungles, mountains, volcanoes and the Great Rift Valley lakes to the east, they continued on, over the moonlit blueness of the savannah plains. At times, the dragon soared high above the clouds, catching thermals and wind currents from far away, or gliding on breezes so close to the ground that the travelers could feel the sun's warmth radiating from the earth below.

The companions said little for the first few days, with the dwelf saying the least. On the seventh day since leaving Kallorm, they made camp in the mouth of a shallow sandstone cave, carved high up on a horseshoe ring of hills, overlooking a gray valley below. Steeply beneath them, amongst the drifting night mists, they could see twinkling specks of light, the glow of fires from a few small settlements. A thick slice of moon waxed yellow and luminous above them, in an almost mocking smile.

Not caring for the wizard's unusual concoctions or Gralen's cooking, Korrun went hunting as Wendya gathered herbs nearby.

"I wonder …"

"What?" asked the dragon.

Mr. Agyk looked up. He hadn't meant to speak aloud. "Oh … I was just wondering where all of this will end. These disappearances. These random attacks. We have paid dearly for our apathy." He shook his head. "How do any of us expect to survive in this strange world, if we do not look after our own?" he slumped down beside the fire as if he wanted to throw himself in.

Gralen knew that grim expression all too well. Any comforting words would be utterly wasted on the old man. "I'll start the meal, I'm not waiting for *Captain Courageous* any longer!" he snorted.

Wendya scrambled from the line of shrub trees below, with a bundle of sweet herbs and vegetables, washed and ready for the pot.

"There's a small stream just beneath that outcrop," she pointed. "It's pure water and look … I found some wild chives and mushrooms. I'll make a broth!"

The wind howled over the ridge as the three friends stoked the fire and prepared to eat. Finally, the dwelf returned, carrying the large carcass of an ibex over his shoulder.

"I hope you like goat," he smiled, throwing it down by the fire.

"We've already made the meal," Gralen scowled, tossing another branch into the flames, as he tried not to drool at the thought of fresh meat.

Korrun glanced at the thin broth and charred vegetables on Wendya's plate, then at the green sludge being dished by the others. "What is it?" he asked, sniffing the slop.

"*Draken Delight*," the wizard smiled.

"I don't think I want to know. I'll get this meat prepared. If you want any, then help yourself." he replied, dragging the creature off to gut and clean it.

Mr. Agyk looked at Gralen, who had started blowing green fire rings into the air. "That was kind of him."

"Humph."

The night grew steadily colder as the travelers finished their meals and settled around the fire. Gralen watched the little silhouette of his friend, his shoulders bent as if he were carrying a heavy load.

The dragon lay on his back, his hands resting on his huge orange belly, as flying embers danced into the darkness. He dearly wanted to see Fendellin, The Kingdom of Dragons, but not if it meant losing the old man. He closed his eyes for a moment, imagining dozens of winged beasts whirling and gliding through the air.

"Tell us about Fendellin," Mr. Agyk asked Korrun, as if reading the dragon's mind.

Gralen glanced at the silent dwelf.

Korrun perched on a tree stump, his back to the fire and his eyes fixed on the horizon. He turned and looked at the others. "Someone should keep watch," he said blankly.

"I am sure we are safe for tonight ... Come, I know nothing of this hidden realm, last sanctuary of dragons," Mr. Agyk pressed, casting a knowing look to Gralen. "We all thought my friend here was the last of his race. We would dearly love to be wrong!"

Korrun shifted uneasily. "King Dorrol knows far more than me. He has given you all that you need, here ...," he pointed to a bundle of curled scrolls in the sack by Gralen's side.

"I would still like to hear tales of it."

The dwelf sighed. "I could tell you *The Lay of Fendellin*. It is a very old ballad, more of a lament really," he mumbled.

The others looked keen, even Gralen. Korrun sighed again and smiled awkwardly, then, twisting a tree branch in the fire, he began. His voice was low and soft and, as he spoke, his eyes never leaving the dying coals, a hint of pain seemed to pass over his face.

> "Pass now beyond the mountains white
> Where frosted rivers leap and spring,
> Amongst the golden grasses light
> Where fÿrrens dwell and soar and sing.
>
> A land as old and fair as stars
> Of snowy peaks and moonlit seas,
> Of darkling woods we travel far
> To gaze upon its silvery leaves.

A flame that springs eternal fire
A city in the misty sky,
A beauty which shall never tire
Amongst the banners flying high.

A sheltered haven, a sacred land
An ancient place of Kings,
A shining sword, a fiery brand
Where magic dwells therein.

Far east beyond heart's lost desire
The birthplace of the eldest kin,
Through rising sun on wings of fire
Lies forgotten Fendellin."

"That was beautiful!" said Wendya, watching the dwelf's eyes as he stared into the fire.

"It sounds like a wondrous place!" replied Mr. Agyk. "Perhaps you will find your dragons there after all, my old friend!"

Gralen smiled but kept quiet, his eyes fixed on the witch and dwelf.

They only had a few hours of sleep. Despite the growing malady that lay heavily on the little wizard, they set off early before the sun had risen. With the wizard's careful tuition, Wendya proved to be a surprisingly quick student, creating a potion that concealed their flight, and helped Gralen combat the tiredness of flying. They sped, unseen, ever onward, reluctant to take more than the smallest amount of sleep.

Eight days and watchful nights passed. By meandering routes, over barren desert and sea, the company drew a little closer to their goal. With Korrun as their guide studying an ancient cava-skin map intensely, he retraced the path he had taken many years before. Once they had passed beyond the great snaking estuaries and flooded lowland plains, the dwelf knew he had found the route he wanted.

"This is it. The great river Indarra. Its waters were released after Indra slew the dra—" he stopped abruptly as Gralen turned his head to glare at him. "Well ... it is called the Indus by the common people. Its course will take us far along the route we need."

By tracing the river to its mountain source and beyond, it would eventually lead them, like a pulsating vein, straight toward Fendellin and M'Sorreck.

They followed the flow of the rushing torrent east and north for many days as it twisted and turned through the changing landscape. It seemed to the dragon that some invisible road was unfolding before him, some hidden force pulling him along, leading and urging him forward and igniting his blood. Somehow, it felt as if he were following a path home; a dangerous, unforeseen path, yet one which he had no choice but to follow.

The river disappeared underground for many miles before reappearing. At times, it dipped and plunged over great waterfalls or dropped into ravines, carving its way through the overhanging cliffs above. The river's rich, sediment-laden waters turned from brown to milky blue, as its churning flow grew steadily colder, flushed with melted snow from the mountaintops far to the north.

Onwards they went, skimming low over the waters. As they flew, an unspoken fear crept upon them, hastening them forward. Wendya kept a close eye on the little wizard, while Korrun watched them both silently.

The days blurred as the group continued northwards. They found a hidden dell, no more than a crease in the rocky cliff-side with the wide gray snake of the river far below, and made camp. After a restless night, all four awoke weary and fretful, with Mr. Agyk the palest and grayest of all. Gralen studied the pallor and pain in his friend's face and promptly declared that his wings needed more rest and that they should depart later in the day. The wizard seemed thankful for the break and soon fell into a listless sleep with the dragon watching over him. Korrun, ever alert, decided to stretch his legs and explore the terrain, leaving the three friends alone at last.

"Take your time ...," Gralen muttered after him.

Wendya sat quietly beside her two companions for much of the morning, listening to the rush of the water and the labored wheezing of the sleeping figure. Oh how she longed for the dappled sunlight and resin-scented shade of her trees again, not this barren hardness of boulder and stone.

"I'll see if I can find some more herbs for a soup. I won't be long," she said, getting up.

"Stay close ... don't go far. It may not be safe," called the dragon, watching as she disappeared behind a spur of rock.

The rocky ground sloped steeply away toward the river, before plunging vertically into the waters below. Wendya climbed up, her woven shoes sliding on the smooth stone, until she found higher and more level ground where the first grasses and vegetation sprang between crack and crevice. She wandered for a while, not caring which way she went. The sky looked blankly down at her. Away to the west, the heavy threat of snow clung to the barren hills they had passed over just days before. Everything looked so mournful and drab. No heat or comfort came from the winter sun. She walked on and found a small hollow surrounded by low scrubby bracken and thorny bushes and sat there staring at the little white flowers and lichens that grew amongst the dry earth. The wind howled down from above and strange bird calls echoed all around. She felt utterly wretched.

"Why?" she whispered. "Why him?"

All fell silent. Wendya fingered the key around her neck. It was hot to the touch and glowed red in her hands. She closed her eyes. She could feel a presence, without shape but dark and fathomless, old as mountains yet thoroughly rotten, a festering malice, a will of iron waiting for its moment, waiting and watching, gathering its strength, gathering all to its command. She remembered Mr. Agyk's words. "There are more monstrous things living in the earth than we know and *he* is awakening them, stirring things that should be left untouched." She felt it now. Evil creatures, demons being brought to life, vomited from the bowels of the earth. Creatures that would follow him relentlessly, that would obey and kill. The closer they drew to Fendellin, the greater her urge to run and hide. Even now she could feel a malice stretching out to ensnare them all.

She opened her eyes and looked around. The birds had fallen silent and she could hear something, or feel something, coming up behind her. She turned. Nothing. Only the swaying thicket and the wind and the empty sky. The noise came again but closer, soft and curling, like breathing.

"Who's there?"

Fear flooded her veins. The key was burning her now, or was it her skin?

"Talliaaaaaa," murmured the wind.

"Who's there?" she shouted.

"Me … Korrun. You shouldn't be out here on your own," he said gravely. He stood nearby, a worried expression on his face. "It's not safe to wander. We don't know these lands … Humans have been fighting all around here and I found fresh tracks of an isso'l'tarr, a snow leopard, not far from here."

Wendya nodded but didn't feel like moving. He came closer, his feet silent on the rocks.

"Korrun, is there any hope for Marval?" she asked quietly, her eyes fixed on the crumbling stones at her feet.

"There's always hope … An old friend told me that," he said with a faint smile.

"King Dorrol?"

Korrun nodded. He brushed past the thicket and sat beside her, his long legs stretching out into the dirt.

"I wish I felt as you do," she murmured, "but this whole journey feels hopeless to me."

"We will find Fendellin and M'Sorreck. Remember, anything that lives can be killed," he said determinedly.

"You sound like Gralen."

He raised his eyebrows. "Uh, thank you," he smiled. "That's encouraging to hear!"

Wendya laughed for a moment, then fell silent.

Korrun looked at her. "The old mage, he means a lot to you, doesn't he?"

She didn't answer but kept staring at the ground.

Korrun continued. "He may be small, but he's stronger than you think. He's always been held in the very highest esteem by all of the Royal House. I know King Dorrol believes in him. One of the wisest and most powerful of the old mages he said. Whatever we face, he is not alone," he said softly, his pale eyes seeming black in the dimming light.

Wendya stared at him. He looked almost as sad as she felt. "So tell me, why is this so important to you? To risk your life for a bunch of strangers?" she said, her green eyes searching his face for an answer. "Why did you try to go to Fendellin when you were younger? The King hinted that you knew about Morreck, that you had some history with him … what did he mean?"

The dwelf looked away and his manner changed. A coldness fell over him, like a door slamming shut, she thought. He paused for a moment, his gaze fixed toward the distant horizon. "King Dorrol was referring to the battles, I think," he answered, his words carefully judged.

Korrun watched as the blank sky deepened to a charcoal dusk and the last glimmers of sunset fell behind the rolling hills. Birds swirled and dived as if catching its final rays, their black shapes all too fleeting. The air filled with their melancholic song as they screeched to any that would hear. Swallows, he thought.

Wendya turned. "Do you mean the battles at Kallorm, when Morreck was looking for his birthkey?"

The dwelf nodded.

"What happened?" she asked, unable to curb her curiosity. "Halli visited me once, after I left, and she told me of a terrible siege ..."

Korrun looked at the young witch as if to gauge her intent, his face austere and mask-like. He turned away and, when at last he spoke, his voice was cold and hard. "It was just as King Dorrol said," he began slowly. "M'Sorreck disguised himself and invaded the city. There was a series of fierce battles that lasted for months. During that time, Morreck disappeared, we didn't know where. We hoped he had abandoned his troops and fled. But no. He'd vanished beneath the city while his hordes kept us fighting above. He must have awoken or disturbed the Gorrgos and been repelled back up to the city ... We were beating his wargols, despite their overwhelming numbers ...," he paused.

"We were winning, forcing them back street by street, bridge by bridge. Morreck re-emerged at the head of a legion of wargols far larger than the others, almost troll sized ... the greatest and foulest wargol was Morreck's chief captain ... Nuroth," the name seemed to catch in his throat. "He slew many good dworlls."

Korrun shifted his weight uneasily, curling and tightening his fingers around the leather straps of his belt. He seemed a stranger once more, withdrawn and remote.

"My older brother, Korrtal, the one that Mr. Agyk knew, died years before. An ambush in the jungles above ... so I became the protector of my younger brother, Sorall. He had been injured in the previous day's fighting," he paused again. "He was recovering in Kallorm's Resting Rooms when Nuroth and a group of wargols headed straight for the White Palace, killing everything in their path. King Dorrol and the Council had been taken to a safe refuge earlier. Finding the King's chambers empty, Nuroth went wild," the dwelf swallowed, his face rigid and contorted in anger. "Then," he spat, "like the filth they are ... they entered the Resting Rooms and butchered everyone inside, including my brother."

Wendya gasped.

"They murdered the healers, the monks in the chapel, every dworll, no matter how wounded or weak they were, even the women and the children ... I ... couldn't get there in time ...," he stopped short and shook his head, trying to control his rage.

"They escaped with M'Sorreck, but the trail of blood they left will never be forgotten or forgiven ... and neither will the sight of a thousand innocent dworlls, slaughtered like cattle, their heads severed and hung by their hair from the palace balconies or thrown into the fountains. They have no honor. They have no mercy. They desecrate everything they touch!" he said bitterly.

He turned, his eyes blazing. The sight shocked her. She'd never seen such hatred in anyone before.

"You asked me why I came with you. I have come to kill Nuroth, and Morreck if I can. Nuroth will feel my sword before this is over! He will pay for my brother's blood!" The dwelf's eyes burned with an intense ferocity, then, as if aware of the witch's shock, he calmed and became himself once more.

He looked at her, his composure and control returned. "That is why I tried to come here before, and it nearly killed me. I couldn't cross the mountains," he sighed. "King Dorrol pleaded with me not to try again and I obeyed. But when you arrived at Kallorm, I could not let this opportunity pass."

"I'm so sorry," said Wendya softly. She placed her hand on his. "M'Sorreck has a lot to answer for."

Korrun studied her face and tried to smile. "Yes," he replied. "Much will be settled."

The wind curled over the rocks and rattled through the bushes with a low hissing sound.

Wendya nodded. "Well ... the others will be wondering where we've gone. I suppose we should be getting back," she said with a smile, and stood up.

"Don't move!" Korrun snapped and grabbed her arm, pulling her down towards him.

"What?"

"Shh ... There's something there, stalking us," he whispered, his hand slowly reaching for his blade, "... just beyond those bushes."

She could hear the noise again, a low breathing sound but much closer this time. She gradually turned her head. Out of the corner of her eye she could just glimpse a shadow, partially hidden in the shrub land only a few feet away, the shape of a monstrous feline creature, twice the size of a snow leopard with a broad head and a protruding ridge of white fur down its back. Through the foliage she could see its feral eyes fixed on hers.

Korrun slowly pushed her behind him. "When I say run ... run for those rocks," he whispered through clenched teeth.

At that moment, the beast charged, leaping forward and clearing the ground between them in a single bound.

"RUN!" shouted the dwelf, spinning round to face the creature as it burst through the thicket.

Wendya turned and, before she had the chance to move a single step, she was confronted by something else rushing through the undergrowth towards her. "It's an ambush! There's two of them ... two of them!" she screamed, as the other creature broke through the ring of thorns. "KORRUN!"

The dwelf looked in horror, but too late, as the first beast pounced on him and he disappeared beneath it in a mass of fur and claws. Wendya screamed and fumbled for her sword as the second monster reared up and lunged at her. She fell back, hitting her head on a rock. An awful sound like a roar and a child's shriek filled the air. Darkness fell about her. She could feel breath, stinking and hot, black eyes upon her and the glint of yellowed sharpened teeth close to her face. She struggled for a second, pinned under the crushing weight, as a brilliant flash of purple fire filled her vision for a moment before fading to black.

Korrun hacked wildly at the beast, managing to pull himself free from under its massive girth. It rolled over in agony, drenching the ground and him with its blood. He staggered back as a blinding ball of light scorched the earth, and vanished in a blaze of sparks. The beast roared, its legs scrabbling about furiously as it tried to get up.

"Give this to your master, you foul fengal!" Korrun cried as he jumped on the creature's back and, plunging his sword up to its hilt, he thrust it through the beast's skull and into the ground with all his force. Dying, tt let out a final and hideous scream.

"Wendya!" he panted falling over the creature "WENDYA?!"

He skidded to a halt. In the growing darkness he couldn't see her, then, slowly his eyes found the burnt carcass of the other beast and Wendya lying still beneath it.

"Oh gods … no … please no … Wendya!" he cried and pulled her from under its hulk, before scooping her gently in his arms. He checked her life signs. She was still breathing, but barely. She seemed unhurt except for a nasty gash on the side of her head and some deep scratches to her arms. "Wendya?" he whispered.

Slowly her pulse strengthened and color returned to her cheeks. He looked at her for a moment and lightly brushed her hair aside as Gralen thundered into view, crashing through the undergrowth in a great gust of wings.

"Wendya? Wendya! … What have you done to her?!" he bellowed, his orange eyes glaring at the blood-soaked dwelf with fiery rage and accusation. "What happened?!"

"She's alright. She hit her head but she's fine. We had a narrow escape," Korrun replied, cradling a piece of torn cloth against her wound.

Gralen came closer and stroked her face, hoping that she'd open her eyes and see him. He stared at the dwelf. "What happened?" he repeated with a scowl.

"We were attacked. There were two of them … like snow leopards or winter lions but bigger, and their eyes were … wrong," Korrun said slowly, shaking his head. "Look for yourself; … servants of M'Sorreck I'd guess."

Gralen turned to the huge beast nearby. Its head lay skewered to the ground with Korrun's sword stuck in it. The surrounding undergrowth lay smoldering as if a meteorite or fireball had exploded there.

He inspected the charcoaled remains of the other creature. "What happened here … to this one? It doesn't look like a fÿrullfr," he said as he bent closer and sniffed the air.

Korrun shook his head. "No … it's not. I saw a bright flash of light, I think Wendya must have done it," he answered. As she stirred in his arms, he became aware that he was soaked in blood.

Gralen turned, his gaze fixed on the young witch. He glanced at the dwelf. "Some devilry of that evil filth I expect," he said blankly. "Give her to me; I think you'd better get cleaned up."

Korrun hesitated for a moment, then carefully passed her over to the dragon. "No more wandering or collecting herbs for her," he said, pulling his sword from the beast. "Every land we come to now is likely to hold more dangers for us."

Gralen nodded and stood silently as he watched the dwelf leave to find a pool to wash in. "Pity we can't leave him behind," he muttered. "I'd never let you get hurt!"

The witch stirred again. She felt ridiculously light in Gralen's arms. He turned to the fengal beasts, their carcasses fouling the ground, and without hesitating he blasted them until only their blackened bones remained.

"That's better than you deserve, scum of Morreck!"

Wendya awoke. She was cold even though a fire blazed just beside her. A wholesome concoction of sweet herbs — crushed white petals of the melliot flower and some wild garlic — was brewing nicely in the pot.

"I just followed one of your recipes," chirped Gralen as she sat up. "How do you feel?"

"Like a tree fell on me," she said, rubbing her ribs and touching her head. "Where's Korrun?" she started.

"I'm here," he replied nearby. "How's the head?"

"Here, drink this; it will help you heal," Gralen smiled, pouring some of the broth into a bowl. "Are you sure you're alright?"

"Yes, but I'm not sure what happened," she touched the small bandage above her left eye and glanced at Mr. Agyk who was still asleep.

"He's been like that all day," murmured the dragon worriedly. "When I heard you scream I came running, but he never woke up. We'll rouse him tomorrow; let him get some of his strength back now."

The next day came and nothing was said of the previous night's attack. Mr. Agyk didn't notice the bruises and cuts on Wendya and Korrun, or the fear on their faces, but appeared confused and tired, as if lost in a fog. The gray dawn beckoned and at first light they set off again with a new urgency.

Three more days rushed past and, with them, the moon, waning towards its last quarter. Following the river through the last tangled forests and stony canyons, the land opened up before them.

Stretching in every direction lay an endless expanse of prairie, its tussock grasses rising in undulating hill after hill, until they joined a thin line of foothills that rose steeply upwards. Above these, like an ominous black shadow across the horizon, stood the first towering peaks of the mountain realm they were looking for. Spurred onwards, the friends continued into the night, passing like a murmur over the grasses. Amidst the darkness, a deeper shade approached, as the jagged mountains loomed ever closer.

"I must stop!" panted Gralen at last, "I can't go any further!"

"Sorry," Mr. Agyk sighed as if waking from a dream. "The burden of travel has been very heavy on you."

"Can you make it to those lower slopes?" asked Korrun pointing to the shapeless, gray foothills that nestled at the mountains feet.

"Yes, but no further!" Gralen grumbled, his wings paining with every movement.

They passed over the twinkling fires of a small nomadic camp and pressed on into the night. Less than an hour later, the four stood on the flattened top of a stony ridge, no more than a series of sloping scree hills. They looked out over the whispering grasslands below, then up at the sheer black walls rising before them.

"That journey will have to wait another day," murmured the wizard, his mind lucid at last. "You are in pain my old friend; I can hear it in your voice. You must rest for a whole day at least."

Gralen glanced at him. He looked so painfully fragile, as if the slightest breeze would break him. "Half a night will suit me better."

They made a small fire and, after a meager supper, all fell into a heavy sleep.

Dawn came early and brought with it the bitter chill of winter. The sky was colorless and a sharp, stinging wind blew from the south, carrying rain-laden clouds over their heads.

"We must go," Korrun said quietly, rousing the dragon from sleep.

The dwelf's face was grimmer than usual and his blue eyes sparkled in the dimness with a look of unease. Gralen was shocked by the sleeping figure of the wizard. In the cold blue light he looked as if he were withered and dying, left to freeze on the barren ground. His hair, though an ungainly tangle, had always been a lustrous silver. It was now dull and gray as his skin, which seemed to barely cover his skeletal frame.

"Look at the staff," Korrun replied softly. "We haven't much time."

Lying beside the little scholar, the staff appeared to be no more than a dead twig. The light, which had always shone so brightly from its orb, was almost lifeless, no more than a faint glimmer amongst the stones.

He looked at the dragon and was surprised to see anguish in this lumbering beast. "We must go," Korrun repeated, placing his hand gently on the dragon. "Come."

Gralen gave him a doubtful glance, sighed and nodded.

"We must leave before the storm," said the tracker, noticing the thunderous sky racing up from behind.

Wendya lay curled up under a heavy bundle of fleecy blankets. The cold morning air swirled around her as she stirred in her sleep. Visions flashed before her eyes of claws and talons ripping and crushing at something, skies ablaze, a mountain on fire, two great horns of crooked rock, a carpet of darkness moving toward her, lightning and rain and tears. Three crying figures … Such terrible grief!

"Wendya?" came a voice through the haze. "Wendya, we've got to go."

The visions seemed to tug at her, wanting to carry her off into the wind as everything blackened.

"Wendya!" came the voice again, only sharper now.

She awoke with a start, gasping for air as if she'd been drowning in some pool of dark water and had only just struggled to the surface. She was weary … another bad dream. She'd been having them since their escape from the Grey Forest, only now they were growing more intense. She blinked the sleep from her eyes.

Korrun looked at her. "Come on," he urged. "We must go now."

She nodded vaguely, her eyes fixed on the little wizard.

Gralen knelt beside his old friend and gently woke him. "Mr. A … it's time."

Mr. Agyk opened his blurry eyes, trying to clear the milky haze that had settled over them. He wobbled to his feet, every movement seeming to put a great strain on the old man.

"Good morning," he mumbled.

Gralen carefully scooped him up and positioned him onto his back. "We're going," he said softly.

"No breakfast?" Mr. Agyk asked.

"No breakfast," answered the dragon quietly, looking at the witch's anxious face.

Korrun kicked over the dying embers and, after a last look around, he joined the others. Minutes later, the four companions were flying high into the blank sky and passing over the first ridge of mountains. The icy wind urged them onwards. The mountains grew steadily taller, rising mournfully from the depths below, until the mighty dragon was overshadowed by their snowy gray flanks.

Gralen climbed through drifting banks of frozen clouds to the thinner air above and the permanent snow-capped peaks that pierced those mammoth heights. Far below, through the shifting mists, the travelers caught sight of mighty crevasses many hundreds of feet deep. Ancient glaciers and snaking rivers of ice sailed by, their surfaces cracked and scarred by a million ages. Above them lay the untouched snowfields of pristine white, their crystals catching in the early sun like sheets of sparkling honeydew. In the far distance rose yet another line of mountains, taller than the others, their upper reaches higher still than the jagged tops they now flew over.

"That is the outer edge of the realm," Korrun said somberly, "the Encircling Mountains are too high to cross on foot. This is as far as I came," he paused. "The Lost Kingdom of Fendellin lies somewhere beyond there."

Gralen flew on, ignoring the ache in his limbs.

The pale sky grew steadily darker around them. As if a shroud had promptly fallen from above to block out the pallid sun they were plunged in a deep shadow. The wind picked up, each gust laced with snow and ice that bit at their faces and wailed past. Gray sheets of rain hid the mountains behind a sleety veil. Korrun peered ahead. Storm clouds raced before them, gathering in the brooding gloom, and the guttural sounds of thunder could be heard rumbling. Gralen smelt the air, sensing a change. Speeding onwards, he climbed higher.

"Hold on!" he cried as he soared towards the approaching storm. "This may get rough!"

The mountain loomed up as a thorny crown above the other peaks, a plateau of ragged rock. Its sharp teeth, bare to the wind and rain, jutted up in ridge after ridge of cruel stone, and though all the lower mountains had been covered in snow, none clung to its pinnacles.

Onwards and upwards they flew, weaving through the fog that rose from the blackness below. Suddenly, a crack of thunder above their heads heralded the tempest, and the heavens opened, sending the rain and hail down in a thunderous deluge. Lightning flashed around them, slashing and zigzagging across the sky, its violent temper illuminating countless other mountaintops still hidden in the gloom.

The sky turned black and all was lost in darkness and pelting rain.

Gralen blew out a long torch of flame that sizzled as the rain hit it, but did little to pierce the thick downpour. With little choice, they flew on blindly until an impossibly high wall of rock appeared before them, reaching up into the clouds. Gralen swerved sharply to avoid it. Beating his wings with all his power, he shot straight through the wisps of cloud and battering rain, hoping against hope not to crash into some hidden outcrop of rock.

As he reached the summit, the storm grew worse. It was as if nature itself were trying to repel them and forbid them from going any further. The rain stung their eyes like acid and huge hailstones bombarded them from all sides while the sheer force of the wind screamed in their ears.

"We've got to keep going!" Gralen shouted, using all his strength to battle on and not be blown into a razor-edged precipice. "Hold one everyone!"

He pushed through the wall of cloud and, in one final effort, they passed over the summit.

Almost as soon as they did, the sky fell silent about them and the wind dropped. Thick clouds filled the air, cocooning them in a strange pocket of eerie deadness. They flew on cautiously through the mist.

Korrun sits on an ancient stele overlooking a glacial lake in Fendellin and guards the company as they sleep.

The blackness and rain lifted, rolling back like a curtain before their eyes, until an unexpected opening appeared and they found themselves in the clear amber sky of the evening. They looked back, and saw the darkness closing up behind them, vanishing into the twilight air, with only a few grumbling storm clouds audible in the far distance.

"Fendellin!" gasped the dragon, forgetting his exhaustion and feeling his heart and blood race as never before.

"Shambhala," Mr. Agyk whispered. "Heaven on Earth!"

The group glided almost lazily over the last sunlit mountains, shaking the rain and ice from their hair and clothes.

There at last lay the forgotten land of Fendellin, The Lost Kingdom of Dragons, the most ancient of all realms. Not a hidden city in some Arctic waste or buried under tons of rock and soil, but an entire land, varied and wondrous and open to the sky. They had found it.

The mountains beneath them, though still great in stature, diminished steadily in size, sloping gently down like outspreading fingers towards Fendellin's outer borders. Those great phalanxes of rock gave way to rolling foothills and twisting canyons, before eventually flattening out into mile upon mile of soft, golden savannah.

Fendellin lay about them, a vast and extraordinary expanse of land that stretched to the distant horizon and beyond. A mysterious kingdom full of spectacular natural beauty, hidden and protected from the outside world by the ever-dominant presence of the Encircling Mountains.

"It's so beautiful!" Wendya gasped squinting into the setting sun. "But … how do we find Morreck?"

"By foot or flight," came the wizard's voice, "by foot or flight."

Gralen hovered, half in a dream. "The Land of Dragons!" he muttered, "I've found it!" A huge smile spread over his face. "I thought I'd only get to see my kin if I joined them in the stars. I've waited my whole life for this!"

He had the distinct feeling that he knew this place, or had seen it before, perhaps in his dreams. Every cell of his body blazed with excitement. All his long life led to this point, to this distant land where legends still existed and breathed in the waking world. Though the skies were clear of any creature, save a circling eagle, Gralen knew for the first time that he was not alone.

They drifted in the air for a moment. Far below them lay a wide glacial lake fed by the mountain streams and waterfalls that cascaded from the heights above and were lost amongst the grasses. From these mountain waters the travelers spied the silver river they had been following, now no more than a small, fast-flowing melt-water stream.

They traced its journey as it lazily meandered from the lowland slopes and snaked through the grasslands, joining springs and clear water pools, before disappearing into a ridge of rounded hills on the horizon.

Gralen swooped towards the glacier lake and its lower shores. Skimming just above the plains, he could not help smiling. They finally set down beside the chilly waters, near a group of broken standing stones and carved steles, their inscriptions the last remnant of some ancient ællfren or dragon culture.

The company made camp for the night, overlooking the startlingly bright azure of the icy lagoon, its color an eerie contrast against the fading light. In the distance, they could see the ghostly, frozen shapes of icebergs gliding silently across its surface.

Gralen ate very little, his attention divided between the sky and signs of other dragons, and the sickly figure of his old friend who grew worryingly weaker every day.

"We must find Morreck …," he whispered, as Mr. Agyk sat dozing and muttering to himself by the firelight.

The witch and dwelf nodded solemnly and the seriousness of the wizard's condition dampened all spirits. Gralen slumped beside Wendya, forgetting his excitement and the aching of his joints.

"I've been praying to Ibell'una every night, to watch over us," Wendya murmured.

"The goddess of the moon?" Gralen asked.

She nodded. "I can't lose him, I can't …," she shook her head, turning aside to stop her eyes from tearing.

"I know," the dragon replied quietly. "Time is short."

They ate silently, leaving the little wizard to rest, and settled down to sleep. They were at last in M'Sorreck's land and, though it was astounding and rare in its beauty, it was also wild and unknown to them — and full of danger. Greater than any other thought was the fear that their search was nearly over and that they could stumble into their enemy at any moment.

"We must post a watch tonight and every night while we're here," said Korrun glumly. "We may have other things to fear than Morreck and his minions. I'll take the first watch. Sleep well."

The dwelf stood up, his eyes mirroring the flames of the fire for a moment; turning, he left the comfort of the circle and scaled one of the larger stones that rose out of the earth like a warning finger. Settling himself on its summit, he sat cross-legged and motionless, his eyes staring into the fading sky, his dark hair and clothes billowing in the night air. Gralen muttered something and stared into the embers, but was soon snoring heavily.

Wendya remained awake for a little longer, staring at the immovable figure of Korrun, almost a statue of stone himself. She had ignored Gralen's little snipes about him — "a cold trout" was one that he liked — because she recognised the loner in Korrun as she recognised it in herself. Yet increasingly, it seemed to the witch, Korrun was troubled by some other deeper shadow of the past, which he would not name.

As the fire cast its last warmth, she fell into a dreamless sleep. The long savannah grasses whispered in the night, swaying in the breeze like a gentle ocean around the company, reminding them of the distant sounds of Kallorm's waterfalls, as the stars above glinted coldly in the blackness.

Chapter Fourteen
The Flame of Fendellin

Wake up! Wake up!" Korrun shouted, as he sent a volley of arrows into the air. "WAKE UP!" Gralen sprang to his feet, Korrun jumped from the standing stone as a torrent of blue and black fire exploded above their heads and a heavy shadow passed low over them, before sweeping into the somber sky.

"Fÿrrens!" cried the dwelf, fitting another set of arrows to his bow.

Gralen, still dazed and groggy, squinted at the early morning sky. High up in the air, there appeared to be a swarm of flying insects or vultures of some kind, circling. He blinked and recognized the shape. The wings stretched out like the gigantic span of a plane, the slender neck coiling, the arched back, the stream-lined body, the tail — more agile than any rudder or tail-fin. Winged beasts, dragons … living DRAGONS!

"Don't just stare! They're attacking, you fool!" Korrun yelled, running past him and springing over the dead campfire to reach Wendya, who had just woken and now sat stunned, her face transfixed on the creatures above.

Korrun grabbed her arm. "Come on! Get the mage!"

The dragon shook his head as if rousing himself from a dream, his senses returning. "… Head for those trees!" Gralen called, pointing along the icy waters to the edge of a small dark wood that skirted the far shores of the lake. "You need cover. I'll fend them off. GO!" he bellowed, and, in one mighty effort, reared up and launched himself into the pale sky.

The creatures circled leisurely overhead, gliding on the air currents and viewing their prey with detached pleasure. Picking up as much as he could carry, Korrun led Wendya, who was clutching a slumbering Mr. Agyk, along the muddy banks of the lake and toward the distant line of trees.

Squally showers rolled in from the west as the witch ran on, glancing down at the sleeping figure she cradled in her arms. He muttered deliriously, his words rambling and slurred; his face ashen gray. Korrun ran beside her, his keen dwelf eyes fixed on the skies above.

Gralen shot like a dart towards the creatures. Higher and higher he climbed. The sky bit with a sharp, lashing wind. The green dragon heard viperous hisses poisoning the skies around.

He flew further upward, both in awe at seeing his own race and horrified at the hideous forms they had taken. A breed quite unlike his own. A race of grotesque things, their noble lineage corrupted and altered inextricably. More serpentine and reptilian, they were also far larger. Their wings were edged with spikes, their heads crested and horned, their eyes slit like a viper and their forked tongues barbed and laced with venom. They wheeled above lazily, as he sped towards them in a blaze of anger.

As Gralen reached them they broke away, spiraling off into different directions like the choreographed movements of a ballet. One scarlet colored creature dived towards the running figures far below.

"Oh no you don't!" Gralen roared, blasting a jet of fire that caught the red serpent's tail and sent him lurching off sideways.

Moments later, and caught off guard, Gralen was suddenly ambushed from above. A mighty vulturine creature twice his size, bore down on him piercing his skin and scales and sinking its talons deep into his back.

Gralen twisted in the air and let out a howl. The vulturine laughed, the blue metallic sheen of its foul hide glinting in the early light.

"Got you now!" it sneered. "Fresh offal! It's been a while since I've feasted on fÿrren flesh!"

"And it'll be a while longer!" Gralen bellowed, lashing his tail back and driving the dagger point deep into the beast's underbelly.

The venomous creature screeched and let go, dropping the green dragon like a dead weight. Gralen plummeted, his back in agony, the wind rushing in his ears while the grasslands below raced up to meet him. With barely seconds to spare he managed to recover. Spreading his wings, he skimmed inches above the ground before propelling himself back into the sky, spewing liquid fire and rage, his senses and blood ablaze.

The other dragons circled and swooped to attack.

"NO! He's mine!" spat the dark creature, clearly the leader of the horde.

The two smashed head-on into each other, a clash of titans, blue and green fire engulfing them both as a deadly bloom.

Far below, Korrun and Wendya — still holding the little wizard — reached the outskirts of the wood and then, daring to look back, they saw the dwarfed figure of Gralen ensnared in the mighty creature's clawing arms. Gralen half-roared, half-howled again as the beast ripped through his wings, breaking one of them at the shoulder joint.

"GRALEN!" Wendya cried, turning to run back.

Korrun quickly grabbed her and held her tightly. "We can't help him!" he shouted. "There's nothing we can do! Think of the wizard!"

At that moment something caught the dwelf's eye. He twisted round to see two serpents pursuing them. "Run! RUN!" he cried, dragging the witch further into the woods as a river of fire fell upon them.

"GRALEN!" Wendya cried, as the other four beasts descended upon the beleaguered figure of her friend. She watched in horror as the creatures dived behind their leader, waiting for the kill and a share of the spoils.

The green dragon struggled wildly, throwing fire into the vulturine's face and towards the others as they closed in, but to no avail.

"GRAAALENNNN!" came a distant voice, as sweet as honeydew to his ears.

He thrashed from side to side, clawing to get free, the talons of his feet and hands trying to rip at the serpent creature that held him in its vice. But still its grip tightened and tightened, its cruel, reptilian, blue eyes blazing with malice and greed as Gralen felt his ribs crack.

Once more he heard the sweet thin voice of Wendya calling his name. His tail stabbed madly at his attacker, hoping to find a soft spot beneath the heavy helm and armor. Even his blasting fire did little damage, only blackening the monster's foul hide, as if the creature were made of stuff far tougher and hotter than any fire a dragon's belly could muster.

"I have you now!" it cackled, the slits of its crocodilian eyes glazing over. "Can you feel your bones breaking?" it said, its tongue flicking out in excitement as it squeezed the dragon harder.

Gralen fought for breath but, through the pain, a great fury boiled inside of him. "By the flame of my forefather's you shall not crush me ... viperous traitor! Scum of our race!" he raged, and, mustering every last ounce of strength, his innards burst into flame and an explosion of green and white fire poured out of him.

Taken aback by such fighting spirit, Gralen's ferocity and force took the beast by surprise and it loosened its grip for an instant. At that moment, a cry went up in the surrounding skies, like a chorus of defiant voices carried on the wind. As the green dragon began to succumb to the pain, he thought he could hear the familiar rush and throbbing sound of beating wings filling the air.

"For Fendellin and all who defend her!" boomed a voice, deeper than the oceans and cracked with age and anger.

The serpentine creature looked up to see the figure of a great dragon, its scales shimmering silver and pearl in the dawn sun, flying straight toward it and, from behind its mighty gray wings, flew at least ten other dragons, their scales sparkling green and golden.

The vile beast reeled back, still gripping a stricken and bleeding Gralen.

"Sedgewick!" it spitted. "This trophy isn't one of your carrion fledglings, it's an outsider. Now go, if you don't want your crows torn apart!" it warned.

"You cannot threaten me Varkul, or any of my kin. Every day brings you nearer to your own death!" Sedgewick roared.

"Drag your carcass any closer, and I'll snap his neck," Varkul sneered, his reptilian eyes turning to a glistening black, "... like I snapped your son's!"

"You will never kill another fÿrren, Varkul!" bellowed the ancient dragon. "I will tear your wings off first!" he thundered, and shot forward.

Varkul saw the wrath in the old dragon's eyes and, dropping Gralen once more, he and the other serpents turned and fled. Sedgewick's dragons followed in pursuit with some swooping down on the remaining beasts that had engulfed a greater part of the woods in a tremendous fire. The old dragon dived to catch the fallen prey of his enemy and, with wonder and puzzlement in his aged eyes, he beheld Gralen and carefully glided down, landing gently on the soft earth near the edge of the burning wood.

The fires raged, sending thick plumes of black smoke into the air as the trees ignited like kindling.

"Always destroying," Sedgewick sighed as two of his kin swooped down, scooped huge amounts of water in their mouths and attempted to quell the fires. "You may now come out," he called in a gravelly voice, his sharp eyes spying a lonely figure emerging through the mists of charcoal and smoke. "Come out. I am not your enemy … your friend here is badly hurt."

Korrun hesitated, his sword drawn. The old dragon was enormous. He was easily twice the size of Gralen, with thickly wrinkled, leathery skin about his throat and face, and pepper-colored eyes that displayed both great wisdom and warmth. He folded his huge wings behind him and his pale scales shimmered in the morning light.

"Who are you?" Korrun asked, suspiciously, as he stepped forward, his hand beckoning to Wendya to stay hidden in the shadows of the still smoldering trees.

"My name is Sedgewick. You have nothing to fear from me, young warrior. I am the greatest and oldest defender of Fendellin and a loyal friend of the High Lord, King Baillum, ruler of this land," answered the old dragon as he watched the tracker draw closer, his sword poised. "You are a dwelf, are you not?!" the dragon asked rather bluntly. "This is a day of strange meetings! We have had no outsiders here for many long years and suddenly we have a dragon I do not know and a dwelf from the annals of history! I have not seen any of your kind since the ǽllfren days of my youth when this land was a realm of both dworlls and ǽllfrs!"

Gralen stirred and muttered something.

Korrun, forgetting any danger, rushed to his side.

"Your friend is badly injured," Sedgewick repeated. "He was brave but foolish to take on so many foes, especially an evil creature like Varkul."

"He is brave," Korrun replied, placing a hand on the dragon's brow, "… and foolhardy. He was protecting us … This is Gralen, a Eurasian dragon of the northern realm I believe, and I am Korrun of Koralan, Royal Guard to King Dorrol of Kallorm."

"Well met. But you said us? I saw only you from the air," Sedgewick said, his eyes flitting toward the wood.

Korrun stared at the old fÿrren, as if trying to read his thoughts; finding no malice or danger in his eyes, he called Wendya. The witch rushed out from the darkness, tears filling her eyes, and fell by Gralen's side.

The dragon stirred as he felt Wendya's hand touch his face. "I'm fine," he whispered.

"No you are not, my friend," Sedgewick replied glancing at the others, his aged voice full of concern. "It is not safe for us to linger here. We must take you all to the Golden City, on the summit of Mund'harr. There is a place there, secret and forbidden to most, but it will heal you. I feel sure King Baillum will allow it."

"There is another who may need it," Korrun replied looking at Wendya.

She opened her cloak, revealing the motionless figure of Mr. Agyk. Sedgewick's eyes opened widely.

"A magus!" he gasped. "I have not seen any magic folk save M'Sorreck, since I was a draken many, many of your lifetimes ago! … This is the work of that evil wizard, is it not?"

Korrun nodded but remained silent. The old dragon looked once more over the little figure, so still and so lifeless before them. "The Corruptor, as we call him, has grown mightier than all wizards. He is as powerful as he is wicked, an accursed and terrible foe to all free Fendellons, dworll and dragon alike. Come, we must hasten, there is little time ... Rollm! Rollm!" he called to one of the young followers who swooped nearby.

"Rollm! Get down here!" Sedgewick's impatience was swiftly rewarded, as a figure came hurtling out of the sky and promptly swept down beside them like a great gust of wind.

The young dragon, smaller and lither than Gralen, had a remarkable resemblance to their friend, though his leathery skin and green scales were of a lighter hue and his belly a pale cream. Sedgewick motioned to the witch and dwelf to climb onto the young draken's back.

He turned to Gralen. "Sleep, my winged brother," he whispered, gently lifting him into the air, his broken wing lolling awfully to one side. "You have been valiant, but rest now, rest now."

As if his words cast a spell, Gralen closed his eyes and fell into a deep sleep in the great dragon's talons. Sedgewick looked at Korrun and Wendya. "You were very fortunate that we were patrolling this area. Varkul, the beast that attacked you, has long been known as The Dragon of Death He kills all he encounters and feasts on the flesh of corpses and living alike, drinking the blood of his enemies. He is the foulest and most evil of M'Sorreck's servants," Sedgewick cast his gray green eyes over the group and nodded. "We go!"

Moments later, they took to the skies. Wendya held the little wizard tightly, as she and Korrun looked in wonder at the lands around them. Countless waterfalls glistened in the sunlight and vast inland seas spread their waters like great mirrored sheets. Onward they flew. Endless miles of golden grasses marched below them, tumbling towards distant mountains and disappearing beneath the whispering shade and serenity of winter woods, their branches touched by spring.

The harshness of winter seemed to have little sway over this magical land.

The company sped on. Amidst the rolling hills, valleys and savannah plains, they saw the first terrible signs of battle. Forests burnt to lifeless charcoal, grasses singed and blackened. Streams and rivers once filled with life were now polluted and ruinous, their channels carriers of death, their banks rotted into mud, their waters thickened into slime.

Nestled amongst these lonely landscapes, lay the ruins of towns and settlements. Glorious architectural creations that had stood in peace and prosperity long before human lands had been tamed and civilized.

Now the buildings lay broken, decaying monuments to the deluge which had descended upon them without warning or mercy, and had left no living creature in its wake.

Sedgewick, carrying Gralen, sighed heavily. "This was once the fairest of all lands under the sun. The first and last realm of the ǽllfrs in the waking world. It was the heart of the ancient Order and the ancestral home of all fÿrren races. Now ... it is a land at war."

Rollm turned his head. "We've been unable to send any word beyond the borders of Fendellin," he said sadly. "Every messenger has been killed, or disappeared," the young dragon looked toward his mentor as if for reassurance. "We've been at war with M'Sorreck's hordes for many years now."

Sedgewick nodded and glanced at the fragile figure in Wendya's hands. "We were hoping that the last remaining Wise of the Order could help us. That if they came here and joined forces, we could repel, perhaps even destroy him. But Rollm is right, no word has been able to reach outside of these lands, and we can no longer spare messengers. Fendellin, as you can see, is already overrun!" he shook his head; his aged eyes looked again with wonder at the strangers. "You do not realize how miraculous your being here is. It is a marvel to me that any of you were able to enter our realm. It has been so many years since outsiders have passed beyond the Encircling Mountains!"

"It was Gralen." Wendya replied quietly, her eyes seldom leaving the green dragon cradled in Sedgewick's arms. "He carried us all."

Rollm stared at the sleeping figure of Gralen. "I had no idea our race still lived in the outside world!" he said with amazement.

"They don't," Wendya replied sadly, looking at her injured friend. "Gralen is the last and only of his kind."

"He is a brave warrior, a true fÿrren, and there are few of those left." Sedgewick smiled. "His lineage is old and noble, and I suspect of a very pure bloodline."

"He is a dear friend," replied the witch, and fell silent.

They sped on as the lands below rushed past in a haze of warm air and beating wings.

As the sun rose high in the pale sky, they approached a solitary mountain, Mund'harr, rising out of the earth like a golden thorn. Standing alone in a sea of grass and low-lying plains, the Golden City on its summit lay shrouded in mist. They flew on. The dwelf and witch became aware of frenzied activity below them, of crisscrossing roads with lines of moving creatures all busy working.

"They are reinforcing the city's defenses," Sedgewick said simply. "We come now to the Golden City of nine rings!"

Drawing closer to the mountain, Korrun could see nine concentric circles spreading out from its base, each wider and deeper than the next.

"What are those?" he pointed.

"These were once the nine rivers of Mund'harr, from the mountain's waterfalls. They were beauteous and fast-flowing. Many of my kindred were born in their fair falls long ago."

"What happened?" Wendya called.

"The war," Rollm answered. "The city has been attacked so many times … the rivers had to be deepened. No longer are they whispering through the grasses but are now deep waters at the bottom of even deeper chasms, too wide to cross. They were designed to stop any ground assault."

They flew over the ravines and excavated moats around the mountain, some of them partly filled with water, others left as gaping voids.

A few temporary bridges spanned the chasms — each one heavily guarded by gates, lookout towers and units of infantry. The activity around these gorges was ceaseless. Great wafts of steam and smoke rose from their abyssal depths. Wendya looked down.

Around each gateway fluttered line upon line of prayer flags, thousands of them, dancing in the cold wind like colorful streamers.

The travelers were taken higher into the air and, amongst Mund'harr's snow-speckled flanks, they saw their first glimpse of the Golden City, Fendellin's capital, and its name was aptly given to this glittering city of gold-drenched spires that clung to the very top of the mountain and snaked in steep tiers about its sides. Perched precariously amongst Mund'harr's upper heights, the city's heart lay within a high circlet of granite peaks. These pinnacles of rock protected the city's largest and most precious buildings. The travelers looked on, astonished by its beauty.

Towers and domes sparkled in the noon day sun. Circular canopies and fortified walls wound round the mountainside as if they had sprung naturally from its rock. The city's overhanging balconies and grand squares nestled amongst its palaces, as hundreds of waterfalls streamed from its sides, making a permanent shroud of mist around the city's feet.

"The gold which men crave …," Korrun whispered.

Not even the beauty of Kallorm's White Palace compared to the city's magnificence.

As they drew nearer, they could see the many pennons of Fendellin's ruling houses and Fendellin's own emblem — a golden mountain entwined by two colossal dragons, one silver and one green, and a sun and moon rising in a shining crown of nine stars. The bell towers rang out, heralding their arrival.

Sedgewick and Rollm flew into one of the large landing squares.

Amongst such mighty company, even the dragons were dwarfed by the sheer size of the buildings. They were greeted by a contingent of silver-clad dworlls and the young captain of the City Guard, Frell: an unusually clean-shaven and fair-skinned dworll with pale amber eyes, auburn hair, and a serious nature. Their armor, showing the royal crest of Fendellin, glinted in the sunshine.

"Greetings, Frell. I must see your father," Sedgewick spoke sternly, bowing to the young captain as he did so. "It is a matter of the greatest importance. These are allies from the outside. They have fought bravely and suffered much. We must see the King."

The soldier hesitated and looked warily at the young girl and with some wonder at the dwelf. Without a word, Frell nodded and beckoned for them to follow.

Sedgewick turned to Rollm. "Stay here and look after our winged friend. I will be back soon," he smiled.

Gralen slowly opened his eyes and smiled at the witch, nodding for her to go. Korrun, with Wendya and the wizard, followed the dworll captain and Sedgewick through the many narrow streets and plazas until they reached the Grand Hall and Senate.

"Wait here." Frell said, disappearing behind a doorway. "I will seek the King."

The friends stood quietly beneath a giant vaulted portico within the entrance of the hall. The chamber reminded Wendya of Mr. Agyk's Great Library, its grandness only eclipsed by its solemn beauty. Its walls were so high that she could barely see the ceiling and, like White Mountain's library, its floors shimmered with a thousand diaphanous colors that seemed to change with every step on its surface. Vast marble and granite pillars towered either side and were looped by galleries and covered balconies.

At the far end of the hall, at the top of a steep flight of steps, stood a raised recess with a canopy of stone. Inside the canopy, sat a large throne with dragon-shaped wings rising from its back.

"Fendellin's seat of power and the heart of the Golden City lies here," Sedgewick said, following their gaze. "The Throne of Clouds."

As he spoke, Frell emerged from an archway with a small band of figures lead by a tall, willowy dworll dressed in stately robes of pale gold and gray.

"Lord Sedgewick! It is always good to see you. My son told me of your coming and the strange guests you have brought," declared the figure, placing his hand across his chest in salute. He turned to the others. "I am Lord Baillum, High King and Protector of Fendellin. Welcome to our fair city," he said solemnly, the depth of his voice resonating around the hall.

He appeared an austere and stern-looking dworll, majestic and lean, with none of the jovial familiarity or the frailty of King Dorrol, and little of his warmth. He was a warrior-king in every sense; almost carved out of stone, it seemed to Wendya, as if no force could bend or break his will and any who tried would perish in the act.

He stepped forward, his hair and beard braided but unadorned. Though his years were long and his bronze hair flecked with silver, he wore few signs of his age. His dark eyes studied each of the group in turn and with some suspicion, as Sedgewick and the others bowed.

"Varkul attacked them," Sedgewick began grimly. "It would seem they no longer fear to fly the skies by day. His boldness is growing."

"Yes, at the behest of his master ... the fÿrren attacks worsen daily," Baillum sighed. Dismissing his soldiers and Frell with a wave of his hand, he looked closely at the witch and with some wonder at Korrun, before speaking again.

"I wonder why you are here," he spoke slowly, his voice cold and full of distrust, each word judged carefully. "How have you managed to cross our borders where so many have failed?" he glanced at Sedgewick as if to reassure himself of their virtue. "You have wounded amongst you and wish to heal them here? Few have dared to ask to use the healing powers of The Flame. Its existence and location are secret, lest M'Sorreck gain knowledge of it!"

"Lord, these travelers have come far and through great peril. Their coming here is by no accident," urged the dragon. "There is no evil in them; indeed their presence is a portent of good fortune. The tides may finally be turning!"

"Perhaps ... perhaps not."

Wendya stepped forward, revealing the still sleeping, ashen figure of Mr. Agyk. She recounted their tale to the King, careful not to mention the finding of Morreck's birthkey.

"Gralen and Marval are all I have, Sire," she said bowing her head.

King Baillum walked over and inspected the little wizard.

"So this is the enchanter. I shall try not to judge him on his size ... but I can see that his hurts are grave. I have seen this malady before. M'Sorreck's evil has drained his life.

There is no power here that can give it back. The Flame may be able to prolong it for a while and give him strength enough, perhaps, to confront M'Sorreck."

"Then you will help?" Sedgewick asked quietly.

Baillum looked over the faces of Wendya and Korrun. "Yes," he answered. "But speak nothing of your quest and plight to any other, unless I first command it. These are dark days and not all ears and hearts are to be trusted," he paused. "Though your quest is a personal one, your arrival here will either prove to be the victory of Fendellin or its ruin. My heart warns me that it may be the latter ... but I see no evil in you. Certainly no dwellfr will ever be doubted in this court and, by your tale, young wicca, you seem to be of close friendship with King Dorrol. Hearing news of him and Kallorm brings me much joy. Long has it been since any news of the outside has reached my ears. Come, I will take you to The Flame ... Lord Sedgewick, bring the injured dragon, *his* wounds at least will be easy to heal."

Wendya, carrying the wizard in her arms, followed Korrun and the King through a maze of twisting tunnels, down into the heart of the mountain. Finally, they reached a small damp cave, little more than the bottom of a vertical well shaft.

Its overhanging walls were lost in the gloom, while dripping mosses clung to its surface, their leafy fronds dangling down in layered, shaggy growths. From some source high up, came a filtered beam of sunlight that lit the dark space in an eerie, green glow.

Mingling with the streams of light came a pouring of clear water sparkling like liquid gold that flowed silently downwards and collected in a shallow pool below.

"The Flame of Fendellin," Baillum announced with reverence. "The healing fountain."

The Dworll King motioned to Wendya. Without a word, the witch climbed the steps to the edge of the pool. The waters danced before her eyes in a million points of light and, from its silence, Wendya seemed to hear the sweetest music in her head.

"Beware of the pool. Do not touch the liquid!" Baillum warned. "Only the enchanter. The everlasting fountain can heal those who need healing but harm those who do not. It has the power to restore life even from the brink of death, or take life from the healthy. Be careful."

Wendya nodded. Kneeling beside the water's edge, she carefully lowered Mr. Agyk onto a shallow ledge of the pool.

"Do not worry. He will not drown," reassured the dworll.

Minutes seemed to pass like hours as she watched over her beloved friend. Mr. Agyk lay motionless, a little wan figure floating on the surface, his tattered robes shifting around him. It appeared to Wendya that the deathly grayness that had clung to him so heavily seemed to lift and a wholesome glow filled his cheeks. Korrun stepped to Wendya's side as life slowly returned to the little scholar and he stirred for the first time since entering Fendellin.

As the two companions looked on in amazement, it seemed to the witch and the tracker that the wizard even appeared to grow a little in size.

"Look at the staff!" Korrun whispered, pointing to the little stick Wendya held in her hand. Once more from its orb sprang a candescent light brighter than they had seen in many weeks.

"His strength is returning," said the dwelf, smiling.

Wendya nearly laughed, relief overwhelming her, as the little wizard awoke.

"Uhh … what? … Oh, I was wandering in a dream, then the path fell from beneath me … where am I?" he murmured, opening his eyes and feeling a strange tingling sensation all around him, as if he were being simultaneously jabbed by thousands of tiny invisible pins "Why am I wet?" he said indignantly, standing up and shaking himself.

The King smiled briefly. "You are alive little magus, and you are in Fendellin. Your friends here have saved you. You were failing fast and nearly beyond our help … I am Baillum, High King of this land. *Narrock see*, welcome all."

Mr. Agyk smiled, and waded to the edge of the pool. He felt invigorated, almost as if he were himself again, but no, not quite, no … he could still feel the emptiness.

As he stepped from the waters, his clothes instantly dried, as did his receding tangle of hair. "Where is Gralen?" he asked, suddenly fearful.

"He will be restored," Sedgewick answered, carrying the injured dragon, his broken wing dragging along the floor. "It looks far worse than it is. Try not to worry," he smiled.

Mr. Agyk leapt down the steps. "What have you done, you reckless fool!" he cried with tears in his eyes. He had never seen his friend so torn and bloodied before.

"He saved our lives … again," Korrun replied, humbly.

Sedgewick gently placed his comrade in the golden waters.

"You have a brave companion here. He challenged Varkul, most feared and powerful of our kind and a match far beyond his strength. But, he fared better than most."

Steam and sizzling vapors rose from the pool's surface, as the dragon's hot skin touched it. The waters lapped over his broken wing. The deep gashes to his back, his bruised torso and crushed ribs were soothed, as the blood and pain was washed away. Within minutes, Gralen opened his eyes and breathed deeply, his ribs and chest feeling whole and healed once more.

"Incredible!" Korrun gasped, unable to believe his eyes. "I have never seen or heard of such a thing!"

"Now do you understand the power of The Flame, and why it must be protected?" replied Baillum gravely.

The dwelf nodded, unable to take his eyes off the wizard and dragon.

Gralen stretched his wings as one who has just woken from a short sleep and a pleasant dream. "I'm starving!" he exclaimed, turning to see the energized figure of Mr. Agyk nearby, so full of life, he sprang from the pool in a single bound and whisked him off his tiny feet.

"Marval! Mr. A! You're well!"

"I am, if you do not crush me into pâté!" the wizard laughed. "We have done a poor job of looking after ourselves … and you have been too reckless as usual … There is much to do."

Gralen nodded and instinctively placed the wizard on his shoulder.

King Baillum stood quietly before the waters, looking deeply into the cascade as if in prayer. He turned to face the group, his face grim.

"Time is shorter than you know wizard, so we will use little of it. You must rest tonight, you have traveled far. I will call you at first light. Then we may talk further. Come."

The company left the cool darkness of the cave with its sparkling waters behind, as they followed the King back up to the surface and the dying afternoon. The friends ate quietly as the shadows of early evening lengthened, then bid each other goodnight.

King Baillum called them early the next morning. The group assembled in the palace's banqueting hall. The travelers, still weary in body and spirit, ate quietly, except for Gralen, who treated the grand platters laid before him as merely an entrée to the main course.

The wizard and dragon appeared fully recovered. Wendya was pleased to see their usual banter return. The friends sat at a dining table that stretched the length of the hall. Large tapestries and marble reliefs decorated the walls and open fireplaces — each hearth already blazing and warming the great hall from the cold morning outside. Lavish crystal chandeliers dangled from the roof trusses above, as attendants buzzed around, dutifully clearing plates, stoking fires and offering Fendellin medeaok, a fine and prized mead, to any who wished it.

"You must forgive my stewards for staring. We have not had outsiders here for many years and none as distinguished as you for longer still." Baillum spoke, allowing a brief smile to pass across his face. "I take it my esteemed ally here has told you of our troubles?" he said, glancing at Sedgewick before turning back to the visitors.

"No doubt you saw the scars M'Sorreck has inflicted on this land. Fÿrullfrs roam the country by night and by day now, hunting in packs. Many, who refused to flee their villages and homes, have been killed, the rest now seek refuge within these city walls. Despite this feast, we have little provisions. Our own crops and fields have been decimated, whole harvests destroyed. It has become far worse in the last few years. In little over a year from now, I fear the people of Fendellin may be starving." Baillum sighed.

"The lands here seem so rich," Wendya said, looking at the spread before them.

"They are. This is a great land, but an immense land; we cannot defend all of it. While we protect our cornfields, our towns are burnt. Other cities and strongholds have fallen under the onslaught. This city, as mighty as she is, was not designed for the entire population of Fendellin. She is not Kallorm. It is a bitter pill for the other lords of this realm to be forced to flee their own halls and seek shelter here," he paused, his face unreadable, his eyes dark. "We are under attack. M'Sorreck's hordes grow stronger every day. His captains ravage the land. Varkul commands the carrion beasts that attack the city from the sky and burn every township and settlement in their path.

While Nuroth, cruelest and most savage of Morreck's demons, commands the wargol legions who issue daily from Kavok, striking fear and death to all …," he paused again and Wendya glanced at Korrun. The dwelf sat bristling with anger at the mention of Nuroth's name, his focus unswerving from the King, as he continued. "Were it not for Lord Sedgewick and his valiant kin, the skies would be a constant enemy to us and all our lands would quickly turn to ash!" Baillum stopped for a moment as if taking stock of his mournful situation and shook his head.

"Wargol demons multiply, breeding quicker than vermin. The mountains, which have always protected us from the outside world, have now become our prison. M'Sorreck constructs endless caverns, which he fills with these filthy creatures. He has not been idle. He is stirring some dreadful evil beneath Kavok. I fear he is raising an army, invincible to any that stand against it. Some talk of ancient evils rising, of dark mytes returning, growing in the darkness, spreading fear like a plague."

"We heard tales of them in Kallorm. What are they exactly?" asked Gralen, chomping another rack of lamb.

King Baillum walked in front of the fireplace, the light seeming to shimmer about him. "Dark mytes are ancient abominations, parasitic demons from the birth of the world. They infect the life force of any living thing they touch. They feed off of fear. If the victim is lucky, they die quickly, before the creatures eat their flesh. The alternative is worse. A murderous madness as the victim mindlessly follows the bidding of their new masters, and preys on the innocent. Such insidious poison turns the virtuous to evil and turns brother against brother. It breaks even the deepest of bonds."

"Turns brother against brother?" Gralen exclaimed.

"Blood may be thicker than water, but it also turns fouler far quicker!" King Baillum sighed, returning to the table.

"We are besieged on all sides," he said. "This mountain is a stronghold but the city is weak," he paused briefly. "We have prevented most ground assaults by the defenses you have seen. Wargols hate water. Our ravines are too deep and wide for them to cross. But such devices have scarred our beautiful land. No more do the nine rivers whisper around our feet …," he made a gesture as close to a kingly shrug as such figures make. "We have fought many battles. The plains which surround this city are soaked with the blood of our kin. I feel certain, as many do, that a final war is fast approaching. We cannot sit idly as M'Sorreck and his armies cover this land in darkness, nor can we continue fighting …," he turned his attention to Sedgewick who stood impassively at the grand north window, his wings tucked neatly behind him as he gazed out across the rooftops below. A regal figure, and an equal to the stoic Dworll King, yet warmer and wiser, Gralen thought.

King Baillum continued. "Lord Sedgewick and his brave warrior-dragons patrol the skies and have long defended our city from the aerial attacks which make it so vulnerable. But they are dwindling in numbers and cannot continue to save us and perish in the act! You come to us now at our weakest" he sighed once more. "As the year fails, it would seem that Fendellin herself may fail … your arrival here is timely indeed!"

He sank further back in his chair, an expression of grim determination in his eyes, as one who knows the bitter truth, yet is resolved to face it.

"May we speak in privacy?" Mr. Agyk gestured, looking at the waiting stewards.

Baillum nodded and dismissed his staff with a cursory glance.

The wizard waited until they had left. "All is not lost," he said, his tone serious and circumspect. "It would be folly to rely on four strangers, but we may bring hope."

Baillum studied the little scholar, intrigued by his manner.

"Can you tell us of M'Sorreck's home?" Mr. Agyk asked.

Baillum met the wizard's eyes. "He has a mountain fortress, mostly underground. A labyrinth of caves beneath Fendellin's highest peak, Kavok. It lies due north and west, ninety leagues as the fÿrren flies. Kavok is his birthplace and seat of his power," he said glumly.

Sedgewick stood beside the King's chair. "Kavok's peak was a place of great evil even before M'Sorreck took it as his lair," Sedgewick began. "Kavok was the greatest of all dragons, the father of fÿrrens many called him. Strongest, bravest, most noble among us. I was a draken when I first heard his name. As revered as he was, as pure of heart as we knew him to be, even he was corrupted by M'Sorreck. The mightiest of us fell from grace and became the most feared. He brought our race to its knees … Varkul is Kavok's offspring, heir to the evil throne which M'Sorreck placed him upon." Sedgewick paused. "Eventually Kavok was killed by an eminent warrior, King Baillum's great grandfather. That is why Varkul hates the King and all his bloodline." He began pacing the room. "We have lost much," he sighed.

Baillum nodded. "It will be seventy years this spring since the destruction of Kasra-Naru and its beloved hanging gardens," the King added. "We cannot force ourselves to redraw the maps, such a grievous loss was that fair forest city. Thousands were slaughtered as the city was burnt around them. That was the last time we marched to war. It was our greatest battle against M'Sorreck and we lost many good dworlls and dragons. Had we known the extent of his forces and how his powers had multiplied, we would have moved against him years earlier. Skirmishes are almost constant now. We choose our battles very carefully now." It was obvious that the King was far from happy about this strategy.

Mr. Agyk looked at Baillum, such a stoical figure. The wizard could see that, like many, he had suffered much at the hands of their enemy. "You may not like the waiting, Sire, but it may have proved the wisest course." Mr. Agyk said, with a glint in his eyes. "You may now have a greater chance of victory than you realize. Perhaps the greatest chance for a long time …," his voice was low and conspiratorial. "We have a precious artifact, something M'Sorreck himself was looking for but could not retrieve!" he said, as Wendya took out a long silver chain with the dragon-shaped key on the end of it. "This is M'Sorreck's birthkey!" announced the wizard triumphantly. "Forgive us for our secrecy, Sire, we had to be careful."

Baillum stared, unsure of what he was seeing. "What? Where did you get this? How?"

"Kallorm," replied the dwelf simply, speaking for the first time. "Morreck's mother took it there long ago and hid it from him, before destroying herself."

"And you found it?" Sedgewick asked in utter astonishment as he stared at the glowing key around Wendya's neck.

King Baillum rose from his chair. "How is this possible? If this trinket truly is the corruptor's birthkey, it is a fortuitous day indeed!" he pronounced. "It is said, and has been proven, that a birthkey will open any barred door and locked passage to the home of its master, be it the most impenetrable fortress! This birthkey will allow us to attack him in the very heart of his home!" The King could barely comprehend the news. "We will have the upper hand … access to him, to his domain, his source of power!"

Sedgewick was equally elated. "At last we can take the battle to his foul door!" he rallied, laughing. "My dear friends, I marvel that you have survived, carrying such a perilous thing!"

King Baillum looked sternly at the wizard, his tone grim. "Does M'Sorreck suspect that you have his key?"

"No, I am sure he does not, yet," answered Mr. Agyk. "But evil has a way of finding out!"

"I agree," replied the King. "He has many spies … but I suspect that if he knew, none of you would have reached our borders alive. With each other's help, we may finally deprive this foul carrion of his life and gain peace for our people, and you, my friend, can regain your full powers," Baillum stood up, his stature seeming even taller than before.

"An alliance then?" asked the wizard.

"Yes, an alliance … of dworlls and dragons and mages and dwellfrs. There has not been such an alliance since the elder days!" He exclaimed, raising a crystal goblet. "I shall gather Fendellin's lords for a war council. They shall be amazed by your tale!"

"We shall be glad to meet them and tell it, but I think it prudent that Morreck's key remain known to us only," said Mr. Agyk quietly.

Baillum considered the wizard's request and nodded. "They are all loyal and their honor is beyond reproach, but as you wish. The birthkey will remain secret." He lifted the decanter and poured a full glass of medeaok. "A last march then. For the freedom of Fendellin and all ancient realms of the earth!"

"For freedom! For Fendellin!" they cheered, draining their glasses.

They talked for most of that day and late into the night, before eventually parting in high spirits to seek rest. Except for Gralen, who, despite his traumas over the last two days, was eager to spend time with Sedgewick and explore the city.

By the next morning, King Baillum had sent word out across the city and surrounding lands to marshal the last of Fendellin's remaining lords, together with their best captains and military minds. Within days, they had hastily made their way to the city's war rooms, to discuss the battle ahead. The fifth new moon passed as an ominous blackness.

King Baillum stood at the head of a huge table made entirely from marble and constructed with twenty segments, each representing one of Fendellin's ruling houses.

There now remained only five including Mund'harr. Korrun looked mournfully at the empty places and wondered what individual fates had befallen the nobles that had once gathered there.

"Let us get the introductions out of the way," Baillum said gesturing. "This is a Grand Magus of the old arts and an adversary of M'Sorreck, Marvalla Agyk. A Eurasian dragon of the northern realms, Gralen. A wicca from Urallaia, Wendya Undokki and an honored dwellfr, Korrun of Koralan! They have traveled far and through great peril to be here."

Hushed gasps and whispers rose from around the table as each figure stared at the four friends in studied disbelief while they recounted their journey.

"Fortune favors us this day, that such honored outsiders sit amongst us. Now, let us introduce ourselves," Baillum smiled, and nodded to a kind but haggard-looking dworll across the table from him.

The figure, unusually tall and gaunt, smiled warmly at the strangers, though his face seemed strained, as if he concealed some harrowing tale that still haunted him.

"I am Lord Lorrin of the Kasra Forest Realm to the north. All our woodsmen and people welcome you," he said, bowing his head, his shock of white hair pulled into loose braids behind him. "May you herald a change in our fortunes, we are much in need of it," he smiled.

King Baillum cast his eyes over the friends. "Lord Lorrin's people and lands have been the worst affected by M'Sorreck. I have told you already of the loss of their capital, Kasra-Naru, but many other sorrows have befallen them since that dreadful day."

Next, a broad-shouldered and sturdy gentleman, stout in frame, with a darker complexion and hazel eyes to match his hair, stood up at the far end of the table and bowed graciously to all. "My name is Nerrus, Lord of the Lakelands to the south," he motioned to a small dark-haired figure beside him. "This is my daughter, Orrla, the last heir of my line. She is captain of our troops and will serve you well," he glanced across the table and smiled at a young dworll, clad in simple deerskin. "She is an excellent horse master, so beware Hallm, she may take your place as the fastest rider in Fendellin!" he laughed and sat down.

Orrla briefly bowed. "*Narrock see*, welcome all," she said, glancing at the witch with a smile, her dark eyes straying toward Frell for a moment.

King Baillum beckoned to another figure, lither than the others, sitting upright only a few spaces away. The dworll stood up slowly, an austere and rather stiff manner to him, much akin with Baillum, Mr. Agyk thought. "I am Lord Perral, ruler of the western realms. Well met to you all," he said warmly. "Your presence here is most welcome!"

Lastly, a jovial figure that reminded them of King Dorrol, yet without his flamboyance, rose from his chair. His violet eyes looked kindly upon the visitors. "We welcome you gladly," he said, and motioned to the dworll in the deerskin that sat beside him. "This is my son, Hallm, captain of our guard. I am Lord Tollam. Many of our people have sought shelter in this fair city. We hope one day to return to our lands and repay its many kindnesses," Tollam said humbly.

Over the next few days, a constant flurry of scouts and messengers flowed to and from the compound, rushing hither and thither at great speed across the lands, while the people of the city looked nervously on.

By now, news of the strangers' arrival, and of a mysterious discovery that could bring a glimpse of hope to all had spread throughout the city and plains like wildfire.

Gralen sat perched high on one of the city's spires, basking in the late morning sun. He enjoyed the cooling breeze upon his scales and the scent of rain in the air. This land was everything he had hoped and dreamed of, a land where he could truly fly free.

"What are you doing here? Why aren't you down there?"

Gralen opened his eyes. Rollm was hovering above him, with a quizzical and slightly irritated expression on his face.

"I thought I'd leave them up to it for a while," Gralen yawned. "They're busy making big speeches in there," he rolled his eyes. "I'll get the gist of it later."

Rollm settled on the ledge beside him. "You're not worried?"

Gralen glanced at him. "I've seen a few battles in my time. There's no reason to suppose this is any different. No, my only worry is for the old man and Wendya."

"Sedgewick believes this coming war is a war to end all wars."

Gralen closed his eyes again. "I've heard that before as well. I just want Mr. A to be alright and Wend' to be safe."

Rollm shifted uneasily. "I think the fate of the future starts or ends here! If M'Sorreck isn't stopped now … it will be too late to ever stop him!" With that the young dragon abruptly dropped off the ledge and glided away.

Gralen watched him soar into the sky and disappear from view. He liked the young draken, even if he was naïve. He sighed and lifted his head to the sky as clouds drifted across the sun and heavy rainstorms gathered pace in the north, obscuring the mountains behind a shadowy veil.

Soldiers and civilians alike were marshaled. Sedgewick called forth every fÿrren of pure heart to the city and every weapon was collected and counted. Horses were gathered, war-wagons stocked and readied, and forges in the city and outskirts were set to work making weapons, shields and armor for all those strong enough to bear them. The days wore on and the wheels of war grinded into motion.

"We have less than a month now." King Baillum said, turning to Mr. Agyk. "We must be ready no later than three weeks from today. It is normally a four day march to Kavok. But we will try to make it in only three, if our pace is swift and we take little rest. By the third night we must be there. It will be the new moon you are waiting for … let us hope that the cover of darkness may prove to be our ally," he reflected, his face troubled. "Are you sure you want to wait, wizard? We could leave sooner. Our people could be ready in … less than fourteen days," Baillum watched the little figure. "If we wait, the timing will be very close!"

"I know. I have little time left, but I must prepare and Wendya must be ready," the wizard replied quietly, looking up at the skies. "In either case, you are right, we must be there by the new moon. If I do not regain my powers by the first light of that new dawn, this battle could be over before it has begun ...," he paused. "Yes, the timing is very short."

Baillum looked at him with pity in his eyes. "So be it. We will wait for a short while before riding out to war!"

Chapter Fifteen

The Silent Watch

Wendya had had another restless night and awoke early. Her room was cold and the city lay silent and pensive. She peeled back the bed sheets and stepped over to the window, wrapping herself in a large, beautifully embroidered quilt. Opening the shutters, she could feel the icy air against her skin. Her eyes were sore. She instinctively touched her face, and only then realized that she had been crying in her sleep.

The olive light outside, not yet dawn, seemed more welcoming than the empty darkness inside. Listening carefully she could just hear the rumblings of Gralen down the hall, his snoring echoing through the heavyset walls, bringing her a measure of comfort, amidst the strange surroundings. She opened the heavy latch on the door, being careful not to make a sound, and left the chamber. Beyond the narrow hall, which stretched the length of the guest wing, lay a series of corridors and stairs. With little direction she headed toward one of them. Feeling the roughness of the hewn stone steps beneath her bare feet, she followed the staircase down until it hit its first opening, a small landing which led to a low arched door and out onto the battlements. She pushed at the door and was suddenly in the chill of the open air.

The crenellations rose and fell in reassuring uniformity, but it was the view Wendya was drawn to. The hills and plains stretched out in an endless blurry patchwork of blues, violets and grays. Everything looked ordered and peaceful as if the coming storm were just a fleeting nightmare that would vanish with the sun. Wendya strolled along the parapet, watching the dark immovable line of the distant mountains; their tops shrouded in mist, their feet plunged in shadow, disappearing amongst the dusky dales and foothills. She found a sheltered spot out of the wind and nestled between the battlements, the cold stone feeling unusually smooth and polished beneath her toes. She sighed heavily. Her heart ached at the danger they all faced.

As she let her mind drift, she was suddenly aware of hundreds of shadowy gray figures moving in endless and soundless streams along the city walls above and below her. The Silent Watch continued their vigil, each cloaked and keen-eyed soldier a member of the city guard, each pair of eyes relentless and fixed on the skies and lands around.

She sat for hours as the stars slowly faded one by one, cradling herself as she had done so many times as a child whenever she felt lonely or miserable. The dawn brought a bitter wind from the north, chasing the clouds before it. The land was so wondrous, so beautiful and majestic. But she missed her little home with its tumbling ivy and clumps of dangling moss, the meadows of cotton grass in summertime and the sweet-smelling blossom of the linden trees. But, despite the harshness of winter, this time of year was always her favorite and brought such peace and snowy silence. Somehow the magic of her forest seemed more real, and certainly more hospitable than this vast open space.

"The snowdrops will be out and the ptarmigans will be getting ready for the coming of spring," she thought.

Grand castles in the clouds were no place for her. Even when she was a child — playing with Halli and staying in Kallorm's White Palace — they'd creep down to the kitchens and servants' quarters to feast at night and find a warm little nook near the hearth to sleep. Snuggling under layers of woolly blankets suited her far better than the silk sheets of four-poster beds. But none of that mattered now. Nothing seemed to matter. The days were drawing closer and time seemed both frozen, and quickening, slipping away from her like the ebbing tide. What could she do in a battle other than get in everybody's way? She was no soldier, nor great sorceress. Her supernatural powers were limited and just as likely to cause disaster as actually do any good … Marval's faith in her was always unrealistic and this time, he was counting on her with his life!

She pulled the quilt tightly round her.

Her only effective skill was her ability to mind-see. Her foresight and her premonitions had often proved right, but it was these which now plagued her daylight hours and kept her awake at night too. No matter what she tried, her dreams always showed the same hazy images … pain, grief and loss. With each new dawn came the sickness and cloying fear that, whatever may come, however the battle against M'Sorreck and his minions might end … she would lose someone dear to her.

Hours and days of waiting and toil rolled past. The green wizard watched the moon and knew his last day was approaching. Preparations continued ceaselessly as the city itself was made ready to protect and defend its walls once the army of Fendellin marched out to war. While the city and its people held its breath, all four companions made themselves busy. The witch divided her time between the old wizard and the dwelf. Under Mr. Agyk's tutelage, she worked tirelessly on a variety of counter spells, invisibility potions, spirit shields and amulets of ancient herbal magic to protect their wearers. Her instruction included spell casts, sorcery techniques and focused on developing and honing her own powers and mind-seeing abilities.

"Again! You must try to focus!" Mr. Agyk snapped. "Focus!"

Wendya sighed and tried again. They had been slaving all day and she was exhausted. She closed her eyes and quieted her breathing, so even the slow, steady beat of her heart faded in her ears. A large marble urn marked with the royal crest rattled suddenly on its plinth, lifted into the air as easily as a feather, slowly rotated and gently hovered above the battlements.

"That is it!" cried the wizard, his eyes unflinching, his voice soft and low. "Now remember it is merely an extension of you, as if you were stretching out your hand. Good. Now... think where you want it to go and move it there."

Suddenly, the jar began to wobble.

"Careful! Focus! Focus!"

Wendya opened her eyes to see it plummet down and crash somewhere below. She rushed over to the walls. "SORRY!"

"Well, I see you've been having fun!" chuckled a voice from behind them.

Korrun perched on a narrow parapet, his legs dangling precariously over the edge as he leaned casually on one of the giant buttresses that supported the city's many towers. His arms were crossed and he had an unusually playful expression on his face.

"Thank you, but that was not quite the idea," Mr. Agyk sighed.

Wendya shrugged. "I'm sorry. I just couldn't decide where I wanted to put it!"

"Well, I think we have done enough for today ...," the little scholar said wearily. "I need to talk to the King and Lord Tollam. I certainly hope their plans are less ... breakable!" he said with a wry smile. "I will see you both at dinner tonight. Oh, Korrun, have you seen Gralen?"

"Yes, he's out with Rollm and Sedgewick again."

The wizard nodded. "They are inseparable these days. Fine, well, she is all yours!" he smiled again and, picking up his tiny cloak, he trudged toward the Senate house.

Wendya sighed and slumped to the ground in an exhausted heap. After the mage's intensive lessons, she always found herself utterly shattered. Though, in truth, no matter how tired she was, she still looked forward to her fighting sessions with the dwelf. Every day, they spent hours together working on defensive and attacking manoeuvers and weaponry skills, trying to ready her for the battle ahead.

Korrun smiled and jumped off the parapet, sliding down the almost vertical sloping wall before landing squarely on his feet.

"I don't think I can move ... really," she complained. "Can't we have a day off?"

The dwelf laughed. "Certainly not. There's still a lot of work to do," he said, gently pulling her to her feet. "I know it's hard, but we're only trying to prepare you. Battle is ugly and brutal ..."

"No more sermons please! I've had Marval moaning at me all day!"

Korrun laughed again, his mood unusually jocund. "Fine. We'll take it easier for today only, but tomorrow we'll have to start on your riding skills!"

The next morning came, raw and bright. It was early and Korrun had already spent several hours in the stable blocks, walking and grooming the horses before collecting a rather nervous Wendya.

"I see you're wearing the clothes Orrla left you. I'm glad. Those dresses of yours … are not suitable," he smiled, his deep blue eyes lingering on the witch.

Wendya stood awkwardly, tightening the belt around her gray tunic shirt. "I'm just not used to wearing trousers," she said, scuffing her heavy boots on the ground.

"You'll be thankful for them at the end of a long day of riding. Here," he beckoned, "we're very lucky. They have the best horses I've ever seen," he enthused, tethering two unusually dark tarpans before saddling them up. He ran his fingers through the bristling mane of the tallest horse, a regal looking creature of great power and even temperament.

"Lord Tollam's son, Hallm, is an excellent horse master. He runs all these stables. He's handpicked some great tarpans for us, very swift and strong. We'll take them out across the flats to start with," he said, turning to pat the smaller black steed. "This is Nallo, she'll be yours. She's good-natured and very fast and the taller one is Enbarr, named after the mythical horse of the elder days."

After a lot of encouragement, Wendya eventually mounted her horse without falling straight off. Gripping the reins in an iron clench, she followed the dwelf down the city's steep and snaking roads until, finally, they left the mountain, passed beyond the city's defenses and found themselves in the whispering soft plains of Mund'harr.

Korrun breathed deeply. "Better than any tonic I know," he sighed.

The young witch remained quiet, watching Nallo's every move intensely.

He laughed. "Try to relax. She won't do anything you don't tell her to … That's it. Remember how I showed you to hold the reins …," he said, watching her fumble with the straps. She seemed distracted today. "You look tired."

"I'm fine … just not sleeping very well."

Korrun looked at her. "Anything I can do?"

"Oh … nothing. I'm just worrying as usual," she said with a nervous smile. "I'll be fine once I learn to ride this thing."

"You're doing well. You're a natural," he lied.

As Wendya's slow and sometimes painful tuition continued, Gralen found himself immersed in a world unlike anything he'd ever known. Every day held a new wonder for him.

Once he had fully satisfied himself that the little wizard had been restored to better health, he was more than pleased to wait for war. Spending most of his waking hours in the company of Sedgewick, Rollm and the other dragons, he felt like a young draken once more, giddy with excitement and full of questions. It seemed an odd coincidence that Gralen was never too far away when the witch and dwelf were training.

Without invitation or discord, Rollm quickly appointed himself as the green dragon's guide and proceeded to take great pleasure in whisking him around the sights of Mund'harr at break-neck speed. Gralen didn't mind, he enjoyed the young draken's company, in fact he seemed to be enjoying *everything*.

As they explored the lofty capital and the intricate beauty of its buildings and open squares, he could not help comparing it to the grand sprawl of Kallorm and its false daylight. Here, no starstones were needed, no artificial day. Here, everything was air and light, not the searing heat of the jungle metropolis. Why have a fake sky when you could have the real thing above you and feel the warming sun on your wings? Gralen smiled, he could so easily live here for the rest of his days.

Gralen watched his young escort as he explained some of the history of Fendellin — of Sedgewick's long lordship over the dragon races, of the battles they'd waged and of the Golden City itself, the most magical and ancient of the world's cities.

"You must see this ... the hanging gardens of Astarri. Whenever I'm in the city I always come here. Most of the dragon gods and fÿrren temples are around here," Rollm said eagerly.

He pushed at a round and heavy-looking copper gate with the weathered head of a grand dragon on it. Gralen gasped at the dappled beauty beyond. A shimmering path of pale quartz led to a wide and breezy tree-lined avenue and the most beautiful garden Gralen had ever seen.

They strolled through the cold sunshine as it streamed through the silver-leaved branches that made a bower above their heads, and gazed at the scene that greeted them.

"Wend' would love this!" Gralen murmured with wonder in his eyes.

"Isn't it amazing? It's as old as the city itself ... but we've had to work hard to keep it this way. If Varkul and his fengal vipers could get close to it, they would have burnt all this to ash long ago!"

The water gardens, as Rollm described them, stretched and curled round the entire southern quarter of the city, clinging to the steepest flank of Mund'harr's south pinnacle and rising up in tier upon tier of draping, lush, green vegetation until they were lost in the mists. Exotic flowers cascaded from every level, dripping from balconies, pillars and trellises as blankets of color. Arches appeared smothered in fragrant blooms almost more exquisite than the views they framed. Fountains danced from pool to pool or trickled into quiet streams as great swathes of dangling vines swayed in the breeze from overhanging struts above. They wandered through the gardens for some time, so dazzling even in their winter splendor. Gralen was led to the many dragon-dedicated temples that lay dotted amidst the vistas and winding steps.

"These are the temples of mighty A'Hia, S'Devra and O'Borros, forbearers and greatest of our kin," Rollm announced, loving his role as guide and tutor. "All Fendellons come here in reverence to give prayer and gifts for their many labors and sacrifices. They helped create this city and many others."

Gralen shook his head. "I don't know them," he replied blankly. "Marval has a great library but I use it for flying practice!" he smirked and fell quiet, overwhelmed by it all. He looked at the domed buildings, at their sinuous carvings and spiraling pillars, each one an entwined dragon, at the frescoes and bejeweled ceilings of their inner vaults, like sparkling grottos, and lastly, at the vast granite tombs themselves. Even the arches that supported such lofty heights were painted and inlaid with fiery gems and the iridescent scales of the honored dead.

Gralen remained unusually speechless for most of the day and for the many days that followed as his draken guide continued the tour of the city's ancient towers, ziggurats and the many statues and dragon sculptures of breath-taking beauty.

"The city of dragons!" Gralen whispered.

He smiled as he listened to the enthusiastic young dragon tumble over his words in excitement. He liked Rollm greatly, in fact he reminded him of himself when he was a growing draken … such impatience and animated curiosity.

However, Gralen followed Sedgewick, the patriarchal leader of the fÿrren order, and eldest member of their kin, doggedly as an eager schoolboy bedazzled by the arrival of a childhood hero.

For Gralen, the wealth of knowledge Sedgewick held was simply mesmerizing. He spoke nostalgically of times long before any of them had been born, of ancient, pre-history, when the world was young and full of magic, and dworlls and ællfrs roamed freely from pole-to-pole and sea-to-sea, ever exploring and seeking the knowledge of all things.

Sedgewick sat rather grandly, his long tail curled neatly into a tight coil at his feet.

"Great ice sheets, leagues thick, covered the world for many life times of man, joining lands and sculpting the earth. We fÿrrens were truly gods back then and our icy cousins in the north thrived, carving great labyrinths at both poles. Why, Ïssätun, the ice-city itself, was first carved and built by the great ice dragons and frost giants to protect our allies from the ravages of nature and from the terror of the Amarrok wolves. While the world changed and the exodus took the ællfrs away, our numbers still swelled," he said proudly. "We ruled the skies and heavens and were freer than the clouds. We were loved and worshipped by all in those early days, as bringers of life and fire, as shapers of stone and crystal and as portents of good fortune. Some were even seen as fertility gods! Those were simpler, more magical times for all folk, especially us," he sighed deeply. "But, there is little value in living in the past; we must look now to our future and remember that it is always the nature of things to change."

Gralen sat for hours listening to the old dragon tell stories and ancient tales of mythologies and histories he never knew; of ruling clans, feuding houses, bloodlines and lineages, different races and even their first dealings with humans.

"Now, Cecrops knew that, as a pure dragon, he would be feared and never accepted by the human primitives, so he visited the Mountain Oracle and sorceress deep in the roots of the Zagros. There he waited for seven long months without food or water and endured many trials, until the eclipse came and he was changed into a half-human. Leaving the mountains behind, he visited the struggling people of the sea-rock, and

167

using his great strength to rebuild their homes and help them with fire and life-giving water, they repaid him by declaring him their savior and ruler. He became the first King of the realm of Attica and the city of Cecropia — now called Athens — was founded." Sedgewick smiled and placed his arm around the Gralen's shoulder. "Now tomorrow, my young apprentice, I will tell you the full and true story of *N'Darra* whom the humans call Indra, and how her jealousy of Varuna caused her to slay her firstborn, the first and greatest of all dragon-kind, and how the skies split asunder and wept, drowning the world in a mighty flood. Every year thereafter, a great deluge falls in remembrance and sorrow of the end of that precious life."

Gralen listened enthralled as an entirely new world was opened up to him. For the first time in his long life, he felt truly whole and complete.

It had been the end of another exhausting day. As rain clouds gathered for yet one more downpour, the dwelf and witch decided to saddle up and head back to the city. Nallo and Enbarr stood grazing beside the rickety stone frame of a granary-house, just one of many ruined and abandoned buildings that lay peppered about the plains, as if some fickle child had scattered its toys in a temper. Korrun and Wendya had spent the last few hours sheltering beneath its ramshackle roof, practicing yet more sword skills as the skies had steadily darkened around them.

"If this doesn't work ... if we lose the battle," Wendya said, shaking her head.

Korrun looked at her, his face impassive. "If we fail ... Fendellin will fall. Morreck will take this land as his stronghold and everyone in it will be enslaved or killed."

Wendya sighed and started pacing the room. "Mr. Agyk believes the whole world is at risk. That Morreck's lust for power won't stop with just our kind. After Fendellin, Ìssátun and Kallorm ... it will just be a matter of time before humans are next."

Korrun nodded. "It makes sense, if Marval is right and M'Sorreck has the ability to take any form he wishes, he could easily assume the identity of a world leader, a ruler of men. With that power, he could start wars, kill millions ... even bring about a global apocalypse!"

"Judging by the actions of most human rulers, he may well have already started!" the witch lamented. "He can be stopped, can't he?"

Korrun looked at her unflinchingly, his face a study of calmness. "I don't know," he said simply, an answer the witch was not expecting from someone so resolute. "But we must try."

"I hate this waiting!" she exclaimed. "This dreadful, endless nothingness. I feel like I can't breathe!" She threw her saddle into the dirt with a loud thud. "Don't you feel it? It's like the air's being squeezed out of everyone!" she slumped down, turning to watch the long grasses sway in the wind like a mass of swirling hair caught in a great current. "Everyone has this ... *look*," she murmured, "like they're waiting for death!"

Korrun bent down and picked up the saddle. "I thought you didn't want this battle to happen?" he asked calmly.

"I don't … of course I don't. I just can't stand this … *nothingness!*" she was aware she sounded like a petulant child, but she couldn't help it. For the life of her she could not understand the wizard's desire to keep waiting … for what? Until the sixth moon came and it was already too late? It seemed utter madness to leave it for so long, with so little time for error. Besides, the old chap seemed revived and almost back to full health, if not size. No, there was something else, something he wasn't telling them, something holding him back.

Korrun looked at her. "Wars tend to happen this way. A short pause before … It won't be long now. The scouts have been sent out as far as the Shudras and a few beyond, all the ruling houses are gathered and Sedgewick's dragons are ready," he glanced out as a roll of heavy thunder rumbled away in the distance and the heavens suddenly opened. "It's only a short burst I think, but there's a storm coming up from the south. We shouldn't stay long."

Wendya stared out of the empty door with a distant look upon her face. "Korrun," she said quietly. "Do you believe that dreams tell us things, that they can become real?"

The dwelf looked surprised by the question. "I don't know. I don't really dream. I suppose they can. Your … mind-seeing? Is that what you mean?"

"Not really. Premonitions are usually different, you see them when you're awake and when you're channeling powers. I mean *dreams*, when you're *asleep*."

Korrun shrugged. "I'm not a scholar or one of the wise," he paused. "Perhaps our dreams are our conscience speaking to us … a way of reminding us of our mistakes."

"I'm sure you haven't made any," she smiled.

"Oh I have, far too many," he laughed awkwardly and fell silent. He crouched down, slowly curling up the battered leather sheet which he had used to carry the many fighting blades and short-swords they had been practicing with, and when at last he spoke again, his voice seemed distant and full of sadness. "I think we all carry burdens … things we need to atone for," he said sadly. "Dreams are dreams; I wouldn't pay them much heed."

Wendya watched him. He was such a grim, taciturn figure, so tall and full of strength and purpose and serious intent, but under that veneer it seemed to her that he was as lost as a child, as lost as she felt.

"What do you mean? … What burdens do you carry?" she asked gently.

Korrun stood still for a moment and tried to smile but couldn't. "Just old wounds," he answered quietly, his eyes betraying a deep sorrow she had never seen before.

"About your younger brother?" she pressed.

He nodded and, taking the leather bundle and saddle, he promptly went outside to Enbarr and the other horse.

The gray rain pounded down like so many angry fists on what remained of the granary roof, the thunderous sheets soaking the dwelf to the skin in seconds. Wendya viewed him in the failing light, his dark hair falling lank about him, his face hidden in shadow. He was a strange fellow, always guarded. She herself had spent so much of her life keeping away from others, safe and unhurt; … never once had she expected to meet someone the same, just as alone, just as lonely.

The horses were restless, their coarse manes collecting the rain like upturned brooms, before they overflowed into twisting little streams that ran down their sides and dripped in thick splashes beneath them. Korrun led them to the adjoining barn for shelter and groomed their coats before returning.

"The horses are jittery," he said, dripping in the doorway as he peered out, his dark skin glistening in the dim light. "We'll have to be careful. Varkul's serpents may be about. It's difficult to see with all this low cloud, but it might be best if we wait for the rain to pass."

"You're soaking!" Wendya said rushing to get him a blanket. "Here, you'll catch a cold."

He took it and put it over his head. "Thank you."

"I'm sorry for … prying," she said softly trying to catch his eye. "It's an awful habit of mine. I ask too many questions and you obviously don't want to talk about it."

He shrugged. "No, it's fine. I just never speak about it. I suppose I should, as I'm fighting in his name. I should at least be honest," he wiped the cloth very slowly over his face, a deliberate gesture Wendya thought, as if he were trying to cleanse himself of some great sin. "My brother, Sorall. I caused his death. I am responsible," he said suddenly.

He sighed heavily and a shiver convulsed through his body as he said the words. Wendya looked at his trembling hands. He sat down, wrapping the blanket over his shoulders as the rain continued outside. He'd never looked so miserable.

"Korrun, you don't need to say anything."

"I know, but it's time I did. It's why I'm here. I'm not avenging my brother, not just … I'm trying to make amends. I thought if I could try to atone for what I did …"

Wendya sat beside him but his eyes and thoughts were fixed elsewhere.

"I was the Captain of the City and Royal Guard, before Urell. The safety of Kallorm and of course White Palace itself, rested on me. It was my responsibility to protect it no matter what …," he paused for a moment. "We'd had wargol attacks before, many of them, but never as bad. The battle was unrelenting. Where the wargol demons came from and how they got in, we didn't know … but they and *he* were there for more than a massacre, they had a purpose to them and it fuelled the battle, made it fiercer and more desperate. If only I'd known then what Morreck was looking for, that it was all a diversion so he could get his birthkey!" he glanced at the chain around Wendya's neck, the glowing key still hidden beneath her clothes. "We had secured several perimeters, inner and outer lines of defense throughout the city. The first lines fell fast. We evacuated the Royal House and the Council Chambers. But the chapels, the sanctuary, the Resting Rooms were still full of the wounded and those tending to them. I should have ordered them out!"

Wendya placed a hand on his shoulder. "It wasn't your fault."

"You don't understand," Korrun sighed. "I left my post! I abandoned my men! I was the senior commanding officer. I was stationed with a contingent of my soldiers in a perimeter around Palace Rock, to stop any wargols reaching the palace. We knew that would be their first target. We were beating them back, we were winning … then … I got distracted. Reports came that the wargols had set fire to the old market quarter, the soldiers there were being driven back by the hordes … I … ," he lowered his head, his eyes fixed on the ground. "There was a woman, the wife of one of the city counselors who lived there. We were …," he paused again, feeling the blood rush to his face. "I abandoned my post, my soldiers, to help, to rescue her … I left my post in the middle of battle. *I left my post!*" he kept repeating the words, his voice sounding hollow and drained. "I wasn't there to stop them … The wargols regrouped and broke through our lines, they … they swarmed over Palace Rock and massacred everyone on it, including my brother," he swallowed, battling to keep back the tears. "I am truly damned. I have the blood of a thousand souls on my hands … how do I atone for that?!" he whispered. "One thousand lives. That is my burden. That is the reason I'm here."

Wendya sat in silence, unsure of what to say. To see him in such pain made her heart ache. "King Dorrol …" she began.

"… doesn't blame me for anything, but he should. Those who were in my battalion and were there and argued, pleaded with me not to leave, see it differently. They hold me accountable. As they should," he said grimly, looking at Wendya to gauge her reaction. "I killed my brother and all those poor souls, just as certainly as if I'd taken a sword to them myself. Do you understand? Even here, my penance is too great to be settled."

"But it was war. You tell me enough, that war is ugly and brutal. You thought you were doing the right thing," the witch implored.

"Did I? … I don't know anymore. Did I abandon my soldiers to help the others or did I leave for my own self-interest? … For a woman I didn't even love?" he shook his head, "I just don't know anymore."

"You thought you were doing the right thing," she repeated. "Even if you had stayed, do you honestly think that you *alone* could have turned the tide and stopped them? Just you?"

"Well, we'll never know," he replied quietly.

The rain had stopped. For the first time that day, the sun pierced the cloud cover, leaching shafts of hazy light down to the plains below. Korrun sighed and watched the light flare toward the west.

"It's getting late. We should go. It's not safe for us to be out here after dark," he murmured with a worried expression. "I'm not quite the shining warrior you were all hoping for, am I?"

"No, you're not … you're more than we could have hoped for," she smiled, and before she knew what she was doing, she leaned over and kissed him tenderly on the lips.

"Sorry!" she said, springing back. "Uh, sorry, that … we should go," she burbled and quickly left.

The dwelf looked almost as startled as the witch. He touched his lips, smiled, and followed her out into the cool dusky air.

It was late and the city was quiet. Korrun had spent an increasing amount of time pacing the battlements alone, while its citizens slept. Occasionally through a passing archway he was aware of activity outside, of the quiet but ceaseless watch, an unyielding presence. He understood the life, the discipline, the routine and the hardships, the hours of cold and the endless waiting. He'd lived his whole life that way, amongst soldiers, and he found their presence comforting.

He found a stairwell leading to a cloistered corridor and an inner courtyard that he had not come across before. The courtyard was overlooked by galleried balconies on three sides and open to the northern plains on one. Yet it felt completely private and as secluded a place as he could think of.

The light from a dozen or so dragon lanterns flickered along the walls. The little reservoir of precious oil that dangled beneath each cup-like vessel, sustaining the flame, gave each lamp its own distinctive colored hue. Amongst the scented vines and the draping climbers that dangled off every pillar and balustrade, he could hear the sound of trickling water. It reminded him of home, of Kallorm's great sanctuary and the serenity of its gardens. He sighed. He had not visited those cloisters since the death of his brother.

The moon's silvery gaze was beautiful but had not yet reached this dark corner. He was suddenly aware of another figure amongst the gloom, deep in thought, moving silently between the beds of mountain orchids and snow poppies. The dappled blossom from the trees of winter cherry fell about her as she passed. He watched for a moment, utterly transfixed and quite unable to move. The figure, dressed in a simple tunic of dark green, with a heavy blanket wrapped around her, moved effortlessly — almost gliding — over the cobbles. From his vantage point he recognized who it was, and saw that she had been crying.

Wendya looked towards the plains, her gaze ever drawn to the north and west as if she could spy the cruel peaks of Kavok and Morreck's lair.

Mists rose from the mountain flanks, like Mund'harr itself was breathing. The wind picked up, growing colder and more unforgiving. She stood still, letting her hair and robes dance freely about her. If she could have grown wings, she would have flown far away.

"Bring me the wisdom of Astarri," she whispered to the stars. "End this uncertainty."

Korrun watched her. Her restlessness reminded the dwelf of himself. He hesitated for a moment. He wanted so much to speak to her, to comfort and hold her, but words escaped him. Reluctantly, he bowed his head, and faltering once more, he quietly turned and left.

The last weeks ticked away and soon the waiting was over.

Lord Tollam gazed out of the western window of his lodging, watching as the sentries changed guard. Korrun sat nearby. After his daily training sessions with Wendya, which he looked forward to more than he should, Korrun and Mr. Agyk had spent many evenings in the company of Lord Tollam and his son, Hallm.

"Our lands stretched over the western plateau from Felleucia in the north, to the Karrun Heights and the southern plains." Lord Tollam explained. "All lands west of the Fenorri River and east of the great descent. Atallum was our capital, in the times of my forefathers. After its destruction, Tolltek and Karu'harr became our home. Now, we traverse between there and here. As the attacks increased, many of our people fled to Fennem, or here, to greater safety." He looked toward his son. "We swallow our pride. The lives and safety of our people must come first. King Baillum has very kindly offered this city as a refuge to all and a second home away from our own." He placed his hand gently on Hallm's shoulder. "We will return to our lands, all of us, when this is over," he smiled.

The old statesman, who was the most beloved of Fendellin's great lords, and the eldest, was a boisterous host full of good humor and hospitality, a thoroughly "splendid fellow", as Mr. Agyk had remarked. Lord Tollam had a darkly comical air about him, as if he had grown to an age where life no longer held any surprises for him. He was as prepared for life or death as anyone they had ever met ... and completely at peace with it.

Korrun watched him relax into his chair. He reminded him of a stouter version of King Dorrol, in character if not looks, who welcomed all guests with open arms. He was quite different from Mund'harr's rather frosty royal figurehead. Hallm, his son and most gifted Captain, obviously doted on his aging father, and seeing the two of them banter made the dwelf quite forlorn.

"Now you must try this vintage; it's the best medeaok in the land!" Hallm smiled, passing another brimming tankard toward his new friend. "How are you getting on with the stallion?"

"Enbarr was a great name for him. He's very swift."

Hallm laughed. "You should see my horse, Forriall, as golden as the grass, as quick as the wind and utterly fearless. I would have given him to you, only I could not bear to be parted from him!"

"It is true, I swear some days he lives in the stables with him," joked Tollam. "He will never find a wife!"

The fifth moon waxed pale in the night sky and began to wane, as finally the last day approached to set out to war.

A heavy anticipation hung in the air, a heady mix of fear and excitement, and a deep restlessness lay on the city and all its inhabitants.

While most of Fendellin's citizens had spent the last precious hours in quiet meditation surrounded by family and loved ones, others had thrown great parties, as if gearing themselves for hardships to come, and grasping joy while they still could.

Gralen enjoyed all aspects of the revelry, happy to be surrounded by his own kindred at last. Mr. Agyk, feeling a renewed vigor and strength, had been pleased to join in with these strange festivities for a little time. But Wendya, like Korrun, was in no mood to celebrate.

As Mr. Agyk bade them all goodnight, Wendya slipped out of the Grand Hall and followed her old friend.

"Marval! Can I talk with you?"

The little wizard stood on the walls overlooking the darkening plains around. Camp fires glittered below in the cool night, like so many fallen stars, and a soft breeze rustled in his silvery hair.

"Have you had enough of the party?" he asked, sensing the witch's anxiety.

Wendya sat on the wall beside him. "Marvalla ... I don't know if I can do this."

Mr. Agyk looked at her. "I wish you did not have to," he said quietly, his voice full of sadness. "The precious waters here have revitalized me, but I do not know if I have the strength left to defeat him."

Wendya's mind was swimming. "Will this end it?"

"If we succeed?"

"Yes ... will Morreck be destroyed once and for all?" Wendya asked.

The old man leaned against the battlements, his little arms folded against the wind and cold. "I honestly do not know."

"But?"

"My heart tells me ... no. Whether it is truly possible to completely destroy a thing like M'Sorreck, and any lingering essence of him, I do not know. Even if we succeed, there are bound to be others. Those he has trained, less powerful, yes, but still a threat, others to take his place." he sighed heavily. "My honest opinion is that this is a crucial battle ... but, the last battle? No. I fear this may only be the beginning of a larger war."

"Then why fight it? If it is hopeless, why fight, why now?"

He looked at her, a mixture of concern and puzzlement over what she was saying.

"I mean ... why not find a way to take the orb instead of destroying it. Surely his power source could ... recharge you, give you your powers back, without you or any of us ever having to confront him!"

"You believe we could slip into his fortress without a battle? No. We must confront him. Even if your plan were to work, where would it lead us? His power source, like the creature itself, will undoubtedly corrupt any who try to harness it."

"But you'd be safe! You'd be whole again, that's all I care about!"

"And the rest of the world? Do we once again turn our backs and close our eyes to the evil in front of us? You know all too well, the enemy you turn your back on, grows stronger in your absence. M'Sorreck has to be stopped, we have to try; there is no other way!"

"You don't need to go tomorrow. We have the key, we have an army! We have a legion of dragons!"

"My dear Wendya," he said softly, his voice seeming to mingle in the air as if it were the sigh of an ocean. "I was going to say the same to you, though I know, as do you, that we are both needed ... This is bigger than just me. I am only a small part of this story. If Morreck defeats me and my full powers become his, he will become virtually indestructible, if he is not already," the wizard paused.

"We must prevent that from happening at all costs. If the battle goes badly for me … I cannot allow him to consume my remaining powers. If it comes to that … I have made my decision, only in a death of my choosing will I deny him what he craves."

Wendya gasped.

"That is a last resort," Mr. Agyk stressed. "Only if it becomes clear that I cannot defeat him, will I take that decision … But he will have a fight on his hands, make no mistake! He has greatly underestimated me, my remaining this size has helped in that, I think."

"You're going to sacrifice yourself?!" cried the witch in horror.

Mr. Agyk sighed. "Only if there is no other way. Listen to me, Wendya. If he defeats us, if Fendellin falls, Kallorm will be next and every remaining dworll stronghold after that. You know this! Our world is fragile, it will fall quickly, and if there are none of us left, the humans will be next. This battle is crucial to all of us, every living thing on this planet!"

"What are you saying?" she asked, feeling the blood drain out of her.

"No matter what happens, you must carry out your part of the plan, you must reach his power source and destroy it. Do not stop or hesitate, not for me or Gralen or Korrun or anyone else. Do you understand? If you falter, even for a moment, we could all perish!"

Wendya nodded. She felt sick.

"Promise me … promise me you will not stop. That when the time comes you will run," he insisted, "and you will not look back!"

Wendya stared into the little wizard's eyes and tried to blink away her tears.

"Promise me!" he demanded.

"I promise … I'll run … I promise," she answered.

"Good, good," the old man's voice became soft once more. "I know there is a great burden on you, on all of us. Time is very short …"

"Don't say it!" Wendya pleaded, the tears now streaming down her face. "Please I can't hear it, not now!"

The wizard smiled, his silver eyes full of gentle sympathy. It was his friends, Gralen, the young warrior Korrun, and this fragile child before him, that made his heart break with worry.

"Just know," he murmured. "That I love you and I always will."

Suddenly, for a moment, he seemed to grow to his real size once more, a comforting old gent with a kindly face and a receding mane of wild, wiry hair. As he put his arms around her, she melted into him, burying her face in his robes.

"You have been the greatest joy in my life … the daughter I never had," he smiled.

Wendya sobbed and felt the wizard lightly kiss her forehead, his strong arms clutching her tightly then slowly dissolving away.

She opened her eyes, but he was gone.

"Are you alright?" called another voice from the darkness.

Wendya sat on the ground, the cold stone of the battlements hard against her back. She hated the night, she hated the moon, but she dreaded the dawn. Her heart felt as if it were ripping apart, an engorged thing twice its size that would burst in her chest and take her with it. She had never felt so miserable.

"Are you alright?" came the voice again.

She looked up and saw Korrun standing there, unsure whether to intrude or not.

"I can't lose him," she whispered.

Korrun came over and gently knelt beside her.

"Everyone I love … leaves me. I can't lose him too, my heart couldn't take it!" she wept.

The dwelf glanced downward. "You'd be surprised what the heart can endure," he said.

He looked at the young girl beside him. The depth of her sadness filled him with a longing and a heartbreak he had never felt before. He wanted so much to just hold her. She stood up, her legs unsteady. She was motionless, her dark hair flowing loosely behind her, her green, watery eyes full of anguish. Her pale skin glowed in the starlight like luminescent porcelain, so fragile, so easily hurt. The dwelf had an overwhelming desire to protect her.

"I cannot lose him," she whispered again, tears staining her freckled cheeks.

"You won't," he murmured, hardly daring to touch this rare flower in case it should wither in his hands. "I promise you, you won't. Marval is strong, stronger than we know. He will defeat Morreck, and all of this will be over."

The words were meaningless echoes in the dark. Wendya stared at the distant mountains, wishing she could sail above those peaks, as free as an eagle, as an empty nothingness.

Korrun tried to catch her gaze. "Believe in your own strength. I know you are frightened, we all are. A wise old man once told me that courage comes from those who are terrified but still choose to face their fears … You will find your strength and Marval will find his."

"I hope you're right," she whispered.

At last she turned her gaze towards the dwelf, his dark skin shimmering in the night, his hair pulled back too sternly from his face. There was something different about him. His eyes caught hers for an instant and she sensed, or recognized, that deep sadness and loneliness, similar to her own, and a hint of something else. He smiled and without saying another word he embraced her tightly and let her weep until she was spent. Outstretching his hand he led her away, and by taking it, she finally turned her back on the night.

Chapter Sixteen
The Last March

At last, the day arrived. Fendellin's bell towers rang out in unison, their clear chimes heralding in the new day and mustering all those who could fight. Rumor of the coming war spread quickly, as the main host gathered in the shadow of Mund'harr. The last march of Fendellin had begun.

Dawn broke over the city. It had rained heavily during the night, cleansing the streets. Mund'harr's waterfalls, swollen by the downpour, roared down the mountainside, sending great wafts of spray into the air.

The surrounding plains lay shrouded in a milky blanket of fog that stretched its fingers for miles. Only the twinkling lights of the gate towers and the city's ramparts below were visible.

Uneasiness fell on the city. All knew that their country's future rested on the success or failure of the battle. A failure would almost certainly mean the fall of Fendellin. Every last resource had now been gathered and would be spent in a final desperate attempt to overthrow the power that had threatened them for so long.

Life stirred in the shadowed streets. Everything lay drenched. Rain dripped ceaselessly from the roof tiles and swilled in little streams down the middle of the cobbled streets. The city flags hung lifelessly in the still air, a bad omen for the day. The last armory and forge fires were doused and the horses and beasts of burden were made ready.

Wendya had not slept at all that night, listening to the howling wind. She joined Mr. Agyk, Gralen, and the others for an early breakfast in the King's banquet hall.

"You know, you were very lucky," Hallm announced, "... to have survived being attacked by fire wolves in the Grey Forest. They're vicious creatures. Attacking Wendya, then all of you ... you were very lucky to escape. So M'Sorreck is hunting individual targets as well as attacking cities like ours, and Kallorm!"

"Yes," answered the wizard quietly, his eyes wandering over to a silent Wendya. "Certainly he wants dominion over all ... submit or perish."

"Do not forget," Mr. Agyk continued, "Wendya is guardian of the Grey Forest. The ancient trees possess a primal magic, very potent and powerful. If Morreck could harness it ... it would increase his strength a hundredfold."

Hallm shrugged and looked to his father. "Well, we shall see his end soon!"

Lord Tollam smiled and raised his goblet. "Hail to that!"

The friends ate a light breakfast before joining the heads of the army and other troops outside, a strange assortment of dworll captains and dragon races.

They gathered in the city's main assembly point, a large open plaza flanked by storehouses and granaries, beneath the columns of the Golden Palace and the Grand Hall. The crowded masses waited in bated silence. At last, King Baillum appeared at the top of the palace steps and climbed onto a tiered rostrum, a ziggurat overlooking the square.

Immediately greeted by a great rumbling barrage of cheers, the Dworll King stood motionless for a moment before raising his hands. He beckoned for silence and spoke.

"Fendellons, free folk of this land, fỳrrens and dworll alike, the time has come to fight!" Baillum's voice rang out clearly in the cool damp air and seemed to lift the hearts and spirits of those he addressed. "This will be our greatest battle and may prove the hardest to win, but win we will! We fight to safeguard all that we hold sacred, our homes, our families, our freedom. We fight for all those who have been lost and taken so cruelly from us." Wendya glanced toward Korrun, who stood nearby, his lips uttering some quiet prayer. Sedgewick too bent his head, as if the King's words evoked a sudden pain. "We fight for our future and the very survival of Fendellin!" the King bellowed.

His voice carried on the breeze. He stepped forward to the edge of the ziggurat. A gust of wind caught his cloak, revealing the King's livery beneath. He stood like a statue of the great warrior-kings of old. His bronze hair, streaked with silver, flowed behind him, and his dark eyes glittered in the gloom with a look of steely determination. He wore a simple crown that shone with a light so brilliant, it was as if he were wearing a crown of real stars.

"The forces of evil threaten to engulf us," he thundered, "and turn this fair land into a hellish country, a realm and stronghold of darkness, which could infect the rest of the world. We must prevent it! If Fendellin, ancient heart of all our peoples, should be lost to tyranny, others will follow and then the planet itself … enslaved by the great Corruptor."

Baillum raised his sword defiantly in the air and roared. "We ride forth! For freedom! For Fendellin!"

"For freedom, for Fendellin!" echoed the troops in a deafening chorus. "For freedom, for Fendellin!" they chanted, their voices and spirits high.

Bell towers rang and trumpeters indicated the start of the great march. Banners unfurled, horses were reined in, and wagons were readied. The city's gates swung open, and led by King Baillum, the army marched forth.

Thousands upon thousands issued from the city confines and down Mund'harr's steep and twisting mountain roads. Feet, hoof and wheel clattering as they passed, through winding tunnels and over high, arched bridges that snaked round the mountain.

Marching across the abyssal moats that surrounded the mountain, they passed the last lonely gate tower before venturing out into the open. Then, as if a curtain had been dropped, they appeared to pass through a bubble and vanish from view.

"It worked!" Wendya cried, watching the long procession disappearing up ahead. "The invisibility spell is actually working!"

"Of course." Mr. Agyk smiled. "As planned, it will veil all from unfriendly eyes. Your powers have grown, my child, I could not have performed that spell without you. But, it will not endure for long … May it give us the cover we need!"

The Fendellon army traveled unseen through the southern plains. Turning west, they skirted the golden mountain, heading northward at a swift pace, toward Kavok and Morreck.

Meanwhile, the dragons, led by Sedgewick, took to the air in a mass of beating wings. Flying low over the heads of their dworll comrades, they too disappeared into the thin blue.

The invisibility spell had worked wonderfully, allowing the marching host to see each other, while cloaking them from the eyes of their foes. In this way, horses and beasts of burden trudged through the landscape oblivious of their appearance, with the only sign of their presence being the muffled sound of hooves and occasional braying.

The great army of Fendellin sallied forth as a shadow and a whisper in the grasses. A silent and unstoppable force that had been set in motion and could not be halted.

At the head of the army rode the King's host, with Frell beside his father. Wendya rode behind them mounted on Nallo, the black steed she had practiced riding on. Gralen, with Mr. Agyk perched on his shoulder, plodded alongside, his eyes constantly alert for any signs of danger.

Behind the royal host were the Fendellin lords and captains, leading their own army contingent, a mixture of trained warriors and soldiers, and inexperienced yeomen.

Korrun rode beside Lord Tollam and his son, listening with interest to their stories, as they discussed everything but the coming battle. "So you have been studying the maps?" Tollam asked. "I am not sure what use they are!" the dworll lord smiled grimly. "Our mapmakers have had to redraw Fendellin's lands more times than I can remember!" He paused for a moment. "Though Mund'harr, the Golden City is the capital of our fair country, Fendellin has always been governed by many city states, each with their own lands and borders. There were twenty ruling houses, now there are just four outside of the Golden City."

"Did M'Sorreck destroy them all?" asked the dwelf.

Lord Tollam looked at the warrior, so serious for one so young.

"Most of them were destroyed by M'Sorreck and his followers. We have all suffered great losses at his hand. Some declined naturally as the climates changed, others banded together. The Lakelands and great seas to the far south and east are ruled by Lord Nerrus. Most of the townships that survived lie next to or on the lakeshores. Its capital, Larroon is an island city protected by very deep waters. Lord Nerrus' people are great fishermen and seafarers."

"Lord Perral's realm lies to the west, a mountainous and volcanic region with very fertile soils. The bread basket of Fendellin! Most of Perral's people are arable farmers, or shepherds. Lord Lorrin's borders lie to the far northeast, the great forests of Kasra-Naru and Tellas. Woodsmen and craftspeople live there. The best armory in the land comes from there," Tollam sighed, "but all towns have declined," he shook his head.

"Never again shall we see the beauty of the Hanging Gardens of Kasra-Naru, unmatched by those in Sumer and Babylon or even our capital. Lorrin's people and his lands have been affected the worst by Morreck."

Korrun looked at the old dworll. "And your lands, my Lord?"

"Our lands have always been in close kinship with Mund'harr, from the great central plateau to the mountains in the north and deserts to the south. Our people are the finest horsemen and herdsmen you will ever see. The tarpans that are here today are Tollamic."

Korrun looked at his stallion, similar in so many ways to the ancient wild tarpans he had bred as a boy; with no forelocks to hide their proud, kingly faces, their thick coats and short, stiff manes bristled in the wind.

"They're beautiful beasts, very impressive," he replied. "Strong, but swift."

"Hallm is probably the best horse master you will ever meet. None can match his skill or speed on horseback."

The captain bowed his head. "They are a fine breed, easy to ride."

"No false modesty, please!" Lord Tollam laughed. "My son knows only too well that I am one of the worst riders in the realm! It is fortunate that he, and not I, trained our soldiers!"

Korrun smiled silently, his mind always wandering back to some dark place.

Tollam studied the troubled young dwelf. "You are different from the others, your friends," he said quietly, "I know their purpose in this. You will help them achieve their goal, no doubt, but there is something else that drives you, is there not?"

Korrun looked at the dworll. "Only my desire to see his evil end, my Lord."

Tollam nodded sadly, unconvinced of his answer and sensing some deeper reason. "Well, when the battle comes, do not be so eager to meet it. I do not know what event has set you on this path, but vengeance can bring nothing but pain in the end. You are too young to carry such hatred, my friend, be careful that it does not blind you," he warned solemnly.

They marched ever northward, denying weariness or rest as the day brightened into a damp February morning and the wind began to pick up. Mr. Agyk looked at the pale sky and watched the dragons glide effortlessly through the misty clouds. Gralen, who had insisted on carrying the wizard and traveling beside Wendya, kept his gaze ever skyward, a look of awe in his eyes as the shadows of his fÿrren kin passed silently above.

As the sun faded, they came to the north-western flank of the Mund'harr plateau, and the sheer drop to the distant gray lands below, stretching endlessly into the dusk. Here, far nearer to the edge of the precipice than Mr. Agyk would have liked, they rested a short while.

"We cannot tarry long," he sighed, peering nervously toward the edge. "The day is failing and we have been lucky... so far... but we should not trust in luck."

"At least the stealth spell you and Wend' concocted has worked wonders!" Gralen smiled.

Dreary hours passed as horse, beast and dworll rested weary bones.

Frell rode over to the group. "We're moving nearer to the Tolltek mountains. We'll make camp there, at the base. They should give us some protection, it is too open here."

"Can't we attempt the pass today?" Korrun asked, anxious to leave the vulnerable heights of the plateau behind.

Frell shook his head. "The sun is setting. We cannot hope to complete the descent before night falls and the pass is too perilous in the dark," he smiled. "We have made good progress. Tomorrow we will descend, then cross the Shudras," he reined his horse in. "Follow us and stay close to your camp. Rest well!" he called, disappearing amongst the throng of riders.

They followed the host along the ridge and toward the mountains behind.

"He's a good man," Korrun said, watching the hooves scrape over the stony ground.

"Who, Frell?"

Korrun smiled. "Yes. But I meant Lord Tollam, he sees much."

Wendya stared at the tracker. "Korrun … thank you for your kindness last night."

The dwelf smiled, lowering his voice. "I know Marval is like a father to you. We're all doubting ourselves. Fear is nothing to be ashamed of, especially fear for others."

"Well I've plenty of that," she answered.

Korrun laughed, his taciturn nature seeming as distant as her home. She looked up at him. In this light, as the shrouded sun threw out its final rays, he looked young, carefree and handsome. His deep blue eyes, almost black now against the graying sky, seemed at peace. Wendya had never seen him look so serene.

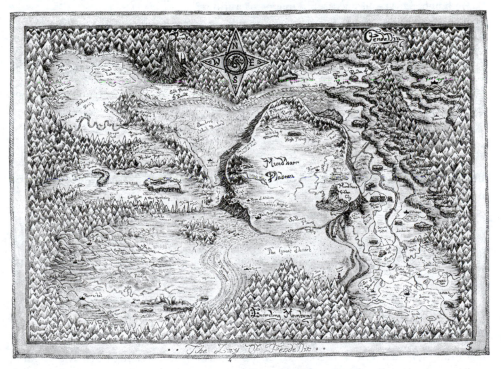

An ancient map of Fendellin, the forgotten 'Kingdom of Dragons'.

They turned south, heading for the line of mountains they had skirted earlier. The sun blazed in a red fury. Into the deepening dusk they marched, until they reached the first outcrops of mountain rock and made a makeshift base beneath its sheltering pinnacles.

Camp fires sprang up, glittering in the gloom, but concealed by the magical veil which hid them from enemy eyes. Sedgewick's dragons rested, perched on the mountain peaks above.

A solemnity fell over them and few found sleep as thoughts of battle and loved ones they had left behind filled their minds. Gralen and the wizard sat silently in the firelight with Wendya close by, a heavy throw wrapped round her to keep out the cold.

"You should get some rest," Korrun said, throwing a blanket over his horse. "The battle will come soon enough. How are you holding up?" he asked Wendya. "It was a hard journey today. Your amulets are working perfectly. The troops are not as tired as they should be."

"So far."

He settled beside her. "Your veiling spell is working. It's kept us from sight and harm."

"I couldn't have done it without Marval."

He laughed. "Are all wiccas and mages so humble?"

Wendya smiled. "Not the successful ones. I've learnt to accept my failures in my stride, as they tend to happen with regular occurrence!"

Korrun stared at her. "I've never met anyone like you," he said, his eyes fixed on hers. Wendya blushed.

He smiled. "You should rest while you can. Tomorrow will be a long day." He stood up, suddenly bent down, and kissed her forehead. "Rest well" he whispered, and left.

Wendya sat motionless and watched him weave his way through the camp until he disappeared in the gloom.

Mr. Agyk looked at the stars, his aged eyes tracing meteors as they streaked across the sky, before vanishing into the blackness. "We must rest," he said wearily. "Good night, dear friends," he murmured, turning his back to the fire and instantly falling asleep.

Gralen looked on in silence, his eyes studying the witch's face, the flush of her cheeks, the smile that lingered on her lips. She finally settled down to sleep.

"Just watch yourself, soldier boy," he snarled under his breath.

The morning came dull and misty. The animals were as restless as the troops. Before dawn fully spread over the grasslands, the entire army was traveling northward again.

King Baillum halted. "Send out word. The pass is extremely steep. Great care must be taken; we cannot afford to lose any. Beasts of burden, wagons, and heavy equipment must go first, and then the cavalry. Those on foot must follow."

The Tolltek Pass lay before them, a steep and treacherously narrow track that clung perilously to the escarpment face, threatening death to those whose tired feet strayed from its path. Progress was painfully slow as the cavalcade trudged on in a ceaseless, winding stream.

The midday sun passed into a hazy afternoon. The last soldiers descended and the host were on their way again, marching at a great pace to recover lost time. The landscape changed around them. Flat plains and rambling hills of tussock gave way to gnarled, weather-beaten rock and thicket beds, their needle-like thorns starkly black against the gray granite.

The ground sloped steadily downward before leveling out, where the barren expanses of rock fell away into mud, reed, and bog. They had reached the Shudras, the silent marshes.

Slimy quagmires stretched out before them as an endless sea. Troughs of stagnant water riddled their way into hazardous, deep pools. Foul-smelling vapors rose from the ground in choking clouds. The thought of crossing such a place lowered all their spirits.

"This was once a wondrous land," Hallm said. "These were the water-meadows of the great Kara Kara River. The pure waters fed Fendellin's rarest orchids here. Grass-pipers, willow larks, and meadow-cranes flitted amongst its grasses. Now, its foul mud clogs every channel and tributary with stagnant filth. Its water sprites and larks have long departed."

"Our beasts cannot cross this!" King Baillum declared, raising his hand. "The pathways should be clear at this time of year. This is the only passage through the swamps! The waters have risen! Another evil M'Sorreck has perpetrated on this land. If we try passing, we shall lose many good horses. Certainly, the wagons cannot cross."

"How far do these marshes stretch?" Korrun asked Hallm.

"Eight and ten leagues at the shortest crossing, which is here," he replied.

The King's stoicism gave way to anger. "How could this happen? We sent scouts ahead to gauge the terrain. Why did they not report this? Bring them here!" he demanded.

Frell whispered into his father's ear. The dwelf watched the King's face change, an unmistakable flash of shock. The news was not good. Korrun glanced at Wendya and the wizard. As if reading his mind, Gralen stepped forward.

"If wheels are no use, wings will have to do," he said boldly. "My kin can take the wagons and the oxen, if the rest of you can find a way through."

Korrun smiled. "He is right, Sire. If the fÿrrens can carry the heavier loads, we should be able to cross. I am a tracker and used to finding lost pathways. I'm sure we can find a way."

"And if the horses are lost?"

"Then my kindred will have more burdens to bear," replied Gralen simply. "A dworll is lighter than an ox!"

King Baillum managed a brief smile. "No obstacles too great? We shall see," he said beckoning to Sedgewick above.

Sedgewick and the other dragons swooped down to carry the various wagons and carts, siege-rams and battle gear too heavy for the marshes. The most careful dragons carried the nervous beasts, zebu, water buffalo, and battle oxen the eighteen leagues north to dry land.

Following Korrun and Hallm, the army began their arduous crossing of the Shudras.

It was well into the night before the last exhausted traveler reached the delights of hard ground once more. They set up camp, the slimy mud and stench of the marshes clinging to each bedraggled member as an unwelcome reminder of the day. A deep unease fell on them.

Korrun sat quietly by one of the campfires, listening to Lord Tollam and Hallm speculate, in hushed tones, on the battle to come.

"It could be a Hal'Torren's choice all over again," Hallm commented.

The other dworlls nodded grimly.

"Hal'Torren's choice? What's that?" Korrun asked.

Hallm shrugged. "It's any situation where the outcome is predetermined or unavoidable, and usually terrible."

Lord Tollam poked the fire, his violet eyes reflecting the glimmer of the flames. "It is an old legend, but a true story. Hal'Torren was a nobleman, strong, incorruptible, a hero and leader to his people. He lived in Oralam, a beautiful city once. One day he returned home to find his family held hostage by his sworn enemy, M'Sorreck. Hal'Torren loved his family deeply, his wife, his three young children. He offered his life in exchange for theirs. But Morreck wanted something far more precious. He wanted to break Hal'Torren utterly," Tollam sighed. "No matter what he did, how he bartered and begged, Hal'Torren was given a dreadful choice. Watch ten thousand of his own people perish, innocent children and families like his own, to save just one member of his family, or save his people and watch all his family die. Now Hal'Torren was a great leader and he loved his people, but like any father, how could he sacrifice his own family?"

Korrun looked at the wise old dworll. "What did he choose?"

"To condemn ten thousand souls to a grisly death, to save one of his family." He shook his head. "Then he had to make the worst choice of all … which member of his family to save. That is Hal'Torren's choice. It is no choice at all. You are damned whichever path you take!"

"How did it end?" the dwelf asked quietly.

Lord Tollam sighed and glanced at his son, as if thanking the gods that he never had to face such a choice. "Tragically of course. He chose to save his daughter, the youngest of his three children. They were then forced to watch his wife and two sons being murdered before them. Naturally, it traumatized the young girl. Only a few years later her father found her hanging from a willow tree. He promptly hung himself beside her. You see why Hal'Torren's choice is impossible. Save one, sacrifice others, condemn yourself."

"Morreck is a fengal beast, a monster!" Korrun said through gritted teeth.

"Yes, of the worst kind," replied Tollam.

Hallm looked at his father for a moment, then turned to the dwelf. "Have you ever faced a Hal'Torren's choice?" he asked.

Korrun shifted uneasily, his face half-hidden in shadow. "Once," he whispered.

"What happened?" Hallm asked, trying to hide his surprise.

The dwelf stood up, his eyes lost in the fire. "I made the wrong choice," he said simply, turned and left.

Despite the foul vapors drifting in from the edges of the marshes, the night air was crisp and clear. The last sliver of moon rose high above them. The army finally settled. Mr. Agyk and Gralen lay sleeping, the green dragon's snoring echoing in the darkness.

"You should be asleep," Korrun stood framed between two high slabs of rock, looking much like a monolith himself, "and you certainly shouldn't be out here alone." He scuffed the ground. Wendya sat on a low mound of earth, her face turned away.

"Wendya?"

She nodded. "Please ... I just need a little time."

Korrun hesitated, came over, and sat beside her. "Look, I'd be happy to leave you alone ... but that giant green thing back there would probably have me for breakfast if anything happened to you. I don't think he likes me very much."

She laughed. "It's not personal."

"Oh, I'm quite certain that it is. It's fine ... I'm not the most likeable fellow. My few friends tell me that!" he smiled.

Wendya laughed again, then stopped. "I'm sorry, I'm just not ready for this, any of this."

"None of us are."

She faced him, her eyes red and puffy. "That's not true. You're ready. You're a soldier."

"Yes, but the old mage isn't, and many others here are just farmers."

"You don't understand," she pulled her knees up. "I've sleep-walked through most of my life. I've wasted so much time. Wasted years, tens of years. I'm not ready for this!"

Korrun looked at her; he didn't know what to say.

"I know it's selfish to be thinking such thoughts, but I'm petrified of losing someone I love and I'm petrified of dying before I've finally woken up and had a chance to live!" She turned to him, her eyes full of confusion. "I'm sorry."

He brushed her hair aside so gently, she barely felt his fingertips graze the side of her cheek. "None of us know what to expect or how this will end," he said softly.

"Please don't ask me to have faith!" she pleaded.

"I wouldn't. That's in short supply with me," he gazed at the campfires dotted around. "No. Fear and anger will take you a long way. Come on, we'll both need our strength tomorrow," he said, taking her arm.

Suddenly, a great commotion could be heard and the sound of shouting. Korrun jumped to his feet and instinctively drew his sword as a group of soldiers burst into view and rushed past, followed by Frell and Orrla.

"What's happening?"

Frell stopped for a moment. "Two of Lord Lorrin's troops have turned!" he panted. "They're attacking the others! We think they've been infected somehow, by dark mytes!"

Orrla nodded. "They've gone on a rampage. They've butchered at least nine soldiers in their sleep!"

"What can I do?" Korrun asked, stepping forward.

Orrla glanced at Frell. "Nothing" she replied blankly. "Go to your beds, both of you. We are handling it!"

"I can help!" shouted the dwelf.

"GO BACK!" Frell ordered and disappeared.

Korrun hesitated and looked at Wendya. "We should go. It is not safe here."

The next day came, featureless and blank. Nothing was said of the disturbing events of the previous few hours, but many noticed the graves clustered together, seventeen in total. After an unsettling night, with little rest or refreshment, the army set off again. Morning waned to afternoon as they drew ever nearer to Morreck's lair. The ground became stony once more as the mountains loomed ominously before them. The highest peak, Kavok, could now be seen clearly, though still at a distance, towering from the lesser mountains and cliffs around it.

The mountain's upper climbs were swathed in thunderous cloud, and rain lashed its cruel pinnacles. Its lower flanks were lost in deepening shadow and a brooding malice lay about it.

"That is it." King Baillum said solemnly. "M'Sorreck's fortress lies at its base, at the head of a ravine cut into the mountain. The valley is always in darkness and is always watched."

At that moment, Frell rode swiftly up with a troubled look on his face.

"Father … Sire, Morreck's forces have been busy", he gasped, as Baillum signaled for the dworll Lords to gather round. Frell continued. "Most of the scouts have returned. The ground ahead is treacherous. They've reported from the Northward Ridge. The land has been scarred with deep cuts, trenches, and fume-filled pits! Worst of all, the approach to Kavok may prove impassable!" Frell took a deep breath. "The salt lake is gone! It's been drained … completely!"

"Drained?" Hallm asked.

"Yes," Frell replied. "Wargols fear water. We were going to use that to our advantage but the waters have gone! It is a wasteland. Dust storms of salt race across it and blind the eyes!"

The Dworll King sighed. "Well, we cannot turn back. You said *most* of the scouts have returned, where are the others?"

"A group is trying to cross now, to survey the land beyond, and report back on the black valley and the enemy's movements."

"Good." Baillum answered, turning his gaze to the golden sky, then away westward. "We have only a few hours of light left, so let us make the most of it!" He nodded to the Dworll Lords. "The time has come to begin our approach. Are your troops ready?"

"Yes, Sire," they replied.

"Then let us begin. Lord Perral and Lord Lorrin you take our outer flanks, Lord Tollam and Lord Nerrus you command our left and right. I shall take the center. We will push through any resistance and give our friends here precious time. Our diversion must work."

"May our ancestors aid us," rallied Tollam, standing tall in his saddle. "And may the stars and the coming of a new moon bring us good fortune!"

Baillum glanced at the little wizard.

"For Fendellin, for freedom!" they chanted, clashing their swords in a defiant gesture.

Bowing to the King, the lords marshaled their soldiers into fighting flanks.

"We go on!" Baillum cried, brandishing his sword.

The army moved as one. Led by each lord, they divided effortlessly into five factions. King Baillum remained at the head of the central flank. Together, the five regiments marched toward the black mountain. The four friends remained with the King's company.

Korrun rode silently for a while, troubled by the scouts' news.

"Will we be able to cross the salt lake?" Wendya asked.

The tracker jolted, as if her voice had brought him back from the brink of some dark dream. "The best thing we can hope for is rain. Rain will stop the salt dust from blinding us."

Gralen plodded along, his eyes fixed on the dwelf and witch. "There he goes with his long hair," he muttered, "I don't know who he thinks he is ... he's just a glorified bodyguard!"

"You have no need to be jealous," Mr. Agyk whispered.

"Jealous?" He scoffed turning his head to face the little wizard. "Of him?"

Mr. Agyk smiled. "Yes, judging by the expression you have had for the last few weeks!"

"That's indigestion," the dragon replied, indignantly. "Too much medeaok and feasting."

"I am glad I am riding on your shoulder and not walking downwind!" the wizard mused.

Gralen grumbled something and trudged on. He wished he were flying with his brothers above, but felt deep relief at hearing the little mage sound like himself again, although his eyes never left Wendya and Korrun.

"You haven't lived in Kallorm your whole life, have you?" Wendya asked Korrun.

"No. I arrived there when I was a child."

"From Koralan, the Sand City?"

"Yes. My brothers and I were born there, only a few years before it fell," Korrun smiled. "It wasn't all desert back then. There were fertile rivers and huge underground lakes."

"I heard stories about it when I was a child," Wendya sighed.

"My memories of it are quite hazy. It was destroyed when I was young. My mother took us to Kallorm, where she was born. It must have been a very difficult journey for her."

"Where is she now?"

"She died shortly afterwards. Kallorm was not the safe place she remembered it to be. She was caught in a wargol attack." A sadness passed over his face.

"And your father? Is he ǽllfr?" she asked softly.

He shifted uneasily in his saddle, tightening the leather reins around his fingers. "Yes. He left," he replied simply.

"I'm sorry."

"It's fine. I am not my father. I stayed," Korrun seemed to stiffen and his voice faltered. "We never knew him. He deserted us. All ǽllfrs deserted this world. Korrtal and I were just children and Sorall was an infant."

"You were close to your brothers?" she asked.

He nodded and smiled briefly, his eyes staring ahead to the mountain. "Especially Sorall. He was very trusting. Not like me at all. He always believed in others — saw the best in them even if he didn't see it in himself."

"And you don't?"

"I believe in the presence of good, I know there is evil. I tend to believe in what I can see and touch and feel." He shrugged. "Are you an optimist like him?"

"I am," she said, and then fell silent, her mind drifting back to the coming battle.

Korrun smiled. "I can't believe that after all those years in Kallorm, I never met you!"

The witch blushed. "You probably did. I very much doubt if King Dorrol's most trusted guard would notice the silly little girl who played with the King's daughter!"

Korrun looked at her seriously. "I would notice," he said.

Wendya smiled. Gralen couldn't take his eyes off them.

The host of Fendellin continued on their course. The sun sank as the dworll army picked their way through the many hazardous obstacles that lay in their path. They passed trenches and pools filled with bubbling acrid substances that burnt the throat and stung the eyes.

At last, they approached the Northward Ridge, a line of high limestone cliffs that overlooked the once great salt lakes below. The wind rose up, howling mournfully over the ridge top and casting Fendellin's many flags and pennons high into the air. The gaping mouth of Morreck's valley lay waiting for them in the distance, staring blackly like a hole of despair between the great mountain's feet.

Suddenly, as the host began their ascent of the ridge, a cry rang out in the skies above. All eyes turned upward as several dragons swooped down through the clouds, led by Rollm.

The young dragon almost crashed in front of the King's horse.

"The battle is upon us!" he puffed. "We have flown high over the salt lakes and Kavok has awoken! It's alive with crawling beasts. Thousands upon thousands of wargols and other foul creatures that we cannot discern. They are massed beyond the flats! They know we're here! They are waiting for us!" the dragon gasped.

"Then this deception has been in vain?" Lord Nerrus exclaimed. "We should have fought at Mund'harr, on the plains we know! We should never have come here!"

"Have hope Lord, and so shall your company. We had no other choice than to bring the battle here," Tollam answered. "At least our deception has brought us to Morreck's fortress unharmed and within hope of victory."

Nerrus nodded, shifting his weight uneasily. "You are right, old friend."

The King looked dismayed. "Where is Lord Sedgewick?" he asked, turning to Rollm.

"He is leading the others," the dragon replied nervously. "They are trying to gauge the enemy's forces. But we are fearful. We have seen no sign of Morreck's winged serpents!"

"Keep the skies safe for us, for as long as you can," replied the King, turning to the others. "So ... the surprise has gone, so be it. It is all the better, for I will not ride into battle cloaked as a thief! Let us be seen!" He raised his arms to the heavens and cried. "Let us be seen!"

As if in response, the spell, which had hidden them since leaving Mund'harr, fell away like the dropping of a curtain, to reveal the last march of Fendellin in all its glory. Banners curled in the dusk, cloaks flew, helms and shields glinted in the fading sun. A mustering of such might had not been seen since the ancient wars in the early dark days of the world.

Rollm took to the air in a flurry of wings and joined his fÿrren comrades, who were wheeling through the amber sky.

"Onward!" cried the King, as the army pushed forward, standards raised defiantly, pennons flickering in the breeze, swords drawn, and battle-axes ready.

They surged forward, each flank protecting the other. Spirits were high.

As they reached the summit of the ridge, they saw the dreadful task that lay before them and their hearts sank. Extending for miles, like a river of shimmering glass, lay the drained salt lakes. Just as the scouts had said, clouds of fine salt dust lashed the dry crusts of the lake bed, smothering everything. Sharp winds whipped and spiraled into mini tornados that tore across its surface, sending great plumes of salt into the sky.

Through the haze of heat and dust, they could see the terror that Rollm had spoken of. There, beyond the salt beds, waiting ... were M'Sorreck's hordes.

An army far greater than they had imagined stretched as far as the eye could see in either direction. An unbroken chain of moving creatures, their crimson armor glistening, their cruel weapons reflecting the last rays of sunlight. Line upon line stood before the mountain's feet and filled the valley behind, a living barrier between them and Morreck.

The dworll host faced their enemy. Baillum looked up at the towering flanks of Kavok.

The mountainside was alive with crawling things, like a nest of ants swarming over its prey. The sight was horrifying and struck fear into the stoutest heart.

"My liege, we should not cross this!" Frell pleaded. "Father ... The winds are against us. We should wait for the enemy to come to us!"

"We cannot wait. Time is our enemy as surely as these foul creatures, or any wind!" King Baillum glanced at the wizard again, turned back to his son, and placed his hand on the young dworll's shoulder. "We press on. Take heart, we shall slay more of them and we shall win the night!"

Mr. Agyk gazed across the white expanse. "The odds are badly against us," he thought. "The Oracle's prophecies cannot be true ... do not lose hope Marval, do not lose hope!"

"Mr. A?" Gralen said, looking at the troubled wizard.

"Promise me, both of you," he said looking anxiously at Wendya and the dragon. "Do not take unnecessary risks. Korrun and the soldiers are ready to fight. Gralen, do not fly off in some thoughtless rage, I cannot save you if you do! Please, be careful, both of you."

They dutifully nodded.

"Onward fair Fendellons ... To victory! March on ... March on!" the King cried.

The dworll army mustered at once. All took heart and courage in the King's words and the flying of the Fendellin banner.

Korrun touched his pendant. "For Sorall," he whispered.

They descended the steep slopes to the salt plains. The sun lingered just above the horizon, its rays igniting the sky in brilliant hues of scarlet and orange, turning the salt flats into a sparkling sea of peach before disappearing in a blaze of molten flame.

The sky darkened and evening fell. Shadows grew ominously. Morreck's forces stood motionless, their red eyes shining. Only the creatures in the valley behind moved ceaselessly, as a boiling cauldron of worms and slithering things.

The host reached the base of the ridge and stood on the dried lakebed.

"Prepare your horses! Shield your eyes!" Frell cried, leading the first flank. "The wind is against us!"

The storm that had clung to Kavok's peak now sent blasts of icy wind rolling down its mountainside, taking with it great choking clouds of salt that blinded the eyes.

From out of this bitter haze came a torrent of arrows, their cruel points poisoned, their reach lengthened by some foul craft. Many found a mark.

"The enemy is upon us!" Baillum cried. "Shields up! To battle!"

Placing their shields before their eyes as best as they could, they pressed forward as arrows whistled about them, flying through the blizzard as a deadly hail.

"Not yet!" Perral cried to the archers. "We cannot fire until we have a target!" he shouted.

"We cannot fight through this!" Korrun cried. "I can barely see my hand, let alone the enemy!"

"We must turn the wind back!" shouted Gralen. "Turn it upon them! Hold on, Marval!"

The great dragon lunged forward and took to the air, arrows narrowly missing his bulk and the little wizard, as he shot straight up into the darkening sky.

Emerging from the dust below, he and Mr. Agyk could see that Sedgewick and his dragons were already assaulting Morreck's hordes at the base of the mountain. Missiles flew wildly into the air and fell back. Spears and lances glanced off the dragons' scales, while the fÿrren swooped lower and lower, pouring liquid fire on the wargol heads. In the growing gloom, Gralen and the wizard could see that this had little effect on the sheer numbers before them, as a spider, though deadly, has little effect on a swarm of carrion flies.

"What are they doing?" the dragon asked. "The wargols ... they're hanging back! Why don't they charge?"

"They are waiting ... They are waiting for *something!*" the wizard replied worriedly.

There, as a dreadful black tide in the deepening shadow of Kavok, Morreck's forces stood. A silent menace as yet unleashed. The dragon and wizard strained their eyes; it seemed to them that this mighty force was now swaying, as if swooning under some powerful influence.

"There's devilry here!" Gralen shouted as he hailed one of the dragons overhead.

Rollm promptly appeared. "Do you see? There's something very wrong here ... they're not moving! They see us ... but they are not moving, even when we attack! What does it mean?"

"It's some foul trick of Morreck's," Gralen answered, watching the skies above. "Look, the dworlls cannot continue, the wind is blinding them. Many good souls have already fallen before a single blow has been struck. We need your help ... can you help us to turn the wind and the salt towards the enemy? Blind *them* instead?"

"Yes, we can try!" Rollm nodded, spiraling into the air toward the ever-blackening spike of Kavok. "Darkness is coming, Gralen!" he cried. "Beware! Not all of us will see the dawn!"

Gralen could just see his brothers and sisters, as small swooping dots against the colossal mountain. Looking up once more, wary of some skyward assault, he and the wizard plunged down into the shifting clouds of salt and disappeared in the gloom.

"Sire, we can go no further!" Frell choked. "We must retreat to the ridge!"

"No, night is already upon us, we cannot falter!" the Dworll King retorted, his shield raised against the wind.

At that moment, Gralen emerged from the clouds to join them, a triumphant smile on his face and a pensive Mr. Agyk perched on his shoulder. "Wait!" he called, "wait ... the wind is changing!"

Almost as soon as he had spoken the words, a great gust of air that nearly knocked some from their steeds drove the salt from their eyes and towards their enemy. Wendya had never seen such a sight. She could just make out a mass of beating wings in the dimness above. The clouds lifted and at last they could see. They had almost crossed the salt flats.

"Remember, there will be no moon tonight. So let our swords light the way!" King Baillum shouted, rearing his horse up. "Our chance is here. To battle!"

They charged forward.

Without warning, the brooding malice of Kavok exploded in answer. The dworll host faltered for a moment, their cries drowned out by a thunderous boom that shook the very ground. The mountain itself seemed to be opening up and from its bowels poured forth an army far greater and more terrible than any they had ever seen.

Firebrands were lit and flames leapt like running water through the ranks of the enemy, spreading through the darkness like flickering eyes.

"Morreck's been breeding an army *tenfold* that of ours!" Gralen shouted, straining his eyes ahead. "This is no battle, this is a rout!"

The salt storm was driven before them, sweeping into the enemy. From behind it emerged Baillum, leading the army and wrath of Fendellin. Released from their swoon, Morreck's forces rushed forward as a solid wall. A hail of darts, some alight, shot through the clouds.

The wargol demons, half-blinded and half-crazed, hacked and hewed at anything that moved, including their own kind. This mattered little, so great were their number. Swords clashed and axes, wielded by strong arms, harvested their deadly fruits. The enemy advanced relentlessly, line upon line, swarming upon the dworlls. Shields and helms were cloven and soon the ground was thick with the bloody and fallen, turning the white plains to crimson.

"Onward!" King Baillum cried, pushing ever forward. "We must reach the valley!"

Protected on either side, Baillum's vanguard forced itself through the wargol lines. Sedgewick's dragons pulled back from the mountain where they had driven the salt-laden clouds deep into the enemy ranks and rushed back to give the King cover.

Gralen, with Mr. Agyk on his back, blasted a fire path through the wargol hides. Wendya, sword drawn and ready, concentrated on her protection spells, increasing the potency of shields and the strength of each dworll's blow.

The clamor of battle lay all about. Baillum's soldiers forced back the hordes, yet as one wargol fell, two or more sprang up in its place. Korrun's sword rang out as he fought next to Frell. Again the wargols charged and broke, charged and broke.

"We must not get hemmed in!" Korrun warned. "They mustn't get behind us!"

"Tollam and Nerrus will prevent it!" cried the King as he hewed another wargol head.

Even as he spoke, a tide of dark creatures was trying to outflank them. Lord Nerrus and Lorrin to the right held firm, but Perral's outer troops to the far left were overtaken.

"Sedgewick!" Tollam bellowed seeing Lord Perral's flank under fierce onslaught, as a large sea of wargols clustered around the legion. "Cover the King! Lord Perral is in need! Hallm, lead on! ... I go to Perral's aid!"

The young captain nodded as he severed the head of an advancing demon, then springing back, he mounted his horse and rallied his soldiers. Tollam rode swiftly, taking a small sortie with him. Rushing through the wargol lines, they breached the enemy siege.

"Well met! I am glad to see you!" Perral called, reining in his horse. "The battle is fierce, my friend! My soldiers are brave but we are badly outnumbered and have paid dearly for the King's protection. We must retreat to the inner flanks or lose too many good dworlls."

"I agree, come, let us forge a path to the King," Tollam smiled, his soldiers hacking into the black mass that surrounded them.

Little by little they fought their way back, though Perral's forces had taken heavy losses.

Hallm rode up. "Father, the enemy is massing. They're trying to drive a wedge between us and the King!"

"Then we shall prevent them!" cried Tollam as Perral's soldiers joined those of his own, and together they drove forward, felling the incoming tide.

The fighting was now furious on all sides as yet more wargol demons issued onto the plains. Fendellin's war-wagons and catapults — huge trebuchets — hurled tar-covered and fire-wreathed shots deep into the enemy's ranks, each one exploding in a shower of flame.

Sparks filled the sky. The heat of battle and smoke mingled with the stench of blood that rose all around. The terrain, now littered with wargol carcasses and the fallen bodies of many dworlls, smoldered as each blazing arrow, torch, sling-shot, and dragon flame hit the ground. The dworlls forged forward and now lay only a short distance from the battlements, the gaping mouth of the black valley, and the fortress beyond.

"To the valley! To the valley!" Baillum boomed above the din.

Suddenly, amidst the tumult of battle, a voice rose up that seared the very air with its cruelty and pierced each heart, wargol, dragon, and dworll alike, with a frozen terror. Something was coming. Thundering down the gorge of the valley and parting the enemy, as a sea riven in two. Terrible cries filled the air, half of fear and madness, half of hideous glee.

For a strange moment, all fell silent. Dworlls stood frozen to the spot, wargols cowered. Gralen flew higher into the blackness trying to see through the smoke, and he and Mr. Agyk were met by Sedgewick, Rollm and the others.

"He is coming!" Sedgewick cried, pointing to the valley behind, his eyes fearful for the first time, his face full of weariness and worry.

"Who?" asked the wizard.

At that moment, as if jolted by a sudden and violent wind, Sedgewick reeled back, his eyes huge and fixed in horror behind Gralen.

"Varkul!" he gasped. "Dive! DIVE!" he shouted and pushed Gralen out of the way.

The evil serpent, talons drawn like knives, hurtled past like a thunderous train and took the old dragon high into the air.

"Sedgewick!" Rollm screamed, as he turned to see thirty or more of Morreck's serpent beasts descending upon them out of the darkness.

Within seconds, the skies were filled with the roar and flame of battle.

"An ambush! Fight! Fight!" Rollm cried, trying to rouse the others from shock then, turning with tears in his eyes to a horrified Gralen and Mr. Agyk, he shouted. "Go! Go! You must look after the wizard, this is our fight. Go!"

"But, Sedgewick!" Gralen gasped, desperate to save his friend and mentor.

"I'll help him! Go!" shouted the young draken as he bolted into the clouds and disappeared.

Gralen shouted after him. "Rollm, no!" He faltered, torn between two friends.

"Go!" said Mr. Agyk calmly. "I will help you if I can. But remember what I said: be careful, think first!"

Gralen turned to his old friend, clearly distressed, his eyes full of panic and concern. "I ... thank you, Marval" he said, then plunged down toward the battle raging below, and toward Wendya who seemed to be in the thick of it.

"I must help Sedgewick," he spluttered to the witch.

Mr. Agyk climbed off the dragon and onto Wendya's shoulder, his eyes shining, his staff blazing. "I know, go my friend ... go!" said the wizard, trying to smile.

Gralen hesitated for a moment longer, agonized over leaving them.

"We'll be safe," Wendya said gently.

Gralen glanced at them both, turned swiftly but reluctantly away, and shot up into the blackness, vanishing from view.

Chapter Seventeen

Kavoh's Peak

Black mist wafted through the enemy ranks as a deathly hush fell over the wargol army. Cries of fear and excitement were silenced as the voices of the foul creatures were struck dumb by the coming of a terrible presence. A shadow was growing, issuing from the valley mouth and moving fast. Within M'Sorreck's army, an ominous black shape approached, moving towards the Fendellon host, cracking the thick salt crust of the lake bed beneath its iron-clad feet.

King Baillum and the dworlls stood firm, their swords ringing in the emptiness, as the heads of their assailants turned to see the horror that drew near, and were swiftly felled for their folly. Panic descended, spreading through the host as the wargols about them parted like a dark curtain.

Korrun stood rooted to the spot, motionless. His pendant ignited in a small, bright flame, burning against his chest, his eyes were fixed on the dark shadow before him. Long years of torment and waiting had brought him to this. His bitterest enemy had come.

"What is it?" Wendya gasped, straining to see its form in the darkness.

"Nuroth!" Korrun muttered slowly, his voice choked and filled with anger, his face an unrecognizable mask.

Nuroth, Morreck's Chief Captain and most feared of his servants, towered above them. A wargol creature far larger than even the mountain demons that were now pouring in from the valley behind. A nightmarish vision, he was hideous and troll-like in both size and features.

He strode forward. On his wide shoulders lay a tangled mass of blood-soaked fur, a fleecy mane that clung in limp strands to his arms and trailed down his back in a curling matt. Protruding from this was a row of barbs growing from his spine like a ridge of serrated yellowed teeth. His eyes were not the bulbous scarlet of the wargols, but a glassy black, reminiscent of the Gorrgos's dead eyes, and they gleamed with a malice and hatred unmatched, save by Morreck himself. These loathsome orbs, set deep into his skull beneath his heavy brow, glistened as he surveyed the quaking insects before him. Foul breath snorted from his nose, no more than two holes drilled into his ugliness, and these were partnered each side by a spur of horn that grew from his cheeks. Two putrid tusks, each already tipped with dworll blood. His skin, unlike the deep blue of other wargols, was a deathly hue of gray and his matted hair fell in foul braids of blackened soot about him.

The very sight of him froze the blood. Horses panicked, reared, or tried to bolt. Lesser wargols flung themselves to the ground or retreated back, half-cackling, half-crying. Even the sturdiest dworlls cowered: their swords limp in their hands, their limbs full of weariness and woe.

"He has the feel of a dark myte," the wizard whispered. "Some foul craft has born him."

Baillum and the other lords shrank back, trying to rally their troops and control their steeds. All of a sudden Nallo, Wendya's sturdy horse, reared and collapsed beneath her. Dead. The witch and the little wizard were thrown to the ground, Frell rushed to their aid. They stood motionless, as if terror had frozen them.

Only one stood firm.

No fear could touch him nor quell the fury that raged inside him, searing his blood, consuming him. He stood as a lonely figure, his raiment torn and his black hair blowing loosely around him. Standing in a bloody and body-strewn circle, his sword gleaming, his axe shining, his eyes as dark as his enemy's. He seemed tiny compared to the thing that towered above him, as terrible as the night, a shadow of death and despair. The creature stared at the dworlls before it and fixed its eyes on the dwelf.

"NUROTH," Korrun spat, hardly able to get the word out.

Flame from the battle above lit the evening skies as lightning crackled over Kavok's summit in reply. Hell had truly fallen on earth. The creature stepped forward showing a hideous smile, spittle dripping from its jaw.

"A dwelf?" it cackled, its very breath reeked of death. "I thought I'd killed you all!" Its dead eyes gleamed. "This is an unexpected bonus!"

Korrun straightened his back and stepped forward, his sword and axe heavy in his hands and his armor like a dead weight upon his shoulders. "I have come here for you," the tracker shouted, his voice strangled, his eyes wild. His heart pounded as if it would burst. "You killed my brother! You murdered him! You slaughtered all of them! I have waited a long time for this!"

"Well, your wait is over, half-breed." Nuroth laughed, the very sound of it turning the stomach and crushing the spirit. "But first, my Master and I have business with an insect wizard and his pet king."

"NO! … You fight me first!" Korrun challenged, pointing his sword to the beast's throat.

The giant turned his full attention and wrath on the small warrior before him.

"Very well … insect," he growled.

Wendya picked up the wizard. "What's he doing? He can't fight him alone! … We've got to help him!" she cried and tried to rush forward. "Korrun!"

Frell grabbed her and held her back.

"NO!" Mr. Agyk shouted. "I was afraid of this. I saw it in his eyes. You cannot stop him!" He said, at last understanding the extent of the dwelf's resolve. "This is why he came," he sighed. "This was his reason … I will try to help him if I can." No sooner had he uttered the words when an overwhelming weariness fell over him.

"Korrun!" she called desperately. The dwelf did not hear his name, but Nuroth did.

"Korrun," he sneered, drawing out each syllable, smiling broadly now and showing his foul, blackened, fang-like teeth. "I know that name. Korrun of Koralan, the Sand City! Son of one of the lesser lords, sniveling Lord Idas, are you not? That simpering fool to the dead King … of course!" he cackled. "Once great lords and Realm Keepers, now tramps and beggars. Yes. I remember burning your city to the ground and you survived!" he laughed in false sympathy. "Left all alone, deserted by your father, by all cowardly ǽllfrs." Nuroth's smile grew wider.

"Korrun … yes, I remember you now. In Kallorm, I took your brother's ring … when I took his head!" he laughed again and the sound of it pierced through bone and sinew to poison every heart and mind with its ugliness.

The wargol reached beneath his foul leather breastplate and drew out a small ring made of dragonsilver, its ǽllfrstone now blackened, its curling dragons a hideous snaking mockery. Korrun felt the burning pendant round his neck, which now glowed with a fierce red light.

"You shall die for the blood of my brother!" he shouted, standing tall before the monster. "You shall die for his blood and for all those you have butchered!" He roared, and, with that, the dwelf leapt forward and brought his sword down with all his strength. "For Sorall!"

The beast stepped back, surprised for a moment by the boldness and ferocity of his attacker. Korrun's sword sliced through the air, glittering in the dark, but missed its mark as the creature sprang to the side, spun round and bore down on the warrior. Steel struck steel, sending a shower of sparks all about them as the two enemies battled. Suddenly, as if roused from some stupor, the dworll host charged forward to protect the dwelf and drive back the wargols who were now gathered, ready to attack.

"I fight him alone!" Korrun bellowed as he wielded his axe and brought it crashing down onto the wargol's shield, shattering it like glass in the wind.

"Then let us at least protect your back!" Frell cried cutting through two of the enemies with one swipe of his blade. "These foul beasts care nothing of honor."

Mr. Agyk, held tightly in Wendya's arms, closed his eyes. "Give him strength," he whispered. "Power of light … cover the dark."

The little mage's staff flamed for a moment, then died again. He looked up at the sky and felt a mist return to his eyes "We must reach M'Sorreck's lair before the night ends. We have only a few hours left." he said to Wendya wearily.

"Then I will take you, alone if need be," she whispered.

She turned and gasped as a wargol axe came towards them and struck the protective shield that now encompassed them both, before evaporating in a flash of light and flame. The wargol stood unhurt but stunned, looking at the witch and his empty hands in bewilderment.

"It works!" she cried, then almost without hesitating, the witch leapt towards the dazed wargol and, brandishing the blade Korrun had given her, she plunged it through his throat and into the chest of another advancing demon.

"We needed a diversion, and we have it! … LOOK!" she cried.

As she pointed, they could now see Lorrin's forces heading the battle, as he drove his legions deep into the enemy's side, and breaching the valley mouth, pushed them back into the dark gorge beyond.

"Now's our chance!" she shouted.

Triumphant yells rose around. Frell reluctantly left Korrun's side and dashed back towards the King, grabbing another horse with him.

"Father, they must go!" he gasped.

Baillum nodded. "Marval, the time has come. Lord Lorrin is at the valley. You must go, both of you."

Wendya mounted the horse, sheltering Mr. Agyk as best she could, as she tried not to look towards the dwelf and wargol.

"Go!" King Baillum shouted. "May speed and luck be with you!"

Through the chaos of battle, Frell ploughed into the wargol throng leading Wendya, the wizard and a small but strong battalion, following the path that Lord Lorrin had blazed.

The witch and wizard found themselves in the advancing company, dwarfed on either side by the granite walls of the valley mouth. The cliffs rose so steeply, and were so black, that it was impossible to see where they ended and the night began.

All lay under a thick cloud of shadow. Only the torches of the dworlls lit the darkness. The flames of the enemy leapt along unseen battlements above, from which a new hail of poisoned and flaming arrows came whistling down in a deadly shower.

Looking northward, following the cruel walls of the valley as they tapered sharply to a point some way off in the gloom, Wendya thought she could make out two giant crooked horns of rock, M'Sorreck's gate towers. From these colossal horned buttresses protruded two immense figures, sentinels of his realm. Hideous serpentine forms seemed to grow out from the black basalt of Kavok itself. Between the deadly clutches of these megalithic guardians lay the entrance and gates to Morreck's fortress.

Wendya shuddered. She had seen this place in her nightmares.

Smoke drifted across the sky. Suddenly amidst the storm clouds and lightning that curled round the summit of the mountain, two mighty jets of flame flashed in the darkness, locked in deadly combat. As if in reply, the surrounding skies burst into flame. Fountains of fire ignited the shifting clouds in explosions of red, gold and green.

Wendya looked up. "Be safe Gralen," she whispered, blinking through watery eyes.

Mr. Agyk's staff glowed once more, then faded. "I have given him all the strength I can," he sighed, turning his face up to the sky. "He will be alright," he said, closing his eyes.

High above the battlefield in the cold clearness of night, through torn and drifting strands of gray cloud, the battle raged mercilessly between Morreck's serpents and Sedgewick's dragons.

Varkul slashed at Sedgewick, talons and teeth ripping at flesh as, together, they wheeled through the darkness, their giant forms twisted and joined together in a balletic dance to the death. They spiraled into the emptiness before breaking free and charging once more with full force. Again they broke, then charged, broke, then charged. Such a fury of leviathans had not been seen since the ancient times. Two writhing and thundering titans in a battle to the death. Fire against fire, engulfing them both like a hideous bloom.

Morreck's serpents slightly outnumbered Sedgewick's fÿrrens, but like the leader of their kin, they were a sickening mongrel breed. Reptilian and serpentine creatures crossed with the ancient pure blood of dragon races had created winged beasts far larger and more deadly than any of Fendellin's great dragons. These foul monsters hissed and swarmed over the dragons, their armored bodies coiled, their forked tongues lashing out into the air, their venomous fangs drawn ready to taste and poison dragon flesh.

"Come!" Lord Lorrin cried as Wendya and Mr. Agyk watched the battle above, trying to find their friend in the darkness. "We have no time!"

Lorrin led his troops deeper into the valley where the fighting was fiercest.

Frell kept close to the witch and wizard. "Lord Lorrin will clear a path," he said quietly, "while Morreck's hordes are fighting him, we'll have a chance to get inside."

He gestured not to the black gates hidden in shadow at the head of the valley, but to an almost unnoticeable cleft, no more than a fissure in the mountainside. As Wendya squinted, she could see other dark slits in the rock at either side of the gorge.

"There is no hope going openly through the gates," Frell whispered. "Even using the birthkey, that path will be defended against us. Secrecy and stealth will be our friend now. These entrances lead to the wargol tunnels beneath. Once inside, the key will guide us to Morreck's lair and open any doors barred to us. Come … hurry!" They dismounted their horses and, as Frell spoke, another surge of wargols poured over the battlements from Kavok. Ahead of these ran a large pack of fÿrullfrs, demonic firewolves, their snarling jaws spewing ash and flame as they ran.

"Hurry! Quickly! To the wall! To the wall! ... HURRY!" cried Frell, grabbing Wendya's arm and running frantically toward the hidden opening as some of their small battalion cleared the path ahead.

As they ran on, they glanced back and saw that the valley mouth was closing in around them. A sea of dark creatures was driving a wedge between Lorrin's forces and the advancing King's company, with the rest of the Fendellin host behind. Looking back now, the entire gorge appeared to be a boiling mass, a cauldron of foul moving shapes, as Lord Lorrin's valiant dworlls were overrun with the shouts and cries of the enemy.

"They are trapped!" Wendya cried. "There is no hope!"

"We cannot linger ... come on!" shouted Frell as they reached the crevice and slipped inside unseen.

Beyond the valley, the battle intensified. Just as the host seemed to be winning the night, Kavok released yet another wave of its poison. More fire hounds emerged from the mountain depths, scrambling over the rocks and running wildly onto the plains. These demon wolves were easier to kill than the wargols, but brought with them the fear of fang and flame.

Amidst the fighting Hallm, whose beloved horse Forriall had been killed while protecting him, ran up to the King. "Sire! Lord Lorrin is besieged! The enemy has him trapped!"

Baillum flashed his sword, hewed through the helm of a wargol demon, and looked up to see the dark wedge being driven between them.

"We must hasten! He will not stand alone! Come Fendellons, your Lord and King need you! Onward!" the warrior-king cried, then turned to Hallm. "Will you ride with me young captain of the plains? If your father will allow it."

Tollam smiled and nodded, as Hallm leapt onto the back of the King's gray steed and together they rushed forward. "To the valley! To the valley!"

Almost as soon as they entered the hidden cleft, Wendya and the others found themselves in a small dark passageway carved into the mountain rock. The roughly hewn tunnel was narrow and ran ahead for several feet before plunging sharply into the darkness. Frell took out a small crystal and cupped it gently in his hands.

The starstone shone to life in his palm, casting a shimmer around them that grew steadily brighter. Frell nodded to the others, and walked ahead, holding the starstone aloft in one hand and a dworll blade in the other. Wendya, with Mr. Agyk, walked a little behind him — surrounded and protected by the small troupe of soldiers, each keen-eyed dworll searching the blackness for the slightest movement or glimmer of red eyes.

They nervously pushed on. The sound of battle, so deafening outside, faded, until they found themselves in complete and eerie silence. With every step they took, the weight of the mountain above seemed to press in upon them. A foul odor, a mixture of wargols, rotting things and some other slinking creatures, hung in the air and grew worse as they proceeded. Wendya anxiously felt the key around her neck. It was hot and gave off a faint, reddish glow.

"The birthkey will lead us to M'Sorreck," Mr. Agyk whispered. "His power is bound with it. It will grow brighter as we get nearer."

"I wish Gralen and Korrun were here," Wendya thought, feeling as if they could stumble into a mass of red-eyed wargols at any moment.

The tunnel continued to drop, descending ever deeper into the mountain's roots. Twisting and turning through the black rock, it was joined by other narrow passageways leading back to the surface or down into some darker place. Onward they crept, as silently as they could and as quickly as they dared, as dark slits opened up menacingly on either side.

"We are lucky," whispered one of the dworlls to Frell. "Morreck has emptied Kavok for the battle outside, we may get far before we have to fight!"

Wendya glanced at her Ikan blade, hoping its strange beauty would bring her some measure of comfort, as it seemed all the more dazzling in that terrifying place.

A creeping dread fell upon the witch, greater and more insidious than any she had felt before, an intense feeling of impending doom. A doom waiting for them, watching their pitiful progress and smiling as they drew nearer. Not even their entombed journey in the catacombs beneath Kallorm had prepared her for this.

The dworlls flanked her, their eyes shining keenly in the dim light cast from Frell's starstone. Shadows flickered on the walls about them, dancing silently above their heads, mocking them, urging them onward.

Mr. Agyk remained quiet and still, a little stony figure gathering his strength. He seemed distant to her now. She longed for their silly chats in front of the fire or his explosive cooking or his appalling attempts to cheat at cards. She longed for them to be anywhere but here. Yet he too, it seemed to the witch, appeared troubled by even more than the task ahead.

They delved deeper into the mountain's belly. The passages, at first jagged and scarred, gave way to smooth obsidian-like black crystal. It was as if the very walls around them had, by some dark power, become superheated and molten like volcanic glass. Frell felt this strange new rock and shook his head as they continued onward.

Tunnels, some narrow, some gaping, appeared all around them. An innumerable labyrinthine maze that riddled its way through the mountain like the spread of some cancerous growth. Every so often, these passages widened and the travelers found themselves in some dark chamber, a watch room or guard station, now deserted for the battle outside. The squalor of rotting meals and wargol filth was strongest in these foul places.

"We are entering the heart of the mountain," Frell said, his voice no more than the faintest of whispers. "As we go on, some of these chambers may be occupied," he warned.

The travelers hurried on as the darkness became blacker and thicker. Frell's starstone shone out, lighting the treacherous path ahead in an amber glow.

"We must hurry," the wizard murmured to Wendya, his voice sounding strange and cold in the gloom. "We have little time left!"

Outside, the ground and the moonless sky thundered with battle. Lightning and flame crackled through the night air as the earth was riven by fire. Fendellin's troops, attacked on every front, drove forward through the shields and helms of their enemy, risking the walls of fÿrullfr flames and the crushing blows of wargol maces, in a desperate attempt to reach their kin, now trapped in the valley beyond.

Kavok towered menacingly above them like a dagger in the sky, its lower flanks and battlements flickering with thousands of blazing wargol torches. Firewolves poured in from every direction in ever increasing numbers onto the bloody battlefield.

Lord Lorrin's forces, trapped deep within the gorge, were losing their battle for survival. Exploding missiles and stone bullets bombarded them from the cliffs above, while cave wargols attacked their dwindling number from the surrounding walls. Lorrin's dworlls, greatly outnumbered, fought fearlessly but without hope.

This diminishing band of brothers fighting to protect each other and their lord, slew many wargols, yet despite their great skill and courage, they could not defeat their enemy. Ever they hacked at the foul beasts, and ever the creatures sprang back in doubled numbers.

King Baillum with Hallm led the charge toward the valley mouth. Nerrus's company followed close behind while Tollam and Perral protected their rear. Battle cries and swords rang out in the chaos.

"The King is coming! The King is coming!" one of Lorrin's young warriors cried out. "We are saved!"

"Not yet!" growled a voice, as the dworll turned in horror to see a huge pair of red eyes staring at him, followed by the flash of an axe.

"NO!" Lorrin yelled, seeing his youngest and most beloved guard cloven in two by a huge cave wargol.

Korrun and the wargol chieftain, Nuroth, were still locked in deadly combat.

The dwelf staggered back. His shattered axe lay nearby amongst the broken and twisted bodies of the fallen. In one hand, he gripped his notched sword, the tip of which was now broken, and in the other a splintered Krael blade. Nuroth strode forward, slashing at a wargol in his way before hurtling another blow towards the tracker.

"Korrun!" a voice cried out of the darkness.

His legs and arms ached with a weariness he had never felt, but a power far stronger than the pain in his limbs drove him on.

"Korrun!" came the voice again as if out of a dream.

Startled, the dwelf looked up to see Orrla, Nerrus's daughter and captain, racing through the battlefield toward him, surrounded by a stout band of riders.

"Korrun we need you! The King needs you! He rides forth!" she shouted, frantically trying to rein her horse in as it reared up before the sight of the wargol beast.

Korrun saw, amidst the carnage, a legion of dworll horsemen cutting through the plains to reach the valley. At the head of Fendellin's force, he could see the banner of the King.

"We are moving toward the valley, you must come!" Orrla shouted, hewing at a demon.

"He'll come ... in pieces!" Nuroth snarled.

Orrla reared back, her brown hair streaming, her sword poised, and was immediately surrounded by her soldiers, who sprang forward to attack.

"No!" Korrun raged. "He's mine!"

The dworlls held back.

Nuroth stopped and laughed, turning his dead eyes toward Korrun once more. "I'll finish you first ... then perhaps the girl next. What pretty bowls your heads will make!" he cackled, with a sickening smile. "I hope you beg and snivel like your brother. He squealed like a pig when I gutted him!"

"Come! Leave him to his poison!" Orrla shouted. "Only Lord Perral and Tollam will stay on the plains, to protect our rear. All of you must come. Let their forces take up your fight, you are needed elsewhere. Come!"

Korrun faltered. His head was swimming. All he could see was his brother and the face of this hideous thing before him. The King was gone? ... He had hardly noticed. They were heading for the valley ... the valley! Marval! Morreck! Wendya!

"WENDYA!" he cried, as if roused from sleep. "They are gone?!"

"Come! Now!" Orrla called again, her arm outstretched, her dark eyes fixed on the dwelf. "Ride with me!"

Korrun stumbled and turned to face Nuroth, who was hacking at two other dworlls to get to him. "NO!" he cried. "Do not fight him!"

Wendya's face came back to the tracker, as his own became reflected in the dead eyes of his enemy. The dworlls reluctantly retreated, leaving the mighty wargol and the dwelf alone in the circle they had hewn.

Korrun stood motionless, feeling the night wind against his face, his blood still running like fire through his body, his eyes staring at the small silver ring, which hung from a twisted braid around the monster's foul neck. He looked across the plains to the valley mouth and knew what he had to do.

"I will finish this! I swear by my brother, I will finish this!" he shouted through gritted teeth, bile catching in his throat.

Then, taking one last look at his hated enemy, he finally turned and took Orrla's hand, jumping onto the back of her horse.

"NO!" Nuroth roared rushing forward. "Half-breed! Coward! Fight! Fight! … FIGHT!"

Nuroth bounded over the carcasses that lay strewn at his feet and, picking up a broken blade, he hurled it towards the dwelf's back. But it was too late. Korrun and the riders turned and, disappearing into the black smoke and haze of battle, they raced toward the valley and their King.

Fumes rose from the ground below and fire split the skies asunder, as Sedgewick's dragons struggled nobly to defend themselves and protect their dworllian allies from the inevitable and savage onslaught of M'Sorreck's viperous crows. So far, this protection had cost them dearly and, though they had managed to keep the serpents away from the troops below, their losses had been great.

Always, Varkul's insidious number swarmed over them, trying to divide them and keep them from reaching Sedgewick and their master. They seemed everywhere at once, encircling them like predators surrounding cattle for the slaughter. Sometimes attacking, sometimes pulling back, sometimes rushing in amongst them and tearing the weak or weary away, before ripping the great creatures apart in a terrifying frenzy.

Outnumbered and trapped by these winged monsters that seared the air with their fire and venom, Rollm, Gralen and the others tried in vain to help Sedgewick, as he fought against Varkul. Every time they flew to the old dragon's aid, they were viciously attacked and driven back. So it was, while Fendellin's gallant and courageous fÿrrens blasted a wall of flame towards their enemy's foul hides, Sedgewick faced his enemy alone.

Lightning zipped and crackled through the air, electrifying the night sky in a flash of brilliant white as the heavens opened and the first rains came.

The mighty dragons, burnt and bloodied, hovered above the black peaks of Kavok, while the storm raged and swirled around them.

"You cannot win, old fool!" Varkul spat. "You'll die as will they. All of them! Fendellin will be ours! Lord Morreck shall have this land once more," he laughed. "A new era is coming! Yours … is already dead!"

"This land will never be his or yours!" Sedgewick boomed, his aged voice cracking as he blocked the pain from his torn wing and the deep gash across his belly, which was now bleeding heavily. "You and he are an abomination to nature and every living thing in this world!" he gasped.

Varkul cackled hysterically, his sharp eyes fixed on the elderly figure before him.

Sedgewick tried to catch his breath; he had never been so weary and so spent. The old dragon glanced below where, lost in the darkness of smoke and rain the battle continued and only a little above it, he could see his comrades hemmed in by Morreck's evil serpents, like a floating ring of fire in the night sky.

Varkul watched the wounded fÿrren.

"They cannot help you! You're nothing but carrion now!" he sneered, his blue eyes gleaming with cold, excited malice. "Your pitiful clan will be extinct before this night is over ... as will you! My master will enjoy using your skull as a decoration ... I have been waiting far too long for this!" he roared, then, like a hideous shadow, he bore down on the injured dragon.

Amidst the deafening clamor from the battlefields, came a terrible heart-wrenching sound. Dworlls and wargols alike turned their faces skyward but could see only the faintest glimmer of a brilliant fire in the skies above Kavok that blazed as brightly as the sun for a moment, before it died. The mountain groaned in response as rock and snow avalanched down its sides tumbling into the blackness.

Fendellin's dragons froze, as did their attackers.

Rollm and Gralen turned, their hearts pounding. Through the storm clouds, they could just see the mighty giants entangled in a bitter and deathly embrace. As they watched, sickened and horrified, the noise came again as Varkul tore through the old dragon's body.

"NO!" screamed Rollm. "He's killing him!"

Gralen tried to grab him but before he could, Rollm had bolted skyward, bursting through the serpents' blockade, toward his dear friend and mentor.

"NO! ... ROLLM!" Gralen shouted as he raced after him.

The encircling serpents, stunned and dazed, tried to regroup and send a barrage of flame-laced venom toward the trapped dragons, but it was too late. Though outnumbered, the Fendellin fÿrrens were united by ties stronger than blood and broke through the siege, scattering their enemies and hurling many of them to their death.

Rollm flew faster than he thought possible as a terrible desperation gripped him. Ahead, through the driving rain and sleet, he could just see the silver shape of his friend and the dark viperous creature wreathed and coiled around him like a sickening vine.

"Sedgewick!" Rollm cried out.

The old dragon's eyes flickered open for a moment. "Do not come ... son of the skies," he thought, but no words came.

Sedgewick turned his weathered face skyward. The rain fell in cool splatters about him. Gazing up he could see the stars glinting clearer and brighter than he had ever seen in all his long life. They were beautiful. And there, twinkling above him in all the glittering multitude, shone the brightest of all, the Dragonstar, like a spike of jeweled pearl and diamond in clear water. It sparkled and its light fell upon him.

"Rollm! No! ... WAIT!" Gralen shouted as he frantically chased the young dragon.

The clouds parted in solemn strands before Rollm as suddenly, in the gloom and blackness, the young dragon saw the vulturine beast raise the limp body of his friend and cast it upon the uppermost spike of Kavok. Searing heat waves pulsed out through the air like ripples on a pond and a blinding flash filled the night as Kavok's peak exploded into a violent fireball of silver and white, lighting the sky and the valley at the mountain's feet.

The flame blazed for a few moments, like a fallen comet, then faded to a smoldering ember and, as the last flickers lessened, they seemed to ignite into a shimmering silver vapor that rose up into the heavens and was lost amongst the stars.

"NO! SEDGEWICK? SEDGEWICK!" Rollm shrieked, tears blinding his eyes as he careered head-long into the huge serpent.

Varkul reeled backwards for a moment. Quicker than a viper's strike, he suddenly spun his bulk around and, using his tail as a blade, severed his attacker's left arm and grabbed the young draken by his throat.

"Two prizes for my collection!" he gloated. "I'll snap more than just your neck tonight!" he sneered as he broke one of his wings.

"No you WON'T!" bellowed a familiar voice rising like a phoenix out of the eye of the storm.

Varkul turned in time to face Gralen's full fury as the green dragon slammed into him with such force that he was sent flying backwards, dropping Rollm as he did so. Gralen lost no time. With no thought of Varkul, he plummeted down at breath-taking speed and caught his young friend just before he too became impaled upon the mountain's cruel summit.

Seconds later, before Varkul could retaliate, the serpent faced the wrath of Sedgewick's loyal dragons as they raced toward the foul beast like the onslaught of some terrible tidal plague.

Utterly overcome with grief and rage, Gralen left Kavok with only one last lingering glance at the broken figure of his beloved friend.

Even in such a desolate and treacherous place, Sedgewick's twisted body looked almost beautiful in the rain, his pale silver scales glinting like treasure amongst the ruinous spires of rock.

Gralen choked. "Goodbye," he whispered, his amber eyes filling with hot tears. Then, carrying the injured draken, he turned and disappeared into the night.

Chapter Eighteen

Turn of the Blade

The battle raged but still the horse ran on, its two riders cutting through the wargol throng, felling grasping arms as they passed, like so many branches in a forest. Orrla proved an extraordinary horse master as her father Nerrus had claimed, weaving herself and Korrun through the chaos with consummate skill.

Korrun gazed up at the moonless sky.

"The battle is turning against us ... Look!" she pointed through the flame-torn clouds to the summit of Kavok, now shrouded in dragon fire. "If your friends do not succeed, all of this will be in vain and Fendellin will fall all the quicker!"

"I know," the tracker whispered as he strained his eyes through the pouring rain to the light that sprang from the mountain peak. "Yes," he said, unable to take his eyes off Kavok, "the battle is turning against us ... and I would have been of more use fighting with the wizard than staying here!"

Orrla spurred her tarpan onward, through the tangled mass of dworll and wargol soldiers, until at last they reached the King.

"Well met!" welcomed Baillum steering his horse forward to meet the two riders. "Things have turned ill for us. Our enemy keeps us divided. Lord Lorrin's troops are trapped and near defeat while the enemy detains us here!" the King shook his head. "If we do not breach the valley within the next hour, Lorrin will be lost!"

At that moment, a great cheer rose up from the front lines. The Fendellin army had finally broken through the heavy bulk of wargols that blocked the ravine mouth.

"Fear not!" Hallm shouted. "Look! We're breaching the valley!"

Catapults and war wagons were dragged to the front to hold the hordes at bay with a flurry of missiles to drive the wargol demons ever deeper into the gorge beyond. Great rams and battle chargers surged forward with rank upon rank of heavily shielded dworlls pushing behind, forcing the enemy to scatter and retreat.

Baillum's forces flooded into the gully led by the King and Lord Nerrus. Moments later, the host of Fendellin had at last fought their way to the besieged and dwindling soldiers of Lord Lorrin — his company now half the number it had been. They swept up the narrow ravine like a tidal wave as triumphant hails greeted them, filling the air and drowning out the howls around. Baillum sped his horse toward a bedraggled and bloodied figure, standing amidst a small circle of guards.

"The King has come!" Lorrin cried, almost too weary to speak.

"Yes, dear friend, and too late!" Baillum answered looking about. "We were assailed and that nearly proved our end."

Lorrin stepped forward and stumbled.

"You are injured!" the King said looking at the dworll lord's right arm, drenched in blood and hanging stiffly at his side.

"I will live, Sire, but many of my kin have not."

Springing from Orrla's horse before it had stopped, Korrun rushed forward. "Where are the others?" he gasped. "Where is Wendya?"

"They are gone," Lord Lorrin replied quietly, clasping the hilt of his sword as if it gave him strength. "But the diversion appears to have worked. Let us hope they succeed."

Baillum looked at the dwelf's worried face and at Orrla's. "Frell is with them and our very best warriors," he reassured. "Do not rebuke yourself, you have slain many of the enemy and the night is far from over!"

"But I was needed here with them!" said the tracker. "My vengeance may have cost us all dearly!"

The Dworll King rested back in his saddle for a moment, a grim look on his face. "Our true attack is through stealth," he whispered, then paused and studied the young warrior once more, as if considering a course of action and its chances of success. "However, if you can follow them without being seen ... I think it would be wise," he sighed. "You may take Orrla, I'm sure her father would allow it, and a few others, certainly no more than a small battalion. We dare not send any more or risk discovery!" he warned, casting his eyes northward towards the crooked horns of Morreck's gate towers and their serpentine guardians. "There is little more we can do to help them now ... Only draw Morreck's forces away from the real danger and defeat as many of them as possible."

Another hail of poisoned arrows whistled over their heads and exploded around them.

Korrun nodded. "Thank you, Sire."

"How will you find them?" Lorrin asked as he was helped onto another horse.

"I'm a tracker ... that's what I do," he replied simply, glancing at Orrla.

The King nodded. "So be it. Good luck ... may luck be kind to us all!" Lifting his sword, he raised his voice to the black skies above in a thunderous and defiant boom. "Come Fendellons! Come! We shall knock on Morreck's door and see if the vile coward will come out! ... To the gates! To the gates!" he rallied.

With a deafening cry, they rode up the valley, driving back any foul beast in their path.

Amongst the chaos and smoke and the mounds of the fallen, which lay strewn about, no one noticed the crouching figures, led by the dwelf, disappearing through a slit in the rock.

The dworlls wandered on through the darkness following only the light from Frell's starstone and the red glimmer of Wendya's key. The tunnels plunged steadily downward for several hundreds of feet. An almost imperceptible glow, no more than a lighter shade of black amongst the pitch, could now be seen in the distance ahead.

"You are shaking," Mr. Agyk whispered looking at the witch's hand. "We are all fearful."

She nodded and walked on quietly, trying to control her desire to vomit and cower in some dark corner.

"Be ready," Frell warned in the lightest of whispers. "We're close to his lair," he glanced at the dragon key around Wendya's neck, which gleamed with a brightness never seen before, and half-smiled. Hiding the starstone away, he added. "We'll have no need for this now."

Onward they crept, swords drawn, breath held, ears listening for the slightest noise amidst the deathly silence that surrounded them. The foul and overpowering stench, which had grown ever stronger the deeper they ventured, lessened now, as if a little clean air from high above had somehow managed to find its way into that dark place.

Though the odor of wargols diminished, the air seemed to grow heavier and more stifling.

As they turned a sharp spur of rock, they found themselves in a widened tunnel mouth, the ground and sides of which had been flattened and pummeled smooth. This small entrance ran on for only a few feet and stopped abruptly between two bending pillars. Nervously, they inched forward until they could see what lay beyond: an immense cavern of almost incalculable size and the source of the strange glowing light.

Frell motioned to the others to crouch down as he quietly crawled to the edge. Wendya felt sick. She was sure the pounding in her chest could be heard by everyone and would betray them like a beckoning drum. Frell gestured to another dworll and together they knelt, huddled at the edge for a moment like two conspirators, before returning.

"It's a huge cavern, but it seems to be empty," Frell murmured checking his sword and looking at Wendya's key again. "There's a door at the far end. It should lead to the inner chambers and to Morreck's power source … or M'Sorreck himself. The key will guide us."

"It will open the door?" Wendya asked, peering beyond the dworll to the cavern beyond.

"It should. We're very close now. Be ready to fight. Keep close to the walls!" he warned.

Frell glanced at the wizard who had remained silent for so long. His voice sank to the merest of whispers. "I hope you are ready, wizard. We may have the element of surprise but that will not help us for long. M'Sorreck is very powerful."

Mr. Agyk roused himself, as if returning from a deep trance. "He will need his strength and you shall witness mine, young captain," he replied sternly, his eyes flaring for a moment. "I will reclaim that which is mine, that which was stolen from me. I will not leave until I have retaken all my powers and broken his! … His malice ends tonight!"

With that, Mr. Agyk became suddenly animated and leapt from Wendya's shoulder. He seemed to glide toward the tunnel mouth, his staff burning brightly about him, his eyes a blazing silver as he gazed over his enemy's domain.

The cavern was enormous, burrowing through the mountain roots for over a mile in length, its walls pitted with hundreds of maggot-looking holes, like black eyes staring at them.

They descended the roughly hewn steps onto a ledge below. It skirted the cavern walls and was broken only by the colossal black pillars that lined the hall, sprouting from the floor and disappearing somewhere in the darkness above. On this narrow and perilous path sat hideous gargoyles, a gallery of grotesque, mocking statues seeming to grow from the pillars themselves. Wendya shuddered, feeling a cold hand run itself down her back.

"This is no mere hall," the little wizard murmured standing on the edge. "This is his home, the heart of it!"

The cavern walls glowed with an eerie diaphanous blue; fathomless and baleful like the bottom of some ghastly ocean trench. Pale lights glinted on the shimmering surface, forming fleeting patterns, before fading. The entire space felt alive; a malignant presence waiting and watching and breathing. The air throbbed with a mindless heartbeat of its own.

They carefully wound their way down the many flights of stairs, which twisted and coiled themselves between the vast pillars, before dividing off into smaller tentacle steps of single width. As they reached the ground, they could see tiny spheres of blue and orange light appear all around the edge of the gigantic floor. Orbs of light bubbled up from somewhere below, pulsating upwards in streams of glowing beads until they disappeared into the gloom above.

Wendya swallowed. "We should leave," she whispered. "Now!"

Gralen bent over Rollm as he phased in and out of consciousness.

"You'll be safe here, but keep out of sight," he murmured, and gently placed the young dragon in a sheltered hollow beneath an overhanging crag of rock. "I've sealed your wounds. You've lost a lot of blood though."

Rollm slowly opened his eyes again.

Gralen smiled. "You'll be fine. I'll be back as soon as I can."

The green draken struggled up, wincing with pain as he held onto the broken stub of his left arm, severed just below the shoulder. "Gralen, find him and kill him!" he spluttered. "Promise me … for Sedgewick."

Thunder rumbled overhead. Lightning flashed across the night as the rain came down even harder. Rollm stared up at his friend, barely able to keep his eyes open.

"Promise me," he whispered, "promise me."

Gralen looked at him. "I promise … now lie still," he sighed. With a sickening dread in his stomach, he reluctantly left his young charge and raced back to the battle.

King Baillum, Nerrus and Lorrin continued up the dark gorge until, at last, they were beneath the mighty granite gates of Morreck's fortress, and under the piercing gaze of its serpentine guardians, the sentinels.

The gate towers rose above them, on either side, like two hideous and crooked tusks piercing the sky with their cruelty. But it was the brooding malice of the sentinels that instilled the most fear amongst the dworllian troops. They loomed above them, monstrous and mountainous, their stony eyes flickering with the threat of life.

"If we are to fight and die, Sire, then let us at least move away from those dreadful things. They freeze the blood!" Lord Nerrus exclaimed.

Baillum nodded. "Yes … M'Sorreck *is* the Master of Serpents. If we cannot force the doors or draw him out, then I too would rather not be pinned under those beasts!" he agreed, looking up at the watch guards.

At that moment, a shifting fog issued from the ground all about and from the mouths of the sentinels, coiling out in seductive fingers. The vapor, a pale, luminous orange, recoiled when touched, as if it were a living entity. Flooding the valley floor, it spread throughout the dworll ranks, unnerving horses and soldiers alike.

"What is this?" Nerrus asked, thrashing the mist with his broken shield.

"Some devilry of Morreck's," the King muttered, looking at the gates before them. "This is far from over!"

Beyond the gorge, on the dark and bloodied salt plains, Lord Tollam and Lord Perral fought tirelessly to lessen their enemy and protect the rear-guard of King Baillum's host. Yet amongst the battle, a strange sense of change permeated the air.

"Where have they gone?" shouted one of Tollam's horsemen.

"They are retreating! The enemy is retreating! … They are defeated!" cried another.

"No … They recoil for another strike!" Tollam replied grimly, his well-lined face staring at the black mountain above through the sheets of rain that now fell in torrents about them.

The old dworll stood high in his saddle, a tall, gracious figure amidst the horror around, his heavy-lidded keen eyes surveying the land and the small pockets of fighting.

"The battle continues," he said, "but it has lessened here and that worries me."

"Let us join Hallm and the King," the young guard answered, "we can do little more here."

Tollam looked up to the dark rain-filled skies and watched the flashes and rumbles up above, his violet eyes full of concern. "Lord Sedgewick's dragons fight bravely … but something is wrong."

"What is the matter, brother?" Perral asked, riding up on his pale horse. "Are we not winning?" he smiled.

Tollam sighed and wearily reined in Dallid, his faithful tarpan. "Look around you. Does this not seem strange? The enemy has all but left these plains. M'Sorreck gives us nothing but vermin to slay. Where have his captains, his prized soldiers, his legions gone? … He is trying to occupy us, keep us distracted. But why?" he shook his head. "I do not think we have won the plains so easily. We stay to protect the King, but from what?"

"That is a good question, Tollam." Perral answered quietly, his eyes scanning the old dworll. "What do we fight for?"

Tollam stared at his friend quizzically.

Perral looked imperious amongst the pouring rain. He sat high and proud in his saddle, his back as straight as a lightning rod, his short, dark hair showing only a few flecks of gray. His pale face denied his true age, with far fewer lines than his friend's, and upon it, Tollam could see an unmistakable excitement and eagerness for battle. Quite understandable he thought, after endless years of tending over fields of emmer and einkorn and crumbling irrigation channels. Perral obviously yearned to recapture the former glories and heroic wars of old. A time less muddled, a simple age where values and loyalties were clear and the destiny of each warrior lay like a river of glass before him.

Tollam studied the dworll lord as he drew alongside him. "What do you mean?" he asked.

A flicker of something, maybe a smile, passed across Perral's face and his eyes glistened darkly. "You think we stand on the brink of a precipice? We have already fallen! Do you really believe we fight for the freedom of Fendellin? Freedom from what? ... From one of our own? An ancient lord, an Ellda, a dwizard of the old realm?"

He paused for a moment, watching Tollam intently.

"Humans — children, as we call them — do we fight for them, these ... primitives?" he said, his voice laced with contempt. "You may not have noticed, Tollam, but we live in a prison already, my friend. A prison! Hemmed in as cattle, caged from an outside world that no longer wants us, or even knows we exist. A world where we were once great lords and kings, masters of our own destiny, where we roamed freely and ruled wisely, and now? We hide and cower like frightened infants. We hide!" his eyes fixed on the old dworll. "Hide from simian creatures, weaker than us, who took our world, poisoned and raped it! They pollute the skies with their chemicals, destroy the seas and the lands, and build ugly cities of concrete and steel. They have no honor, no power, no history, except that which we gave them. They were animals when we were kings. We allowed them to breed, to spread and infect this planet like a plague, while we did nothing! Why? Because the Order told us to!" he ranted. "We were the chosen ones; we were the guardians of this world, our world. Why should they rule and ruin it, rule and ruin us? Should we really allow them to destroy us as they destroy themselves and everything they touch? ... Do you really believe you are free?"

Tollam remained tight-lipped and silent.

Great wafts of drifting smoke enveloped them, isolating them from the other troops. Time seemed to stand still. Even the noise of battle and the rain seemed a distant drone. Perral smiled, his manner friendly and unguarded.

"Fendellin is large but not limitless. Her glory has long since passed. She is no longer a nation of grand city-states, of great wisdom and glorious achievements. She is weak. These primitives have a thirst to conquer all. They will never stop ... One day they will come. They will find us. Fendellin's great mountain barrier cannot hide us forever." Perral's eyes searched Tollam's for any sign of agreement. "And what will happen when they find us, when our borders crumble? Will we again scurry underground like rats? Or will we fight to preserve and reclaim what is rightfully ours?"

His eyes gleamed with an agitated fire that Tollam had never seen before. He had known this dworll his entire life, since childhood. A brother-in-arms, a great friend and a ruler to his people, fair and just, a man of words, of reason, a brother in kind.

With an awful clarity and a sickening dread, the undeniable truth struck him. Tollam knew the stories, as they all did, of those who had undergone 'the change'. Stories of transformations, corruptions that could infiltrate any brotherhood, deterioration that could silently slide into the minds and hearts of even the most loyal. Of deathly harbingers, whispering into the ears of the sleeping.

Some had turned overnight and withdrawn into darkness and insanity. Most had exploded in psychotic violence. Rumors had spread of fellow soldiers turning, of skirmishes in the night that had been kept quiet. Tollam knew the signs and what to look for, but never had he imagined that Perral, one of the few ruling Lords of Fendellin, would fall victim.

Lord Tollam said nothing in reply but inched his hand toward the hilt of his sword.

"M'Sorreck is not our enemy," Perral continued. "He is our savior! We should be embracing him instead of fighting him! He will reclaim the world, all of it, for us, for our children, he has the power to do it. Only Morreck can restore the planet again and give us true freedom! ... The simians have had their time and look what they've done! Do you not see? M'Sorreck will restore the Ancient Order as it should have been and the earth shall be a paradise for all our peoples!"

Tollam responded calmly. "Freedom is not his to give, Lord Perral, none can offer that. You have changed, old friend. We had our time, now it is theirs, the world does not belong to us anymore. Evolution ... nature ... has chosen them."

"Nature!" Perral spat, his face suddenly contorted. "Nature is mindless and savage, and they care nothing for it! They will destroy this world, will you help them do it?" he shouted, quickly regained his composure, and tried to smile. "I talk of magic, of restoring the old ways as they were, before the great mages, Oracles and ǽllfrs left. Before the exodus, when we did not have to hide in tunnels and dark cities. I talk of light! Light! Of restoring our citadels, reclaiming our heritage! Think of it ... reclaiming what is rightfully ours!" his face had a manic quality to it, his pupils dilated, as one possessed by a great fervor.

Tollam sighed and shook his head mournfully. "I never thought it would be you, Perral. I am ashamed to admit that I suspected ... I had misgivings about Lord Nerrus." he sighed again. "So ... when did you become M'Sorreck's puppet? When were you corrupted by his poison?" he asked quietly, feeling a weight of sorrow fall upon his shoulders as his fingers curled and tightened round his sword.

"Poison! Poison!" Perral laughed. "*You've* been poisoned by false promises, not I! I see more clearly than I ever have! I'm fighting for a future, a future for our people! The path ahead is clear, as is what we must do. There are others ... Lord Morreck has many followers, in every ruling house, every council, every government in our world, and theirs. Devoted followers, poised to move, waiting for him. There are too many to stop, Tollam!" he sneered. "The war began long before now; this is only an insignificant battle, a precursor to the main event! The final battles are to come. Open your eyes! We see the great mistakes for what they are. The sacrifices you make are meaningless. The hardships you endure are futile. The result is the same, caged like animals. We see the truth, not what a frightened weakling coward feeds us. The King of a prison is no King at all!"

The old dworll stared at him. "You would turn against King Baillum? Turn against us?"

Perral's eyes narrowed. "I am a true patriot!" he exclaimed. "Are you? I will protect this land and protect our heritage. If that means the death of a floundering King, then so be it. Choices have to be made. Do you have the courage and the clarity to make them?" he studied Tollam closely. "You are a strong leader, Lord Tollam, your people will follow you. Join us. Give your followers a chance, fight for *them*, not for some fool of a King! Join us!"

"Never!" Tollam bellowed. He drew his sword and, in one deft movement, pointed it at the dworll lord that he thought he had known so well.

"So be it." Perral smiled coldly. "It is better this way, old friend."

Tollam turned to see one of his young horsemen silently standing nearby, looking stunned and confused at the exchange between two such prominent lords. "Go!" he shouted. "Warn the King! Perral has turned! Go!"

The young soldier nodded and mounted his horse, but as he did so, two arrows rang out and caught him in the throat.

"NO!" Tollam shouted, as the dworll fell dead to the ground and his horse galloped off.

The old lord spun round. Through the mists he could see that his troops were dispersed across the plains and mingled with Perral's, with many of them still fighting the enemy dregs. Arrows suddenly filled the air, flying around him in a blizzard, and in the dark he could hear wails and cries as they found their marks.

"TRAITOR!" he screamed, turned to Perral, and lunged forward.

The sentinels, massive stone dragons and guardians of Morreck's fortress.

Perral laughed and reared his horse back. Raising his sword high into the air in a gesturing signal, he smiled. "Dishonesty is an underrated virtue, Tollam. I'm glad the pretense is over," he sneered. "The time has come! Attack! Attack!"

The thousands of carcasses and bodies that lay slumped in piles around them, stirred. Bodies and limbs moved in the darkness. Groans could be heard through the rain. The dead were awakening! Terrified cries echoed through the night as, amongst the fallen, hundreds of red wargol eyes appeared and, rising beside them, their eyes now horrifyingly dead, were Perral's soldiers, thought killed in battle, forming an unholy alliance with the enemy.

"You should have joined us!" the traitorous dworll cried, glaring at Tollam with eyes as dark as jet. "You have just sealed your fate, and that of all those who follow you."

Tollam's soldiers lay scattered and bewildered, horror-struck by the movement all around them, as the dead came alive once more. The rallying cry of their beloved leader brought them to their senses. As Perral's treachery was revealed, they came together, a united force.

"Traitor! … Traitors!" they cried.

The deathblow was swift and merciless.

Tollam's dwindling soldiers and those few of Perral's who had remained loyal and knew nothing of their master's treachery, or the poisoning of their comrades, were dispatched in the first and second wave of arrows. Like the tightening of a deadly net, which had been trapped and baited, their enemy surrounded them on all sides.

A few warriors fuelled by outrage and courage broke through but were quickly felled by the wargol demons that had lain in wait. Tollam fought bravely, his horsemen protecting him as he ploughed through the enemy ranks trying to reach Perral, but the fight was futile. Amidst the cries and clashes of shield and metal, a dworll axe struck and found its target.

Tollam lurched to one side, falling from his horse. His soldiers rallied round and fought wildly about him, but were killed one after the other, their bodies crashing to the ground, as the traitors closed in.

Lord Tollam lay on his back gasping for breath. His horse-guard lay dead beside him. The last of his brave warriors were slaughtered. He was alone. He blinked the sweat and blood from his eyes and looked in delirious disbelief at the fallen bodies of his kin, so many of them young with families. He raised his eyes to the sea of wargols and dark dworlls about him.

"I shall see you all rot in the Chasms of Kallimal!" he roared and pulled the axe blade from his chest. "Your reward for this treachery shall be everlasting! You are damned, all of you!"

He slashed wildly at his enemy's legs, but his cloven breastplate and the blood that now gushed from the mortal wound inside, could not be mended.

He looked to the glittering multitude above, the stars glinting pitilessly in the dark. "I have failed you, Sire," he spluttered. "Forgive me, I did not know," he whispered, falling back as a pair of red eyes bore down on him. "I did not know."

Exploding missiles showered into the valley, cascading over the battlements and cliffs like waterfalls of fire, while rivers of orange mist flowed through the Fendellin host below.

"Sire, these gates are held by more than just iron and granite! The battle rams have had no effect! We cannot force them!" Lord Nerrus called, looking at the black gates as arrows whistled past. "We need shelter from this!"

"Our shields must suffice," King Baillum answered sternly. "What we need is magic."

"Or flame," Lorrin replied looking upward. "Our friends may help us there."

Baillum felt the battle slipping away from them. "Yes, the time has come for greater aid. Let us hope the battle above has gone well, so we may use their talents here!"

At that moment, a commotion could be heard from the soldiers behind. Something was coming up the gorge, weaving between the carnage, approaching very fast. The dworll army stood ready. Amidst the shower of darts and the constant foul cries from the black cliffs above, silence rolled up the valley floor toward them.

"Don't shoot!" Hallm cried. "Don't shoot! They're ours."

"It is only a horse … no, two horses," Lord Nerrus said, standing up in his stirrups. "There is something behind, at the valley mouth. Riders! It is Perral's flag! The plains must be won!"

"Then victory must be close," King Baillum said, relief passing over his face.

The approaching horses galloped wildly onward, as if fleeing a great terror. Hallm raced forward and leapt in front of them. Catching one of their bridles, he jumped onto the older horse's back and managed to slow them, stopping just before the King's company.

"You truly are a horse master, young Hallm!" the King smiled.

"Wait!" Lorrin cried as he walked towards them. "I know these horses," he said taking the reins of the larger gray beast. He looked up at a silent Hallm, whose face was turned aside and full of sorrow. "This is your father's horse, this is Lord Tollam's!" he whispered.

Baillum looked at the young captain. "Are you sure?" he asked.

Hallm bent his head and, placing his hand on the nervous beast's neck, nodded. "It is his horse," he replied quietly, fighting his grief away.

"He may still be alive, just thrown perhaps," Lorrin said, staring at the startled beast.

Hallm looked at them and shook his head. "Dallid does not throw his master," he answered solemnly, his voice faltering as he tried to calm the horse. "There is only one reason he has returned without his master," he said, slipping from the horse. He gently removed its bridle and armored harness. "No others shall ride him."

"Does this night have no end?" Baillum muttered. "How much must we suffer?"

The sky thundered in reply. The swirling wind and rain danced gaily amongst the cruel rocks and fiery battlements above, but in the ravine, a storm approached.

"Lord Perral draws near!" Nerrus hailed.

As soon as he had spoken, Perral's forces swept up the gully. As they drew nearer, the vicious reign of missiles that had showered down from Kavok seemed to lessen.

"Look! He has driven fear into the enemy's heart!" one of the soldiers cried.

A hushed silence filled the air once more, pierced only by the pounding of hooves and the feet of the approaching host. Perral rode triumphantly at the head of his soldiers, a returning hero and warrior-lord, proud and defiant.

The Fendellin army, exhausted and weary in body and soul, rejoiced at the lord's arrival. Dworlls cheered and stamped feet or clashed shields together. The battle was nearly won! The valley and the plains were taken and Morreck's hordes had been slain or driven back into the mountain roots. Victory was at hand!

"My old friend!" Lord Nerrus welcomed his friend. "Well met!"

Lord Perral passed without a word and stopped abruptly before the King, his face troubled. "I have news, Sire," he said, his voice strangely cold and hard. "The plains have been taken but at a great cost. The battle was fierce," he paused. "... Lord Tollam has fallen."

Hallm stood nearby. The others bent their heads in deference, but the young captain remained silent, staring at the dworll lord.

"A mountain wargol, one of the larger demons, killed him," Perral continued quietly, his eyes fixed on the old King. "He fought valiantly."

Fires flickered above their heads but still the enemy lay quiet.

"It is as we feared," Baillum sighed at last. "When Lord Tollam's horse returned without its master, young Hallm here knew that his father had died."

Perral sat motionless in his saddle, his face an unreadable mask.

"Are you injured?" the King asked, sensing a change in the dworll.

"No ... only in spirit, Sire," he replied through cold eyes.

The King nodded in agreement. "Your troops ... why are some of their eyes shielded?"

"The salt was blinding, Sire, we had to protect ourselves," he retorted, his eyes never leaving the King.

Hallm slowly stepped forward. "Forgive me Lord, but where is the body of my father?"

Perral glared at the young captain. "Do you doubt me?" he snapped.

Hallm bowed low. "No Lord ... I only wish to have my father's body so that I may place him upon his horse, and carry him to a place of rest amongst the battlefield."

Lorrin agreed. "Even in such a place as this, it is customary of our kin, and certainly our lordships, that they are borne away and not left amongst the fallen to be desecrated."

Perral glanced at him and turned once more toward the King. "I am aware of our customs and do not need telling of them. But, alas," he said, trying to soften his voice. "There was little for me to bring, or I would have done so. He was, I'm afraid, terribly savaged before I could reach him." Lord Perral, every muscle rigid, every sense acute, watched Baillum and the others cross their arms over their chests in sign of mourning. Poised as if on a razor's edge, his eyes suddenly blazed and without warnin,g he lunged forward.

"And so it shall be with you!" he cried raising his sword.

In that instant, Perral's forces waiting for a signal from their master, broke rank and turned on their dworll comrades. The sky crackled with wargol howls and dragon screams, and the air itself was singed with fire.

As Perral's sword went to strike its deadly blow and sink into the helm of the King, it struck steel instead. Hallm, never taking his eyes off Perral, had moved silently towards the King's side, while Perral had spoken of his father. As the traitorous dworll raised his sword, so too did Hallm, in response.

"Traitor!" he shouted, as he leapt in front to protect the King.

Baillum reeled backwards as if bitten by a snake.

"Die! All of you! Die as the slaves you are, as the cowering fools! Die in this prison you love so much!" Perral snarled, his face horribly contorted by wild madness and murderous rage, as he charged his horse toward the young captain.

"Treachery! Treachery! To arms Fendellons!" King Baillum hailed as his forces were waylaid "Look to your backs! We have been betrayed!"

Perral's ranks cackled. The Fendellin host could now see thousands of red-eyed wargols streaming up the valley towards them and through hidden slits in the black rock.

With a perfect and abhorrent lucidity they all understood. The plains were lost and they were now trapped, like cattle in an abattoir, ready for the slaughter. Through Perral's treachery, Morreck had known everything. He had been waiting for them and they had fallen unwittingly into his clutches. There was no way out.

"Oh, gods! … This was his plan all along … to bring us to him! To wipe us out, all of us! We have walked straight into his grasp!" Nerrus shouted looking around frantically, his troops besieged on all sides.

There was no way to survive this.

A thundering boom shook the ground and echoed in every ear. Fendellin soldiers looked up in abject horror as Morreck's gate towers ignited into flame and with a sickening sound and the sliding judder of a great iron bolt, a door opened with a cracking noise .

"Fight! Fight! It is a trap! Fight to the death! For glory, for Fendellin!" Baillum rallied as the enemy swarmed over the cliff edges and M'Sorreck's black gates finally swung open.

In that same instant, more howls and screams filled the air as boulders and great splinters of rock showered down from above, crushing any beneath them.

"Look! The sentinels! The sentinels are alive! Save us! Save us!" they cried in disbelief.

Cracked and blackened like the mountain itself, the sentinels moved, two monstrous and serpentine things rising from the rock face, groaning into life, breaking free of the stone shackles that held them in place.

"Run! Run!"

The creatures, mindless and driven by only one purpose, flexed their stony spines and wings and, in one swift movement, they careered down upon the fleeing dworlls. Crushing them like ants beneath their huge clawed feet, while the wargols cheered on.

The young captain stood between Perral and the King's company.

"You treacherous scum! What did Morreck offer you? Rule over Fendellin? A share of the bounty? Your own kingdom?" Hallm roared, his sword raised.

Perral smiled insidiously, his face a hideous mask. "Of course. Actually, I believe your two nubile sisters were also part of the bargain!"

"You filth! My father was your friend!" the dworll cried as Perral's steed bore down on him. "You shall pay for your treason and for murdering him!"

The young captain lunged forward, but in his rage fell over a body slain on the ground. Perral smiled and reared his horse up to crush him. Suddenly it screamed and fell forward throwing its rider, a sword thrust into its belly. Hallm rolled out of the way and scrambled to his feet. He pulled his sword from the poor beast as it thrashed and kicked its legs in agony.

"Curse you!" Perral screamed as he rushed toward the young dworll. "Die!"

Hallm could hear heavy, iron-shod feet behind him. Standing firm, he did not swerve from Perral's sight. He held his sword aloft, and quickly jumped aside as a large wargol came up behind him, spear in hand.

The enemy's spear pierced body armor and flesh.

Perral dropped to his knees, stunned. A crude lance impaled through his chest, skewering him to the ground. Hallm wasted no time. He sprang onto the dazed wargol's back and slit his throat. Striding the foul carcass, he calmly stood before the treacherous lord, trusted for so long and by so many.

Perral's eyes blazed like a creature possessed as he looked up from the impaled spear and sneered through red gritted teeth. "You cannot win!" he hissed. "There are too many of us!"

Hallm took a deep breath. For a single moment the cloud of battle around seemed to diminish and fall silent.

"Faithless villain! Traitor! You are the scum of Morreck. You gave no mercy … and you shall receive none!" he bellowed through clenched teeth, as he brought his sword down upon the betrayer's head.

Lightning flashed across the sky in horrid zigzags as the black rain continued to fall. Gralen raced onward, keeping low over the mountaintops and out of sight of the wheeling serpents above, until he reached the plains. But, to his alarm, everything lay still. He circled the salt flats, trying to find some movement, some friend or foe amongst the smoldering piles and nightmarish scenes below.

Something was terribly wrong. Nothing stirred, no wargol or dworll. The battlefield lay silent and dead, a graveyard of twisted limbs and straddling smoke. In desperation, Gralen looked ahead and his keen eyes could see that the fighting was now concentrated in the gorge, and the fiercest of this was at the valley head, directly beneath the menacing towers of Morreck's fortress.

He turned and sped on, passing over the black rocks and battlements of Kavok's outer defenses, skimming low over the narrowing canyon and the masses below. The entire ravine was alive with fire and crawling things, like a mound of black beetles slithering and squirming in a sea of mud, and in the far distance two large and ominous shadows moved, pounding through the gloom.

The dragon faltered, unsure of what he was seeing. "How can this be ...?!" he gasped and flew northward.

The gruesome sight that finally greeted him was worse than any foul trick or vision he could have imagined. The Fendellin army lay in tatters, divided and swamped by overwhelming numbers of wargols and fÿrullfrs, but worse, far worse, was the sight of dworll fighting dworll.

"What's happening? They've gone mad! A madness has taken them!" he muttered in disbelief. Then he saw them; ... two colossal moving mountains of rock sculpted into serpentine creatures and both racing toward him.

He veered off to the side as one of the sentinels swiped at him, its stony bulk too heavy to lift off the ground.

"What madness is this?" Gralen gasped spiraling into the air as the other launched towards him. He blasted them from above, but his fiercest flames had no effect and only blackened them further. "Alright ... stone with stone!" he cried and plummeted straight toward them at incredible speed.

The sentinels were instantly ready, their craggy hands stretching out to grasp him. Seconds before crashing into them, he swerved and shot over their heads. Turning swiftly to claw him, they struck each other instead, their stone arms crashing into the other and crumbling in the force of the impact.

"Not too bright, are you?" taunted the dragon as the limbs and half of one of their faces, shattered to the ground.

The green dragon quickly launched himself at them again, this time firing jets of flame before him, which hid the boulder he now carried. Again he dived just above them and sent the rock crashing down upon their heads, fracturing one and completely destroying the other.

Gralen attacked again and again, until at last the dreaded sentinels were reduced to no more than twitching piles of rubble. Almost paralyzed with fear for his lost friends, the dragon swooped into the valley — desperate to find them amongst the throng.

Spears glanced off him or struck hard flesh for a moment before falling away. He dove lower. Skimming above the enemy, he took many heads as he flew and scooped the larger wargol demons in his talons, delighting in dropping them from a great height or impaling them on any jutting spike of rock as Varkul had done to dear Sedgewick. Suddenly, amongst the deafening howls of the enemy, a voice, clear as glass pierced the din.

"Gralen! GRALEN!"

The dragon swerved and circled back.

"GRALEN!" the voice called. "Here! It is King Baillum! Here!"

The dragon searched the crowds and finally saw, amidst a ferocious cluster of fighting, the Dworll King. Only a few hundred Fendellin soldiers now remained, being cut down rank after rank as quickly as wheat harvested from a field. Missiles and serpent bombs — fireballs laced with venom — continued to explode around them, sending sparks and flame into the air and making it hard to breathe.

He arched his back and roared, the thundering sound sending a wave of terrified wargols running before him and giving him just enough space to crash-land.

"You are well met!" the King shouted.

"What's happened here?" Gralen demanded.

"Devilry and treachery! Betrayal of the worse kind!" the King replied stoically, as he clutched a bloodied scarf to his head, then turned and looked toward the sentinels. "You have saved many by taking those things down, our swords and spears had no effect at all! ... But it will not be enough, we are overrun!"

Lord Lorrin approached, himself badly injured. "Sire, there are too many of them, we will not last another hour if we stay here! We should retreat, if we can, and rally for another assault or at least find some shelter!"

"We cannot go back ... but help is at hand," Baillum answered, looking at the dragon. "We need Sedgewick and the others now ... Can you bring them?" he asked.

Gralen hesitated, then nodded. "I will," he replied mournfully and took a deep breath. "But Lord Sedgewick ... has fallen," he paused, casting his eyes briefly to the summit of Kavok before looking away. "Most of Morreck's serpents have been slain or have fled across the mountains, the others are giving chase ... I'll call as many of them here to help you as I can. But first, please tell me...," he swallowed nervously.

Baillum smiled. "The mage and the young wicca are safe, at least they were when they left us," he answered. "That part of the plan at least has worked. Korrun has followed them along with Lord Nerrus's daughter, Orrla."

Gralen sighed.

"I am glad to see you relieved, but news of Lord Sedgewick's death pains me. Things here have also turned evil," replied the King, with pain in his eyes. "Lord Perral and his forces have turned on us! That is why you see dworll fighting dworll. A trusted friend he was. Never did I think I would see an evil day such as this!"

"Perral!" Gralen gasped, looking at the old dworll.

"He is dead. Hallm killed him to protect me, but not before the traitor murdered his father, Lord Tollam."

"Lord Tollam is dead!" the dragon cried in utter disbelief.

The warrior King nodded. "Perral's treachery has caused the death of many, and may prove the death of all!"

"Are all his troops turned?" Gralen asked quietly, watching the fighting around.

"Most of them, yes," Lorrin answered. "Corrupted and poisoned ... when, we do not know. But it is too late for them. They are followers of M'Sorreck now, dark dworlls, their minds gone, their hearts as black as their foul master's. Those who did not turn, who were unaware of the betrayal, were probably slaughtered," he shook his head in dismay, "I too never thought I'd live to see such a day!"

King Baillum felt the weight of such a defeat heavily on his heart. He had led them to their death, all of them, with little hope of victory, and now Mund'harr and the Golden City lay waiting for Morreck to grasp it. Never in all his long life and the lives of the great rulers before him, had such an accursed tragedy occurred.

"Do not give in to despair, Sire," Lorrin said watching the old King falter. "The night is far from over."

"This is an evil turn of the blade!" the dragon gasped, feeling a cloying sickness swell in him. "That's how Morreck knew of our attack. That's how he knew we were coming and was waiting for us!"

"I would surmise. But now is not the time for riddles. The battle has turned against us and we must fight," Baillum retorted, stirring his weary horse into action. "We must give the wizard more time."

"WAIT! Wait!" Gralen cried, his heart pounding in his great chest, his head reeling as a horror slowly gripped him. "If Perral was a traitor and he told Morreck of our plans, then he must've told Morreck everything. Morreck will know our plans, about Marval and Wendya! He'll know everything!" he shouted. "He'll be waiting for them! ... They'll be walking into a trap! ... A TRAP!!"

Chapter Nineteen

Cavern of Souls

A suffocating dread choked the air, as the group continued through the cavern. They walked quickly now, their footsteps falling silently on the glassy floor as they weaved between the pillars, keeping close to the walls and out of sight of the grotesque gargoyles.

At the far end of the hall, they could just make out a tall, narrow doorway at the top of a steep flight of jagged stairs. Surrounding it lay strange deformed carvings that grew from the stone and branched over the walls in spidery tentacles.

Frell ran on ahead, his keen ears and eyes scanning for the merest sound or movement.

Mr. Agyk followed, appearing to glide, as he led the rest of the group. Wendya ran uneasily behind. Fear crept over her with every step, filling her limbs with a sick lethargy. Her body felt like lead, as if she were trying to awaken from the clutches of a dark sleep.

The cavern walls began to undulate, sending out slowly rippling waves like the viscous film of some deep pool. She watched, mesmerized by the flickering orbs of blue and orange light that flashed into the darkness, and the pale luminescent veil that ebbed and flowed with the shifting surface, inviting her to touch it.

She outstretched her hand.

"Do not touch the walls!" Mr. Agyk whispered sharply. "They are not rock!" he paused. "Something is alive in here ...," he added nervously. "There is a presence. I can feel it ... watching us. We must hurry!"

221

They ran on, as Wendya's key burned brightly against her skin.

Suddenly the floor trembled and swelled, as if it were alive and was now taking its first breath.

"He knows we are here!" the wizard murmured, panic filling his voice.

A splitting sound filled the air as the walls bulged inwards, throbbing and pulsating like the chambers of a giant heart.

"The walls are alive! The walls are alive!" they cried.

"Don't touch them! Quickly, to the center!" Frell called.

"This entire hall is alive!" Mr. Agyk muttered, feeling a buzz and tingle of electricity surrounding them. "He knows we are here! This is a TRAP!"

At that moment, every orb of blue and orange light changed to milky white, tracing up the cavern walls like thousands of empty eyeballs. Groans and murmurs emanated around, and deathly faces appeared in the rock before the horrified group.

Ghastly waifs and ghostly apparitions strained their skeletal faces, moaning and gaping in agony, their torsos writhing and stretching beneath the skin of the stone. Pillars animated into life, moving with outstretched hands, rising and sinking in tidal unison. A sickly orange vapor bubbled from the ground, spreading across the floor towards them, as the air became almost un-breathable. A paralyzing fear took hold of the company as the wails of the fallen souls grew louder.

"Welcome," a voice boomed as if from the very bowels of the earth.

The amber mist encircled them, curling into the air like a twisting snake. Raising his arms aloft, the little wizard uttered an incantation and in response his staff burst into a brilliant flame, shrinking the vapors back with a hiss as if they were hurt by it.

Before the eyes of his astonished companions, Mr. Agyk stepped forward, a steely expression on his face, as he grew in stature, instantly overshadowing them.

"We have come for you, M'Sorreck! I have come for you!" he bellowed. His comrades stared at him in shock and disbelief. "Your tyranny will stop this night! I reclaim that which you stole, foul wærloga! Now show yourself!" the wizard's voice rang out.

"Here I ammm …," a licentious voice whispered into every ear, playful in manner and so chillingly close that each dworll turned to see the speaker.

"Enough of your tricks!" Mr. Agyk shouted, his eyes ablaze, his voice breaking like thunder. "Show yourself M'Sorreck, breaker of oaths, corruptor of hearts!"

Laughter rumbled in the darkness above. Frell and the other dworlls readied themselves.

"I have heard my name so many times, uttered in so many tongues, whispered on ten thousand trembling lips," the voice replied. "I have been waiting and watching far longer than you can surmise. And you come to me with this pitiful band of ants to assail me?" hissed the voice. "I can feel your fear, you are drenched with it!"

"Do not listen to him!" Mr. Agyk rallied. "He is a feeder of souls and hope! He is a master of demons and all the fetid creatures that slither in this world! He will corrupt you if he can! … Show yourself!" he demanded.

With that, the stone door at the far end of the cavern shuddered and the sculpted tentacles surrounding it came alive, as the door itself groaned open. All eyes were fixed as the door gaped wider and wider, stretching the rock apart like elastic, and from its yawning mouth issued a thick black fog. The fog hovered for a moment, lingering at the top of the stairs and from within its depths came a strange glowing liquid.

The dworlls stood motionless, spellbound as the liquid poured itself languidly down the steps. Trickling onto the floor it gathered itself, rising up into a monstrous globular mass, devoid of any form. Frell and the others stepped back, aghast, as the thing slowly came towards them, rising in stature and taking on the appearance of a hooded figure.

The terror and dread it brought had never been felt by any in the group before and they struggled to catch their breath, as if they were being asphyxiated.

"Save us! Save us!" a soldier howled as he broke ranks and dropped to his knees.

Another wailed and fled, screaming down the hall tearing at his hair and face.

"Stay together Fendellons! Stay together!!" Frell rallied. "Remember who you are!"

"Oh gods! A shape shifter! A changeling!" exclaimed another. "We cannot fight that!"

"I will fight it! Do not forget your strength Fendellons! Listen to your Captain!" the wizard shouted, his voice silencing other sounds and filling them with defiant hope.

Unable to avert her eyes, Wendya stared at the creature. It was as if they were looking at the very face of death, their own gruesome death, as both a spectator to the horror and a helpless victim of it. It held a hypnotic power over them.

The thing approached, moving without a sound. Then, stretching its form again, it grew in height once more. "Marvalla A'Gyk. Welcome to my humble home," the figure spoke, seeming both youthful and as aged as the mountain in which they were entombed. "So, you have come to match wits with me?" it murmured mockingly, its silken voice caressing those it addressed.

"Enough of your tricks foul wærloga!" Mr. Agyk retorted sharply.

The shape towered before them, ominous and fathomless, a pit of ruinous despair. Hairline cracks spread like fine fingers on the floor around its feet, igniting the vapors that covered the ground. The fog that enveloped around it spun faster and faster, flickering as a dark flame, before rising to reveal the creature inside.

Morreck stood before them. The embodiment of a living god.

This divine figure appeared untouched by time yet ancient beyond their reckoning. A first order magus of a once noble line and the last remaining Ellda, he was a creature of immeasurable power. Millenniums of dark magic and festering malice ran through his veins. Untold years of slaughtering and consuming the powers of others had changed him forever.

Gold and ochre robes lay beneath his dark mantle and the flash of scarlet that lined it, . His alabaster skin, hard and smooth as marble, yet tissue-thin, glowed with a sickly phosphorous light, a strange luminescent substance which, in its translucency, scarcely concealed his frame. A terrifying force coursed through him, akin to electricity.

They watched in silence as his hood fell away to reveal a face perilously fair and beautiful, a reincarnation of the Sun-God Ra, or Gilgamesh perhaps, heroic and handsome but undeniably dangerous. Despite his attractive features, he could not disguise the rottenness that emanated from within and seeped out through every pore like an infection.

A dreamy expression drifted across his face, as his eyes remained closed. He stood for a moment, swaying. As he did, the cavernous hall moved with him. He breathed and the cavern breathed. The company shifted uneasily, waiting for some dreadful vengeance to crash upon their heads.

Morreck moved again, floating effortlessly toward them before stopping only a few feet away. His pale hair danced in the air, a halo of finely spun gold that shimmered about him.

The figure, his eyes still firmly closed, seemed to survey the intruders before him. He lingered on the wizard and smiled broadly, then turned his attention toward Wendya.

"A witch child ... no, a sorceress, an infant magus queen! There is a presence in you ...," the creature tilted its head, pausing as if contemplating something, a puzzled expression on its face, half-fascination, half-questioning. "You are powerful, girl."

Morreck opened his eyes. The horror of his countenance struck terror. Eyes burning like two empty orbs ablaze with fury from within, he stared straight at the witch. "Yes ... you are very powerful, though you do not know it ...," his eyes were unflinching, his voice curling inside her head and shattering her thoughts like glass. "Not ripe yet ... but you could be picked."

Wendya felt her knees buckling, her body falling, spiraling downward.

"Do not look at him!" shouted a muffled voice nearby. "Wendya! Do not look at his eyes!" the voice came again, only louder and clearer.

She squirmed beneath the scorching glare and the soft whispering voice in her head.

"Look away NOW!" Mr. Agyk commanded; his graveled voice like a jab in her side.

Wendya jolted, blinking through the mist clouding her vision. She felt as if she were drowning. Frell caught her and quickly covered her eyes.

"Face *me*, M'Sorreck!" Mr. Agyk shouted. "Face me, coward and corruptor!"

To all that watched it seemed that the old wizard's anger ignited in him. He stepped forward to meet the figure, and holding his staff in both hands, he pounded it upon the floor in an explosion of light that surged forward and protected all those in the company behind.

"You will not murder or steal another soul!" he bellowed, his voice thundering around the hall which such force that even Morreck appeared to flinch for a moment. "Your evil stops this night! The Order may have allowed you to escape them once, but we shall not!"

Morreck smiled, his white eyes fixed on the old mage.

"Good, good! This will be far more enjoyable. The others, your pitiful *friends* were weaker. They were too easily taken, too easily consumed. I knew you would be stronger ...," he answered, barely able to contain his excitement. "It has been many years since I have had food as rich as you! One of the last great wizards you were, once. Not an Ellda but close enough. I shall have to cross the dark divide to A'Orvas to find another like you ...," he sneered mockingly, his words a cancerous sneer.

"I was hoping you would have some fight left in you, green wizard," he laughed, "if only for a more entertaining death!" his smile spread. "But I have been deceived. I see now that you have more power than I was told. It was wise of you to keep your true strength hidden, but your efforts are futile …," he paused, his eyes flaring with a blistering malice. "How delicious that you should have carried out my own plans ahead of time by leading these deluded fools into a war they cannot win. While Mund'harr and the Golden City are left virtually undefended! How will it survive the night I wonder?"

The warlock laughed, the honeyed tone of his voice falling away, a malignant hatred so powerful that it shrank the courage of all. Even Mr. Agyk faltered.

"Once I destroy you and consume your remaining few powers, I shall add your soul to my collection here. Then … I will enjoy entertaining your friends … especially the girl!" Morreck smiled at Wendya, then turned to the dworlls. "I have no use for these insects!" he said dismissively, and casting a hand idly over the group, the entire battalion were suddenly tossed into the air and violently thrown down the length of the hall, as if they were mere rag dolls.

Before Mr. Agyk could react, Wendya was hurled across the floor. Slamming into a pillar, she hardly had time to catch her breath before hundreds of grasping hands sprang from the stone, pulling and dragging her in.

"Join us! Join us!" they wailed, their spiny fingers clawing and scratching at her.

The hands stretched outwards, curling round her ankles, clutching the flesh of her legs. She screamed and struggled for a few moments.

"NO!" she commanded as they tore her dress and the cloak from her back before she pulled herself free.

"Wendya!" the wizard cried, suddenly finding himself frozen to the spot, his legs paralyzed.

"Going somewhere?" Morreck sneered.

Mr. Agyk faced him. "Your tricks will not save you!" he shouted and, pounding his staff on the floor, he cast off his enemy's spell.

M'Sorreck raised his arms slowly, in a grandiose gesture of power and dominance, and black electricity sparked between them, leaping in jagged crackles along each limb and fingertip. The dark fog still hovered above, gathering in size and depth, spinning ever faster. Then like a bolt, it shot down the hall.

The dworlls lay in utter disarray. Bruised and bloodied Frell picked himself up. His shoulder was dislocated. Through clenched teeth he snapped it into place. A fellow dworll, a good friend, lay nearby, motionless, his neck snapped by the force of the fall.

"On your feet! Up Fendellons!" Frell shouted, struggling to help the others. "We must fight! On your feet!"

The figures of the wizard and their enemy were mere specks in the distance now.

"Captain, look!" gasped a dworll in horror.

Racing toward them came the black fog again, boiling and hissing with venom. The dworlls dropped to the ground as it skimmed just above their heads and disappeared into every maggot-hole in the cavern's walls.

"What was that?"

"I don't know, but it can't be good," Frell replied. "Come on, we must help the wizard! Onward!"

The witch scrambled to her feet. She looked ahead, her gaze fixed on the two wizards as they confronted each other.

The smaller figure of Mr. Agyk floated just above the floor, his tatty robes wafting about him, his receding mane of gray hair glistening with a brilliance of its own. But towering above him loomed the warlock. The very air around Morreck darkened and sizzled, scorching the lungs. Silver and green flames rose from Mr. Agyk's staff striking at the figure, as sparks filled the air.

Wendya instinctively ran towards him, desperate to help. But with every step she took, listlessness fell upon her. Her limbs felt leaden, as if wading through thick mud. Suddenly a faint voice cried out behind her, Frell's voice.

"We cannot move! A spell has been cast! We cannot get any closer! You must help him!"

At that moment the black fog reappeared with a snarling, rushing sound, spilling out of the holes and doorways and darting forward to envelop its master once more. From behind it, as if awoken or summoned, emerged an army of red wargol eyes.

M'Sorreck quivered with anticipation, his eyes changing back and forth from blank white to a shimmering opalescent.

"Did you really believe that I could be deceived so easily? That I do not know exactly where every creature in this land resides, that I cannot perceive their thoughts and their pitiable plans? I have eyes everywhere," he laughed, his voice shaking the cavernous space. "You thought I would leave my home unprotected?" Morreck mocked as fumes, poisonous and reeking, spewed from his mouth. "Everything that has transpired has been to my design. You cannot win Marvalla, green wizard of the gray rock!"

At that moment, hundreds of wargols poured into the hall from every foul crevice.

"If we cannot get closer, we must turn and fight!" Frell rallied, as the demons streamed down the steps howling and cheering towards them. "Come Fendellons, to glory or death!"

"To glory or death!" they roared, readying their axes and swords to face their enemy.

Wendya stood transfixed as a blanket of darkness fell upon her.

"No hope, no hope at all," whispered a voice in her head. "Give up … give in …"

"No," she murmured, and closed her eyes.

Mists swirled in her mind. Slowly the clash of wizard fire and shrieks of battle melted away. She felt her body suspended in air, cushioned by a moving liquid mass, and, though her senses told her to panic, to resist, a strange calmness fell upon her.

Her mind stretched through the rock and earth. She saw a night sky ... it was on fire. Beating dragon wings blocked out the stars and thick smoke clung to the mountainsides. She could see Gralen crying and Korrun running frantically in the dark. The entire heavens burst into flame and the valley exploded in violence. Hordes filled it, terrible, sickened creatures and amongst them she could see the dworlls outnumbered, desperately fighting their enemies ... and themselves? Dark dworlls ... traitors, corrupted and merciless! The King was cornered, trapped and ... Sedgewick, Tollam, Perral and countless others all lay dead, their corpses beckoning to her through the mists.

"NO!" she shouted forcing her eyes open. "Get back!" she cried thrusting her hands out and rejecting the visions.

Searing pain stabbed her in the chest, spreading outwards, flooding her body and burning her veins. She screamed and fell onto her knees in agony.

"What's happening to me?"

Minutes passed like hours and slowly the pain subsided and ebbed to a nauseating throb. But a power, faint at first, thengrowing stronger, began to pulse down her arms, snaking through her wrists and radiating through the skin of her fingertips. Wendya stared at her hands in terror as she looked up to see the darkness evaporating around her. Suddenly she saw a wall of wargol demons thundering towards her.

The wargols wavered, unsure. Streams of light flowed and entwined round the witch like fine gossamer ribbons, before dissolving into the air. Some cowered or ran away, others changed course to pursue Frell and the other dworlls, but the largest creatures merely snarled their hatred, converged and charged.

She couldn't outrun them and she knew it. She rose to her feet as another surge of strength pulsated through her, igniting her blood and heightening her senses; an utterly overwhelming strength she had never felt before, alien yet strangely familiar.

With trembling hands, she drew the sword Korrun had given her, and clutching the burning key around her neck, she faced the demons alone.

Electricity and flames crackled as the two wizards struck each other, locked in combat.

"*Kaero kaiata wairua!* Diminish, soul taker!" Mr. Agyk bellowed.

Fire sprang from the wizard's eyes and re-ignited his staff into a blaze more brilliant than before. Morreck responded, blasting at the old mage. Sickly yellow bolts emanated from his dead eyes and lightning coiled about him, attacking the wizard like hundreds of fiery vipers. "You pitiful fool! You are weak." Morreck hissed. "I have the strength of ten thousand mages coursing through me!"

"Strength you stole, strength you murdered for!" Mr. Agyk shouted.

M'Sorreck laughed again and closed his eyes at the wondrous pleasure of it all. "I can taste your fear Marvalla ... that at least is wise of you. You *should* fear me." He opened his eyes once more, and to Mr. Agyk's horror they seemed to boil, engorged on power. "I can feel your powers draining from you, you sense it. A weakening of your cells ...

power leaving you and becoming mine. Death awaits you and an eternity of torment as my newest toy. Everything you have and are shall be mine!"

"You will never take my soul, never! You will be hunted the rest of your miserable life!"

The warlock cackled hysterically, his robes and golden hair flying wildly about him and the sickly tissue of his skin glowed.

"Hunted?" he scoffed, "by whom? The Council of Kallorm? The Mages' Guild? The Ellda Order? They had little power in their time and now they have none. They knew who I was and what I wanted from the very start. They stood by and watched. Sniveling cowards every one of them! They had their time. We have all lived by and suffered from their mistakes for too long and I live by them no longer! The world shall witness my wrath. I will purge the earth of any who oppose me, scorch it clean of these human vermin ...," his excitement was palpable. "I have prepared for this longer than you can perceive," he smiled. "The day of reckoning is here. The world shall be cleansed and reborn; it is the cycle of nature!"

"Nature!" Mr. Agyk laughed grimly. "You are an *abomination* to nature! You twist and corrupt everything you touch! ... All you seek is to dominate and destroy ... you are planning global genocide!"

Morreck laughed. "Would you call destroying an ant hill *genocide?*" He studied the old man. He was stronger than he had expected. Almost worth saving, if he could be persuaded.

"A war is coming, Marvalla, you know it as well as I. Judgment Day as the primitives call it," he stared at the aged scholar, so utterly different from himself. "It cannot be stopped, old man. I cannot be stopped. Despite their 'technology'," he scoffed, "these primitives are as weak-minded and superstitious as they were when we first encountered them, groveling around in the dirt like the animals they are. Show a human true magic and they mistake it for divinity ... then follow it blindly anywhere," he sneered, narrowing his eyes. "I am baffled why you want to save these simians. For what purpose? To allow them to poison this planet you purport to care so much about? They maim, rape, kill ... for profit, for land, for their 'divine gods' ... for no reason at all. You would choose them over your own kind?"

"Do not bandy words with me, wærloga!" Mr. Agyk snapped. "You do not serve 'our' kind or any other, you serve only your own ruthlessness and ambition! I would choose any form of freedom over your tyranny! You offer only death!"

"They are parasites! Parasites!" Morreck spat, as if the mere mention of humans contaminated him. "I will purge this planet of their filth and rule it as it should be ruled!"

"Never!"

M'Sorreck smiled, his eyes burning intensely as he stared at the wizard. His tone softened. "You could still join me, Marvalla A'Gyk. Tell me where the others are, those last few of our kind. They cannot hide from me forever."

"Never! I am no betrayer!" cried the old wizard, his voice faltering.

"You cannot defeat me. I shall be ruler over all, first our world, then theirs. Fendellin will fall, then Kallorm and Gwallor and all the remaining dworllian realms. Every magus, every wicca, every magic-caster will be hunted down. My hounds are very good, but you know that! Those that do not join our cause will suffer and die. The cities of man will be destroyed one by one. Perhaps I'll start with those you favor most!"

Each word was carefully chosen and laced with cruelty to inflict the greatest damage.

"I have lain quiet for many long ages, old man, but I have not been idle," he continued, hovering menacingly above his adversary. "Forces are at work that cannot be halted. I have an army ten thousand times that of which you see now, an army that speaks in every tongue, that whispers in every government in every continent and country across this globe! They wait for me. The great cities of man will submit or fall. These primitives should make good servants, don't you think?" He smiled again. "Earth will be a dominion of dark magic once more!"

He suddenly lunged forward, blasting the wizard and sending him flying back.

"Now DIE!" he roared.

Regaining his balance, Mr. Agyk felt an icy grip tightening around his rib cage, an iron vice squeezing the life out of him. He fought back, blasting a shot of fire towards his attacker, who was slowly encircling him. The old mage could feel himself weakening. A substance akin to ice, but stronger than steel, grew around him, thickening round his legs, encasing his arms and rising up and over his head in a deathly shroud.

Mr. Agyk struggled. He could feel his heart slowing and his blood coagulating as it began to freeze. Beyond the icy cocoon, he could just make out the ominous figure of his enemy hovering like a carrion crow above him, willing and waiting for him to draw his last breath.

"I will not succumb! NO!" he cried, though he could barely move. "If I die this night … it will not be like this, it will not be like this!"

M'Sorreck glided above him, a hideous and gloating expression on his youthful face.

Mr. Agyk quietly gathered himself once more. Then, channeling all his strength, he began to move. Cracks, fine at first, then growing larger, appeared in the ice around him. Morreck hesitated and moved back, suddenly uncertain. The ice shattered into a thousand sparkling shards and the wizard freed himself, emerging with his staff as a flaming brand in his hand.

"You will not win, foul carrion beast! I cast you back into the bowels of darkness where you belong! Back, back!" he bellowed, his voice powerful, his silvery eyes enraged.

Morreck hissed, his face contorted by fury. "You will die Marvalla, as will all those you love!" he spat and unleashed wave upon wave of lightning bolts, each violent burst more powerful than the last. They broke like surf upon the old figure and with such incredible force that he seemed to diminish with each onslaught.

Mr. Agyk flew back, trying to shield himself, but the bolts were too strong. Again they struck and again, each blow weakened him, each blast becoming dozens of invisible sharp, clawing hands lashing and tearing at him.

The warlock smiled. "Do you know nothing?" he sneered. "I am a God amongst you. Even if it were possible to destroy me, which it is not, you would only quicken my ascension. I will transcend this mortal plain, my transformation cannot be stopped.

Ultimate power! If this body, this shape I occupy, is killed … I will grow stronger. A formless power can never be destroyed!"

M'Sorreck's eyes glistened. He leaned forward, opening his mouth, and from it issued a thousand stinging darts, like crawling insects, covering and swarming over the wizard. Once more, Mr. Agyk blasted at these foul wrappings but was met by a ferocious black fire. Engulfed in the full force of the inferno, he screamed in agony as Morreck's dark flames rose around him, consuming him whole.

Wendya was fighting one of the larger wargol demons. The terror of the beast and the stench of its hot breath sickened her. She struck it hard and the tip of her blade snapped off in its shoulder. It barely flinched. It then lifted her up, threw her to the ground, and beckoned for more wargols to join it. Snarling, its foul teeth gnawed for the chance of sweetmeat, its red eyes unafraid of the light that flickered like streamers about her. Wendya scrambled backwards as it bore down on her. Suddenly something caught its sight and made it smile. Horrified, Wendya followed its gaze and turned to see Mr. Agyk devoured by fire.

"Marval!" she screamed, but her voice was lost in the din.

"You are weakening, old fool!" Morreck spat, striking the wizard again.

Mr. Agyk tried to clutch at the warlock, but was beaten by scorching flames.

"MARVALLLL!" Wendya cried.

Once more she felt a dizzying power quicken inside her, fuelled by rage and fear. The wargol creature straddled her, savoring the moment. It drew a long serrated knife, curved like a scimitar. The demon bent over her, its weight pinning her to the ground, crushing her ribs, its stinking breath hot on her face. Instinctively, she grabbed the knife that was pressing against her neck. Staring defiantly into the blood-colored eyes of her attacker, she melted the blade in her bare hands. The wargol blinked and stumbled back in disbelief. But before its slow brain could muster itself for another assault, she jumped to her feet, and without thought or effort, she tossed it high into the air, smashing it against one of the pillars.

Instantaneously, hundreds of hands appeared out of the rock, grasping at the wargol as they dragged it, screaming, into their deadly embrace. Within seconds the screams were silenced as it disappeared into the stone.

Wendya turned swiftly to her enemies and outstretched her hands. "Be gone!" she shouted.

A blast of icy wind, like a solid wall or tidal front flowed out of her body and raced toward the advancing wargols, sweeping them aside like leaves.

"Marval!" she cried and, picking up a wargol axe, she rushed forward.

"Yessss!" the warlock laughed, his awful white eyes reflecting the torment in the wizard's face "You see your own death now, do you not?"

Morreck twisted in the air, his body contorting and writhing in glee, his robes sparking with electricity, his face a deathly grimace. "You are dying," he smiled. "Once I have you ... I shall have the girl! She does not know her full power yet, but she will ... I shall teach her."

"NO!" the wizard bellowed. "You shall have neither her nor me!" His green robes exploded in flame as he sent a wave of lightning toward his enemy. "Die foul beast! Corruptor!" he boomed, mustering his strength for another attack.

Morreck let out a cry and floundered for a moment, but it was not enough. He recovered all too quickly and rushed at the exhausted wizard. "No mercy!" he hissed.

The dworlls battled on defiantly as the cavern swarmed with demons.

"There are too many!" one of the soldiers cried.

"Watch out!" Frell warned as a large wargol came up behind the young Fendellon.

The dworll turned to see the demon plunge a lance into his body and smile.

"NOOO!" Frell cried as the youngster dropped to his knees and fell.

"We can't survive long! They're a different breed to the others!" another dworll wailed.

Frell sprang forward and thrust his sword into the gullet of an attacking demon, then cut his way back to the others.

"Keep the circle!" he cried, re-joining them. "Keep the circle! ... These beasts must have been bred with dark mytes!" he shouted, swiping at the legs of another advancing wargol. "We have no choice. We must give the green wizard and the witch more time! Be strong Fendellons, let anger be your ally. Remember these beasts can still be killed!"

Wendya ran now, her feet hardly touching the floor, her torn skirts billowing behind her like great sails as she raced towards the two wizards. In the void above, she could see her old friend ensnared in a squirming mass of fiery snakes. Dark flames surrounded them, sizzling through the air and hitting the walls and pillars, sending chunks of masonry crashing to the ground in huge clouds of dust. She ran on but with every step the old scholar's words returned to her.

"Wendya, whatever may happen, you must find the orb, his power source and destroy it! Do not stop, not for anyone, not for me. If you try to intervene, you will fail and that will seal all our fates. We must stop M'Sorreck at any cost. This may be our only chance. Everything we hold dear depends upon it. Promise me, that when the time comes and you see your chance, you will run, just run!"

"I can't leave you ... I won't!" she argued, shaking her head.

The walls tingled and rippled with excitement. Wargols continued to flow from every hole, but the way to the stair and the door lay strangely clear. The witch hesitated, then ran on, her hand clasped tightly around the hilt of her sword, eyes fixed on her stricken friend and the thing that hovered above him. But, amidst the deafening howls and the throbbing of the air, Wendya could hear the thunder of footsteps again, closing in around her. The footsteps abruptly halted and foul cries of triumph and fear echoed through the hall. Wendya turned. A line of wargols stretched across the entire width of the cavern floor, straining forward and swaying as if under a spell, their evil eyes glinting scarlet in the gloom. They were euphoric about something. She looked away and fell backwards, confronted by the worst terror of all.

Nuroth stood, towering above her, his mouth a blood-stained and drooling smile, his black eyes glistening with anticipation and fixed on only her.

"Well, hello my pretty," he hissed.

Outside, the skies were on fire.

"LOOK! Fÿrrens! The dragons are coming! We are saved!" Hallm shouted, pointing to the heavens as they filled with beating wings and jets of colored flame.

"Gralen was as good as his word," King Baillum replied, as flocks of Fendellon dragons cut rivers of fire through the wargol host. "But we are not saved yet. Trap or no trap, let us hope that victory is grasped within the mountain or all of this will be in vain!"

Wendya recoiled in horror.

The wargol chieftain stepped closer. "It's a pity I have no time to carve you into my new play thing," Nuroth sneered as he stood over her. "I'll let you choose which part of you I eat first!" he smiled, bending down only inches from her face "But I shall keep your pretty head as a memento."

"You'll have to take mine first!" replied a cold voice behind him.

Nuroth turned to see a bloodied but determined Korrun striding towards him, sword readied, eyes dark.

The wargol captain laughed. "The coward returns! Ha! Look at you … you can hardly stand! Good! Now you can see her die!" he snarled as he swiftly spun round and brought his black sword down upon the terrified witch.

"NOOOOO!" shouted Korrun, throwing his Krael blade as he raced forward.

The dagger caught Nuroth square in the back. He stumbled, his blow falling wide.

"RUN!" Korrun yelled as she scrambled away and he faced Nuroth. "Leave the girl. Face me and die like the vermin you are!"

Korrun's sword clashed with Nuroth's as the great demon kicked the dwelf in the face, sending him flying. Wendya got to her feet as Nuroth pulled the dagger from his flesh, licked it and threw it towards her, catching her in the shoulder. She screamed and fell back.

"Wendya!" Korrun cried, rushing to her.

"Thanks for that!" the wargol laughed as he faced his enemy's wrath.

"I'm fine, I'm fine!" she gasped. "It's not deep," she lied, clutching her shoulder and the knife that pierced it.

The dwelf stood tall, his face a mask once more. "Go! Help the wizard! GO!"

Wendya lingered for a moment, and then staggered on.

"Pretty girlfriend you have there," Nuroth grinned, bringing all his weight down upon the tracker. "Maybe I'll make her watch you die, before I take her."

Korrun gritted his teeth, his heart pounding in his ears as he grabbed a broken sword nearby. "This ends tonight. NOW!" he cried lunging at him.

The witch half-ran, half-stumbled until the pain in her shoulder grew too great. Biting her lip she grasped the hilt of the dagger and pulled the knife clean from her shoulder. Darkness returned, clouding her vision.

"Be strong!" she whispered, blinking back the mist.

The cavern moved beneath her, surging and shifting under her feet, its sides pulsating, bowing inwards, blackness above, terror behind. Lights flashed and flowed in a dizzying haze and always the chorus of wails could be heard from the pillars and walls. She closed her eyes, gathering her strength, shutting out the sounds.

Spinning wildly in the air like some ragged plaything, Mr. Agyk hung listlessly above her, encircled by lightning and lashed by evil shapes. His enemy floated in front of him, a being of immense power that was visibly getting stronger with every passing minute.

Wendya stared at her beloved scholar, as his silver hair faded to an ashen gray, before turning white. His green robes became dusty tatters about him. Morreck paraded before him, the warlock's head a blaze of gold and orange flame, his skin growing evermore luminescent, his ghastly eyes intent on only the wizard. Mr. Agyk fought bravely, his sword and staff shining in the gloom, but he was fading fast.

"He's dying!" she gasped.

At that moment, as if the very heavens were falling, a deafening boom echoed round the cavern, rocking the floor beneath them. The old mage struggled. His sword fell from his hand and shattered upon the floor. Still he fought with the creature, clenching his staff against the onslaught. It blazed for a moment as a white molten rod, brighter than Wendya had ever seen it, then suddenly it cracked and splintered into a thousand glittering shards that burned like falling stars in the darkness, before extinguishing.

"NO! MARVALLLLLLLLLLLLLLL!" she cried, but he could not hear her.

Every cell, every part of his being, all the strength of his long years, all the knowledge of his ancestry, all the power of his bloodline flowed through him and before him, stretched out as an endless carpet, a great winding path leading him away from this place. He saw all the pain of his friends, the tears of the past and of the future. He saw Wendya floating on a still pond, peaceful, cold, her hair a tangled mass of weeds about her. He saw Gralen overcome by anger and grief, a blazing comet soaring into the night and disappearing amongst the stars. He saw Korrun bloodied and weeping, a broken figure, despair and vengeance his only companions. And everywhere Mr. Agyk could see fire, consuming whole mountains, filling skies, burning fields, woods and cities, all ablaze. Fendellin lay as a charred skeleton, Kállorm a ruin, White Mountain destroyed. He saw humans running and screaming. Dead, millions of them, billions, great metropolises leveled, reduced to heaps of twisted metal, concrete and ash. Floods, plagues, and every conceivable natural disaster blighting the world. All at Morreck's command.

"NO!" he cried, his voice weak and lost amongst the din. "I will fight you!"

"Of course you will." M'Sorreck smiled. "Unto death, and yours is very close now!"

Wendya stood rooted for a moment andwatched the two wizards with tears streaming down her face. *Do not stop, not for anyone, not for me ... Promise me, that when the time comes and you see your chance, you will run, just run!* Mr. Agyk's words echoed in her ears.

"I can't! I can't leave you!" she cried out.

"You must!" came a voice in reply, a graveled voice she knew and loved.

Mr. Agyk closed his eyes and the faintest flicker of a smile traced his lips.

"Do not break your promise. You must go my child, for me, for us all," said the voice speaking softly inside her head. "Go now and do not falter. This is your chance. Now RUN!"

The dragon key around her neck burned like never before and the blood in her veins seemed to be boiling. She forced herself to look away to the stairs and the carved door beyond, still quite a distance away. Somewhere inside lay Morreck's inner sanctum and the source of his power. Wendya looked up, tears burning her sight.

"Go now!" whispered the voice.

She nodded, and casting one last anxious glance at her dear friend, she reluctantly turned. Clutching her shoulder and running as fast as she could towards the steps, she passed quickly and unseen beneath the black cloud that engulfed the two wizards. Once more, the strange power returned, growing inside her, throbbing in tune with the air, coursing through her tissue. The cavern floor quaked in response, rising and falling beneath her feet in waves of excitement that made her disorientated and weak.

A disturbing feeling crept over her. An unsettling sense of recognition, vague but undeniable. As nightmarish as the thought was, she seemed to know this place.

She ran on, listening to the battle behind and the crackling of power above, and another sound, distant at first but growing louder, like the coming of a monstrous train. Wendya strained to hear any word or sound from Mr. Agyk, but nothing. Only silence, mixed with a rumbling laughter that pierced the heart with its cruelty.

Chapter Twenty

Morreck

"Orrla!" they cheered, as the young captain and another group of dworlls appeared in the cavern, slaying a path as they went. "It's good to see you Frell!" she smiled. Their faces were full of relief at seeing each other. "Korrun thought you could use some reinforcements," she laughed grimly. "I see he was right!"

Frell smiled at her. "Well met! Our secret plans were betrayed … we had not the numbers for an open assault! … My father?"

"… is fine or was when we left him. He was riding to Lord Lorrin's aid," she replied.

He stared at the small number of troops she brought with her. "How goes it?"

Orrla sighed. "Difficult. I cannot say who will win the night. Most of the tunnels behind us are clear and Korrun's dealing with Nuroth. But … there is something coming … we heard it up there," she gestured to one of the passages.

"I can hear it!" A soldier shouted nearby. "Another evil of M'Sorreck!"

"No doubt. It does not matter," Frell cried launching himself against a dazed wargol. "We have no choice but to fight, devilry or no."

The wargols hesitated, aware of some new danger drawing close. A few demons withdrew, while others listened in stunned silence.

"Whatever it is, they hear it too … look at them!" Orrla replied. "It's coming this way … fast!"

Frell looked at the faces of their enemy. "You're right and I'd say they fear it. That is a good sign at least!"

"Really? Anything that is so terrible it strikes dread in even a 'gol's thick head, is something I do not want to meet!" Orrla laughed.

Frell glanced down the cavern to the distant figures of the wizards, swallowed in flame and lightning. "In either case we will not last much longer … the old mage had better do what he came here to do … and quickly, we're running out of time!"

Running on in fear and desperation, Wendya's heart sank. She could see the steps clearly now, just a little ahead, but gathering at the top of them stood twenty or thirty large mountain demons, alike in size and malice to their foul chieftain, yet somehow different.

"No!" she cried, utterly exhausted. "There's no way through!"

A strange silence descended as an unmistakable and thunderous rumbling echoed somewhere in the bowels of the mountain, growing nearer and nearer at an alarming pace. An eeriness fell, as the cavern began to shake. Something was coming. Like a roar of wind or water sweeping down the passages towards them.

"Ready yourselves. Here it comes!" Frell shouted.

The walls trembled and cracks appeared from the mouth of one of the tunnels, spreading outward like jagged fingers. A giant ball of flame, green as jade, exploded into the hall. The wargols shrank back. Some looked to their master for guidance, others fled back to their holes.

The flame came again, and with it a terrible rushing sound that filled their heads, blocking all other noise. None had heard such a ruinous sound before, save Mr. Agyk and the witch.

Wendya spun round, her face full of hope, as a large green and orange creature burst into the hall in an eruption of fire and flying rock.

Nuroth stumbled back in surprise as the dragon swept overhead, to a hail of cheers and cries. Korrun lay injured at his feet but, in that instant, he saw his chance.

Weapon-less and bleeding badly, he fumbled for one of the broken arrows that littered the floor. Quickly rising in one supreme act of will and hatred, he thrust it into the wargol's throat, pushing it up with all his force until he drove it deep into the demon's brain and the splintered tip of it protruded from its foul skull. Nuroth's jaw gaped open and his head tilted. Tottering backwards, he tried to clasp his throat. Korrun rose slowly to his feet, his eyes triumphant and wild. He would remember this moment. Nuroth's black eyes fixed on the dwelf in an almost comical expression of stunned horror and amazement.

"My brother is finally avenged! That was for Sorall," panted the tracker, his stare unflinching. "… and this is for ME!" he roared as he picked up a notched sword and, turning swiftly, took the wargol captain's head off in one clean swipe.

Nuroth's massive body slumped to the ground, his head rolling towards the dwelf who promptly kicked it away. Bending down, Korrun found the foul braid around the base of the creature's severed neck, and pulled at it. He had at last recovered his brother's ring.

He clasped the ring in his hand and closing his eyes briefly, he kissed it. "Be at peace, Sorall," he whispered. "My debt to you is paid, dear brother … rest now."

He opened his eyes and placed the silver ring on his finger. Almost immediately the black ǽllfrstone changed color to a sparkling blue, as the hideous snake creatures that surrounded it, uncurled before his eyes to become the proud dragon guardians they once were.

The dworlls gave another cheer as Gralen bore down upon their enemies, blasting their hides or taking their foul heads with his talons. Fear of the dragon swept through the enemy ranks, scattering them in all directions. Wendya had never been so happy to see an old friend.

"Bloody caves!" the dragon muttered, as he swerved, avoiding the spears that showered down on him from the ledge above.

Gralen swooped. In one blast and flick of his tail, he swiped tens of wargols off the parapet to their death. Wheeling once more, he sliced through the throngs of wargols below, sending jets of molten flame down every maggot hole he could see. Pausing for a moment, he tried to find his lost friends amidst the chaos.

Korrun stared into the mounting gloom and saw the distant figure of Wendya, trapped at the foot of the stairs. "Why have you stopped? Keep going!" he muttered, and saw the deathly black shapes beyond, blocking her way. "Wargols ... no ... dark mytes!" he gasped.

"I see them!" boomed a voice above. "Help the dworlls, I'll deal with this!" Gralen cried shooting forward.

The dwelf hesitated, his eyes drawn to the witch. Turning aside, he found his own broken sword amongst the debris, and looked at the body of his defeated enemy.

"The mighty can fall," he murmured and prized Nuroth's black blade out of the beast's dead hands. "Now, for the others!" he said, rushing to help Frell.

Gralen sped on, as Mr. Agyk's voice filled his head. *You must help Wendya, not me! Only she can destroy the orb. M'Sorreck cannot be defeated unless the orb is broken!*

He flew quickly, looked up and saw the stricken figure of the wizard now far above him in the darkness, lost amongst a tangled mass of smoke and light.

"Hold on!" he pleaded. "I'll do what you asked ... but I won't abandon you!"

Flying on, he darted toward the witch.

The creatures blocking her path seemed to melt together, their eyes gleaming, their shapes shifting. Clearly petrified and shaking, Wendya stood her ground, as a dread, like frozen teeth gnawing on her skin, gripped her.

"Y ... you cannot stop me!" she shouted, her voice quivering. "Your master will fail!"

They burst into simultaneous laughter as streams of black vapors trickled from their mouths and curled towards her. "You think we are afraid of a girl and a pet dragon? Your fear is food to us!" they answered. "We are death!" they hissed, descending the stair.

"So is this *pet*!" Gralen bellowed as he dived down and blasted the demons.

They cackled in reply as the fiery torrent enveloped them, and then fizzled harmlessly away.

"Fÿrren fire cannot touch us," they taunted, their voices speaking in unison. "Your weakling powers are no match for us!"

Without warning, they suddenly changed shape, sprouting arms and legs from their backs and growing in height and darkness. Hideous black beetles they became, scuttling forward, their jaws protruding as pincers and dripping with venom.

Wendya staggered backwards. "Oh gods!" she cried.

"Dark mytes!" Gralen gasped, feeling himself stifled by a gut-wrenching fear. For the first time, the dragon understood the terror that came with the name. "Dark mytes ... they're changelings too!"

Wendya felt herself swoon. Despite her revulsion, she could feel an irresistible urge pulling her forward, beckoning to her.

Gralen gathered himself, shutting his mind to the horrors before him.

You must help Wendya ... Only she can destroy the orb. The old man's words resonated again.

The dragon nodded, and in one smooth movement, he scooped the witch up and flew high overhead. Wendya struggled frantically for a moment as the beasts scrabbled below.

"Wend'!" Gralen called softly. "It's alright. It's me, it's me!"

She wilted in his arms, a weightless thing. "I'm alright ...," she murmured.

Gralen glided down and rested the young wicca at the top of the steps, only a few feet from the door. "Please be safe," he pleaded, his amber eyes like huge saucers as they gazed into hers.

"I will ... and you too," she paused and pressed her hand softly against his scaly cheek. "I will see you when this is over," she smiled.

Gralen looked at her wistfully, wanting to say so much more than the moment allowed. He released her hand slowly and nodded. "You'd better go ...," he said quietly, "I'll deal with these foul beasts!"

He watched her for a second as she turned and ran, then reluctantly turned himself and shot towards the advancing creatures.

"Right! If I can deal with a 'mighty' Oracle and your stone sentinels outside, I can deal with you cockroaches!" he boomed. "Can't be killed by fire, eh? What about being buried?"

In one almighty effort, the dragon heaved a huge piece of masonry and slammed it on the demons' heads as they raced to catch the witch. "I've had just about enough of bloody caves and tunnels!" he roared, "... and the stench of creatures like YOU!"

As promised, Wendya did not hesitate. She ran as fast as her legs could take her, half-stumbling, half-crawling. The pendant blazed fiercely against her skin. As she looked at it, she could see it was writhed in an intense scarlet flame that grew brighter with every step.

Morreck leisurely spun the green wizard, as if he were slowly roasting him on a spit.

"You could have joined me," he smiled, his voice seductively silken. His golden beauty shining with a ferocity as bright as his malice. "Now you are nothing ... merely fodder for my transition."

Mr. Agyk looked through cloaked eyes and saw the tiny figure of Wendya far below, racing to the door. "Good," he thought. "It is as it should be."

The old wizard's mind flickered with images past. His first encounter with Gralen when he had found and rescued the infant draken, no more than thirty years old or so, and how the young dragon had suffered. Long years had elapsed since then, as starlight upon deep water, passing quickly but forever remembered. Travels and adventures they had shared flashed through his thoughts; the fall and desolation of Koralan and the other great cities of old; the last sorrowful exodus, friends gone forever now. He would join them soon enough.

Outside, he could sense dawn was approaching fast. The young witch's face blazed before him. "Protect her," King Dorrol had implored. "Watch over her, she is … very special."

Mr. Agyk closed his eyes. Pain blighted him, dissolving his strength. The aged scholar felt himself fading, his body becoming heavier, the irresistible pull of the ground. "Hold on" he thought, "… just a little longer!"

M'Sorreck laughed, his luminous face a hideous mask, his eyes crazed. "I can feel your power, a power of ages … secrets, knowledge … all mine. You are a strong magus, far stronger than I ever guessed. I should have taken your soul centuries ago, I—"

Morreck suddenly faltered and his smile disappeared.

At that exact moment, somewhere in the darkest recesses of his mind a creeping doubt sprang, piercing his thoughts, a faint but undeniable sense of imminent danger.

He looked away from the dying figure before him and gazed over the carnage below… his minions, the insignificant dworlls, and the futile and pathetic efforts against him. He would deal with them all later. But through the noise and gloom, Morreck's lifeless eyes perceived the threat and, for the first time, the great warlock felt fear.

Far below, away from the others, was a tiny running figure, and there, dangling around her neck like a shining red beacon, was a key … The birthkey he had long been looking for. Almost identical to his own, the one he had consumed, that now burned intensely inside his rotten flesh.

"The key!" he gasped, his eyes widening. "It is the key … it's glowing! It is her! It is HER!" He floundered for a moment, stunned by the sight. "I have found her at last!"

The realization hit him, then the danger.

"No! NO! I have been tricked! Tricked!" his eyes blazed as he saw the young wicca running wildly towards the door, she had nearly reached it! "NOOOOOOOOO!" he boomed, his voice cracking like rock.

In an instant, he left the dying mage and hurtled towards the witch, his eyes engorged with madness and fury.

Wendya slammed against the door, ripping the burning key from her neck. At either side of the door, the carvings began moving, tentacles of stone tearing themselves from the rock-face, coiling and grasping at her.

"Where's the lock? Where's the damn lock?" she cried as she heard a terrible roaring sound behind her that seemed to twist inside her body and stayed her hand.

She turned and screamed as a monstrous and hollow blackness descended upon her and, at its core, two consuming white eyes and a scorching halo of gold hair.

"He's coming!" she spun round, her fingers fumbled and found a dent in the door. "Come on! Open! OPEN!" she screamed and slammed her fist against the crack.

Suddenly, like a black slit, it opened and she fell inside.

"NO!" Morreck roared as he plunged toward the witch, only to see her disappear inside the rock-face. "NOOOOOOOOOOOOO!"

His wrath shook the cavern, masonry rained down from above. The walls screamed and a huge chasm opened up in the floor that swallowed many wargols and some dworlls.

"No you don't!" shouted a rough voice, as Gralen flew up in front of him.

Morreck's body burst into an explosion of black flame that overshadowed the dragon. "Out of my way, carrion!" he bellowed. "DIE!"

Gralen found himself being strangled by hundreds of invisible snakes, coiling about him. Mr. Agyk opened his eyes wearily, feeling the trap loosen.

Far below the dworlls battled on. "To the door!" Korrun cried, rallying those around. "Move! Now!"

Gralen fought against his invisible assailants, as M'Sorreck thundered past in a cloud of black and crimson.

"NO!" the dragon shouted, his belly burning with rage, his strength forcing his attackers apart. "I'm not *that* easy to dispose of!" he shouted and blasted fire after the warlock, engulfing his robes in flame.

Wendya found herself in total darkness. The key flared in her hand, its cold, burning light changing from red to a deeper shade of crimson and casting a glimmer amongst the pitch. She struggled on blindly. The ground felt strangely spongy under her feet and, as she sank into it, a feeling of dread came over her, greater than that of the cavern, a feeling that she had actually fallen inside the belly of some living creature.

Suddenly the ground shifted and gave way beneath her like stretched elastic. She struggled wildly for a few moments, exhaustion plaguing her every move. Something icy clasped her, grabbing at her ankles and roughly pulling her down through the floor. The darkness engulfed her within seconds, swamping her ears and eyes as she disappeared.

In the valley outside, the battle still raged, as the sky grew ever paler. In the distance, the snowy peaks were glowing pink in the first rays of light. Dawn was racing eastward. Time was almost out.

M'Sorreck returned the dragon fire, his contorted body pulsing with energy. Again Gralen dived after the warlock to block his way. The creature hissed, growing in size to dwarf the dragon before it, then in a blinding flash of yellow light, it lashed out. Bolts of energy, akin to lightning but more destructive, coursed from its rotten flesh striking the dragon repeatedly. Venomous tongues issued from its mouth and nose and flowed from its dead eyes as its entire body blazed with power.

Wendya opened her eyes. A huge bulbous object pounded above her, like an engorged heart. For a long moment she lay still, unable or unwilling to move, floating in some sort of drifting current. Not water, almost sand. She tried to focus her eyes. Shadows and shapes moved in the dimness. Energy rippled in tiny specks of fast-flowing light. Every sense in her body was alive and on fire. Despite the pain and the fear, she felt strangely at peace here. She was suddenly aware of a figure before her. A slender woman sat crying, cradling an infant. She looked like Wendya, only her doleful eyes were the deepest violet flecked with gold and amber. Her long dark hair fell loosely over one shoulder, black as jet. She placed a small silver key in the shape of a dragon around the child's neck, kissed it tenderly on the forehead, and disappeared. A waterfall roared nearby, then nothing. Now a man appeared, his face masked and hidden from view, but a rage emanated from him, a terrible, merciless rage. He was frantically looking for something … or someone.

Wendya blinked. He was gone.

She was alone again, slowly spiraling inside a vortex, a giant whirlpool of dancing images. Colors flew past her, collided, separated, or exploded in showers of dazzling light that changed constantly, intensifying or growing darker. Sounds and voices echoed through her head. Her body felt light, not hers somehow. Wendya struggled to stand but found she could not. Looking ahead now, through the misty blur of shapes, she could see a bright, pulsating center, an almost blinding golden light with a tiny crimson core beating within. She glided towards it, inextricably drawn to it. The voices became louder.

"Destiny, destiny," they echoed. "Power beyond end. Take it. Claim it as your own! Bond with it. Unite, unite, unite!"

Shielding her eyes from its brilliance, she drew nearer. She could glimpse something moving inside the light, the source of it … a floating orb, red, metallic or mirrored, rapidly spinning and no bigger than her fist.

"Where am I? What is this place?" she whispered, her voice sounding strange to her own ears.

"You know," replied the voices.

"Who are you?"

"Who are you … you … you?" they whispered.

"I don't understand."

"You … Only you …"

Wendya looked down and opened her hands. They were bleeding. Suddenly the key, which she had clasped so tightly, burst into flames and, rising from her palms, it hovered for a moment before her, then placed itself on the broken chain around her neck. Wendya felt a huge surge of blood and power rush to her head, making her swoon. She closed her eyes, trying to steady herself, and slowly outstretched her hands. Her fingertips found the sphere, racing over its smooth spinning surface. She took a deep breath, seized it in both hands, and clasped it tightly to her breast.

"You must unite with it, with him! The power will be yours. Destiny!"

Never had she felt such strength before, cold and dark and incalculably terrible, yet inviting, enticing. Its icy tendrils spread through her veins, insidious and relentless, freezing blood and bone and sinew.

"Join with us, join with him. The power is yours!"

She felt herself weakening.

"Marval, where are you? Please … I need you! … I can't do this … NO!" she shouted, forcing the orb back and holding it above her head. It looked so beautiful, so perfect … how could she destroy such a wondrous thing?

"I love you and I always will," came Mr. Agyk's voice, *"… the daughter child I never had."*

Tears clouded her eyes. "I won't fail you … father. For you! For us all!" she cried, mustered her remaining strength and what little will she had, and released the orb, sending it shattering to her feet.

The explosion caught her off-guard, flinging her into the air in a blast of searing light that seemed to splinter the mind and all around it. Shockwaves, one after another, crashed upon her like great tidal surges. The air thickened with screams, fire spread everywhere, choking the oxygen, no way to breathe, no way out!

Flame and sparks filled her vision. Molten rock spewed around her. The ground trembled and shuddered in its final death throes, then cracked.

Blackness surrounded her. A pain in her chest, piercingly sharp, told her she was still alive. The key had burnt its dragon shape into her flesh, branding her just below the throat, a permanent scar, before it melted away.

She lay down at last and let the darkness take her, she saw the sad woman with the long, flowing hair surrounded by gushing water falling.

Gralen howled in pain as black lightning ripped through his body.

"Gralen! NO!" the dying wizard cried, desperate to help his friend.

Morreck's face, bloated by hatred, bore down on the green dragon. "Now, out of my way foul draken!" he snarled, sending the dragon plummeting to the ground as he rushed past to reach the door.

"Hold on!" Korrun yelled, leading the dworll charge as they swept through the hall, scattering wargols in their wake.

Gralen smashed into the ground in a cloud of dust and smoke. He looked up through weary blood-stained eyes and saw the creature tearing towards the door.

"Wendya!" he muttered in exhaustion and pain.

He tried to drag himself up when something caught his gaze. Rising all around him came an awful chittering sound and, with it, a blood-curdling realization ... the dark mytes had gathered and they wanted their prize!

M'Sorreck's hand had barely touched the door when he suddenly stopped. His body went rigid, as if he had been paralyzed. He faltered, swayed unsteadily, and his giant mass grew smaller. The stone tentacles framing the door wailed inconsolably, before crumbling to dust at his feet. The dark mytes which swarmed over the fallen dragon like deathly scavengers screamed and fell back in madness. The black cloud around their warlock master began to hiss and fray at the edges as if it were being torn apart from the inside.

"NOOOOOOOOOOOOOOOOOOOOOOOOO!" came a howl rising to a deafening screech, a juddering boom that shook the entire cavern and the mountain above, instantly silencing the wargol hordes.

Gralen valiantly tried to stand, to claw his way back to Morreck.

"Stay back!" came Mr. Agyk's voice, weakened but stonily determined.

The tide was turning.

The old scholar looked at his wizened, gray hands in amazement as his color returned and he felt his former strength begin to course through his body, tingling down every nerve and artery. "Wendya! You did it!" he gasped. "Now, finally ... I will finish this!"

His chance had come at last.

The mist lifted from his eyes. Slowly but surely Mr. Agyk felt his power leeching out of his nemesis and flowing back to him, vibrating through the pores of his skin to every cell of his being, invigorating his blood, filling every tissue and sinew with life and energy. The old mage threw back his tattered cloak. Emanating from somewhere deep within him came a light, pure as day, glistening silver, green and lilac. He closed his eyes, built his strength, and broke the strangling holds around him.

M'Sorreck stood like a flickering darkness, shapeless and fathomless. Trails of vapor escaped from him, climbing higher into the air, changing from black to crimson to sickly yellow. The walls around groaned, the figures trapped within writhed not in agony, but in ecstasy and excited victory. His countless victims would have their revenge this day.

Mr. Agyk glided towards his enemy, his robes whole once more and flying about him like a glorious trail of summery green sails. His unkempt mane of wild hair sparkled silvery-white and his eyes glimmered as clear as a starlit stream. Twinkling shards glittered in the gloom, reforming themselves into his staff.

Despite his revival, his face betrayed a greater weight of age than just his years, as if the battle had drained him to a point too far for a complete recovery.

"It is over!" he called, his graveled voice aged but echoing stronger than the foul foundations he stood on.

M'Sorreck turned, changing from a shapeless mass back into a figure, full of wrath and hatred. The tall warlock was clearly weakened, but still immeasurably strong. His face, once so wondrously fair to look upon, now a grimace of death, his golden locks a rancid ochre, his empty eyes fixed on only Mr. Agyk.

"Let's finish this!" he sneered, lunging at the wizard with all his fury. Wizard struck wizard and the cavern cracked beneath their feet, crumbling steps and sending pillars crashing to the ground.

"The power of my ancestors belongs to me alone!" Mr. Agyk shouted, though far from full strength, he knew their task had succeeded. "I reclaim it!" he bellowed, his eyes ablaze with ferocious silver light.

Outside, King Baillum looked to the sky. "I hope the wizard has succeeded. Here comes the dawn!" he cried, hailing the new day as it caught Fendellin's great plains in a haze of shimmering gold and raced westward toward Kavok.

As the dawn sun hit Kavok's peak in a blaze of light, another chasm opened up in the floor deeper than the first. Mr. Agyk grabbed M'Sorreck's hand. Instantly, power sprang from the warlock's deadly eyes and pulsed back into the old wizard.

"Breaker of oaths, soul taker, corruptor! Many names you have, wærloga, and all of them evil! I purge you of all my powers and cast you down to oblivion! *Ngaro urupatu kore!*" boomed the green wizard.

Morreck struggled desperately to break free, to break the bond, but could not. "I will bathe in the blood of all those you love," he snarled. "They will suffer and die before you … Then I will have you!"

"Morreck, master of demons, words cannot avail you! Be gone, fengal creature, back to the darkness where you belong!" cried Mr. Agyk.

A blinding flash sparked between the two wizards and blasted them apart, slamming them into opposite walls across the chasm. Mr. Agyk sprang to his feet and instinctively felt his chest.

Whole at last! All his power and strength returned!

The warlock regained his composure, his appearance becoming beautiful once more. He laughed as if his designs had been fulfilled. He stood smiling callously at the old scholar from the other side of the chasm. When he finally spoke, the cutting malice of his voice brought a new terror with it.

"You simple-minded fool! You have no idea what you have done," he whispered. "You are stronger than I thought, magus, but not as strong as me … nor my kin, my heir, a true darkling child!" he said, looking closely at the wizard. "You know now of whom I speak, though you only wondered before. I have been searching for her for many long years. It was foolish of Dorrol to keep her a secret from me and perhaps from you … I will repay his kindness in time," he smiled and his white eyes glowed with a ferociousness that struck fear into the wizard's heart.

"I will visit you both again. I shall enjoy watching her blossom," he said the words slowly, his black tongue relishing every syllable. "I shall not rest until I have taken what is mine. She will bloom and I will reap the harvest! Like father, like daughter, Marvalla!" he smiled.

"YOU WILL NOT GO NEAR HER!" the wizard roared.

Morreck laughed. "You want to kill me, do you not? Come! I invite you to try … kill me!" he cackled. "You understand nothing! … Kill me and I will only grow stronger," he laughed again, his white eyes challenging the old wizard.

"Let us see how strong you are *without* my powers!" Mr. Agyk shouted, conjuring a barrage of flying arrows towards him.

M'Sorreck laughed as they fizzled away before they could touch him. "You have helped me transcend, old man," he sneered, then suddenly vanished and reappeared beside the aged wizard. "I will see you and her again, Marvalla!" he hissed into his ear.

In that instant, Mr. Agyk knew his mind.

"NO!" he cried. "STOP!"

But it was too late.

M'Sorreck reappeared again on the other side of the chasm, and stepped to the edge of the abyss, his eyes fixed and burning on the wizard, a malignant smile playing on his face.

"Formless but even stronger!" he cackled. "Give her my love! I will join with her soon enough!"

Without another word, he stepped off the edge and fell into the abyss, disappearing into the darkness below. Mr. Agyk rushed forward and peered into the void. For a moment, he saw two white luminous eyes laughing, taunting, staring back at him intently, before the warlock vanished into the depths.

Mr. Agyk slumped back, exhausted and fearful. "Wendya! What have I done?" He whispered. "I am a fool, this will prove ill for us all."

Chapter Twenty-One
Into The Light

endya ... Wendya?" The young witch could feel arms stretching across her, gently lifting her up. "Careful, she is hurt!" came the voice again, soft and aged. "Wendya, come back to us."

"Am I dead?" she murmured, opening her eyes.

"No," chuckled the voice. "But we must leave, the cavern is unstable. Can you stand?"

She focused her eyes and, amidst the blurring light and dust, she could see an anxious, familiar face with a scruffy beard and a shock of wild, wiry hair.

"Marval?

"Yes, it is me," he smiled.

"You're alive!"

"Yes, we are both alive ... though only just," smiled the wizard. He was clearly battered and utterly exhausted, but full of life. His hair, though whiter, shone with an inner brilliance and the silvery-gray of his eyes sparkled in the dim light. A deep sadness lingered over him and he tried to hide a troubled expression.

Wendya touched his cheek, seeing that the familiar creases and signs of age lay far deeper than before. "Are you alright?" she asked.

The old mage laughed, the same graveled chortle he always did when someone was being ludicrous. "Come on," he smiled. "Are you able to stand?"

"I think so."

"You're injured," said a voice beside her.

Korrun touched her shoulder and took a torn piece of material from his belt. "Use this," he said softly, his bruised and bloodied face showing an uncharacteristically warm smile.

"Korrun! You're here and alright!" she gasped. "Where is Gralen?!"

"I'm fine, if anybody wants to know," he grumbled nearby, "just a few cuts and tears." The green dragon stood watching a few feet away, and couldn't disguise the anxiety and relief on his face.

Mr. Agyk gently wrapped the bandage around her shoulder and arm and tended to the cuts on her head. "Good, the bleeding has stopped at least. There, that will have to do for now," he paused and looked earnestly into the young wicca's eyes. "Well done, my dear, very well done!" he smiled, squeezing her hand and kissing her on the forehead. Wendya hugged the old wizard tightly and wept with joy. She couldn't remember feeling so happy.

"Careful!" he teased. "I am not a youngster like all of you!"

Gralen shifted uneasily. "We'd best be going. There are things I must tell you, but not here ... This place looks like it could cave in at any minute!"

"Quite right. Come, there are still many wargols about, and fouler creatures perhaps. I fear the battle still continues outside," the wizard sighed, peering through the gloom as the mountain groaned above them.

"Morreck!?" Wendya suddenly cried out, her face full of fear for a moment.

"Gone," the dwelf replied simply, picking through the debris to find any useful weapon.

Mr. Agyk looked tense. "I will explain later, this is neither the time nor the place...," he said nervously. "I will only say ... that he is gone," the wizard sighed heavily and his age seemed to burden him. "Perhaps it is for the best ...," he murmured. Wendya stared at him, puzzled. There was clearly something troubling him deeply that he would not voice. "We must leave quickly. Let us hope that we do not have to battle our way back to the surface. I am thoroughly spent!" he added.

The friends kept close together, picking their way through the bodies and debris that littered the cavern floor, while Gralen took immense pleasure in trampling over as many foul wargol hides as he could, as if he were squashing grapes for a fine vintage. There were no signs of the dreaded dark mytes, not even their crushed bodies could be seen.

Soon, they were joined by Frell, Orrla and the remaining dworlls.

"Well met my friends!" Frell called as they came closer.

Orrla stood beside him, a clear look of amazement on her face. "I am glad to see you all ... nearly in one piece!" she said glancing over the bedraggled group, before her gaze stopped on the wizard, "and back to your full size!"

"And full powers!" Frell added. "Mr. Agyk has defeated our greatest enemy!"

The wizard stared at the small number of dworlls before them. "You have suffered great losses ..."

"We have," Frell answered, casting his pale eyes over the soldiers, "... but I think it a miracle that *any* of us are standing, given the number of our foe!" he paused. "This night shall never be forgotten!"

Mr. Agyk placed a hand on the dworll's shoulder. "Yes ... the night is over at last and the first light of dawn has broken outside, but I fear the fighting is not over yet. Let us celebrate our victory when we have achieved it and are safely back in our homes!" the wizard said grimly.

"Do any of your injured need carrying?" Gralen asked.

Orrla shook her head. "We're all walking wounded, as are you!" she smiled, glancing at the dragon and witch, then lingering on the dwelf's injuries.

Korrun nodded, a bandage of sorts pressed against his bleeding side. "We cannot pause here. We must get back to the valley," he said.

"You will not like what you find there," Gralen replied sadly, "... things have gone badly."

Mr. Agyk and the dworlls looked at him with questioning faces.

"Lord Sedgewick and Lord Tollam are dead ...," the green dragon paused for a moment, unsure of what to say or how to say it. Korrun lowered his head as Gralen continued, his voice full of sorrow. "There has been treachery amongst the Fendellon ranks. I'm only glad that none of you were … turned," he fell silent and would speak no more.

Mr. Agyk studied his old friend and knew there was more to tell, and none of it good.

"We will go," Frell replied quietly, looking around with some nervousness. "Many wargol demons still lurk, driven mad by their Master's demise, and are bent on revenge. We will need reinforcements to hunt them out. For now, we should leave this evil place. Stay close to the pillars but do not touch them, and watch the ledge above, two of our number have been killed by snipers already!"

The survivors wound their way through the cavern until they reached one of the few unbroken stairways. Heading for the tunnel that they had come from earlier, they climbed slowly. Gralen ignored the pain in his torn wings and took to the air, circling overhead to look out for ambushes and hidden wargols. Every so often he blasted a jet of green flame down the many holes and doorways that lined the cavern. After three or four small skirmishes, the group at last left Morreck's lair behind.

Wendya stood for a moment, framed in the tunnel mouth, and watched the walls shimmer and ripple with a peaceful ebbing movement of their own.

"I hope they're at peace," she sighed.

"Who?" Korrun asked.

"All the poor souls trapped in those walls."

Mr. Agyk watched her. "Come on," he said gently, taking her arm. "A new day is dawning … it is time we climbed, it will be light outside. We must help those who have fought so valiantly."

Wendya took one last look, as if reluctant to leave, turned her back, and started the long, dark journey to the surface and into the light.

The ascent was steep and difficult and signs of Korrun and Orrla's battles were clearly evident. In places the tunnels divided off or were blocked by rock and wargol bodies, stacked one upon the other. The mountain around them groaned and shivered. Great cracks opened up in the pathway, too wide to cross or jump, each time forcing the travelers to double back and try another passage.

"I hope the King is safe …," Orrla said quietly, as she smiled at Frell.

Gralen sighed but said nothing, as he followed behind. The horror of what he had seen and the thought of what they might yet find, filled him with dread and kept him silent. Were any of them left alive? And always his thoughts returned to Rollm lying badly injured and alone, and his beloved Sedgewick, gone forever.

Mr. Agyk looked at the dragon, as if sensing his old friend's anguish.

"How far?" Wendya murmured, her limbs feeling heavy again.

"Not far now," the wizard smiled as he helped her along. "Oh, it is good to be whole once more."

Wendya clasped his arm tightly. "I was so afraid I'd lost you," she whispered.

Onward they trudged, higher and higher and, slowly, the path became easier.

Korrun gazed at his brother's ring, lost in thought. "Wargols are just mindless drones," he muttered, as if answering a question, "they cannot survive long without their master. The worst of the fighting should be over."

"Let us hope so ... but remember, a dying bee may still sting!" the wizard warned.

"True enough," Orrla said, looking past the dragon to check the passage behind. "You saw those creatures; many of them had gone mad!"

The wizard sighed in agreement. "Fendellin may have been saved, but I fear she may be plagued by troubles for a while." He turned and glanced at Wendya who walked in silence beside him, "... a victory, yes, but at what price?" he thought. "I fear there are troubled waters ahead."

They slogged on, climbing the steep winding passages of Kavok, helping each other along the way, until at last they saw a faint glimmer of light ahead.

"Daylight! We are there!" Frell cried, quickening his pace.

The group cautiously emerged from the mountainside. The cold blue of dawn bathed everything in an eerie stillness. The scene that greeted them could not have been worse.

Everywhere the bodies of the dead — dworll, wargol, enemy or friend — lay strewn waist-deep, so great was their number they could not be counted. The group stood in stunned silence. Nothing moved. No sound stirred amongst the piles and mounds of the fallen. All was silent, even the skies.

Eventually Frell spoke.

"Where are they all?" he whispered, bewildered and horrified in equal measure.

An acrid smell filled the air, catching the back of the throat. Wafts of brown smoke drifted through the gorge in straddling fingers, carried on the morning breeze. Steam rose from the ground in curling wisps and issued from the fissures in the mountain. Everywhere blood lay in thick black puddles mingled with the night rain.

"Madness!" Mr. Agyk muttered.

Frell stared at the bodies, his eyes caught by the sight of so many slain dworlls. He knelt down suddenly. Amongst the carnage lay two dworlls that he knew well, locked in deadly combat with each other, one from the ranks of Perral's army and another from the King's company, and each impaled on the other's sword.

Gralen's warning had not prepared them for this.

"I don't understand ... what has happened here?" Frell cried, turning to the others.

The dragon spoke quietly, as if a stray word would bring destruction upon their heads. "Treachery," he replied sullenly. "I don't know much, but when I came here the King told me that some of the troops had 'turned'. It was the reason I had to follow after you. Morreck knew of our plans, he knew everything!"

Mr. Agyk looked at his friend and nodded grimly as if he finally understood. "Who was it?" he asked solemnly.

"Perral ...," Gralen answered, "amongst others. He was corrupted. Hallm said he turned traitor on the King and killed Lord Tollam, then set dworll upon dworll. I'd never have believed it ... ."

"M'Sorreck's poison has spread further and deeper than we know," sighed the wizard.

A mournful silence fell on the group as they walked through the detritus, looking for signs of life. There were none. They collected a few weapons where they could, and the pennons and flags of the Fendellon ruling houses. As they reached a protruding outcrop of rock, Korrun, who had walked a little further ahead, stopped and crouched low to the ground.

"Listen!" he whispered. "I hear something! Fighting up ahead!" He pointed northwards through the thick smoke towards the horned gates. "Let us see if we can finish this!" he shouted and darted off, as if weariness and injury had left him.

They followed. Within a short time, the group came upon the first pockets of fighting. By now, most of Perral's forces had been killed or driven into the mountain with their wargol comrades. Only the stronger, fearless and most loyal followers remained, determined to fight to the death and slaughter every last Fendellon.

Korrun headed into the throng without hesitation, with the others close behind. Gralen, glad to be free of the confines of Kavok, spread his wings and took to the air, passing low over the valley.

As the tearful hue of dawn brightened into a pale, somber yellow, the battle at last ceased, and the troupe were reunited with King Baillum and the remaining Fendellin host.

Cheers arose and echoed round the canyon, as Korrun and the others approached, holding aloft the tattered but triumphant flags they had gathered, like a trail of flying tails behind them. The old King stood lost in conversation with Lord Nerrus, his fallen horse beside them, amidst the boulders and broken ruins of M'Sorreck's gate towers and the crumbled remains of the mighty sentinels.

"Victory at last!" Nerrus hailed and rushed forward to hug his daughter. "Never has a Lord of the Realm been so glad to see his captain!" he laughed before addressing the others. "We are most glad to see you all! We knew you must have succeeded, the moment M'Sorreck's fengal creatures started deserting the field and skewering themselves on their own spikes!"

Gralen flew over the soldiers' heads and landed amongst the rubble.

"You are well met," smiled the King, turning to the old mage. "It is good to see you at your full height. I see you have regained your strength!" he paused, his face somber once more. "We have been hard-pressed. We would not be standing here now if you had not defeated that evil thing."

Mr. Agyk looked at him gravely. "My Lord, it was not I who ended this. Morreck was greatly weakened and knew it. I suspect he feared that he could be destroyed."

"I'd have gladly done it!" Gralen muttered.

The wizard sighed, his silver eyes full of worry and doubt. "In the end, no action of ours caused his defeat … he threw himself into the chasm, and deprived me of the pleasure!"

King Baillum held his gaze for a long while. It seemed he was trying to guess the cause of the wizard's troubled heart. "That news greatly surprise me … yet, ever has that abomination been ruler of his own destiny. Nonetheless, no power on this earth would have driven him to such a decision if he were not so 'weakened' as you say," the King smiled again. "Praise is fitting."

"And for you father," bowed Frell. "The battle has been bitter since I left you."

"The bitterest," the King explained, looking over the fallen bodies of his people, many of them close friends and allies he had known since he was a young dworll. "The cost has been far greater than my worst fears. We have lost countless souls because of Perral's villainy."

Baillum stood, as a statue, his raiment catching in the breeze, his stern eyes full of sadness. "That was the cruelest blow to endure," he said grimly, "and the most difficult to explain to those waiting at home." He shook his head, his brow heavy with weariness and worry. "We have won the night and the day. M'Sorreck's terror has at last been lifted from our lands. Now, we must attend to the injured and burn this accursed place to the ground!" he paused and sighed. "I can only hope that the defenses left at Mund'harr were sufficient."

Mr. Agyk remembered Morreck's words and an aching fearfulness filled him. He looked at the smashed tower gates and the shattered bodies of the sentinels, then to the broken walls beyond. He cast his eyes down the gorge, as if he could pierce the smoke, to find some green blade of hope in the lands beyond. In the east, the sun was climbing high, casting its pale rays across Fendellin's grasslands, stretching its waking touch to the salt flats and the scarred peaks of Kavok. Away to the far southeast, Mr. Agyk thought he could glimpse dark smoke climbing into the misty sky.

"This night has at last ended," Baillum announced. "May we never see another like it!"

Korrun stuck the Fendellin banner into the ground and looked at Gralen. "What of the fight above? What of Sedgewick's fÿrrens?" he asked anxiously.

"Half have flown to the city to protect it. The others are on a rout, scouring the mountains, hunting for Morreck's serpents," explained the King. Hturned and looked solemnly at the green dragon, "We could not have won this night without them, or you. Thank you."

"But they have paid dearly for helping us," Nerrus sighed. "Lord Sedgewick, our greatest friend, has fallen and many of his kin."

Mr. Agyk nodded. "Gralen told us of his passing."

The dragon gazed up to the skies, his orange eyes lost in grief. "I must go," he murmured. "Rollm ... I have a friend who needs me ... and a promise to keep."

The wizard nodded. "I know," he said sadly. "Rollm will be safe. And you be careful. Our losses have been heavy, my heart could not bear it if anything happened to you!"

Gralen glanced at the old man and Wendya and half-grinned, then shot up and disappeared into the early morning haze.

"He will be alright," smiled the wizard. "The battle is over."

The skies brightened further as Hallm emerged from what remained of the fortress gates behind.

"We have secured the main causeway inside and the keep beyond ... and have succeeded in taking the first, second and third halls. Now that their master is dead, most of Morreck's hordes have scattered, stricken by madness and fear. Are we to pursue them further into the mountain?" he asked.

"No, Kavok is a labyrinth … We have neither the soldiers nor the resources for that, yet. No, secure what you have and barricade the rest. Every tunnel, every doorway, every rat-infested hole in or out of that place must be blocked … and the valley entrances too," King Baillum's face hardened. "We will seal the whole gorge and trap them like the vermin they are!"

"And then, Sire?"

Baillum paused. "Once we gather more reinforcements and strengthen our position, we will flush them out and drown them in fire!"

Hallm nodded and went to leave.

"I am sorry to hear of your father," Korrun said quietly. "Lord Tollam was the truest of all."

The young captain flinched as if the name pained him. "Thank you. Many good Fendellons have fallen, but for me, none better than he!"

"Now is not the time. But his people and lands will need a leader after this," replied the King, solemnly placing a hand on the dworll's shoulder. "I can think of none more loved or more worthy than you, Hallm. You were his first choice as successor."

Hallm hesitated. "I cannot think of that, Sire. My only desire is revenge!"

As they talked, a dark cloud passed overhead dimming the sun for a moment. A faint cry, barely audible, carried on the wind and echoed over the mountaintops. Wendya and the others turned to see the dark cloud returning, swooping down out of the east against the rising sun. They strained their eyes as the cry echoed again from the north. A warning cry … it was Gralen's voice, but too faint to discern … and too late.

"VARKUL!" the wizard gasped in horror, as the creature hurtled towards them.

Within seconds, the dragon ploughed into the group, slammed into the wizard and crushed Hallm and the King under its massive bulk. Nerrus and Korrun lunged forward wielding anything they could grab and were thrown aside by one casual flick of its tail. Frell too raced forward and was sent crashing against a rock, shattering his already damaged shoulder. Orrla rushed to his aid as Wendya ran toward the stunned mage.

The creature blasted jets of blue flame toward the other dworlls, forcing them back. Arching its back and spreading its huge wings, it hoisted itself back into the air, hovered for a moment, then dived again.

"WATCH OUT!" Korrun yelled, running wildly forward.

"WENDYA!" Mr. Agyk cried, as he scrambled to his feet.

The witch spun round to see the blackened creature descend upon her, his leathery wings blocking out the sky, his reptilian eyes an icy sapphire and intent on only her.

"GET DOWN!" Orrla shouted, as she darted in front of Wendya, pushing her to the ground and managing to throw a spear into the beast before it swept them both up and shot into the sky.

Varkul flew straight upwards, with Orrla in one arm and Wendya in the other.

"NOOOOOOOO!" Mr. Agyk bellowed and cast a freezing spell to paralyze the beast. But it simply shattered like glass upon contact. Again, the wizard blasted the creature and again, to no avail.

"Your feeble magic cannot harm me, wizard!" it snarled, savoring the moment.

The look of sheer desperation on their faces was a delight to him, their efforts against him utterly futile. He wished he could prolong their agony, but already his keen hearing could sense a change on the wind, the unmistakable sound of approaching wings. Sedgewick's crows were on their way!

Nerrus sprinted frantically forward as the beast hovered just above the valley, its eyes fixed on the wizard and the King, its ears listening to the roar and wrath of an advancing dragon.

"ORRLA!!" Nerrus cried.

"Move and they die!" Varkul sneered. He smiled crookedly, showing his blood-stained teeth. "Here, have your daughter back!" it spat. To the horror of everyone, something fell from its huge talons … a head followed by a body.

"ORRLLLLLLAAAAAAAAAAAAAA!" howled Nerrus, as his beloved daughter fell amongst the stones.

Wendya screamed and struggled to free herself from the iron vice around her, as she dangled beneath the creature's belly like a mouse caught in the claws of a great eagle. She tried using what powers she could, but they seemed to have left her.

The wizard, far below, kept blasting the creature with lightning, fire, freezing bolts, anything he could muster. None of them had the slightest effect.

Varkul smiled. "A passing gift to remember me by!" he hissed.

Taking the struggling witch in one hand, he snapped her neck like a matchstick and dropped her for a long fall to the ground.

"NOOOOOOOOOO! WENDYAAAAAAAAAA!" Mr. Agyk screamed, stumbling over the rocks and shooting wave upon wave of green lightning toward the creature.

Varkul swerved, then seeing Gralen and a host of dragons racing towards him, he turned and fled over the mountains and was lost amongst the snow-covered peaks.

Mr. Agyk and Korrun dashed forward as Nerrus and Frell scrambled towards the broken body of Orrla, and collapsed in grief beside her. The wizard outstretched his arms and sent out a cushion of soft air which caught the falling witch and gently bought her down to rest amongst the ruins.

"Wendya!" Mr. Agyk cried rushing to her side.

Korrun fell to his knees before her. The witch lay very still, her body contorted, her head awkwardly lolling to one side. Her green eyes fluttered, as if she were waking from a long sleep.

"Marval?" she whispered faintly. "I can't see you … I can't see you …"

"I am here my darling."

"I can't feel my legs," she murmured.

"Lie still my child," he whispered, gently brushing her hair aside. "Lie still …"

A gust of bitter wind blew in from the north as Gralen swept down in a blaze of anger, and the shadow of five or six large dragons flew overhead in pursuit of their enemy.

No sooner had his great wings taken him over the last jagged peaks and into Kavok's rocky gorge, had Gralen seen the figures of his friends, frozen like praying statues. The green dragon faltered, his eyes widening in shock and disbelief, stricken by a terrible groping horror. There, twisted as a tiny rag doll amongst the carnage, lay his beloved Wendya.

King Baillum and Hallm, injured by Varkul's attack, hobbled over to their fallen friends. The soldiers gathered round them, escorting the King while nervously watching the skies in case of another assault. Utterly grief-stricken, Nerrus sat cradling his daughter's severed head in his lap and howled in despair, a broken figure. Frell gently placed his cloak over Orrla's crumpled body and wept.

"Wend'?" Gralen called as he crashed into the valley and careered over the rocks and boulders to the fallen witch. "WENDYA?!"

Wendya's eyes flickered once more and a tear traced itself down her cheek.

"I'm alright," she whispered, her eyes feeling heavy now. "I'm fine ..."

She looked up at the white sky as it fractured into thousands of swirling shapes like silk scarves dancing in the wind, lacing in and out of each other.

"Wendya?" the wizard called, stroking her hair.

A long sigh almost like relief or happiness escaped from her lips and her body relaxed.

"Wendya?" he called softly.

The witch didn't move, her eyes fixed on the heavens above.

"WENDYA!" Gralen shouted, tears blinding his sight. "WENDYA!" he roared.

The young witch lay perfectly still, a calmness descended upon her pale face. Korrun gently took her small hand in his and kissed it, tears filling his eyes.

"Wendya, please!" he whispered.

He held her hand tightly until he felt the warmth slowly leave her, taken by the cruel and bitter air.

"No! NO!" Gralen shook his head, fire consuming him, filling his blood, exploding in his chest and head. "NOOOOOOOOOOOOOOO!" he screamed, a cry that could have riven the sky in two, so clear and haunting it was. "Do something ... DO SOMETHING!"

Mr. Agyk closed his eyes and placed his hands gently on either side of the witch's brow.

"Let my life energy flow to her," he whispered. "Take my life, not hers ... I beg of you, take me ... please!" he started to chant, frantically and quietly in languages unknown.

A searing light coalesced in front of them; millions of tiny star points which sprang from the wizard's aged hands and passed onto the witch, illuminating her beneath a sparkling veil. Yet, as each point of light shimmered and touched her, it rebounded back into the air, feathering into streams before flowing back into the old mage.

"Try again!" Gralen begged, slamming his fist into the rocks.

Mr. Agyk could hardly contain his grief, could hardly form words. It wasn't working, he knew it, he could feel it. "Please!" he implored, desperately trying to focus, to hold back his tears. "Please! I give my life for hers!" he said and began the chant again. Again the light sprang from the wizard to the witch and recoiled back. Again he tried and again and again.

"It's not working!" Gralen cried. "Why isn't it working?"

Mr. Agyk stroked her head, letting the tears finally stream down his face. "Oh gods!" he cried. "Because ... she is gone!" he choked.

He kissed her lovingly on the forehead and closed her eyes. "Oh gods! She is gone!" he murmured touching her face. "She is gone ... my darling sweet girl is gone!" he wailed, rocking her in his arms.

The sun shone coldly above them and all the world lay still and gray. With grief overwhelming him, and the accursed Oracle's bitter words ringing in his head, the old wizard finally succumbed to grief and wept as he had never done in all his long life.

Chapter Twenty-Two

Mund'harr

Time passed slowly. Korrun closed his eyes, grief and rage choking his throat like bile. "You're wrong! You're all wrong! ... She's fine," Gralen insisted, roughly pushing the dwelf aside to cradle Wendya in his arms. "Come on ... wake up!" he cried, shaking her, "Please, PLEASE, wake up!"

Korrun placed a hand gently on the dragon's shoulder. "Gralen ... she is gone," he whispered, his eyes meeting the dragon's. "Marval is right. She is gone. Let her rest."

The dragon shook his head, refusing to accept the truth, his eyes wild and unseeing. "No! I won't allow it ... not her, not her!"

Mr. Agyk slumped over, a weary figure overwhelmed by grief. He outstretched his hand in a pleading gesture. "Gralen, do not ... Leave her! It is over, it is all over!" he wept.

"It's not over!" Gralen raged. "Don't you dare give up! You've wasted years concerning yourself with the troubles that humans bring upon themselves and not concerning yourself with the extinction of your own people! It's not too late! I know it. We can save her, we can still save her!" he cried angrily, searching for a sign of hope in the old wizard's eyes. Suddenly, he turned to the King. "I can save her!" he gasped, "... and I know how!" Before anyone could stop him, he whisked Wendya's lifeless body into the air and shot out of the gorge.

"Gralen! ... NO! NO!" the wizard shouted, but the dragon did not hear.

In an instant, the dragon had left Kavok and the valley behind and was racing over the great salt plains towards the northward ridge and the Silent Marshes beyond, onward to Mund'harr and the Golden City.

"Hold on," he whispered softly, tears burning his eyes and running down his face in hot sizzling streams.

The great dragon's chest pounded as if it might explode at any moment and consume itself in a raging ball of fire, a burning comet tearing through the sky. Never had he flown at such a speed, every inch of his will, every muscle and sinew worked together with one purpose, desperation pushing him on. The boggy landscape of the Shudras loomed below as a passing blur, featureless and gray, only the noxious fumes gave its presence away.

"Hold on. You'll be alright ... hold on!" he whispered again.

He flew on, his vision a stinging fog that could focus on only one thing. Fendellin lay before him, silent and shrouded. As the morning grew brighter and a fresh spring-like rain fell lightly from the pale clouds above, all remained dark to him save the course ahead.

Hours passed as the sun traveled across the sky and the dragon sped on, racing over league upon league. The afternoon hazed into dusk when Gralen could at last glimpse the dark line of the Mund'harr plateau, rising up in the distance as a sheer line of limestone cliffs. If he kept going through the night, he could reach the city by dawn.

Clutching Wendya gently to his chest, his great clawed hands cupped her lifeless head as her hair streamed behind. "I'll never give up on you, I promise," he whispered.

The stars took flight. The land faded away with the fading sun. It started raining. As the cold chill of the wind cut cruelly against him, Gralen felt utterly alone, speeding as fast as his wings could bear without breaking.

The night deepened as the dragon crossed the last of the marshes and swooped above the plateau ridge. The first grasslands whispered below, as strange glowing lights appeared around him. Thousands of fires could now be seen, spiraling high into the air, despite the rain. As he approached, he could see fields and ancient woods ablaze, farmsteads and whole villages alight. Gralen looked down in despair, and through the drifting strands of smoke and ash, it became clear that Morreck's serpents had attacked mercilessly, burning anything they could see. Fear for the city struck his heart.

He raced on into the night. As the first light of dawn appeared once more in the east, misty and gray, Gralen caught sight of Mund'harr and the golden spires of the city glinting in the rising sun. Tall and ominously about them towered giant plumes of thick, black smoke and the unmistakable glow of flames. The city was on fire!

Gralen shot forward, skimming low over the charred villages and devastated towns that dotted the plains. Even the bridges spanning the many twisting rivers that criss-crossed the central plains were completely destroyed. As the dragon approached, the damage became ever clearer. Varkul's serpents had indeed broken off and attacked the city, while the battle raged at Kavok. Left with only the protection of the City and Prairian Guards and the few dragons Sedgewick could spare, Fendellin's capital had burned under the onslaught. Miraculously, the night rain had brought blessed relief, curbing the worst of the fires from spreading, and saving many of the ancient buildings from utter ruin.

To Gralen's surprise and delight, a great number of Sedgewick's fÿrrens, scattered from the battle, now patrolled the skies, wheeling above the city in ever widening sweeps. Their keen eyes scanned the lands around while others carried large wagons of river water to quell the fiercest fires.

Suddenly a call went out, reverberating through the air as a rumbling echo. A dragon warning call. Gralen had been spotted. Swift to action, five winged guardians appeared from nowhere and darted towards him in attack formation, as the city's bell towers rang out in response.

"I am Gralen! I am a friend!" he bellowed.

Recognizing the portly green dragon, they broke off their attack and waved him past quickly, then continued their vigil.

Smoke billowed over the city's blackened ramparts and clung in swirling wisps to its rooftops and turrets. The few remaining City and Prairian Guards marshaled all able-bodied souls to help extinguish the flames and keep watch. Despite the fires and chaos, most of the capital's great palaces and citadels such as the Chapel of Kings, had been spared from major damage. However, the beloved Archive — a library equal to that in ancient Alexandria — lay smoldering, no more than a crumbled pile of embers. The most precious of their resources, containing countless books, scrolls, tablets and other materials chronicling over 120,000 years of dworll, ǽllfren, fȳrren and Fendellin history, was gone. In the ensuing firestorm, people had risked their lives to save as many of the priceless maps, volumes, and artifacts as possible before the entire building had collapsed.

Gralen landed, unhindered, amongst the smoky haze and disappeared through the Grand Hall and down into the heart of the mountain. Less than an hour later, the dragon entered the last chamber, the sacred cave, and stood before The Flame of Fendellin.

Gralen stared at the sparkling cascade and the pool below. The shimmering waters knew nothing of war or pain or grief, and somehow, in that quiet place, they seemed to sing to him.

"This will help you," he whispered softly.

He knelt beside the pool, its shallow waters moving silently, as gold sparkled and rippled across its silken surface.

"Please ... please help her," he pleaded as he gently placed her in the precious liquid. "I beg of you, I'll do anything!"

Wendya lay still, her hair a dull tangle of weeds in the water, her lips a pale blue, her face icy to the touch and as white and smooth as marble. The dragon gazed at her, willing her to open her eyes and smile at him.

"Wake up ... please," he begged, the words catching in his throat. "Come back to me ..."

He looked at the young witch's face, so serene, so beautiful. Shafts of green and yellow light streamed down from high above and danced upon her, igniting the water in hundreds of golden sparkles. But still the sleeping figure showed no sign of movement or life.

"I love you," Gralen whispered, his voice seeming loud and brash to his own ears. "I love you … I have always loved you … please don't leave me!" he wept.

Ignoring King Baillum's warning not to touch the water, he scooped some of it up and poured it over her. His huge hands fumbled with her bandages. Removing them as carefully as he could, he looked at her injured shoulder. It had stopped bleeding, but it had not healed, and all her cuts and bruises still remained.

"It has to work!" he sobbed, lapping the waters over her until he could bear it no longer. "This is my fault, my fault! I left you! I should've stayed by your side!" he howled. Overcome by loss, he wept uncontrollably, his body finally giving in to exhaustion and grief.

The rest of the day passed.

By the early light of the next dawn, the first battalions eventually returned to the city, escorted by Fendellin's brave warrior dragons. Mund'harr's bell towers rang out, in a chorus of victory, rather than a fearful warning of another sky assault. Despite the fanfare of horns and the warmth of the roaring cheers that greeted them, a mournful and muted procession they were, battered soldiers returning with their honored dead. All who witnessed the heroes returning were shocked at how few there were and how many had fallen.

When Mr. Agyk and Korrun eventually returned to the city, they found their friend sleeping next to the pool, with Wendya still floating upon its waters.

King Baillum leaned heavily on his crutch refusing aid, his leg broken and left side crushed after Varkul's attack. He watched solemnly as Mr. Agyk sat beside the exhausted dragon. Korrun retreated to the shadows, a ghostly, broken man, his face gaunt and stricken with grief, his dark eyes fixed on Wendya.

"Is there any hope?" Korrun asked, his voice the merest of whispers.

The King shook his head. "I am sorry. The waters can do many things. They can heal the gravest of wounds, or harm those who have none. They can bring a person back from the brink of death, but they cannot help those who have passed beyond it. They cannot give life to the lifeless … I am sorry," he explained softly.

Mr. Agyk sighed. "Then I will stay here beyond hope, for her and for him," he replied, looking at Wendya and Gralen, then lastly at Korrun.

"As you wish. I will leave you. My city and people need me. I will return and help if I may," the King paused, his weary eyes drifting over the fallen girl. "I am sorry Marval, as Lord Nerrus now knows, to lose a child as young and as fair … I would not wish that pain on any. I will send word to King Dorrol of Kallorm if I can. He will be greatly grieved by this loss."

"Do not send word yet," whispered the old scholar, "… not yet."

Baillum nodded. "There will be much grieving this night and for many long days and nights to come. Then the task of rebuilding must begin. Farewell." Bowing his head, the proud dworll left the friends alone at last.

Mr. Agyk stood transfixed, gazing blankly into the pool, before he turned to the figure of his old dragon friend. Dragon tears stained the green scales of his face and lay glistening like amber crystals at his feet. The wizard had never seen him so utterly crushed and wished with all his heart that the bitter events of Kavok had struck him alone, and not those he loved. He bent down and gently placed his arm on the dragon's shoulder.

"Gralen," he whispered, "old friend."

The dragon stirred and opened his bleary eyes, and turned immediately to the pool. His hope vanished.

"Gralen," Mr. Agyk called again, his voice like the deep echoes of a dream. "Let her go." He held the dragon firmly. "Let her go … our sweet child is gone."

"It didn't work? … Why?" He looked searchingly into the wizard's eyes. "But it has to work!"

"I know … I would gladly give my life a thousand times over if I could save hers, but she is gone," he whispered mournfully, tears filling his eyes yet again, his face heavily lined and ashen gray with grief.

Mr. Agyk slumped down on a bench, his legs feeling weak beneath him; full of woe and weariness, he wept. The dragon did not move, his body frozen beside the pool, his pale orange eyes dry from tears and staring at the lifeless girl. Korrun remained silent in the shadows, his back pressed tightly against the cold rock, his head hung, hardly able to lift his eyes, until he too finally gave in to sorrow.

Time ebbed. The morning and the afternoon came and went. The sun blazed above the frenzied activity of the city, then sank in a bloodied haze as more exhausted troops arrived back from Kavok, and new ones were sent out to scour the lands for any marauding wargols.

Darkness fell once more. A thin sliver of new moon rose high in the star-filled sky. All around the city and plains, the fires had at last been extinguished, but were now replaced by funeral pyres. Mourners wept openly in the streets, while others kept bedside vigils over their wounded and dying.

Amidst the sorrow, as each mourner bade the spirits of their loved ones to soar amongst the heavens, there came a requiem for the fallen. The proud and familiar words of *The Lay of Fendellin* carried on the wind, as a soft lamentation, then a growing chorus uniting all.

"Pass now beyond the mountains white
Where frosted rivers leap and spring,
Amongst the golden grasses light
Where fÿrrens dwell and soar and sing.

A land as old and fair as stars
Of snowy peaks and moonlit seas,
Of darkling woods we travel far
To gaze upon its silvery leaves.

A flame that springs eternal fire
A city in the misty sky,
A beauty which shall never tire
Amongst the banners flying high.

A sheltered haven, a sacred land
An ancient place of Kings,
A shining sword, a fiery brand
Where magic dwells therein.

Far east beyond heart's lost desire
The birthplace of the eldest kin,
Through rising sun on wings of fire
Lies beloved Fendellin."

The shattered helm of Lord Tollam was all that could be found on the battlefield. It was brought into the Chapel of Kings, together with the body of young Orrla, to be laid amongst the honored dead. A heartbroken Frell stayed by Lord Nerrus's side throughout, until the time came for them to say their final goodbyes. Insisting on carrying their burdens alone, Hallm bore his father's helmet and the pennon of their house, and Lord Nerrus bore the body of his beloved daughter into the sepulcher and laid them to rest amongst the great warrior Kings and Queens of Fendellin.

Lord Lorrin, badly injured in the battle and blinded in one eye, could not be deterred from leaving his bed and paying his final respects, at Lord Tollam and Orrla's funeral procession.

Sedgewick's dragons held their own ceremonies for the fallen, a haloed circle of many colored flames that rose from the plains for miles into the sky. Their ancient kin were honored by the dworlls, strengthening the bonds of friendship between the two races.

Hailed as Sedgewick's protégé and heir, despite his youth, Rollm however, lay fighting for his life in the Temples of Healing.

The three companions slept, prayed and wept. Gralen's tears boiled on the surface of the water, bursting in flashes of green and amber, until he too was utterly spent and could cry no longer.

Bells tolled mournfully as the dawn of the third day came and light crept over the plains outside. King Baillum returned to the chamber.

The dragon still lay beside the pool, his great chest heaving. Korrun lay asleep in the darkness. Only the old mage remained awake, sitting as a statue lost in thought.

"Marval," called the King softly. "It is time."

Mr. Agyk looked up slowly, his face haggard and drawn and aged terribly.

"It is time my friend," repeated the dworll, his amber hair swept majestically back in braids of copper. "She should be taken out of the water and laid to rest amongst the honored."

"I know," the wizard murmured. "We will leave."

Baillum nodded and quietly left.

Mr. Agyk woke the dragon softly. "Gralen, come away ... let her be at peace."

The dragon looked pleadingly into his friend's eyes and reluctantly agreed. The wizard helped his old friend up, then stood and looked at the girl he had known and loved for so many long and wonderful years.

He saw the curious child so full of love and impetuousness, and the child prone to melancholia, a child who had known such pain and loss and kept her heart closely guarded. He saw the little girl he had cared for and loved all her life. The babe-in-arms he had been entrusted to protect. He remembered early summer days in the woods and meadows of her home, sunbathing on the snowy slopes of White Mountain, and her first flying lesson aboard Gralen. He smiled at her hilarious and often disastrous experiments in spell casting, her frustration at failing, and her untamed jubilation when she succeeded. He saw the girl who had brought so much joy and life back into their staid lives. How she had changed them from two stubborn old hermits. How she had encouraged his strange culinary creations and expanded his knowledge of all the trees and plants and living creatures on the planet!

He saw the girl who brought sunshine with her wherever she went, the girl who had been the child and daughter he had never had but always wanted.

"Protect her," Dorrol's words haunted him. He had failed. "I am sorry," he whispered. "I am so, so sorry!" Tears streamed from his silver eyes and caught like diamonds in his beard. "Sleep sweet princess," he murmured. "May stars and angels guide you to your rest."

Finally, he turned, took the dragon's arm and together they left the cave for the city above.

Korrun remained, hunched and forgotten in the shadows, his eyes dark and red-rimmed. Shafts of dappled light rippled on the walls as the dwelf stepped over to the pool. Wendya floated peacefully. Korrun touched her hand, it was icy and hard.

"I wish I had known you before all this," he whispered, gently brushing a few wet strands of hair from her face. "I owe you a kiss." Tenderly and lightly he kissed her on the lips. "The kindest, fairest person I have ever known ... I love you," he murmured as hot tears stung his eyes.

A wave of anger and grief washed over him and he fell back. "Why? Why her? ... I love you, I love you ... I should have told you!" he spluttered. "I should have told you!"

Korrun gazed down at his brother's ring, then without hesitating, he slipped it from his finger and placed it on Wendya's hand. "This belongs to you, not me," he sighed and closed his eyes.

Hours passed as a myriad of dreams danced before the tracker's eyes. Dreams of Wendya whirling in his arms, of shared laughter, of flying, sailing through the air. Korrun woke in dusty darkness, alone. The ground felt dry and sandy beneath him and a faint smell of candle smoke and sulfur hung in the air. The dwelf sat up, trying to get his bearings. Torches flickered in the gloom. He was not in the cave chamber anymore, and these were not his guest quarter's either. A draft of warm air channeled past him. He was in the passageway outside. Scrambling to his feet he tried the door. It was locked.

"Oh gods! Gralen? Open the door!" he hammered. "Gralen … don't do this! Open the door! … Wendya wouldn't want this … Open the door NOW!"

Desperately, he threw himself against the door and tried to break the iron hinges and the lock, but he could tell from the bulging frame that great slabs of rock had been stacked against it, barricading it from the inside. With not a moment to spare, Korrun turned and raced toward the city above.

Outside, the day had waned and a fine evening drizzle glistened on the cobbled streets. The first stars glinted through gray rain clouds and the funeral pyres, which still blazed in the plains below. Frell stood alone, quietly watching over the main gates, his arm in a sling, as the dwelf sprinted up the steps towards him, shouting wildly.

"Korrun? Wait! Wait!" Frell called as he rushed down to meet him. "What is it?"

"Frell!" Korrun panted. "You must get the mage. Where is he?"

"He and the dragon and you, I thought, were all staying in the guest quarters with the King, up in the Court Palace," the dworll replied, puzzled.

"Good … you must get him, tell him his friend is dying, Gralen is dying! … Tell him to hurry or he'll be too late! … Go!" he dworll captain nodded as Korrun dashed back to the chamber. Within moments it seemed, Mr. Agyk and Frell arrived with several of the City Guards. Korrun had managed to buckle the lock and lever the door a little, but it wouldn't budge any further.

"It's blocked from the inside!" he cried.

"Out of my way!" Mr. Agyk snapped. "I am a fool! … I should have known he would try something!" He shouted, "stand back!"

Korrun and the others retreated into the corridor as the wizard mumbled an incantation under his breath. He placed a single hand on the door and an awful groaning and cracking sound filled the passageway. The door shattered into a thousand tiny fragments, and the fallen rocks that blocked the entrance inside crumbled into dust before their eyes. The old scholar rushed through the dust cloud and into the chamber.

Afloat in the water beside the young witch lay the dragon, his scales dull, his immense body filling the pool, his torn wings and lifeless tail spilling out over the sides. The constant fire in his belly was now little more than a glimmer.

"You fool! You blasted fool!" Mr. Agyk cried racing over to him. "I cannot lose you both!" He took the dragon's cold hand in his and a faint smile of relief flickered on his face.

"Thank the stars! The waters have not taken all of your life energy, nearly … but not yet. We have come in time!"

Mr. Agyk gestured to Korrun and the others and together they heaved the great body out of the water and onto the mossy floor.

The old wizard cursed again. "You fool! She would never want this!"

He knelt beside his friend, and as he had tried three days earlier with Wendya, he placed his hands on either side of the dragon's head. A fiery light, green as jade, sprang from the wizard and passed into the dragon, slowly filling him with life force once more. The others looked on in stunned amazement as the mage worked his magic, and gradually, the burning ember in the dragon's belly glowed brighter and brighter.

"Careful!" Korrun warned, grasping the wizard's arm. "Do not drain yourself!"

Mr. Agyk sighed and stumbled back. "Yes. You are right ... no more. He will live," he gasped, as the dragon stirred. "Thank you, Korrun. You have saved his life. If we were any later ...," he sighed. "Well, it is done."

The wizard sat beside the great beast, utterly exhausted, and felt the fÿrren's two hearts pounding evermore strongly inside his cavernous chest.

"I could not bear to lose you both ... my heart has not the strength to mourn for you too!" He heaved a deep sigh as Gralen slowly opened his eyes.

"I'm sorry," the dragon mumbled, every part of him aching as if he had been asleep for a thousand years.

"The fault is mine. I should have known you would try something. Reckless to the bone!

I should never have left you alone ... even to sleep," Mr. Agyk smiled, wishing he could sleep himself, for an age.

Gralen sat up stiffly, his great orange eyes full of sadness. "It didn't work then?"

The wizard shook his head. "Come," he said softly, taking the dragon over to the pool. Korrun looked at them and remembered Wendya's own words about the wizard, the night before they had left for battle, and his eyes fell once more upon the young girl.

Wendya lay drifting in the waters, a picture of some ancient and tragic princess: her beauty had not faded, her skin glowing, her raven hair sparkling in the water as black gossamer.

"We should take her from here. She needs to be at rest," the wizard murmured. "She could stay in Fendellin, or we could take her back to the Grey Forest, and let her sleep amongst the trees she loves ..."

Korrun watched the young wicca. His eyes seemed to be playing tricks on him. In the dim light, he thought for a moment that he saw her eyes flicker.

"The forest," Gralen whispered, his heart feeling as if it were lead. "She'd want to be there, that's her home," he said quietly.

The wizard nodded. "Come. You need to rest properly and recover your strength, as do I. We are all burdened by grief and heavy toil," Mr. Agyk motioned at Frell and the City Guards to finally lift the young girl out of the pool. "Please ... be gentle," he implored, as Gralen averted his eyes, unable to watch.

Korrun stood, spellbound. "WAIT!" he shouted, staggering forward to gaze at the figure. "Wait ... I saw something! She's moving! Wendya ...? Wendya, come back to us!"

As if in response, a finger flexed in the water.

"LOOK! See?" Korrun cried, his heart throbbing.

The friends stared, hardly daring to move or breathe.

Wendya's hair was no longer dull, but shimmered and danced in the waters, sparkling with life again and a luminescence emanated from her skin. Her fingers twitched, then her toes. As they watched in rapt hope and excitement, life slowly crept back into the young witch.

"It worked!" Gralen bellowed, hardly able to contain himself.

Suddenly, Wendya's chest heaved and she gasped her first breath for nearly four days.

"Wend'?" cried the dragon overwhelmed with joy. "Wendya!"

"My child, come back to us! Open your eyes!" Mr. Agyk commanded as the young girl stirred.

"Marval, is that you?" she mouthed the words, her voice so slight that only those closest could discern it.

"My dear!" Mr. Agyk leapt into the pool as if he were an exuberant child himself, and cradled her in his arms. "My sweet, sweet child! I am here, we are all here!" he laughed and peppered her forehead with kisses.

"Where am I?" she asked groggily.

"You are safe … you are alive, my dear sweet wonderful girl … my daughter child! You are alive!" the wizard wept, squeezing her tightly as his tears fell on the witch's face.

"I was flying," she murmured. "I was flying above a white sea and I heard someone calling my name." She blinked through the mist clouding her sight and looked into the aged wizard's face. An elderly man, whom she hardly recognized, smiled back at her. "Where are we?"

"Mund'harr, the Golden City … we are safe," he smiled.

"It's over?"

"Yes, at last it is over," he said softly, hardly able to form the words. "Oh … we thought we had lost you! But by some wondrous miracle and the stubbornness, foolishness and bravery of a dragon … you are returned to us!" Mr. Agyk carefully scooped her up and lifted her out of the water. "Gralen sacrificed his life for yours and nearly lost the fight, if Korrun had not alerted us…," he shook his head, "but now, I have you both!" he cried.

Wendya glanced at the dragon, her face full of confusion.

At that moment, voices could be heard coming down the passageway, as King Baillum and a small host of trusted soldiers burst into the chamber.

"What is this?" the King demanded, then hesitated, his skeptical eyes wide with wonder as he looked upon the young witch and the wet wizard beside her. "How? … You are a powerful Arch Magus indeed, to bring back the dead!"

Mr. Agyk raised his hand. "I will tell you, Sire, but for now we need some dry clothes and a healer's hands for both of these," the wizard explained wearily, helping a fragile Wendya to stand.

"A powerful mage you are, but I would say you need a bed and full rest, my wizard friend, before you fall on your feet!" the King smiled, his usual stoic nature confounded by the scene before him.

"Oh … and a hearty meal!" Gralen added with an impish grin, feeling as if he were dancing on air. "I'm starving!"

The King bowed. "Indeed … though the pyres have burned to honor our dead, it is time to honor our brave living and the victory we have snatched from the jaws of defeat! We shall feast and celebrate this night!"

The party left the cave in a mass of excited noise and uplifted voices. Only a single forgotten figure stayed behind in the darkness, standing silently in the shifting light, his face staring at the floor, his body motionless, his lips smiling, and his dark eyes full of joyful tears.

Wondrous days and nights of celebration followed. Fireworks and feasting filled the city and surrounding lands, spilling out of halls and homesteads alike, bathing every square and balcony with color. Yet, amongst the revelry and the flowing of fine ales was the bitter-sweetness of a victory against Morreck the Corruptor: a victory with such a heavy loss of life.

Lanterns and candles lined the cobble streets in tribute to each fallen soul. Some were taken high above the city to the pinnacles of Mund'harr where they shone like beacons in the clear night. Others were placed in small wooden boats and cast over Fendellin's many waterfalls, where they fell like stars in the deluge.

Healers tended to the wounded and worshippers tended to the troubles of battle. Final ceremonies of honor were given, and a strange peace fell over the city, the first it had known for many a long age.

Nearly two weeks passed and young Hallm was elected as heir and successor to Lord Tollam. On the twelfth night of celebration and the sixteenth since the death of his beloved father, Hallm was knighted a Lord of the Realm by King Baillum and given lordship over the lands from the northern plains and highlands of the Felleucian Range to the Sand Hills of the southern realms. As reparation for the treachery that killed his father and so many of their kinsmen, all of Perral's lands were given to Lord Hallm.

Gralen's injuries healed fully. He divided his time between visiting Wendya and Rollm. Korrun also healed quickly but kept to himself, preferring to wander alone amongst the towers and battlements of the Golden City. During the day he busied himself in the stables or helped to rebuild the many burnt and destroyed buildings that littered the city state. He visited Wendya daily, usually when the others had left and often in the twilight hours before dawn, when most of the city slept. He found comfort pacing through the starched white corridors of the Temples of Healing and watching the young witch sleep, with the wizard snoring gently in a chair beside her.

"Come over," whispered the old man opening an eye.

"I thought you were sleeping!" Korrun blurted, feeling a little awkward.

The wizard smiled. "Sometimes I am."

Korrun looked at Wendya as she slept, her eyelids flickering rapidly as if she were having a nightmare. "Will she be alright?" he asked worriedly.

Mr. Agyk sighed as if he had been pondering and struggling with the same question for some time and was still no nearer to knowing the answer ."In truth … I do not know," he said at last. "Her body will heal, but some experiences change a person. None of us truly know what she has been through."

Korrun looked puzzled by his reply, the old fellow was being cryptic again.

Mr. Agyk half-smiled. "Let us trust in her, and help her when she needs us. That is all we can do. We should let her rest now."

The dwelf nodded and quietly left, walking through the marbled corridors and into the moonlight. A slight smell of camphor lingered on the night air, mixed with the smoke from a thousand lanterns. Korrun wandered aimlessly for a while until he spotted a familiar face staring out across the plains. A lonely figure lost amongst the battlements.

"How are you?" Korrun asked softly.

Frell wiped his face and turned to the tracker. "How is Wendya?"

"Getting better, slowly. She's been through a lot."

Frell nodded. "I am glad," he sighed heavily, his auburn hair catching in the wind, his pale eyes full of despair. "I am not one to give advice. The gods know I rarely follow it. But if you are fortunate enough to find someone special … tell them, while you have the chance." He looked away sharply.

Korrun could feel his anguish. "I am so sorry. Orrla was …"

"… wonderful, extraordinary …," Frell looked at him through weary, bloodshot eyes. "Don't leave it too late," he whispered. "Tell her."

As predicted, Wendya took many long weeks to recover, and remained ill, on and off, for many months. Her friends did their best to boost her spirits, but Mr. Agyk in particular noticed her changed manner and the disturbed terrors of her sleep. Yet Wendya always smiled when pain or shadow passed over her and she kept any troubled thoughts to herself.

"It must feel good to be yourself again," she had commented one afternoon, watching the old wizard sipping a draft of ale while rocking the chair he was slouched in.

"You are awake? Good! Very fine medeaok this," the wizard burbled.

Wendya smiled. "I was saying that it must feel good to be your real size again."

"Oh yes. When you are small you certainly do pay attention to the minutiae of life!" He paused, a twinkle in his eyes. "Now, I know the monks will protest but I am taking you out for a late lunch! I have it on good authority that Gralen has prepared a feast even you could not refuse … lots of roasted vegetables I believe! And Korrun has picked the perfect spot!" The wizard chuckled, fussing over her and wrapping a blanket around her shoulders.

"So what are you bringing?" she laughed, happy to go along with him.

He smiled broadly, his nose as bright as a cherry. "I may or may not have perfected a human sustenance you rather like," he replied teasingly "… yeast spread sandwiches!"

Wendya smiled silently, as if a shadow had passed over her.

"What is it, my dear?"

"I know we do not talk of him … but is Morreck really destroyed?" she asked suddenly.

Mr. Agyk looked stunned for a moment. He gazed seriously at her, as if trying to read her mind, smiled and finally took her hand. "I truly believe he is gone, perhaps forever but at least for a long, long time. I cannot sense any part of him. The King and the others will be vigilant. This is their country, they will defend it."

"And Kavok?" she asked, a cold shiver running through her as she said the name.

"Kavok will have a permanent garrison of the best guards until they can finish blocking all the passages. Then, when that is done they will collapse the entire labyrinth under there, permanently. It is over. Wendya, you do not need to worry; the fear has passed." he said gently. "I have even been working on the old craft of mirror-seeing … I have made some new and improved mimmirians, four actually! One for Fendellin, Kallorm, White Mountain and you, so we will be able to keep an eye on each other … *and* speak to new friends," he said, winking.

"Thank you," she sighed. She grabbed his arm tightly and they strolled out into the golden warmth of the afternoon sun.

Chapter Twenty-Three

The Long Journey

The last remnants of winter finally gave way to a short but glorious spring. A touch of summer seemed to have come early as the days grew steadily warmer, and from the shimmering grasslands below Mund'harr and the seas of blue mountain poppies sprang many tarpan foals and young spring calves frolicking in the sunshine.

Numerous skirmishes, all of them costly, had arisen since the great battle, as the most defiant of Morreck's forces attempted to wage war on the people of Fendellin. Many of the outer territories, especially those whose borders lay close to Kavok, were constantly assaulted and remained too dangerous to venture into. Yet, under the watchful vigil of Sedgewick's brave and battle-hardy dragons, life slowly began to return to normal.

Four more wondrous months passed in the Golden City under pale Fendellin skies. While the heat of July deepened on their backs, the time came at last for the travelers to leave the blessed Kingdom of Dragons.

"Preparations have been made. Are you certain you cannot stay longer?" King Baillum asked, as he walked beside the wizard in the glow of the late afternoon sun.

"I wish that we could, but no, it is time we left. Wendya has healed as much as she can here, as much as she may anywhere."

"You worry for her," the King said quietly.

The wizard looked off into the distance and sighed. "I do," he replied. "It is a miracle beyond my understanding that she is here at all. She has endured an ordeal none of us can imagine. Returned from a place none return from. She is strong, far stronger than any of us surmised, but, I fear she may always be haunted by her experiences here."

Mr. Agyk paused, his eyes full of sorrow. "She may never be completely whole again," he sighed and cast his gaze over the plains below.

Baillum studied him. The dworll had never fully understood or trusted magic-casters and it was clear to him that despite the wizard's good nature, the old magus was concealing something important, and something that troubled him greatly. "Is she more likely to heal in her own home?" He asked. "It was destroyed, was it not?"

"Yes. We will rebuild it. The forest should nurture her. Perhaps, if she is surrounded by the trees she loves, it may help lift her heart a little," Mr. Agyk tried to smile. "She has agreed to stay with us in White Mountain, for a while. We will be glad of her company!"

The King saw the concern etched on the old man's face, and for the first time he grasped the paternal pain of the wizard. "I will make the arrangements," he said. "We will accompany you as far as our southern borders and give you any provisions you may need for your long journey ahead."

"Thank you," the wizard replied. "We will remember your kindness and your sacrifices."

"And we shall remember your bravery and great service to our people and to all of Fendellin. Come, let us feast tonight and forget our troubles in a roaring fire!" Baillum smiled.

It was a fine morning. The sun felt reassuringly warm on their faces although a bitter wind cut through the air — the first sign of the approaching autumn. Wendya and Mr. Agyk found themselves amongst the lush pastures and plains that surrounded Mund'harr beyond its encircling chasm-moats.

Endless chalk paths fiddled their way through the thin, soiled grasslands, crossing this way and that without apparent reason or destination. Wendya passed her fingers through the tops of the grasses as they wandered through the open prairies.

"Some kind of emmer," she murmured.

Mr. Agyk sighed and breathed in the soft scent. "I could end my days here quite happily," he mused.

Wendya looked at him sharply for a moment, then walked on, glad to be quiet and free.

After a long afternoon of walking, they rested amongst the tall grasses, out of the wind's reach. Wendya sat engrossed, staring at her hands, at the texture of her skin, the imperfections, the lines, the badly bitten nails and the chewed surface around the quick.

"Are you alright?"

Mr. Agyk stood above her, the wind billowing his hair into its usual tangled mess. He sat down, his long, spindly legs stretching out into the grass like two knobbly sticks. She smiled.

"It is good," he said, "… to see a smile."

She looked at him. "It's a sunny day."

"A little brisk for me," he shuddered. "How are you today?"

"I'm fine."

"Umm … *fine*," he mulled over the word, "you do not have to pretend for me."

"What d'you mean?"

"You are not *fine*," the wizard paused, unsure of how to phrase it. "I have sensed a change in you since—"

"… since I died?!"

The old man looked hurt at the remark. "You should not be flippant!"

"I'm not … I'm … uh, I don't know," she shook her head.

"Wendya, what happened to you inside Morreck's lair?" he asked, rather more timidly than he had meant to.

A flash of anger seemed to cross her face, but was quickly gone again. Mr. Agyk could feel her withdrawing from him.

"What do you mean?" she said blankly. "I followed the plan. I destroyed the power source. That's it."

"Could you describe what it was like in there?" he pressed.

"Not really … It was dark. I don't remember."

He looked at her and sighed. "Umm … well … when you do remember I will be here to listen," he said softly, then gently squeezed her hand, kissed it and left.

She watched him struggle, almost comically, down the grassy incline, half-sliding half-falling backward, until he reached a path below and wandered back toward the city. He turned just once and waved, then disappeared round the hill. Wendya sat staring after him for a long while, hardly realizing that she was crying.

Another week or so passed and slowly the friends packed their few belongings and said their goodbyes. At last the wagons and caravans were made ready. Fendellin flags and banners lined the roads for miles around and danced in the cool morning breeze, as the bell towers rang out over the glistening rooftops of the Golden City.

Rollm stood on the parapet overlooking the main city gates.

"Well, it's time," Gralen said glumly, as he lumbered over and looked at the young dragon's injuries.

In the early morning light, Rollm looked painfully young. Gralen wished he could take him with them. The young draken stood quietly and smiled at his friend.

"It'll heal, I'll fly again," he said cheerfully, as Gralen glanced at his broken wing and the bandages round his shoulder.

"Your arm …?" he asked.

"Mr. Agyk gave me this wonderful fizzing potion for the pain … it works a treat, maybe a little too well!" he chuckled. "Don't worry, I'll be fine. Who needs two arms anyway?!"

Gralen sighed and stared seriously into the young dragon's eyes. "We are brothers, Rollm, you and I. If you ever, ever need me … anytime, I will be there. Remember: use Marval's mimmirian to call me. Understand?"

Rollm nodded. "P … erhaps I could visit you sometime, if the others permit it, when I'm better?"

Gralen smiled. "I'll expect it! Besides, you are the head of the Wyvern Order now, make your own rules!" he grinned. "I'll give you a grand tour of White Mountain … and you'll have never tasted heaven 'til you've had Mr. A's codswobble and habsquibble surprise!"

"What's the surprise?" Rollm asked innocently.

Gralen chortled. "That anything that looks and smells that bad, can taste so good!"

The two dragons laughed and embraced as brothers. Then, with sad hearts and misty eyes and too much to say, they said farewell.

The cavalcade rolled out of the city gates in a fanfare of bells and horns and cheers, and made its way down the twisted and cobbled mountain roads until they reached the foothills and last city battlements. Crossing each of the chasm-moats and the last tower bridge, they turned south and passed over the grassland savannahs, past colorful prayer flags flying high in the cold sunshine.

Mr. Agyk and the King Baillum rode together at the front of the procession, with Frell, Korrun and Wendya close behind. Gralen trotted beside Wendya's horse and kept a quiet but constant eye on the witch.

Hallm and the other lords rode with them for a few leagues then one-by-one they said their farewells and watched as the caravans passed out of view. To them, and many watching that day, it seemed as if they were witnessing the last great exodus of theællfrs and magic ones, a passing of knowledge and mysticism to realms beyond their reach, and a melancholic longing filled their hearts.

"We will return," the wizard smiled as he turned to watch the Golden City, perched high upon Mund'harr's pinnacle, grow smaller in the distance.

He stared at the mountain. Its thunderous falls sparkled in the morning and rainbows sprang at its feet. There, rising clear above a blanket of white mist stood Fendellin's highest tower, like a burnished spur of gold, before disappearing behind a haze of cloud.

"Farewell," Mr. Agyk whispered and glanced at the green dragon.

"We'll be back," Gralen sighed, meeting the wizard's eyes. "*Here be dragons!*" he joked, then fell silent.

The friends chatted quietly as the Southern Plains gave way to lowland heaths and gorse-covered hills. Descending from the central Mund'harr Plateau at its lowest point, the Harrem Crossing, they skirted the southern deserts. They turned westward and climbed down a series of snaking scree slopes: large steppes that leveled out into a wondrous landscape of spectacular terraces and rich, volcanic soils.

They made camp beside a small glacier lake.

A haze of gray rain cascaded from the Encircling Mountains that now loomed in a dark line before them.

Within moments, a mass of circular tents sprang up amidst the stony ground, their canopies billowing in the night wind. Fires ignited, crackling and blazing cheerfully as groups huddled round them, swapping tales of times and travels past. Yet, amongst the gentle conversation, none mentioned the terrible battle at Kavok, nor the countless skirmishes that had plagued them since.

Wendya sat silently throughout, staring into the fire, a distant expression playing on her face, as if distracted by something dark and disturbing, which she chose not to share with the others.

"She grows stronger," King Baillum noted, seeing the wizard watching her once more "... We fear the same thing, I think."

Mr. Agyk jolted. "What?!"

"The future," the King replied calmly. Whatever the mage was hiding, it was clearly preying on his nerves.

Mr. Agyk laughed awkwardly. "Oh ... yes, yes, the future is always uncertain ...," he answered, his eyes straying over to the young wicca.

"It is not uncertainty I speak of, Marval, or battles," explained the King quietly. "But war. My seers tell me that, despite the outcome at Kavok, a great war, akin to the terrible wars of old is coming! I believe M'Sorreck is vanquished utterly, but the evil he seeded will not die as quickly. It may only be a matter of time I fear, before another rises up to take his place, a darkling successor."

Mr. Agyk stared at the stars as they drifted past and the color blanched from his cheeks. "That is my fear also," he replied grimly. "Though I trust nothing that Morreck said; he did boast that his followers are far greater in number than we know. It is fair to assume that others, in both our world and the human one, have already been corrupted by him and are carrying out his nefarious orders as we speak."

King Baillum nodded in agreement. "Yes ... that would certainly explain many of the insane conflicts you have told me about, that humans commit against each other. Nevertheless, I believe a great war is coming, my friend, sooner or later!"

The night passed peacefully. A perimeter of guards was posted to keep watch, but within the camp circle, one by one succumbed to sleep. The fires died, their embers glowing dimly in the night air. All slept soundly, except for two.

Korrun sat hunched against a large boulder, poking the coals with a stick, as the witch sat beside him.

"Can't sleep?" she asked.

"No," the dwelf smiled. "Probably the thought of all that stomach-churning dragon flying!"

Wendya smiled. "I never find it as comfortable as Marval. Poor Gralen, he has quite a burden with all of us."

"Not to mention the burden he has accumulated after a few months of Fendellin's fine cuisine!" Korrun chuckled. "Most of these wagons are filled with food for him!"

Wendya laughed, then fell silent. The dwelf looked down at his battered leather boots, at the broken stitching and countless repairs and shifted uneasily. His heart was pounding in his chest, his mouth suddenly dry when Wendya finally broke the silence.

"I wanted to give you this," she said holding out a beautifully carved silver ring with a large blue ællfrstone at its center. "I didn't know when to do it. It belonged to your brother, you should have it, not me."

Korrun looked at the ring, then at Wendya. "I gave it to you, it's yours. I want you to keep it," he said softly.

"Why?"

He hesitated for a moment, his somber demeanour softened in the firelight. "It is a gift, to remind you that I will always be there if you need me. I made that promise to my brother once, and I didn't keep it. I don't want to break it again. It reminds me that I still have someone to look after … if she wants me to," he said nervously, his eyes darting to the fire.

Wendya blushed, her green eyes trying to catch the dwelf's. "Thank you."

Korrun smiled again. "So, you will be going to the mage's home first?" He said, glad to change the subject.

"Yes, just until I've rested a while, then I'll head back home and start rebuilding. I need to see if there's anything left of my little cottage."

"I'm sure it will still be there. Tell me about your home?" he asked, relaxed once more.

Wendya sighed, it seemed a hundred lifetimes since she had last seen it. "I have two homes really, my summer and winter homes. They're not grand but they're beautiful," she murmured. "They are set deep in the Grey Forest amongst the trees and water meadows."

"Sounds restful."

"Oh it is, well, it was. I'll have to take you there one day, to the oldest parts of the forest, the Llrinaru, to see the glens, the whispering springs, the meadows of cotton grass."

"I'd like that," the dwelf replied leaning forward, his dark eyes reflecting the firelight.

The witch smiled and fingered the ring in her hand. "It's a magical place," she continued, wishing she was there, "very peaceful. I could take you to see the Silver Greenwood trees and the house I have in the canopy."

Korrun stretched out and held the witch's hand, then slipped the ring back onto her finger. "I have to return to Kallorm," he said quietly, "once I have settled my affairs, I would like to see you again, and your home."

Wendya smiled, but gently took her hand away. "You will," she murmured. "We'd better get some rest now, there's a long journey ahead of us."

Gralen watched them silently, as they said goodnight to each other and returned to their beds. The dragon's heart heaved in his chest as he turned over and finally closed his eyes.

Night winds howled dolefully over the camp, as clear skies glittered above them, beckoning the first frost of the season. Wendya slept uneasily. Warning calls sounded in her dreams, moving shapes in the dark, blood spilt, black as tar in the moonlight. She woke suddenly, wet with sweat. Something was moving outside. Warning horns were blowing. A face appeared at the entrance of her tent, it was Korrun.

"Stay inside!" he shouted.

"What's happening?"

"Wargol attack. Stay inside!" With that, the dwelf disappeared and joined the others scouring the camp for the invading enemy.

Wendya sat completely still, listening to the shouts outside — a clash of metal on metal — shrieks and heavy footsteps thundering past, slowing, then stopping. In the darkness, she could make out a bulging shape, something pressing against the canvas, then a tearing sound. She fumbled for a blade amongst the furs and bed coverings. The tear grew wider and through it came an enormous black silhouette, followed by two more.

Even in the gloom she could see their eyes and smell the stench of them. With no reason or discernible thought, Wendya dropped the blade she was holding. The creatures needed no other invitation and, seeming to smile at their victim, they rushed towards her.

She closed her eyes and lifted her head to the sky, as if she could sense the stars through the canopy. The largest brute grabbed her but as his clawed fingers touched her skin he howled in agony and burst into flame. The other wargols froze began to scream in pain and, one by one, they disintegrated from within, in a flash of light, and were reduced to nothing but dust. Wendya stood perfectly still, her hands outstretched, her eyes closed. A faint smile flickered across her lips.

"Are you alright?" Gralen shouted, as he burst into her tent, closely followed by the wizard.

The witch slumped down on the bed. "Perfectly fine," she sighed.

Gralen sniffed the air. "Those things were in here!"

"Yes, they ran away when they heard you coming," she looked dazed.

Mr. Agyk narrowed his eyes and stared at the young wicca. "They ran away?"

"Yes," she nodded.

"Doesn't surprise me," Gralen panted. "Filthy things are cowards. A group of them killed some of the sentries. Korrun and the others are checking the camp now. You sure you're alright?"

Wendya nodded and smiled weakly, though the old wizard knew she was shaken by something else.

"All the same, I think I will stay with you until sunrise," Mr. Agyk said gently, wrapping a blanket around the young girl. "Gralen, the camp could use some illumination. Could you light the fires again, make sure there are no more unexpected visitors?"

"No problem. Try and get some rest you two, dawn is still a few hours away," he added, then left quickly and took to the skies.

Dawn arrived to reveal the carnage of the previous night.

A mournful air permeated the camp as the bodies of the fallen were placed in makeshift rafts and set alight upon the icy waters of the lake. Throughout the sadness Mr. Agyk noted, with admiration, the steely resolve of the Fendellons. After a silent breakfast, the travelers were ready. The camp was left behind as they journeyed on for the last few miles. Scaling a steep embankment at the base of the mountains, they traveled in single file until they reached the top and unburdened the horses.

King Baillum stood tall against the milky sky, one of the last great Warrior Kings, the Fendellin crest emblazoned across his chest and a genuine sadness in his eyes.

"It is time to say farewell, my friends," he smiled. "May your journey be safe and uneventful. We have many trials to overcome and a land and people to heal, but your aid has been invaluable to us. We will forever be in your debt." The Dworll King looked closely at each of the party in turn. "Korrun, young dwellfr and last of your great and noble people. Gralen, bravest and fiercest of warrior dragons. Wendya, jewel of these lands, fair and courageous. And of course, Marval Agyk, wizard among wizards! We thank you all. The tyranny of M'Sorreck has been defeated and with the skill of Mr. Agyk's mimmirians, may the bonds of friendship between Fendellin and White Mountain grow ever stronger and never diminish! Peace be upon you!"

"And with you!" the travelers cheered.

They embraced, and with heavy hearts, but longing for their own lands, they parted. Frell and his father waved them off as the great dragon took to the air. Gralen circled twice overhead before Mr. Agyk cast his invisibility veil and they disappeared from sight.

They lingered for a moment, each saying a last farewell to the Lost Kingdom of Dragons, before they became lost amongst the mountain mists.

Gralen bore the burden of his cargo well, rising above the mountaintops and jagged peaks, as Mr. Agyk, Wendya and Korrun clung to the dragon's back. They had not been flying long, when a blanket of thick fog appeared as a solid wall before them, hemming them in. Once more an eerie deadness fell.

"Goodbye Fendellin, found and never forgotten," Gralen whispered and shot through the tunnel of mist.

After some turbulence, welcome patches of blue sky appeared and suddenly the world lay before them. Clouds laden with snow and rain rolled by and as they flew on, the worries of their travels seemed to fall away into the whiteness below.

The day waned and by nightfall the group had passed over the last gray mountains and they were flying low over highland steppes and waterlogged paddy fields, the moon glinting back at them amongst the dark reed beds.

The travelers found a shelter for the night in a jungle copse. After a few hours of rest and another large breakfast or three, they started off again, southwest, as the pale sun rose over the water fields behind them.

Days merged until, slowly, the friends began to recognize the blurring lands and twisting river deltas beneath them. By the end of the second week from Fendellin, they had crossed great stretches of rocky desert, craggy coastline and dry grasslands and both Wendya and Korrun began to see the familiar volcanic landmarks of their childhood and the winding rivers and hills of the old African dworll kingdom.

"Kallorm!" The dwelf gasped. "I never thought I would miss it, but I have."

By the shade of early evening the companions had set down in the rainforest and were following Korrun to one of the tracker's hidden entrances. The air was cool and fresh and amidst the incessant jungle noises, Wendya thought she could hear the faint whisper of a river or waterfall somewhere far below.

The moon shone full and waxy, a friend at last. Mr. Agyk smiled at it from beneath the jungle canopy.

"Are you sure you cannot stay, even for the night?" Korrun asked, glancing at Wendya and the wizard. "King Dorrol would be greatly pleased to see you all and learn of Morreck's defeat!"

The scholar's jovial demeanour changed at the mention of the old King's name. The dwelf thought he could detect a flash of rage on the wizard's face.

"We cannot," he replied, his eyes straying to Wendya who had remained quiet and withdrawn since they had left Fendellin. "I will speak to Dorrol soon enough; ... we have much to discuss," he said coldly, unable to hide his anger. Even Gralen noticed.

Korrun studied the wizard. "Well, I will see you all very soon, I am sure. Take care of each other. I will use the seeing-mirror, the mimmirian, whenever I can," he said, glancing at the witch.

Mr. Agyk smiled warmly at the dwelf, becoming his usual affable self once more. "Thank you for all of your help, Korrun," he said, then hugged the tracker. "Try not to worry, we will look after her," he whispered, as if he could read the dwelf's mind. "You have been a great friend to us. Be safe and remember you are always welcome at White Mountain."

"Thank you, Marval." Korrun felt an unexpected wave of melancholy at having to leave the old mage. He turned to the dragon. "Thank you for saving our hides. You've been a good friend to a stranger ... even a cold fish like me!" he grinned.

Gralen looked vaguely embarrassed and smiled awkwardly as he shook the tracker's hand. Finally, the dwelf turned to the witch, his eyes sparkling in the dim light.

"Remember … if you ever need me," he murmured.

Wendya touched the dwelf's face, so tired, so alone, so like her and, to his surprise, she kissed him on the lips.

"I owed you a kiss," she said. "I will not forget anything. Goodbye, Korrun. I will see you soon."

Korrun looked as stunned as the others and blushed slightly. Bidding them all a final farewell, he turned and disappeared down the forest path and was soon lost amongst the tangle of trees.

"Well, I still say he's strange!" Gralen grumbled, sauntering off in the opposite direction with the wizard close behind.

Wendya stood leaning against a large tree fern and stared down the path after the dwelf, as if she could still see him.

"I love you too," she whispered.

"Are you coming?" called a gruff and plainly irritated voice behind her.

She smiled and joined the others.

By dawn the next day, the three travelers were flying over the last stretches of jungle, turning due north towards White Mountain. Gralen felt lifted, as if a worry had been removed from his shoulders. They flew onward without rushing, and stopped frequently to enjoy meals and take rest. The witch always remained distant to them.

And so, nearly a year since they had left White Mountain, the three adventurers crossed the Mediterranean or Silver Sea, and flew over rolling hills and vineyards and little woods, towards the clear white peaks ahead. In less than half a day, the companions finally glimpsed their beloved mountain home, rising above the other heights as a pinnacle of pure white.

White Mountain at last.

The dragon landed amongst the powdery snow, enjoying the sensation of it between his scaly toes. Soon the exhausted friends were inside sitting round a roaring fire. Mr. Agyk, in particular, seemed immensely relieved to be back and quickly fell into familiar routines, as he slumped into his favorite chair.

"Well, that's all over at last!" Gralen announced with a profound sense of achievement.

"Is it? Is it … I wonder? "

Gralen looked at him. "Morreck's gone and may he rot in his own filth! I know you're not convinced but Frell and the others are sure he's dead — *nobody* could survive a fall like that! Anyway, Baillum and his folk'll have Kavok fumigated in no time. And you're back to rights again … it's all over!"

The wizard and witch remained silent.

"Well?" prompted the dragon, feeling his triumphant mood slipping.

"It is just … it feels like the beginning of something, not the end," Mr. Agyk muttered. "I wonder if it really is over."

"Well you're a barrel of laughs! We've won and you're moping around like a bowl of cold porridge!"

Mr. Agyk laughed. "Well, I shall just have to perk myself up. After all it would not do if we were *both* grumpy old fools!"

"Hey!" Gralen smiled.

"It truly is so wonderful to be home though!" Mr. Agyk sighed and kicked off his grubby boots. "I shall not travel anywhere now, not for a lifetime!"

"No 'expeditions' then?" Gralen grinned with a raised brow.

"Definitely not!" He laughed. "I shall sleep for a month I think. Then, I will make more of my mimmirians, for all our other cities and sanctuaries around the globe. I think it is more important than ever that we all keep in close contact," he said. "Knowledge is a torch in dark places, ignorance breeds evil." He paused. "Actually, I shall have to return to Ïssätun," he said quietly. "There is much to do there."

"But not yet," Gralen smiled. "I will help you clean the place up and melt those ice dungeons to puddles!" He chirped. "But for now, we need to rest."

"Agreed," Mr. Agyk sighed with a smile.

The dragon stretched out on the rug, his hands behind his head. He was keen to forget, for a little while at least, the adventures and troubles they had endured. So, joining the wizard in familiar routines, he gazed up at the ceiling. "The stars are looking bright tonight," he said contentedly.

Wendya remained silent, staring into the fire, lost in the roaring flames.

Mr. Agyk glanced at her. Still so frail. He had worried that she would never fully recover and he feared it was so … but another fear gnawed at him. He had waited as long as he dared, waited for her strength to return, waited to be sure, but knew he would have to tell her the truth and he dreaded it as he had never dreaded anything in his life. Morreck's insidious voice still whispered in his ears: *like father like daughter*. A thousand questions raced through his head but none could quell the fury he felt towards his old friend and ally, King Dorrol of Kallorm. Why had Dorrol chosen not to tell him, not to tell *her*? WHY? How could he have kept it from them? How could he have been so stupid, so blind? With every passing doubt, everything the old King had said now made perfect sense: *protect her, she is very special*. "Yes, she is," he murmured in response.

"Mr. A? You alright?"

Mr. Agyk looked up and saw Gralen's puzzled face staring at him.

"Yes, well, I think it is time we had something to eat. I was thinking up a new dish, I am calling it *Mund'harr Surprise!*"

The friends looked at each other dubiously.

"Actually, Mr. A," the dragon replied, sitting up quickly, "why don't you take a load off and let me cook tonight? I know just the right thing, it's quick and it's tasty."

"Oh … gladly," Mr. Agyk muttered.

Wendya winked at Gralen and mouthed, "Bread and cheese", before he disappeared toward the kitchen. The old mage knew he would be in there for a long time, guzzling most of the contents of his cupboards. He settled back into his favorite rocking chair. They sat in silence, listening to the crackle of the fire, the witch's face full of sadness and worry.

Mr. Agyk watched her and sighed. "What is it, my child?" he asked softly, fearing the answer.

"I need to talk to you, it's important, but … I don't know where to start," she stammered, keeping her face turned to the fire, "… it's about Kavok. And me."

Mr. Agyk's heart sank and he shifted uneasily in his chair. The moment he had dreaded had arrived. Wendya drew her legs up and rested her head on her knees.

"Something very strange happened to me in that mountain. I couldn't remember at first but I've been having flashbacks, images coming back to me … haunting my dreams," she paused, trying to clarify her thoughts. "I felt a power, an *incredible* power I've never felt before. An overwhelming strength … I don't know what it was or where it came from, except that it was coming out of me, through my fingers, out of my skin!" she looked at her hands as if she half expected them to start glowing.

"There were streams of light," she continued. "I had the strength to push people away, wargols, anyone, just by willing it … I … I *melted* a knife in my bare hands!" She turned at last to face the old wizard, desperate for answers. "And when we were attacked in the camp … I touched those awful wargol creatures and they just … *disappeared!*" She shook her head. "No, not disappeared, that's not right. It was like … I vaporized them — they just burst into flames when I touched them!" She paused. "In Kavok, the power almost took me over. I could hear these strange voices in my head and I seemed to grow stronger the closer I got to the door, to M'Sorreck's power source," she sighed as if trying to unravel what she was saying. "I saw things there, in the chamber … images, I don't know what they were, or if they were real, but my heart tells me they were … They seemed to know me, to connect to me. I saw them again when I was floating in the pool … when I died."

The old magus sighed and closed his aged eyes for an instant.

"Perhaps they were tricks but," she shook her head again, clearly agitated, "there was a woman crying; she looked like me."

Wendya suddenly stopped, aware of the wizard's silence. At that exact moment, a sickening truth hit her. "My gods! You know something … don't you?" she asked, her eyes full of hurt and childlike questioning.

The wizard sighed again and nodded. He turned his face towards the fire. "I do … or at least I have guessed much of it. I was never told the truth … you must believe me. I was deceived the same as you. But the small pieces I was told do fit together now."

"Tell me!" Wendya gasped, suddenly afraid of what he might say. For the first time in years, she couldn't read him, his thoughts; his expressions were all alien to her now, as if a shroud had covered his face from her.

Mr. Agyk turned to his beloved Wendya. "Kavok revealed the truth to me also. I never knew before … I swear it! Any oath I have taken, I would have gladly broken to tell you the truth … a secret that should have been revealed a long time ago."

"What secret? Whose secret?" she asked.

"The true identity of your mother. *Her* secret," the wizard replied simply, "I am certain that the woman you saw in your vision was your mother."

Wendya looked stunned.

"It is a long story and I only know parts of it, or have guessed parts of it," he said slowly.

"Go on!" she urged.

Mr. Agyk took a deep, labored breath. "Many years ago, when I was an advisor to the Council of Kallorm, I was unexpectedly asked to protect a child, to look after it as a guardian, and ensure that its identity was never revealed. I myself was never told. I was bound to a secret oath and instructed never to ask any questions. Out of misplaced fealty, I agreed because I was glad of my task. The child was a marvel to me, fair and full of energy and life and love; I was happy to live in ignorant bliss. I just wanted to look after her and love her as if she were a daughter child of my own. *You* were that child. I would have looked after you whether I had been instructed to or not."

Mr. Agyk sighed again, as memories flooded back to him. "Living in Kallorm, you probably heard of the tragic *Tale of Tallia*, though only Dorrol knows the full truth," he said.

Wendya froze at the name. She knew it. She had heard it, spoken in her dreams, whispered on the wind.

The old man continued. "Princess Tallia was a beautiful daughter of Kallorm, the youngest sister of King Dorrol. She was both radiantly fair and unusually gifted with her own natural abilities. Unfortunately, as a result, it was not long before she attracted the attention of an ambitious young magus," Mr. Agyk paused, watching confusion flicker over the witch's face.

"Garroll was his name, a handsome young suitor who had visited Kallorm on numerous occasions and had become very influential in both political and magical circles. He rose through the ranks of Kallormian society with extraordinary speed and quickly became a favored son amongst the members of the Ellda Order. I know only the details of the story that most folk know. He became obsessed with Tallia and by some foul art, he enchanted her and … forced himself upon the young princess. Perhaps he did love her — as much as he was *capable* of loving anything."

Mr. Agyk paused, then started to pace the room. "An unforeseen result of that unhappy union … a pregnancy," the wizard shook his head. "In my dimness, I never pieced all the facts together until Kavok … Then … there was the simple fact that I knew Tallia a little and that as you grew older you began to bear a striking resemblance to her. Your mother was very kind and very beautiful, just like you."

Wendya stared at him blankly. "What! What are you saying?"

"Princess Tallia was your mother. The woman in your dreams and visions."

The young witch sat motionless, bewildered by it all. Eventually she spoke. "King Dorrol is my uncle? Halli is my cousin?"

The wizard nodded.

"And this monster, Garroll, was my father?" she asked.

Mr. Agyk nodded, hardly able to continue. He so wished the dragon would interrupt them. "Yes," he said quietly. "I could never understand Dorrol's fears for you, they seemed completely unfounded ... until Kailla and Vallok, your adopted family, disappeared."

"That was because of me?" Wendya gasped, horrified at the thought.

"NO, no. You are blameless in all of this!" He sighed, weary with worry. "I still do not know what happened to them and I believe Dorrol knows nothing ... but clearly, it scared him and he begged me to take you out of the city. You were so devastated by their disappearance that you wanted to leave anyway. I only started to wonder about your birth parents many years later. Dorrol refused to tell me anything," Mr. Agyk repeated.

Wendya shook her head. "I still don't understand. Why all the secrecy? Even if I *was* born into dreadful circumstances, if I *am* Princess Tallia's child, then why hide me? Why did I need to be protected? From whom? ... From Garroll?" Wendya asked, staring harshly at the old wizard's face.

Mr. Agyk hung his head and sank back into the chair, his eyes fixed on the fire, avoiding Wendya's gaze. "Garroll, after he had ... accosted the princess, left the city for a time. He knew nothing of the pregnancy or baby, which was a blessing. When Garroll returned, he scoured the city looking for Tallia, tore it apart to claim her as his own again. When the final truth about him was revealed and his disguise was discovered," the wizard fell silent for a moment, "a terrible battle ensued. They managed to expel him from the city. It was at this time that Tallia finally returned from hiding. The truth must have horrified her. I suppose she must have realized that she and the child would never be safe or free. That he would sense or gain knowledge of the child's existence and identity. So she sacrificed herself for her baby. She hid the baby's birthkey and, in madness and despair, she threw herself from the Falls of Tarro and thus safeguarded her child and ended her own torment."

Wendya stared down into the fire and shook her head.

"All these deaths and disappearances! They were protecting me?"

"They all loved you, as do I."

"What truth? Who was he? Who was Garroll?"

Mr. Agyk looked at her and the scar at the base of her throat where the key had burned its dragon shape into her flesh. "... I should have guessed a connection when we recovered the birthkey in Kallorm. It should never ignite like that in the hands of anyone other than its owner or someone of the same bloodline ... like Korrun and his sillvaf'yrren pendant and the ring of his brother. Dragonsilver is linked to its owner and any blood relatives."

He stared back into the fire for the longest time and his face seemed gray and wizened with worry.

"Marval? *Who* was Garroll?" the witch asked.

A creeping horror struck her, making her sick to her very core. "If you are saying that that was *my* birthkey in Kallorm and not Morreck's, then ... how could it open doors in Kavok?" she stammered.

The wizard slowly shook his head, resigned to the awful truth of it. "That must have been the secret Dorrol kept, the dying wish of your mother ... that you should never know," he replied quietly. "But you should know ... you *should* know!"

"Know what? Why was Tallia in such danger? Why am I? Who is my father? Who is Garroll? Tell me, Marval ... Tell me!" she shouted, searching the wizard's eyes, willing him to say anything but the name she was terrified to hear.

"Dorrol should have told you ... he should have told me," he muttered.

"Who is Garroll? Tell me! I NEED YOU TO SAY HIS NAME!"

Like the pieces of a splintered jigsaw, the blanket of denial slowly fell away, leaving only the exposed bones of the truth, and they were hard and cruel and bitter.

Mr. Agyk looked at the young witch with an expression of perfect clarity and, like a bolt of crystal to the brain, she understood the horror of what her friend was trying to say and the knowledge of it was like a scream in her head.

"Garroll had many names and many disguises, Kirrem Hal, Molloch ...," the old mage paused. "Garroll is another name for M'Sorreck ... your father."

"Your father is Morreck."

Lightning Source UK Ltd.
Milton Keynes UK
UKOW051013041012

200013UK00002B/46/P